JUNIOR MIDSHIPMAN BULLER WAS
LEARNING WHAT THE ROYAL NAVY
WAS ALL ABOUT . . .

Personnel: flogging, and keel-hauling in extreme
cases, were the only means of keeping discipline.
Diet: salt beef and pork were nourishing and what
the men liked. Compulsory lime juice against the
scurvy. Grog to keep them contented and as an occasional reward—"Always believed in the stuff.
Nothing like splicing the mainbrace for a happy
ship." (And he did just that with his third brandy.)
Ordnance: nothing like smoothbore muzzle-loaders. Simple to load and fire; encourage a commander to lay his ship alongside the enemy where
you can see the whites of his eyes. "That's what he
did for the Frogs and Dons!" And ships: back to
"the wooden walls." Last forever. Sails keep the
men busy, out of mischief. The rubbish they build
today's out of date at the end of the first commission.

BULLER'S GUNS

RICHARD HOUGH

CHARTER
NEW YORK

A DIVISION OF CHARTER COMMUNICATIONS INC.
A GROSSET & DUNLAP COMPANY
51 Madison Avenue
New York, New York 10010

Published by arrangement with William Morrow and Company, Inc.

First Ace Charter Printing: August, 1982
Published simultaneously in Canada
Manufactured in the United States of America
2 4 6 8 0 9 7 5 3 1

Acknowledgments

The extracts from Queen Victoria's Journal are reproduced by the gracious permission of Her Majesty the Queen.

My warmest thanks are due to Lieutenant Commander P. K. Kemp, O.B.E., R.N. (Retd.), and to Lieutenant Colonel C. C. Mitchell, for guidance and information.

Richard Hough

BULLER'S GUNS

PART ONE

Chapter I

On August 14, 1864, a party of workers under the supervision of their foreman, Tom Maclewin, took the train on the private Elswick railway line from the Armstrong Gun Works in Newcastle-upon-Tyne up into the hills and moors north of the city. Their carriage was open and one of only three in the train. The second was a small closed carriage containing the other passengers in the party, a number of officials of the Works headed by Sir William Armstrong himself, and three naval officers in the ordnance branch.

The third piece of rolling stock was a long, articulated flatcar to which was secured the barrel of a 68-pounder naval gun, laid out like an object of sacrifice to some heathen idol and prepared for destruction: an analogy that was to prove only too accurate.

Sir William Armstrong, fifty-four years old, heavily bearded, and grave in manner, had made his fortune originally from machinery, especially hydraulic and electrical machinery, which were the fruit of his own inventive genius. More recently, his mind had turned to gun manufacture.

The shortcomings of army artillery had been demonstrated in the Crimean War. The gun had developed very little over several decades, and like most originators, Armstrong was irritated by mechanical inefficiency and conservatism.

Guns were still made of cast iron, and—as in Nelson's time—were loaded from the muzzle, a clumsy procedure which required running the gun back after firing in order to sponge out the barrel and reload the charge and the projectile.

One day early in 1855, Armstrong had sat down at his desk and in a few moments had sketched out on the back of an envelope a new design for a compact field gun. A prototype had been made in his Works and in less than six months it was ready for firing. It was made with an inner tube of steel, rifled with spiral grooves. But the first innovation was the wrought-iron wire which was wound spirally in ribbons and welded together at white heat into a tube. The second innovation—although not entirely new—was the method of loading at the breech where a block was dropped in and made fast by a hollow screw.

The wire-wound breechloader was to become the standard gun in the army and the navy of every country. It was much more resistant to pressure and far more accurate—seven times more accurate, it was shown, at early trials. Much larger wire-guns were built at the Armstrong Elswick Works, an ordnance factory was set up, and a proving ground for gun trials—to which this private train was destined—was established. In 1861, the first British ironclad—the mighty H.M.S. *Warrior*—was armed with Armstrong 110-pounder and 70-pounder breech-loading wire guns. Almost overnight, the Royal Navy led the navies of the world by a wide margin in ordnance.

And the millionaire-inventor-industrialist, who already owned much of Newcastle and for whom so many of the "Geordies" worked, appeared destined for greater-than-ever honours, power, and wealth.

Tom Maclewin had been employed in the construction of

the prototype Armstrong gun. He was a self-educated and ambitious young Scot, newly married. He was recognized as a first-class welder, and after a year, when their first child was born, he had been able to afford to rent a second room in the back-to-back house in Groom Road. When this new 68-pounder with revised breech mechanism had been proposed, Tom Maclewin had been put in charge of the welding in the small welding shop set up for the work. His interest in guns grew to become a fascination. The shop manager encouraged the clever young Scot and this had led to Maclewin's becoming foreman.

On this August day, the gun was due for its first firing trials. On rare days in the summer, with a mellow wind from the west, Northumberland can be hot. As the train wound its way up the gradient out of the valleys and onto the moors, Tom Maclewin, along with the other men sitting on the wooden seats, took off his cap and eased the kerchief round his neck.

Tom was a Lowland Scot, son of a farm labourer. When times had been particularly bad in the late 1840s, Tom had left the croft where they lived south of Edinburgh and, like so many youngsters, headed for the new industrial towns south of the border to seek employment. He had arrived almost penniless in Newcastle in 1849, the year Robert Stephenson's cast-iron bridge across the Tyne was opened. It seemed to signify new prosperity for the city.

Now, fifteen years later, a married man with an infant son and a daughter of three, Tom Maclewin could have looked forward with hope for the future. Instead, he was to die on that warm summer day, with the burns flowing pure in the valleys and the purple heather at its finest and the larks singing so loudly they could be heard above the panting of the locomotive.

The accident happened late in the afternoon after they had a break for tea. The crane lifted the big gun off its carriage. The weapon was secured to the mounting especially prepared for it, and the usual safety procedure carried out to check the area for anyone who might have missed the warning signs and numerous red flags about the firing area.

As usual, a single reduced charge was used for the first shot. The 68-pound projectile, handled manually, was inserted into the breech, the silk bag of powder followed it, and the block dropped in. Sir William made a brief inspection, and the entire company retired to the safety pit while the gun was fired by remote control.

The mechanism failed twice. On the third failure—a most unusual occurrence—Tom Maclewin left the pit, taking out the earplugs they all wore as he did so. He thought he knew where the failure in the firing mechanism might be. He intended to touch nothing, only to examine, and he had the manager's consent. There was seemingly no risk involved.

He was three yards from the gun's breech when the gun exploded. His body was torn to pieces, and very little of him was ever found among the ruins of the gun, its mounting, and two nearby iron and wooden huts.

The range was a place of explosions, and no one in the nearest village three miles away nor a party out shooting grouse suspected that there had been an accident. Newcastle did not know about it until late that evening, when the train returned to Elswick. Only when the minister called did Doris Maclewin learn that her husband had been killed. The twenty-month-old boy, Roderick, fretful from the heat of the evening, was in his mother's arms when there was a knock on the door of the house in Groom Road.

As a result of these events, Rod Maclewin never knew his father. To be fatherless was not unusual among the children who lived in the narrow cobbled streets which led down steeply to the Elswick Works and the Tyne. There were few safety precautions in the welding shops and the machine shops, the sawmills, the fitting shops, and the plate shops of the factories where the men worked. Others died in their prime from tuberculosis or pneumonia as a direct consequence of malnutrition, cold, and poor housing. Drink, an escape from the miseries of reality, took more lives.

Rod grew up in the belief that his father had been a brave man, a hero who had given his life for the safety of others, which was the way the accident had been recounted to his mother. Meanwhile, the family lived in penury. Mrs. Maclewin earned a few pence looking after the children of neighbours, who also helped out—a bowl of soup, a jug of milk, a loaf of bread—when they could. The parish provided her with a shilling or two a week, and the Elswick Works contributed a small pension—nothing like enough to live on, but a pension of any kind was considered benevolent.

The burst of that experimental 68-pounder Armstrong was not the first or the last for these new breechloaders, and the Ordnance Committee, which was responsible for purchasing guns for the Army and the Navy, reversed its policy from excessive enthusiasm to excessive disapproval. The Navy suddenly opposed them, too, discovering that their muzzle velocity as well as the penetrating power of the shells was less than that of similar-caliber muzzle-loaders. Who cared about accuracy anyway? Tactical policy had not changed much since the eighteenth century, and Admiral Nelson's voice saying that "you could find little fault with a Captain who laid his ship close alongside the enemy" still echoed about the quarterdeck.

At Newcastle, the Armstrong ordnance factory was closed down, and many men were thrown out of work. The depression lasted for years, years when Rod Maclewin was growing up, and there was much suffering in the tight-packed back-to-back houses. The Elementary Education Act came into force when he was eight but it was slow in being established, and after a short time at a dame school, the only education he received was from his mother. Doris Maclewin was pure Geordie, her family line going back many generations in Newcastle, typically tough and resilient and self-reliant. She passed on to Rod and his sister, Kate, what she had learned at her own mother's knee.

Doris Maclewin was popular and admired. Although she was a pretty, fair-haired woman—short but sturdy (Rod had inherited his father's wiriness)—and could have had any number of young men, she showed no sign of wanting to remarry. For some twelve years after the loss of her husband, she devoted her life entirely to keeping her children fed, clothed, and housed—and educated.

The three were very close, and when Kate left home at the age of fifteen, to "go into service" as a junior parlour-maid at Sir William Armstrong's immense citadel of a place, Cragside outside Rothbury, Rod and his mother were both desolate. But it was equally important for Rod to find work, and that was almost impossible in the Elswick Works where men had been unemployed and almost destitute for years.

It was no help that Rod appeared undersized. Shop people accused him of putting up his age, and judged him (quite wrongly) to be physically weak. After much pleading, he got temporary work in a butcher's shop, but when there was need for economy, he was the first to go. He had six weeks, at a shilling a week, helping with a newspaper round. He was taken on as a temporary apprentice fireman on the footplate of Great Northern Railway goods locomotives and learned the elements of driving a Stephenson from a sympathetic old driver. But a supervisor, taking one look at the undersized boy, had sacked him on the spot one day.

Then nothing. Rod would go to the Armstrong Library every weekday to look through the employment columns in the local newspapers. Then, in the *Newcastle Journal* for April 2, 1877, he read a small advertisement. "Join the Royal Navy," it ran. Boys of fourteen and over were welcomed if fit and had parents' consent and a suitable recommendation.

Rod had often seen similar advertisements and posters, and although he had been fourteen for three months, the possibility of joining the Navy had never registered. The Navy was for young men who were unemployable ashore; and he had no romantic notions about the sea anyway. But later in the day, with nothing to do, Rod went for a walk, crossing the Tyne by the swing bridge. On the way back, he had to wait while an ironclad passed down the river, attended by several paddle tugs.

She was a fine-looking ship, returning to sea after a refit at one of the yards upriver, the two turrets flanking the single funnel amidships giving an impression of invincible power and menace. There were more guns behind ports fore and aft, and the great ship carried three masts, the fore and main ship rigged, the mizzen barque rigged. The hull was shiny black with a single white gunwale band, the deck almost white from holystoning, and the brasswork gleamed like the stars on a clear night.

Rod could make out the Captain on the quarterdeck, surrounded by officers and Petty Officers, and the two helmsmen at the wheel. He could also see a number of sailors, some of them boys looking no older than he, horse-playing on the deck about the funnel. Most of the older men wore beards and sennit hats. Rod especially noticed a tall, upstanding seaman with a fine red beard standing at the rail and holding a clay pipe. Their eyes met for a moment, and the sailor was just near enough for Rod to see him smile and briefly wave the hand holding the pipe in his direction. He might have been saying, "This is a fine day, and this is a fine life. Come and join us!" Rod waved back.

On the way home, Rod walked slowly. It was late in the afternoon and getting dark. The men were pouring out of the Elswick Works, carrying their dinner boxes, some in cloth caps, some in bowlers, all in clogs that set up a clamorous rattle against the cobbles, a characteristic sound twice a day in Newcastle. At every street corner there was a pub, and almost all the men headed for one or another of them, pushing aside the swing doors eagerly for their second drink of the day, most of them having had one on the way to work at six o'clock in the morning. Precious, hard-earned money poured into the pubs, often leaving too little to clothe and feed the family. Too hard work, too little work, and drunkenness were three of the unhappy things about Newcastle, and Rod sometimes wondered if he would get drunk often like the others when he was older—if he ever got a job.

But he was not thinking of that now, nor did he notice the men still pouring out through the factory gates, nor the barefooted children standing by the gates calling out, "Any bread left? Any bread left?" He did not see in the last light of the day the tall factory chimneys belching smoke into the evening sky, the smoke from countless house chimneys rising to form a vast and sulphurous cloud above this sooty dark city. He did not see the children, some wearing only an old vest, playing in the street—hopscotch, an old hoop, a skipping rope—or hear their voices. He did not notice the women in long black dresses and clogs at the doors, arms akimbo or carrying an infant, toddlers on the step beside them, or hear the rich Northumberland voices calling out to a neighbour. He did not glance into the street-corner pubs and was deaf to the roar of men's voices harsh in complaint or anecdote as he passed.

Rod was thinking about the Navy and was blind and deaf to everything about him.

The house at 19D Groom Street was approached through an archway that led into the yard dividing one street of houses from the next, with the privies shared between eight houses running down the center. The Maclewins' two rooms were upstairs, the windows looking east over the yard. Rod's mother was at the iron range where she was cooking supper. She looked up and smiled when he came in. "Well, Roddy, an' what's been doing?"

"I've been doing some thinking, Ma."

Confident in his mother's trust and wisdom, Rod had never practiced guile. It had never crossed his mind that he should deceive her or even fail to tell her everything as it came to his mind.

"I've been thinking—I'll not be getting any work here in Newcastle. Never."

"There's no such word—no word 'never.'"

"It seems never, Ma. I could join the Navy. Then I'd be earning money and could send some back to you."

Doris Maclewin turned and sat down suddenly at the scrubbed table. She had grown pale and the ladle she was holding fell to the floor. He picked it up and as he gave it back to her he said, "I wouldn't if you didn't want me to. But I must be doing something, Ma, and making the family some money."

Rod's mother never held back anything from her son, either, and she spoke her feelings now as she registered them: she would miss him, she would be lonely, she would be afraid for him. Then, "But if you want to go, if you think it's right, I'll not stop you, love. Not forever, just for a few years till things get better. But you may not be right for a sailor—not stand those heights up the masts, or the sea-sickness. And you'll miss your friends here—and perhaps me."

"Of course I'll miss you, Ma. Terribly. And home." He repeated, "I'll not be getting any work here in Newcastle," pronouncing it "Newcassel" like every good Geordie.

"You'd best take a letter. The minister'll write one. Else they'll not be believing your age again."

Then for once Doris Maclewin kept her thoughts to herself. She was thinking at that moment, as the vegetable stew quietly bubbled on the range, "The Navy killed my Tom; please God don't let it kill my Roddy."

Chapter II

In October 1743, Captain Alastair Buller of the frigate *Frobisher 26* captured the Spanish treasure ship *San Salvador* off Jamaica after a day-and-night-long pursuit and a brisk action. It was all in the best traditions of semipiratical semilegitimate activity practiced so profitably by naval commanders from Drake to Anson himself. A Spaniard would have as swiftly and ruthlessly attacked and captured the *Frobisher* without a qualm if he had possessed the courage, gunnery, and fighting prowess. But this was not the golden age of the Spanish Empire, and in 1743 there were few Spanish captains resolute enough to take on an English frigate.

Captain Buller's share of the prize money was not far short of £75,000, which was a great fortune. After thirty-five years in the Royal Navy, Buller retired, bought a thousand acres in Gloucestershire, and commissioned Sir William Chambers to build a house worthy of Buller, now created a Baron by King George III for "tickling the Dons" off Jamaica.

By the time the Honourable Archibald Buller, age twelve,

was sent to the naval training ship *Britannia*, four generations of naval Bullers had resided at Weir Park—if residence can be defined as a brief infancy and boyhood, before going away to sea, and marrying and begetting new young naval material between commissions and occasional periods on half pay.

The Bullers and the Royal Navy were synonymous. Portraits of Alastair Buller and his three sons (one served under Howe at the Glorious First of June and the other two under Jervis at St. Vincent) hung in the hall and up the wide main staircase alongside Vice Admiral Gordon Buller, Rear Admiral James Buller, Lieutenant Hillary Buller who had fought off three Spanish ships of the line for nine hours near Trinidad and died on his quarterdeck in hand-to-hand combat when his ship had been boarded, and Archy's father, George, now a Rear Admiral.

The women in the Bullers' lives, the wives and daughters and those cousins and nieces unfortunate enough to be born female, were also painted, several by Gainsborough, and the gilt-framed pictures hung in the drawing room and in the women's sitting rooms upstairs. The Bullers loved their women dearly and, although like most sailors they left their marriage lines behind at Gibraltar, remained loyal and steady husbands, treating them with great gallantry, making sure they avoided the walls with the toppers on the hunting field, showing concern for them in confinement, and insisting on their enjoying the best of everything, from a sufficient number of personal servants to the finest of silk dresses—from Paris, of course—during those brief intervals when they were not fighting the French.

But except for the drawing room and the bedrooms, Weir Park was essentially a masculine place, and nautical masculine at that, the billiard room being called the gunroom, and to confuse things further, the real gunroom, the magazine. The smoking room was the wardroom, and the stairs inevitably the companionway. Distinguished visitors were not actually piped on board, but there was a great deal of saluting, which came readily to the menservants who were mostly re-tired Warrant Officers and able seamen.

Weir Park was built just below the summit of a south-facing hill, with views on clear days far across the upper Thames flatland to the Wiltshire Downs. A river, which flowed over a weir by a watermill and eventually found the Thames after a circuitous journey through villages and between water meadows, ran through the valley below the house's terraced gardens, and on the other side was a seventy-acre deer park. Gordon Buller had built a small, gemlike Cotswold stone church in the center of this deer park in gratitude to God for His having saved his life and the lives of his officers and men in a Caribbean hurricane in 1794. The entire family and the forty-eight servants from laundry maids to the housekeeper walked there every Sunday, across the bridge that Chambers had returned to design in 1795.

The house itself graced and blended in to perfection with the Cotswold landscape. Chambers had designed it in the full flood tide of romanticism, with deep low windows on the ground floor looking out over formal gardens to the north, and the descending grass terraces to the south. The bedroom windows on the first floor were much smaller, giving the house the fashionable high-waisted appearance, the stone remaining unrendered there.

Also in accord with the taste of the 1770s, Chambers had not hesitated to unbalance the frontal aspect by adding a conservatory to the west side, which also concealed the ser-vants' block, the stables with their yard, the coachhouse, the wash house, the mangle room, and other ancillary buildings.

It was a house built for house parties and for pleasure. Fifty—even thirty—years earlier, Weir Park would have been a place to be visited reluctantly and as a duty to one's estate, before returning thankfully to the delights of Town. By 1770 the country had become a joyous place, nature was beautiful, hunting and coursing were all the rage, and re-spectable people were being painted on horseback. With a network of new turnpikes through the land, it was even quite pleasant and speedy to get there.

In the century since it had been built, Weir Park had mellowed, the stone losing its newly quarried harshness and blending in with the landscape. A cedar tree which Chambers had planted fifty feet from the southeast corner had matured and acquired majesty. (Lady Buller complained that it took the morning light off the breakfast room.)

Archy Buller did not consciously love or admire Weir Park. His home was simply a part of his life, as taken for granted as his spaniel Junus, or, say, Clarke, the head groom, or fat Thomas, his father's valet. He liked them all. In fact, he liked almost everything and everyone in his life as it had so far been lived. But he was not much of a one for defining his feelings. People were there, things happened, and he enjoyed himself. Almost always.

For Archy Buller, Weir Park was no more than a background for real life, which was on board a man-o'-war at sea, and preferably in combat. He had understood, without any questioning, that he was destined for the life of a sailor. Everything pointed to the sea, things like Millais's painting "Raleigh's Boyhood," a copy of which hung in his bedroom; ship models in the library and billiard room; the half cutlass hanging in the gunroom belonging to Great-uncle William Buller (the other half had gone three inches into the timbers of a French 74 after cutting almost in half a Lieutenant Comte de Guienne); the length of chain shot draped above the front door after doing its worst at the Battle of the Saints; and numerous other relics and mementoes. All these, and the portraits and paintings, suggested that the only other life outside Weir Park was at sea in the Royal Navy.

Closely related to this maritime influence, which Archy Buller had absorbed from infancy, was his father's failure to experience combat, unlike all his ancestors. George Buller resented this deeply but, suffering under the misfortune of serving through a period when there was almost no fighting at sea, there was nothing he could do about it. He would sometimes say to Archy, "I hope you won't go through life as I have been forced to do, without hearing a shot fired in anger, or defending my country."

"A shot fired in anger!" This was a phrase that echoed and echoed again through Archy Buller's childhood. He was determined that he would not experience his father's frustration —his fearless father who would have fought as bravely as all the other Bullers. Archy would fight to defend his country against her enemies. He would hear the sound of shots fired in anger. Of that there could be no doubt.

Archy Buller enjoyed himself especially on the morning of September 7, 1877. He got up early, raided the kitchens for some breakfast (to the giggles of mock disapproval of two of the young kitchenmaids), whistled up Junus, took his new Purdy from "the magazine," and went out on a rough shoot on his own. He shot a brace of partridge and a fat buck rabbit.

As Archy walked up the gravel drive with Junus at his heel, his father entered the Park through the lodge gates, receiving a curtsey from Mrs. O'Mara and a doffing of his hat from her husband. The train had brought him from London to Cirencester, and his own coach had picked him up at the station. He brought good news with him. But the first reason for his returning to his place was to see off his youngest son to the training ship *Britannia* and give him some last-minute advice.

Before turning the last corner, which revealed the house half a mile away, Mason slowed the coach and called down: "Young Master Archibald, sir. Shall I pick him up?"

George Buller let down the window and looked ahead. His son, with hair too long and blowing in the wind, was standing a hundred yards distant on the grass verge, smiling and waving his bag, Junus obediently sitting at his feet, tail brushing the grass. George Buller had a special affection for the boy as the afterthought (his straight-talking wife called him "the last mistake") of his family, conceived when George was forty-five and Cecily thirty-eight. He liked the spontaneousness of the boy and his sunny nature and reckoned that time would cure his impulsiveness, which was engaging in boyhood but a disadvantage in a career, and the occasional sharp outbreaks of temper.

"How fast he's grown! My youngest son almost as tall as I am," George Buller was thinking as the carriage halted and Mason got down to open the door. "And one for the ladies in a few years." He noticed indulgently that Archy had torn his breeches again and that he had probably not even run a comb through his dark-brown hair since getting up. The *Britannia* would see to that sort of thing.

"How are you, my boy?"

"Perfectly splendid, Papa." Mason took his gun, but Archy held on to his bag, which he opened to show his father sitting opposite.

"How are you, Papa? And how was London?"

"I have some news. But that can keep until luncheon. Are you looking forward to tomorrow? All your kit shipshape?"

Cecily Buller at fifty was almost indistinguishable from her portrait, painted ten years earlier and hung at the far end of the dining room above her customary place at dinner parties. Many guests noted the fact—noted how the hair had retained its rich chestnut colour, gleaming with health, noted the same discreet lines beside the full mouth, the same warmth in her hazel eyes, the same little creases of good humour about them.

Lady Buller (her husband had succeeded to the title at about the time this portrait was painted) was as full of vigour as ever, taking an active part with her housekeeper in running Weir Park, supervising Baines, the head gardener, riding to hounds twice a week, organizing tenants' balls and county charities, sitting on the bench, and many other responsibilities. Ever since she had married George Buller in 1848 when he was a Lieutenant R.N. and at sea for long periods, she had accustomed herself to playing the part of both husband and wife at Weir Park. It was the price of a naval marriage.

Cecily Buller did not find her life exacting. She thrived on work and every sort of activity, and she weighed not a pound more than when she had walked down the aisle on her father's arm at twenty-one, the most alluring bride anyone could hope for.

She greeted her husband in the hall as he came in, dressed in a dark-brown suit and matching short coat with silk cravat and hatless as always when out of uniform. He had filled out over the years, especially since shore appointments had come his way, but he was not a fat man, and at fifty-seven, with a thick full naval beard and iron-grey hair, he looked the very apotheosis of a senior naval officer at the height of his power.

George Buller embraced his wife and then greeted the house steward. "Will you be good enough to ask Grey to bring up a bottle of champagne. And we'll have another with luncheon. Where are the older boys?"

"I understand they are upstairs packing, sir."

Guy and Henry, identical twins of nineteen and soon due to take their Lieutenant's examinations, were returning to their ship at Portsmouth the following day, by coincidence the same day that Archy would formally join the Royal Navy as a cadet.

They sat down to luncheon at 1:15, six in all—Sir George and Lady Buller; Guy and Henry in the undress uniform of Midshipmen of blue, single-breasted jacket with nine buttons, three buttons on each cuff, and stand-up white collar; a grey and rather nondescript aunt in a black dress (Aunt Pidgy she was called, who had not married, and many years earlier—no one could remember quite when—had been invited to stay by her brother and had remained, seemingly forever); and Archy.

They were all—even Aunt Pidgy—inclined to be cheerful on the first bottle of champagne. Guy and Henry, tall, good-looking young men with strong fair hair that would one day turn grey like their father's, spent some time teasing Archy about the horrors of the *Britannia*, the tortures and fagging, the salt beef and weevil-ridden biscuits, the bitter cold of a yardarm in a howling winter gale. When they got to the flogging and keel-hauling, Archy, who had continued to eat without any reaction, interrupted to say, "Rubbish—the last flogging in the fleet was in 1867, and even you said the food was jolly splendid." He had got the measure of his older brothers years ago and could give as good as he got so long as they did not resort to fighting.

"You're going to have some Royal company, Archy," said his father. "I was at Hatfield House the other evening, and Lord Salisbury said that the Prince and Princess of Wales are sending Prince George this year. And his elder brother, too, to keep him company."

"I bet they won't keel-haul *them*," said Archy, taking three more slices of mutton offered to him by the footman. "Shall I have to call them 'sir' and stand up when they come in?"

"No. You'll find they are treated like all the other cadets. But they'll have their tutor with them. And they may sleep in special quarters. They're nice, rather gentle boys who have never mixed much with others outside their family, and they may get bullied. See that you don't—that would be cowardly and dishonourable."

Buller nodded. "All right, sir. Is there much fighting?"

The twins chimed in here. "Every morning, Archy. Before breakfast," said Guy with a severe expression.

"Three of the biggest boys beat a New unconscious—a different one every day for a month."

" 'Corporal punishment of Boys,' " intoned Guy, " 'is to be inflicted with the Birch, as supplied from the Dockyard; the birching is to be given over the bare breech, and is never to exceed 24 cuts or blows; it is to be inflicted by the Ship's Police . . .' Article 691, Queen's Regulations."

"You are becoming tiresome, boys," said Lady Buller firmly. "Archy is much too sensible to listen to this nonsense. You are looking forward to it, aren't you, dear?"

Lady Buller was quite right. Her son had no anxieties about the *Britannia*. He was so accustomed to enjoying things, that he had no reason to believe (in spite of his brothers' persistent efforts to scare him) he would not enjoy his time on the River Dart. After two years as a weekly boarder in a private school in Cheltenham, he had gone to Dr. Ransome's Establishment in Gosport; which specialized in preparing boys for the naval entry examinations.

Gosport had accustomed Buller to being away from home. He had been given a few bloody noses and learned to look after himself, but not how to control his temper, for which he had been beaten a couple of times.

"And now," said George Buller in a voice which ended all the flippant talk, "I will tell you my news, unimportant though it is by comparison with a twelve-year-old entering the *Britannia* and two more of my sons facing the onerous examinations for their commissions. I was told something else at Hatfield House. Mr. W. H. Smith was also there, and he always hears from the other side of the House what is going on in the Navy. I understand I shall shortly be appointed Third Naval Lord with the rank of Vice Admiral and given a G.C.B. as well for my work at the Admiralty."

George Buller was incapable of being pompous, and he covered up any suggestion of self-importance by laughing and telling his sons that if they wrote to him officially, they would have to address him as "My Lord" in future.

Cecily said, "My dear, it's what you've always wanted. I'm so glad. And proud." She raised her glass and the boys stood. "To Vice Admiral Sir George Buller, Baronet, G.C.B. My handsome husband."

"I'll second the first part, Mama," said Guy.

"But not the second," said Henry. "Unless he gives secret orders to the examination board to slip us through."

Then George Buller rose and held his glass towards Archy. "Success in the *Britannia*," he said. "And a plague on your brothers."

Archy, who had been given a whole glass for the first time, smiled at his father and thanked him, but decided he would not get up as he was not fully confident that his legs would function.

The next day, September 8, Cadet Archy Buller took the train from Cirencester for Dartmouth. He felt very new by himself in his obviously new dark-blue uniform and cap.

Clarke had seen that his sea chest went safely into the guard's van and had bade him good-bye. No one else saw him off. He was, he had been told, a young man now and could look after himself. At Taunton another boy in cadet's uniform got into his first-class carriage, and two more at another station. At Exeter they changed onto the train from London, and there were many more boys already on board, leaning out of the windows and calling to one another as if they were old friends.

One compartment had a reserved sign stuck to the window, and Archy caught a glimpse inside of a rather severe-looking man and two cadets. A fair-haired boy with a disdainful expression on his face who was boarding the train at the same time as Archy said in a drawling accent, "Those are the Wales boys. They're going to get a drubbing from the Threes."

This seemed like a new language to Archy, and the train had reached full speed, winding in and out of the Dawlish tunnels with the sea shimmering alongside the track, before he had worked out the meaning. He glanced across at the fair-haired boy, who was impressing a craven-looking neighbour with some anecdote and smoking a cigarette.

He decided then that he might not like everyone at Dartmouth, and that there might be quite a lot of fighting ahead.

But an hour later, and with a sudden spasm of excitement, he decided he did like the look of the *Britannia*. At Dartmouth station they all climbed into one of a fleet of horse buses, which in turn went clattering out of the station forecourt and up the Dittisham road. The *Britannia* and her consort, the *Hibernia*, came suddenly into sight as they rounded a corner.

The two great three-deckers, little different from the ships of the line of Nelson's time, the *Hibernia* having been launched before Trafalgar, lay anchored between the high banks of the beautiful river, the Devonshire hills clad with beeches and high-hedged fields above them. A cutter was taking out the first batch of boys, the men at the oars pulling in long, muscular unison. So this was the Royal Navy.

❧ ⚜ ❧

Chapter III

═══════════════

Rod Maclewin's last three pennies went to the waterman, the big callused hand closing round the coins and depositing them into his pouch pocket. The three-decker First Rate anchored off Mount Wise at Devonport might have been ready to sail to the Battle of Trafalgar, with her cream masts and spars. Nothing in the scene appeared to have changed over seventy years, until a ferry chugged out of Torpoint and headed east for Keyham, its paddles churning the water white and trailing a wake across the smooth waters of the anchorage.

"So ye are wantin' go t'sea, lad?" The waterman was pulling with short, seemingly effortless strokes, but the boat was making rapid progress towards the training ship.

The Devonshire accent was so alien to Rod's Geordie ear that it was a moment before he understood what the waterman was saying.

"Aye, sir. That's what I hope."

" 'Tis a hard life, and for a little whippersnapper as you. You'll be set to clean everything fro' the mess deck to t'seven seas."

The waterman back-oared to bring the boat alongside the staging, and Rod jumped out, grasping the rail with one hand, holding tightly to the canvas bag of his possessions with the other.

He was to remember for all time the climb up the steps to the gangway; the first time ever on shipboard; the smell of paint and tar, even here outside the bulwarks; the size of the timbers; the sudden sight of a great black cannon muzzle, brass tampion gleaming, as the steps took him past an open port; and the sudden darkness of the deck as he went through the entry port. Here there was the smell of brass polish and newly scrubbed wood.

"And what d'ye need, little Midge?" A heavily built figure who was later identified as the Quartermaster stepped forward out of the darkness and looked down at Rod. He had a great red beard and spoke amiably enough—indulgently even.

"I want to join the Navy, sir."

"Best come along with me, Midge. The Jaunty'll look after ye."

The Quartermaster led Rod along the deck aft, knocked on a door, and handed him over to the Master-at-Arms in his quarters. In turn he took Rod to the ship's sick bay, where he was ordered to strip to his vest and weighed. A pole was held against his back and he was ordered sharply to stand up straight.

Then came the words of doom. "Ye're not measurin' up, boy. Ye've got to be four foot ten—ye aren't even nine. Take 'im away, Nobby."

Rod had to hold back his tears as he was marched silently back along the deck the way he had come. The whole process of rejection had taken less than five minutes. And what was he to do now, with no money and only the papers he had brought with him, and the spare shirt and worn blanket in his bag?

The waterman was still there, as if accustomed to rejects, and he said he would take him back to the shore for nothing as he had to go anyway. Rod was about to step into the boat when a voice boomed out from high above.

"Where are *you* off to?" A grand-looking figure was leaning over the rail of the upper deck. Rod caught a glimpse of epaulettes and gold braid and a red face peering down.

"I wanted very much to join the Navy, sir."

"Speak up, young man."

"I wanted to join the Navy," Rod shouted in a desperate voice. "I were too short, sir. Just a mite too short, sir."

"Quartermaster!" The voice must have carried to Devonport; and when the red-bearded figure appeared at the head of the gangway: "Quartermaster, see if you can stretch this little fellow. He looks a likely number." The epaulettes and gold braid disappeared, and the Quartermaster ordered him on board again.

His acceptance was as rapid as his rejection had been. Before Rod had time to consider the reversal in his fortunes, he had handed over the papers showing his nationality and parentage and religion, and the Newcastle magistrate's letter of recommendation. He had been given in exchange a ditty box for his possessions; his kit of uniform—"Jacket, monkey one, trousers, duck two, handkerchief, silk, black one," and so on, ending with "Half boots, pair of, one" but "They're only for landing and wearing in t'sick bay"; three pennies ("Holy Joe") for his first week, the sum it had cost him to get to the ship. Finally he was given a form and told to make his mark.

"So ye can read, lad," the Master-at-Arms commented in surprise as he saw Rod looking at the lines on the form, and then using the pen to write his name rather than making the usual cross. Rod saw that he was committing himself to serve ten years after he reached eighteen, fourteen years from now—why, he would be middle-aged! And everyone knew what happened if you deserted your ship . . .

During the following months, there were times when Rod despaired and sank into a state of suicidal gloom when he contemplated the loss of the best years of his life. There were other times when he felt buoyant with joy at successfully conquering some skill and receiving a word of praise for it. And for many months, the homesickness and the thought of his mother struck him like a blow against his stomach in rare moments of idleness during the day, or as he lay in his hammock awake in the morning.

From the moment when he was sent to the new entrants' mess ("the Nozzers'") on that first morning, he was made aware of what a tough life he had let himself in for. There was much justice and some injustice. There was much fear at first, especially high up in his station on the main royal yard with the winter wind biting at his bare feet and hands and threatening to tear him from his hold.

There was, on the one hand, the satisfaction of comradeship and the team spirit with his opposite number (Rod was in the starboard watch) and the unpleasantness of dealing with the ship's bullies—heavy, stupid, ugly oafs of boys who might knock you down one minute and try to climb into your hammock in the middle of the night and make you touch them, which was worse.

The food was as heavy and as coarse as these boys: a basin of greasy cocoa and biscuit or bread for breakfast, bread and cheese for supper, and only one proper meal a day, dinner of salt beef or concoctions of dough and meat and vegetables like "schooner on the rocks" or "toad in the hole." And the routine was demanding for boys still growing, from the call "All hands" at 5:45 A.M to 8:30 P.M. "pipe down." There was much holystoning of decks in the grey light of dawn with water sloshing everywhere; much cleaning of brass and wood and messtraps and kettles and dishes; much inspection and marching; furling and unfurling of the sails; lessons in seamanship and knots.

Always they were aware, and often physically conscious, of the bo'sun and Petty Officer instructors who took them in hand from their first days, ready with "the stonachies" and "the ticklers"—the pieces of short rope or canes used for keeping discipline and keeping the routine going at a rate.

Only three weeks had passed on board the *Impregnable* before Rod heard the same words that Archy Buller was to hear under such different circumstances—"Article 691, Queen's Regulations: Corporal punishment of boys is to be inflicted with the Birch, as supplied from the Dockyard; the birching is to be given over the bare breech . . ."

But on this occasion the words were not in jest. Rod heard them spoken in the solemn tone of authority while standing, like the others, cap in hand on the upper deck. The ceremony of punishment was carried out before dinner, with the Captain reading from *Queen's Regulations*. When he closed the fat volume, caps were resumed, and the Master-at-Arms was ordered, "Carry on."

Rod felt a cold shaft of terror and disgust as the boy (he was one of the bullies, but that made it no better) had his trousers removed and was told, "Bend over that hammock," by the Master-at-Arms. A canvas band was then tied above and below his buttocks, and the Master-at-Arms took up his birch with an expression of dutiful satisfaction on his hard face.

They had all been shown this birch in order to ram home to them its deterrent power. Rod had thought it a terrifying instrument and had decided that as far as he was concerned he would steer clear of any trouble while on board this ship. The tight-bound birch twigs were about two feet six inches long, and the boys had been told that they were always soaked in hot vinegar before application in order to harden them further.

Now the Master-at-Arms raised the birch high above his head. There was not a breath of wind blowing that morning, and they all heard the sickening swish as the birch came down, the thwack as it struck the victim's buttocks; and the scream of pain might have been heard above the sound of a gale. After three strokes, each registered by the calling of the number, blue weals crisscrossed the boy's buttocks, and at the fourth, Rod saw the blood spring from his flesh. Then he shut his eyes.

At a dozen, he opened his eyes again and with a feeling of sickness and degradation saw the boy's backside being covered with a blanket by the ship's doctor, who then hustled him

34

away, half-carrying him, as if he were an object to be removed from human view—as indeed he was.

It had been difficult to bite into the salt beef and swallow the greasy gravy of dinner after that experience. It had been less difficult the next time, and the punishment soon had no effect on Rod's appetite.

"I am getting hardened," he told himself in some dismay as he swung in his hammock one night. "My feet are getting hardened, and my hands—and my heart. What is the Navy doing to me?" Then he fell asleep, weary from his fifteen-hour day, some of it spent on the main royal yard, where he had been rated upper yardman, and some of it at swimming lessons, where he and a boy on the starboard watch called Ben Cuddiford were well in advance of the others.

Less than a year passed before Rod fully understood how essential the toughening process was, as well as the swimming lessons. During that time, he gained his Good Conduct Badge and went to sea for the first time in a 600-ton brig for a short voyage up-Channel, across the North Sea to the Dutch coast, and back along the French coast to Devonport. Rod was sick twice, but in the worst storm he was so busy holding on aloft that he forgot the state of his stomach.

Then, on an afternoon in early November, he was counted off to report with a hundred more boys on the upper deck. After a few minutes, the Captain appeared, stood them at ease, and said: "You may thank God for your good fortune in your prayers tonight. You have been selected to proceed on a long voyage to the West Indies, returning to these shores before Easter next year. Your ship will be the finest training ship in the Royal Navy, the ex-frigate *Eurydice*, and your commander one of the most experienced in the Royal Navy—a personal friend of mine and a great officer, Captain Marcus Hare."

Chapter IV

Lady Buller poured a second cup of tea and said to her husband, "I do not understand a single word of Archy's letter, George. Kindly listen to this and explain."

She held the letter up to the morning light at the breakfast table and read from the sheet of paper with the "H.M.S. Britannia" heading:

"We had sea gull for Sunday dinner but no one eats it. We News get knocked about a bit and have to fag but I don't mind. I went over the futtock, the first New to do so. Most News use the lubber's hole. The Chief Petty Officer says, 'keep one hand for yourself and one for the country' when you're aloft. A Four called Suddaby put a cockroach upside down in the service telegraph lens during firing practice. The bo'sun said to the officer, 'There's a cutter out there, sir, with tossed oars.' Wasn't that a grand joke? Suddaby got Mod."

Lady Buller passed the letter to her husband. "Kindly translate, George."

Sir George Buller cast his mind back to his training days

half a century ago when the Navy was all sails and rigging and smoothbore 36-pounders, with flogging at the gangway commonplace. "When you go up the mast, dearest," he explained patiently, "you come to a platform called a top. Now, you can either follow the ratlines, which means going half upside down like a fly on the ceiling and then over the lip of the top, which is quicker. Or you can go through a hole cut in the top close to the mast—'the lubber's hole,' which is strictly for beginners or cowards. The French, I need hardly tell you, dearest, *always* use the lubber's hole."

"It sounds horribly dangerous." But Cecily Buller laughed. With sons and a husband all sailors, she had long ago reconciled herself to the risks of the mariner's life. And the reckless style in which she hunted suggested that she did not regard danger with great seriousness anyway.

George Buller glanced down his half-spectacles at the letter again. "As to the food in the *Britannia*, I happen to know that it is healthy, varied, and more than adequate. Fit for a King. And, talking of Kings, my dear, I see our boy refers to the young Princes as being quiet and shy and getting knocked about a bit. That won't do them any harm so long as it doesn't go too far. Wales told me last week that he wants them treated the same as all the other cadets. They'll be getting 'sea gull' too, which is really very good chicken.

"Finally, my dear, Mod is a form of punishment. An hour's marching and drilling without rest with a Black Bess. And that rifle weighs all of thirty pounds. Stiffens you up, I can tell you."

Cadet Archibald Buller was feeling just that, stiffened up. He was ready to drop when he went below for a belated breakfast. There were only a few cadets at the table, one of them Prince George, and Buller sat down opposite him. The Prince looked at him with concern. "I say, that's a whopper of a black eye. Does it hurt much?"

"If it does, I can't feel it. Can't feel anything, old top, after that marching."

"It was jolly decent of you, Buller. If there's anything I can ever do for you, you must let me know."

It was "that beastly temper of yours" that had done it. That, plus righteous indignation and an instinct to help the underdog.

The cadet who had smoked on the train and aroused this response in Buller was Alan Marchmount, a member of the banking Marchmounts. Like his friend, Duff-Davies, he had a natural aptitude for leadership and for attracting sycophants. He was a good-looking boy, his appearance slightly spoilt by a heavy chin and jowls. He possessed a very considerable charm and was popular with the Petty Officer police and the instructors. He was also bright and had finished second in the Second Term examinations.

During the first weeks in the *Britannia*, Buller had been unable to make up his mind about the boy. He was normally very polite, although quick to call for a fag, and often gave a reward of a penny or two for an efficiently carried out task. (Money meant nothing to him: Marchmount was renowned as having limitless resources, like his father.) He had been almost ingratiating to Buller on the few times he had called on him, presumably because he knew his father was Third Naval Lord. Then, one day Buller had seen him slap a New of half his weight across the side of his face so hard that the boy had stumbled and fallen to the deck. A Petty Officer policeman happened to be passing, and while Marchmount disappeared, had ordered the boy to his feet and given him a Mod on the spot, no explanations listened to, for fooling on deck.

Buller now realized that Marchmount was a bully of the first order. He had already heard that he had knocked down Prince Eddie. Then on one Saturday afternoon, Buller saw him summon Prince George to his quarters and order him to go ashore and buy him some tuck (which was against the rules) and bring it back within the hour.

As Prince George turned to carry out the fag, Marchmount tripped him up, laughing with satisfaction as he did so. The Prince fell to the deck, picked himself up, and to Buller's amazed admiration, threw himself at his tormentor. It was a spirited attack but had no chance of success. Marchmount laughed again and parried the blows of the boy, who was three inches shorter and twenty pounds lighter than he was, intoning provocatively, "Young Mr. Grandboots—thinks he's grand and needn't fag. Young Mr. Grandboots . . ."

He had then punched Prince George on the nose, sending him to the deck again. The Prince's face was pouring with blood when he turned, groping for a handkerchief.

Buller would have intervened earlier but for the unwritten rule that only cowards fought two to one. Now he ran to help the Prince to his feet and told him to go to the sick bay.

"Little Prince Milksop," sneered Marchmount. "Go and have a good cry with the surgeon." His voice turned suddenly harsh. "And then you'll do my fag or I'll know the reason why."

Buller turned on Marchmount, all discretion and caution tossed aside by the gale of outrage that had overcome him. "That beastly temper," as his nursery governess used to describe it, had seized him again, so that he became a victim of impulse, throwing himself at Marchmount, fists pummelling and calling out, "You beastly bully!" twice, and then a threatening but uncompleted sentence, "By the time I've finished with you . . ."

They were in a clinch, wrestling, evenly matched in weight and strength, Buller beating against the boy's kidneys as he himself was forced backwards until he thought his spine would break. When he finally gave way and fell, he succeeded in twisting sideways so that they crashed to the deck together. Buller was quicker. He tore his right arm free and landed a sharp blow on Marchmount's mouth, feeling the teeth sharp against his knuckles. He heard a grunt, felt himself being lifted up, felt a counterblow to his own face—right in the eye.

Then they were rolling over and over as Marchmount resumed his tight grip, and they hit the wooden bulkhead together, both half-stunned by the blow.

Hands dragged them apart. A corporal and a Petty Officer tore the grip each had on the other, cursing the two boys and ordering them to get up.

They stood facing each other, Marchmount bleeding from the mouth, Buller able to see with only one eye, panting for breath.

"Now what's all this?"

"Please, sir, Buller just went for him. For no reason, sir."

Except for Prince George, whose testimony was not even heard, the little New sycophant who made this accusation was the only witness. The police chose to ignore Buller's explanation, too, and he was ordered two hours' "Mod," with the threat of being "put in Second Class" or receiving a birching if he did not behave in future.

Buller found it easier to accept the injustices of life than did some of his contemporaries. His cheerful disposition helped. So did his experience in having two older brothers, and his year at Dr. Ransome's. He held no special grudge against either Marchmount or his snivelling chum for turning false evidence. He would watch Marchmount more carefully in future but did not promise not to fight him again if necessary. Moreover, he would do better next time, too.

After that, attempts by Marchmount to blacken Buller as a coward were not successful. It was difficult to brand Buller as a funk. A few days later after tea and with the upper deck clear of authority, Buller was unable to resist going aloft to stand on the truck.

Buller did not just possess a good head for heights. He did not know what fear was high up in the rigging. He had always been a nimble tree climber at Weir Park. On board the *Britannia* the cadets were encouraged to climb the rigging and lay out on the yards at any time when they were free from duties, loosening and furling the sails for practice.

He had used the lubber's hole only once, and thought it

a slow and clumsy means of getting aloft. Some of his term had not gone over the futtock by the end of the first term. Others were almost as quick as Buller. But no one enjoyed it as much as he did, up here on the yards, with its marvellous views over Devonshire.

"I'll bet you can't touch the jack!"

Buller rose to the challenge without hesitation, skinning up the ratlines like a veteran hand, up, up to the foremast's crosstrees and then reached up to touch the iron bar—the "jack."

Only two days later, again after tea when they had time to themselves and authority lay low: "I'll bet you can't touch the truck."

This time Buller told his challenger to put down three-pence, to which he added the same sum and put the total in Prince George's charge.

The task presented Buller with no special problem, and it was as easy—if higher and more awkward—as the jack, though the wind was rather troublesome. There was nothing higher, except the lightning conductor.

A week later he was standing on the eight-inch truck, the ultimate and rarely achieved accomplishment. This time it was not in answer to any challenge, and no one knew that he was attempting this dare, strictly forbidden by the training ship's rules. Afraid that he might be accused of showing off, Buller left the mess table early, and while most cadets were still eating, he came up on deck, slipped off his shoes, and grasped the lower ratlines of the foremast.

It was a faintly misty, late autumn evening, the air still and smelling richly of fallen leaves from the Devonshire beechwoods. Buller went over the futtocks as if he had crawled half upside down all his life, paused momentarily on the top, and then continued the climb. A minute later he was reaching up for the mast's cap. Then he drew his legs together over the signal sheaves and round the masthead and eased himself up, hand over hand, until he could reach up his right hand to the truck.

He still experienced no fear of falling. But there was fear in his heart. Fear of failure, fear that he would not be able to rise to this supreme challenge, that his arms might not be strong enough or that he would be unable to draw his legs up . . .

The only way was to use the lightning conductor, secured firmly—he hoped, firmly—to the truck. Its metal was cold to the touch. He gripped it, eased his legs up the mast a further six inches, then a foot, two feet, so that he was crouched just below the truck.

He had a thigh over the truck now, a buttock, and was sitting there comfortably at ease, waiting for his breathing to slow for the final effort.

It was, in the end, easier than he had thought. He just moved his hands farther and farther up the conductor and got one heel, then the other, onto the rounded top of the truck. And drew himself to a standing position.

He looked down at the River Dart, at the mellow fields, some already ploughed for spring sowing, at the red-tinted beech tree tops so far below. But the mist obscured the broader panoramas he had enjoyed the other day. He could make out the wake of a cutter sailing downstream from Dittisham, some figures moving about the narrow streets of Kingswear. And finally, but still blurred in the mist drifting across the river valley, a group of cadets on deck, white faces pointed upwards: anonymous, unidentifiable figures, seven in all.

It was Buller's only disappointment. He had relished the climb as always, relished the challenge; now he enjoyed the view and this sense of possessing the whole world. But for some perverse reason that he did not attempt to analyze (he was no great self-analyst at any time) he was sorry that he had spectators. This was an accomplishment he had wanted to keep to himself.

❧ ⚜ ❧

Chapter V

March 24, 1878, a bright but cold early spring day, with a brisk north-westerly blowing. At 2:20 on that Sunday afternoon, a cutter's crew consisting of the two Wales boys, Archy Buller, and the third-termer, or "sixer," Harry Duff-Davies, untied the boat from alongside the *Britannia*. Duff-Davies was extremely resentful at having to consort with such lowly beings on his Sunday afternoon. However, Mr. Dalton had made it a condition of his two charges' going sailing that a senior cadet of experience and responsibility should be in command, and the *Britannia*'s commanding officer had arranged matters accordingly.

All four cadets wore boots, thick white drill trousers, monkey jackets, and the uniform cadet's peaked navy blue caps.

After supervising the letting go of the painter and the hoisting of the sails, Harry Duff-Davies took no further interest in his comrades or the cutter, settling down in the bows with a book on navigation. Buller and Prince George did most of the work, with Prince Eddie occasionally taking the tiller while they tacked slowly upriver.

By 3:30 P.M. they had followed the River Dart, which flowed here between high rolling hills, up as far as the village of Dittisham. Here Duff-Davies began to take an interest in events again. There was a well-known sweetshop which doubled as the post office, and he put away his book and ordered Buller to take the cutter alongside the little jetty.

Addressing Prince George, Duff-Davies in his lazy, affectedly drawling voice ordered him ashore. "You're to get me a bottle of pop and half a pound of bullseyes."

"Can I have some money, please?" To go shopping was against regulations, as they all knew, but the Prince also knew that it was useless to argue.

"I'll pay you when you come back." Duff-Davies was back with his book, but added in a soft voice which only Buller heard, "Or might."

Prince George was already running along the jetty towards the village when Buller said challengingly, "You *will* pay him, I'll see to that."

Duff-Davies turned on him sharply, his cheeks flushed. "Don't you cheek me, you whippersnapper, or I'll throw you to the fishes."

"You wouldn't dare. You're a coward and a bully, Duff-Davies, and everyone knows it. You *never* pay the Wales boys—I've seen you."

The senior cadet appeared to be retreating in the face of this onslaught, but added in defense, "They're made of gold —soft and rich, both of them."

Prince Eddie, aroused at last, said, "That's not true. We get a shilling a week, and no more."

The argument was halted by the arrival next to them at the jetty of Old Paul's ferryboat. He was a local character, well into his eighties, with hands like shoe leather from pulling to and fro across the Dart, and a face as red and wrinkled as a Devonshire ploughed field. He claimed to have been a powder monkey in the *Victory* at Trafalgar. No one had disproved the story, which was sure to benefit him a tip of a penny or two from strangers as they were rowed across from Devon to Cornwall.

When he had helped ashore his one passenger, a young girl in a bonnet with a bag of shopping, he turned to the boys. Old Paul always enjoyed what he called "a yarn" with the cadets, though he did all the talking. He touched his cap to Prince Eddie and remarked, "It's comin' up rough for ye youngsters." He pointed upriver to the north where dark clouds were building up.

"We don't mind getting wet," said Buller cheerfully.

"Rain's one thing, river's another. Minds me of that arternoon arter t'battle." Duff-Davies affected a loud groan and said, "Here we go," without raising his head from his book. But Old Paul was half deaf, had been, from the guns, for seventy-three years, since "t'battle," and carried on. "Of course Lord Nelson, 'e knew. Down in t'cockpit 'e might've been, bleeding 'is life away for 'is country. But 'e knew. Warned 'is Captain, I 'eard 'e say so. But no one took notice and we lost 'alf our prizes and our fortunes—I'd be a rich man now . . ."

Prince George, carrying the bottle and the bag of sweets in one hand, was letting go the painter when Old Paul turned and touched his cap to him. "What are ye up to, young sir? Not going out in t'river—not with this squall comin' up?"

Duff-Davies told the Prince to carry on, but Buller intervened. "You listen to Old Paul—he ought to know this river."

"I've just about had enough—"

"You do as ye're told." Old Paul's voice was very firm suddenly, as if he were back on deck as a Chief Petty Officer. "Take down those sails, make fast t'painter—and then ye runs for it." He looked up at the sky again, and no one could mistake the threatening nature of the great black cloud sweeping down across Dartmoor. "Ye feel that wind—eh?" It had backed suddenly to the northwest, setting the sailhoops rattling against the mast. "That's the sort of squall to capsize a ship if she's not properly handled."

The first snow flurries hit them like pellets, and the four boys, suddenly alarmed, kept their backs to the rising wind as they struggled to get the sails down. Before turning to run for shelter, Buller glanced back across the river. Though half-blinded by the driving snow, he could see that the placid waters of the River Dart had been transformed into violent turbulence, and the waves that must have swept them to their death were already pounding and breaking over the jetty.

In the diminutive cabin of the schooner *Emma*, 137 tons, were several well-worn charts of the east, southeast, and south coasts of England, a copy of Nares's *Seamanship*, a manual on signalling at sea, and copies of *The North Sea Pilot* and *The Channel Pilot*. On page 379 of this last book, whose binding was stained by seawater and torn at the spine, was a descriptive passage typical of these essential guides:

> The Coast between St. Catherine's Point and Dunnose consists of a low cliff, behind which rise large masses of rock named the Undercliff, which is again backed by a precipitous rocky wall nearly 500 feet above the sea, with Downs rising higher still in the rear.

The *Emma*'s Captain knew this southern coast of the Isle of Wight as well as he knew the configuration of Flamboro's Head, the cliffs between Dover and Folkestone, or Selsey Bill. For three years, and with a crew of five, he had been running between Newcastle-upon-Tyne and Poole, Dorset, bringing coal to southern England from the rich seams of Northumberland, as sailors (including Captain Cook) had done for centuries. On Sunday, March 24, 1878, he had left Poole harbour and by 3:45 P.M. was sailing close inshore between St. Catherine's Point and Dunnose, with a stiff breeze just abaft of his port beam.

Captain William Jenken had expected a satisfactory and uneventful day's sailing until shortly before this time, when he had seen the building up of black cloud to the north over the hills of the island. Suspecting a freshening wind, but certainly no significant trouble, he had hauled down the flying jib, main-topmast staysail, and topsail, and altered course a point or two to keep well under the shelter of the high cliffs. Like the coastguard at Bonchurch a few minutes earlier, he took note of a frigate about three and a half miles out on the same course as the *Emma*, under a full press of sail, including stunsails set on the fore and main topmasts. He calculated her speed as a full 8 knots, perhaps more, and as the black cloud approached and became darker and more menacing in appearance, Captain Jenken wondered at the seeming rashness of the frigate's commander under the circumstances.

He said something to his mate on the subject, and the mate shrugged his shoulders. " 'e's Royal Navy—'e should know."

Almost at once the two men on the schooner's deck felt the sudden chill of a breath of wind from the north. Within less than half a minute, it had become a breeze, and soon after that a brisk wind. Before Captain Jenken had to give all his attention to his own ship, he saw the frigate, now heeling heavily to starboard, suddenly become shut off from sight by the snow squall; as if *The Flying Dutchman* had been briefly glimpsed again, and then, like any other phantom ship, had dissolved into the weather.

"She'll be feeling it," Captain Jenken said.

" 'e's Royal Navy—'e should know." The mate was not a man of original thought.

The little *Emma*, too, was engulfed by the onrush of snow coming off the high land of Luccombe Chine. Captain Jenken felt no anxiety for his schooner. Close inshore and a few miles west of Ventnor, he was well protected, but he could hear the fury of the squall as it beat its way down south from the island into the Channel like some rampaging fiend.

The storm took almost an hour to wear itself out. Then, as suddenly as the sky had closed over the sea, it was clear again, the sun came out as brightly as before, and only the shining deck and the thin spread of white over the Downs and the dripping shrouds gave evidence of the ordeal. The frigate appeared to have weathered the squall so successfully that she had disappeared round Dunnose, and there was no other ship in sight. Just crystal-shining sea for as far as the eye could reach, with the sun lower in the western sky now.

Rod saw the black cloud over the Downs a moment before Ben Cuddiford came up on deck and tapped Rod on the shoulder. "The glass's falling, falling like a diving cormorant," he said.

Rod could not take his eyes off the great dark shape that was already half filling the sky over the Isle of Wight. He said, "Why doesn't the Captain give the order to take in sail? And close the ports, for that matter?" At the same time he recalled the Scottish Chief Petty Officer's sharp comment a day earlier, before they had raised the Lizard Lighthouse: "So, young Maclewin, y'ken all the answers, noo? Y'cuid teach Captain Hare a lesson—after six months in the Queen's Navy?"

All right. So he and Ben hardly knew a nave-hole from a navel hood, a gunwale from a gaub-line, but they did know that a rapidly falling barometer and the sudden threatening appearance of a cloud as black as tar from the northwest called for action of some kind. And none was so far forthcoming. Not an order from Lieutenant Randolph, officer-of-the-watch, or from Captain Marcus Hare, standing there beside him on the poop deck close to the wheel.

Both officers had their heads back, staring up at the ship's sails—courses, topsails, topgallants, royals—all well filled by the brisk wind as the *Eurydice* headed for Spithead at a little over 8 knots. It was 3:45 P.M., sunset was at 6:17, and at this spanking rate they would be at their anchorage well before darkness fell, something they all wanted.

Unseen, the glass that sharp-eyed Ben Cuddiford had observed falling with ominous and spectacular speed, was now down to 29. The wind had suddenly dropped. At first sight of the beech woods, the green meadows, and the Downs themselves voluptuously rounded and rolling from the

Needles east, the pattern of hedgerows not yet green for spring—at first sight of all this, Rod's heart had lifted, after the months away from England. Now he could recognize only the menace of the black monster creeping across this landscape, across the sky towards them, betokening a line squall, and a strong one at that.

Why was nobody doing anything?

There was a schooner between the *Eurydice* and the cliffs, well inshore and heading for Dunnose Head. There was no other sail or smudge of steamer smoke in sight, as if all shipping, not deceived by the bright sunshine, had scurried for shelter.

Ben scrambled up the rigging to see better.

"That schooner'll be all right," he called to Rod, and swung himself down to land lightly on the spotless deck beside him again.

There was much bustle now, but it was not related to the threatening squall. In fifteen minutes it would be eight bells, and the first dog watch would soon be taking over from the afternoon watch. This would coincide with Prayers, so as many as 200 of the frigate's company of 320 would shortly be on deck.

Among them would be passengers—Colonel Ferrier of the Royal Engineers, a consular official from Barbados invalided home, and several Army supernumeraries. The duties of others kept them below, and Ordinary Seaman Second Class Alfred W. Watter, who had deserted ship January 7 at Grenada and been recaptured, was in irons and securely locked in the cells as he had been for the entire passage from the West Indies, and no doubt would be for much longer when his sentence was eventually made known.

When the black cloud cut off the sun—and it was as if all the lanterns on the mess deck had simultaneously been doused —Rod became aware of a change in the air as rapid as in the light. The wind. Of course it was the wind. The newly developed responses of a young man whose life was now bound up with the sea's cruelty and deception told him at once. It had freshened and backed to the northwest, bringing with it air that might have come straight off the polar cap. Then gusts, as if the heavens were short of breath.

The sky was overwhelmingly black, all black, with only the thinnest line of sunshine playing on the sea fifty miles down Channel, like light from under a door. The temperature had dropped as sharply as the barometer had.

A rustle of discomfited canvas, the first whine of wind through the shrouds, beating like a boxer who is still only teasing but is hellbent on destruction. And above these sounds, Captain Marcus's voice from the poop deck:

"Furl the stuns'ls!"

Rod's bare feet were already dancing up the lower ratlines, hands racing forward in unison, up, up . . .

"Furl the fore royals, furl the main royals, furl the mizzen royals, furl the fore t'gallants . . ."

His Captain's voice followed him, fading.

Rod was at the first yardarm truss and there were others of the watch above and below him, Jack Watt's bare feet in his face, Arthur Brewer's hands striking his own feet, calling out. "Look sharp there, get up there . . ."

The wind was biting at them—razor cold, already bringing flurries of snow. Someone below, not the Captain, was shouting, "Port watch, take in the royals." But before anyone was halfway to the mizzen royals, another voice, more like the Captain's, was shouting, "Come down! Come down!" And with a note of despair, "If you can't let it go, cut it loose!"—an order which Rod found puzzling.

For a moment there was pandemonium in the rigging, with some of the watch still struggling up while others, already panicking, fought to get down. Rod was flung to one side, almost lost his grip, was kicked in the leg, regained a hold. He leaped the last ten feet to the deck and at once fell over onto his back. The frigate had taken on a heavy list to starboard, which he had failed to notice while climbing down the ratlines.

The squall had struck the 900-ton *Eurydice* as if she were

a fragment of flotsam, driving her off her course. Ben was lost in the sudden crowding of hands on deck. There were shouts and—the first of many, and more chilling than the gale—screams.

Rod could just see that there were six men at the wheel, among them Sub-Lieutenant Edward Gifford, all straining and leaning as sharply as the ship herself in their combined and fruitless effort to get the helm over and prevent the frigate from capsizing. But at once the snow, driving horizontally across the deck, cut them from view, and Rod could only just make out the terrifying sight of the water rushing over the lee netting along the starboard side, tearing off the big cutter from the booms and throwing it out of sight into the snow as if it were a piece of newspaper.

Rod seized the mizzen shroud to prevent himself from following the cutter to destruction. But the *Eurydice* could no longer offer him safety. She was going, there could no longer be any doubt of that, and Rod—through the fear that gripped his throat as tightly as his hands clutched the rope—exclaimed, "So fast! How could it happen so fast?" He might have shouted it aloud, unable to hear his own voice, though he could hear, above the cries and screams of men and raging wind through the rigging, the voice of his Captain, "All hands for themselves!"

Captain Marcus Hare's last order was also the least needed. Survival was already a one-man and desperate battle which some had lost—another seaman and then another as the order was repeated, crashing down the near vertical deck and, arms and legs flailing, into the sea.

Forward, intermittently seen, a number of sailors were stripping, their clothes flying away, at once lost in the driving snow. Some had a lifebuoy, but not many, and Rod remembered that most of the lifebelts had been painted the day before and had been hanging to dry over the ship's starboard side to catch the best of the sun. A bitter stroke of fate, that.

He managed to get a grip on the weather netting and pulled himself onto the ship's port side. There were hands gripping the edge of one of the open ports, and Rod managed to drag the man up. He did not even glance at Rod before plunging fully dressed into the sea and being swept away.

The Captain was on the ship's port side, too, standing hatless near the quarter boat, suddenly bereft of responsibility or even of anything to do, momentarily a pathetic figure. The open ports were like a line of guilty evidence.

Rod kicked off his trousers. He was one of the *Eurydice*'s strongest swimmers, but he did not relish the touch of the choppy sea. Many of his shipmates were on the side of the doomed vessel now, some naked, others half clothed, some sitting; those who were standing were leaning into the wind and against the angle of the hull. One, clutching a lifebelt, jumped in, and as if relieved of a great weight, the frigate gave another lurch, revealing her red keel through the waves.

There were five men in a small boat, slipping past at a pace. It rose on a wave and capsized, throwing the men into the water. Before it faded from sight, Rod saw two of the men (one he recognized as a fellow Geordie, Peter Wint) clambering onto the bottom.

The frigate was going, digging in her near-horizontal bows, sailing to the bottom under a full spread of sail. They had all been warned of the suck, the dreaded suck when a ship goes down, drawing with it anyone near.

Suddenly the snow was blinding, so that Rod could barely see his own bare feet against the black-painted ship's side. It was time to go. He enjoyed a grain of comfort by noting that the water could not be colder than this biting wind, which—in any case—must soon hurl him into the sea.

A quick prayer. "Almighty God, heavenly Father . . ." The church at the end of Armstrong Crescent. Kneeling there on Christmas Day. His mother slipping him a penny for the collection.

The sounds of the storm and of desperate men had faded. In respect for his brief prayer? Or because the sea had swallowed most of the *Eurydice*'s sails and rigging, and most of the ship's company were now in the water, or already beneath it, cries silenced?

Rod joined them, for life or death, walking in over the deep keel that, exposed like this, deprived the frigate of the last of her dignity, like her unfortunate commander. The sea was so cold that Rod was thrown up one side of a wave and fell fifteen feet into its trough before he began swimming. And almost at once, the first pair of desperate arms clutched the shoulders of champion swimmer Maclewin, and then his neck.

As Captain Jenken of the *Emma* was about to order sail to be made, he caught a glimpse of a mast and rigging. It was the flapping of white canvas that had attracted his eye—royals they were, white naval sails, as effective as any marker buoy for what could only be a wreck. It was less than two miles away, in the exact spot where the frigate had last been seen, driving along so bravely for Spithead. Captain Jenken could see all three topmasts, certain confirmation that it was the same ship, one of the topmasts apparently snapped off. It was not deep here, maybe ten or twelve fathoms, and she must have capsized, taken in water, and righted herself before touching bottom.

"Get aloft, Jack," the Captain ordered one of the hands. "There'll have to be survivors."

The mate and the other hands were setting sail, and Captain Jenken brought round the helm of his schooner so that they were making for the wreck. He could hear faint sounds of shouting, and there was a lot of flotsam in the water but no sign of any survivor until a voice from aloft called down and the lookout pointed ahead. "There, in the jacket . . ."

The *Emma* stood towards the figure in the water, head and shoulders showing above the cork jacket. A waving arm gave proof that the man was still alive. The schooner tacked once to fetch him, coming alongside while one of the hands dropped a knotted rope over the side. It took four of them to drag him up and over the gunwale, where they laid him out on the deck.

Captain Jenken saw that he was little more than a boy, perhaps fifteen or sixteen, naked except for a grey vest, his skin shrivelled from the cold and wet, but brown from the sun except between his waist and upper thighs. His eyes remained closed until he began retching and he was then seized with a fit of coughing. One of the hands held him to a sitting position and put a rug round his shoulders, and the boy opened his eyes and looked about him.

"Thanks, mates. There are others out there," he managed to say. "Not many but some." He spoke in a rich west-country accent, like that of the crew of the schooner, which added to their relief at the rescue.

"Get him below, lads, and give him a good rubbing and a mug of rum." The Captain addressed the boy. "We've got a boat in the water and we'll pick up any still alive. What's your name, boy?"

"Ben Cuddiford, sir. From Plymouth. Thank you, sir." His eyes had a wild look, as if still enveloped in the nightmare of his ordeal, and he was shaking all over from the cold and the shock.

The tide was on the ebb which helped the boat crew by bringing the survivors towards them. At first it seemed as if there might be a number of them, but they turned out to be loose lockers or other fragments of wreckage. But four more were dragged, limp and only half-conscious, into the boat and laid out unceremoniously in the bottom. One was a 1st class seaman, who was in the best condition and was able to give his name as Sydney Fletcher. An Army officer was identifiable as a Colonel by his uniform, and there was a Lieutenant R.N., very weak, and a Petty Officer whom Fletcher identified as Bennett, who was dead before they reached the *Emma*.

The schooner's total complement of six were employed in lifting on board, as gently as they could in the choppy seas, the three survivors and the one dead man. It took another ten minutes to get them below, where two of the hands were employed as nurses, massaging and giving sips of rum to those who could take it.

No one noticed the figure spread over a wooden locker which had drifted on the tide against the schooner's port side. But when the *Emma* got under way again, the locker was driven down the length of the hull, banging against the ship's timbers as if knocking for attention. They all heard it, and one of the hands ran across the deck and spotted the locker and its passenger as it drifted astern.

"If you starboard the helm, sir," the hand shouted, "there's another here." Then, "He looks a goner, though."

The *Emma* bore up on the wreckage rising and falling on the waves, and two of the crew leaned over in time to prevent the head from striking the schooner's side.

"Ease him. That's it, get his other arm. Mind his head again."

They were both strong Cornishmen, but even a lightweight—as this boy appeared to be—took a lot of lifting up from the sea. He was stark naked and, like his shipmate, brown-skinned from the tropical sun, except where he was white from wearing shorts. He was quite limp and appeared lifeless, his head falling back before they laid him out.

Captain Jenken left the tiller and bent over the body. He had been at sea for many years and had seen many drowned men washed up on the shore or plucked from the ocean. But this one, so young, not yet fully grown, like the other two below. It was heartrending, no doubt of it—plain heartrending. What a waste! And the thought crossed his mind that the frigate had been a training ship, manned mostly by boys like this, boys without the experience to shorten sail in time.

He leaned down to tuck the blanket close about the boy's neck, noticing the soft down on his cheek. Then he placed his right ear close against the boy's heart. And, as if from a great distance, he could just hear the faintest beat of life.

Queen Victoria had arrived at Windsor the previous afternoon by train, accompanied by her youngeset daughter and constant companion, Princess Beatrice, and attended by Lady Abercromby, Colonel J. C. M'Neill V.C., and her private secretary.

The following day, March 24, broke fine and clear though with a cold northerly wind. The Queen attended to her regular duties with state papers during the early part of the morning, and then, in spite of a tiresome cough, took a short drive in Windsor Park with Lady Abercromby and the Honourable Horatia Stopford, Princess Beatrice complaining of being unwell. She had hoped for a second drive later in the afternoon, but when she went to the window of her drawing room and looked out across the park, she saw a great black cloud filling the sky to the north and fast approaching.

The Queen therefore gave instructions to cancel her carriage and observed what she described as "a sudden violent snow storm" build up. "It continued snowing for some time."

Windsor Park, and for as far as the Royal eye could see, was still white the following morning, and the Queen noted that there was nine degrees of frost, an unusually low temperature for the time of year. Princess Beatrice, she was informed, was less indisposed but would not be down for breakfast. The Queen's own cough was still very troublesome and remained so all day.

But such trivial observations were driven from her mind when she sat down for breakfast and started to read the day's news. Later she recorded in her Journal: "Horrified at seeing in the papers, that yesterday, during that snow storm, & gale of wind, the 'Eurydice' a training ship, was lost, literally blown over, and went down in a moment." Noting how few had survived out of the total complement, she added, "Too awful! Three others were picked up, but died of exhaustion. It happened near Ventnor, almost within sight of Spithead. The 'Eurydice' was returning from the West Indies, all the families awaiting them. It was quite calm before, & they had all sails set—too fearful! Could think of little else . . ."

Immediately after breakfast, Her Majesty composed a message of condolence to the relatives and friends of all those who had drowned, and a further message of sympathy for the Admiralty. She also learned that Commander Lord Charles Beresford, a friend of her eldest son's, the Prince of Wales, had already opened a fund for the support of the dependents of the men lost in the disaster.

Rod could hear Ben's voice, rising and falling but always faint, as if he were talking in a normal voice while on the yardarm in a gale. Rod missed a lot of what he said, but he did not much mind as the words served only as a reminder of the torment he had endured so recently.

"It was the cold that did for them, sir. It was terrible, right through into your bones . . . I had to kick them off— I had to. It wasn't nice, sir, your own shipmates, but we'd all have gone under. They knew I was a good swimmer, sir. Seaman Maclewin and I, we won all the prizes . . ."

That had been the worst part, Rod recalled dimly, tearing hands from your neck and throat, desperate hands. He had even bitten one when he had been forced down and was half-choking. And kicked off others. Brutally. It had weakened him dreadfully, and he had been ready to give up, with the cold like shafts of ice probing deep into his body. Then the locker had knocked against him, and he had struggled to get onto it. Had it taken an hour? It had seemed like it. It had probably been only a few minutes, though.

There was a face leaning over him, grave and bearded. A hand passed to and fro across his eyes, and he followed it; a voice—deep and authoritative—said, "This one'll be all right." Then, "How do you feel, little 'un?"

It seemed a long time before Rod was able to speak, but the face was still there, blue eyes and a rather big nose. "I'm all right, sir."

But Rod was still only intermittently aware of what was happening about him, and what had happened to him, and his spirits and state of mind rose and fell as that locker had done during that one hour and twenty minutes of suffering and pain.

One moment it was a voice saying gravely, "He's gone, I'm afraid, John."

Then it was—clearly, indisputably—Ben's voice again. Ben alive! Where was he? He wanted to talk to Ben, to ask him how he had beaten the cold and the sea.

A new voice spoke in the darkness. "Yes, sir, I told the Cottage Hospital at Bonchurch to be ready. Yes, twenty beds, sir."

"I wish we were in need of that many, John. I'm afraid this soldier is going."

Up and down, up and down. First the fight in the water, then the locker, then this cabin, and always his hopes and spirits, going up and down.

There were the sounds of the schooner tying up alongside, and more voices. There was a lantern hanging from the cabin roof, and now it stopped swinging. Rod could see up the hatchway. Figures were coming down the ladder, carrying stretchers, and behind them was the dark night sky.

And it was then, and not until then, that Rod Maclewin noted that everything was at last steady, that the undulating had at last ceased, and that in conformity with this wonderful new sense of peace, his spirits were so high that he felt heady with the knowledge that he was alive, and overwhelmed with thankfulness to Almighty God for sparing him.

The *Britannia*'s chaplain extended prayers by ten minutes on Monday morning. The 200 cadets, bareheaded and kneeling in the chapel, listened to the deep, reverential voice.

"This tragedy touches our hearts not only in its scale, and because so many of those who died were so young and scarcely older than any of you, but also because they were lost at sea, an element which can be awful when aroused, an element upon which so much of your future lives will be spent.

"Gentlemen, the sea is . . ."

Then they had sung "For Those in Peril on the Sea."

Afterwards, Prince George said to Buller, "Come with me a minute. Eddie and I have to see Mr. Dalton before lessons. He wants to show us Grandmama's message. 'It is very moving and noble,' he says."

Eddie joined them and they hurried aft, past the Commander's cabin, to Mr. Dalton's quarters. John Dalton had been the Princes' tutor and governor for seven years now.

The boys greeted him, and Mr. Dalton rose from his desk, a copy of *The Times* in his hands. He read aloud the message Queen Victoria had sent to the relatives and friends of all those who had been lost in the *Eurydice*, and then handed the newspaper to Prince Eddie so that all three boys could read the opening of the long account.

Just before they entered the classroom, with a written message from Mr. Dalton to explain their lateness, Prince George said in a low voice to Buller, "Do you think that was the same squall?"

"Of course it was. And that would have made an even bigger story, if you and Eddie had been drowned."

"Shall I ask Grandmama to give Old Paul a decoration?"

Buller laughed softly. "You say nothing to anyone, or you'll never be allowed sailing again."

At the end of their sons' third term and three months after the *Eurydice* disaster, the Prince and Princess of Wales came to Dartmouth to present the prizes. It was a day of ritual and celebration and colourful formality, with pulling races in the river, speeches, and the inspection and prize-giving at the end.

The Prince of Wales, portly and of rather below average height, dressed in a black suit with waistcoat crisscrossed by gold chains and wearing a black Homburg hat, paced decisively across the deck. Inspections and parades figured prominently in his official life, and he was not going to waste any time, that was clear, as he walked up and down the ranks, the Admiral, the *Britannia*'s Captain, senior Lieutenant, and Warrant Officer behind him.

The Prince's eyes glanced along the line of faces, occasionally dropping to check gleaming webbing belt and white shoes. Once in every row he paused to speak to a cadet. Archy saw him stop at the boy immediately in front of him, heard the boy say, "Yes, Your Royal Highness, very much," and saw the back of his neck redden with embarrassment.

Then it was with a curious feeling of excitement that Buller saw the Prince of Wales standing in front of him, a puckish smile on his round, bearded face. He was about Buller's own height, his eyes were brown and slightly protuberant, Buller recalled later, and there was a glow of good health and good living to the Royal face. The Captain must have pointed Buller out at the Prince's request, for he began talking to him at once, using his name.

"My sons would like you to stay with us at Osborne later this month, Mr. Buller. I saw your father at dinner the other evening, and he had no objection to our claiming a few days of your time. Do you?"

"Yes, sir, yes . . ." Buller found himself stumbling over his words and pulled himself together, encouraged by the broadening smile. "Your Royal Highness, it is a great honour to be asked, and yes, sir, I—I accept your—"

"That's good. The Princess and I will be very pleased." He was already three cadets away, walking firmly down the deck. An equerry paused in front of Buller and said, "You will be informed of details this evening, Cadet Buller."

"Yes, sir."

The rest of the hot summer day passed like a hazy dream, broken by a brief period of backbreaking endeavour in a pulling race. Buller was starboard bow oar, and Prince George pulled the port bow oar on the same thwart, their ten-oared cutter being one of four in the race.

There was a brief moment before the start, which allowed Buller to say quietly, "Your Papa has asked me to stay at Osborne."

"That's grand," said the Prince. "I asked him to. You'll like Osborne. There are all sorts of jolly things to do."

Chapter VI

Commander Lord Charles William de la Poer Beresford, second son of the fourth Marquess of Waterford, was a rising naval officer of great charm, accomplishment, and eccentricity. He was a close friend of the Prince and Princess of Wales and, inevitably, a member of the "fast Marlborough set" and was regarded as a great buck about town, where he was a source of scandal and fun.

Beresford had entered the Navy, passed out of the *Britannia* in March 1861, eighteen years earlier than the Royal Princes and Archy Buller; had cruised the world and doubled the Horn under sail; had possessed numerous beautiful women; had gambled recklessly, to the near-despair of his father; and had commanded the Royal Yacht *Osborne*.

By 1878, however, he was becoming what his friends described as "settled down," although in his case this was only a relative phrase. He was thirty-two years old, had become a Member of Parliament, had found someone he believed he could love steadily and had decided he would marry if she would have him.

By strange coincidence, he proposed to Miss Ellen Jeromina Gardner on the day the *Eurydice* went down. She was the daughter of a Countess—a plumpish beauty, who made up heavily at a time when only prostitutes and actresses were expected to do so, and did not care what people said of her. "Dot," as her future husband called her, was as disregarding of public opinion and convention and quite as eccentric as Lord Charles was. One member of the nobility claimed that he thought he saw "a butterfly fluttering in the draught" above her head. "I reached out and grasped and dislodged an eyebrow," he recounted later. And her future husband referred to her as "my little pinnace with a new coat of paint on." In later years, fellow naval officers called the couple "The red Admiral and the painted lady"; and fellow Parliamentarians, "The windbag and the ragbag."

On that squally March day, Dot agreed to marry the rising Commander R.N., and the date for the marriage was fixed for a month and a day later at St. Peter's, Eaton Square. Their home was to be number 100 Eaton Square for the first ten years of their married life.

During that early spring of 1878, Lord Charles also became deeply involved in less happy events. As soon as he heard of the sinking of the training frigate, almost within sight of the eagerly waiting friends and relatives of the young men on board, he wrote a letter to *The Times* and started a fund for their support. However frivolous and wild he might be, for Lord Charles the Royal Navy was the most important thing in his life. He was also a very kind man. Recognizing the damage to the recruiting and to the reputation of the service the disaster could inflict, he determined that these dependents and relatives should at least suffer as little as possible financially.

Lord Charles was also determined to discover the cause of the *Eurydice*'s sinking and with his powerful influence quickly contrived an invitation from the Admiral-Superintendent at Portsmouth Dockyard to participate in the salvage operations and the investigations.

It was a busy time for the young Commander. Besides his Parliamentary obligations, Lord Charles was also serving in the brand-new, mastless, innovatory battleship *Thunderer*. His duties were demanding and included the reception of visitors, and these were many, for there was great curiosity about this massive ironclad that heralded a new age of fighting ship.

Two of these visitors were Gilbert and Sullivan, who wanted to ensure that they had got the details right for their opera *H.M.S. Pinafore*, shortly to have its premiere. ("Quite excellent!" Lord Charles commented.)

Another was Queen Victoria, who noted sadly how her dear late Prince Albert would have been so *deeply* interested in the mechanical miracles of the ship: its torpedoes, its engine room, its great turret protected by fourteen inches of steel. She found the ladders rather steep for her little legs and unsuitably long dress. In the evening she had a dinner party for the officers at Osborne. Lord Charles had recently displeased the Queen with his goings-on, but now she noted merely that she found him "Very funny. A trifle cracky, but clever and a good officer."

Lord Charles wished to question at length all three survivors of the *Eurydice* and did so as soon as they were fit enough to leave the hospital. On Monday April 1, 1878, he and Rear Admiral Foley set up an informal inquiry, to precede the official one, at Portsmouth Dockyard. At three o'clock in the afternoon, Ordinary Seaman Roderick Maclewin was called from the waiting room outside the Admiral's office.

Rod's recovery from the ordeal had at first been rapid, and he had been impatient to leave the Cottage Hospital. He had been given further massage on arrival in the ward. Hot blankets had been applied to his body, and he had been given a sharp-tasting drink which made him fall into a long and deep sleep.

It was after he awoke that he became restless and complained to the nurse that he was well enough to dress. Ben Cuddiford, in the next bed, felt the same, and when permission was refused, they grumbled together and then ate a hearty meal. The Press, they learned, had arrived in force and were anxious to question all three survivors who had been blessed with such good luck and remarkable tenacity to have lived for so long in such cold and rough seas. None of the reporters was allowed in, and the only other person Rod saw was his mother.

The police called at 19D Groom Road early on the Monday morning, and for one terrible moment as she stood in the doorway in answer to the officer's knock, Doris Maclewin thought that Rod had drowned, believing that the presence of police meant only bad news. She was quickly reassured, and as she heard the words, "Your son is one of only three survivors," she had to be helped to the kitchen chair.

"The telegram says he is not in any danger but is in hospital," continued the policeman, who then gave her a Navy railway travel warrant and instructions on how to reach the hospital.

The reaction for Rod set in the following morning. He awoke dizzy from what he later learned was delayed shock. He was unable to lift his head from the pillow, the room revolved slowly about him, and the objects were faint, as if seen through a haze of smoke.

Emerging from this mist there later appeared the beloved face of his mother, and momentarily Rod believed that he was dead and that she had come to mourn him. But Doris Maclewin's face was only anxious, not grieving. He heard her say, "You're going to be all right—there's my bonny Roddy."

After a while, he was able to say a few words of thanks and to inquire how she had got there. He felt her hand holding his, then he drifted off into another long sleep.

Doris Maclewin stayed in Bonchurch for two days, and when she left, Rod had almost completely recovered. With the other two, he was transferred to the barracks at Portsmouth. He knew that the loss of a ship always entailed a court-martial, and he had tried, with the help of the others, to piece together the sequence of events which had led to the capsizing of their ship. Now, at the preliminary inquiry, he was being asked to tell his story and to answer questions.

Of the two officers across the table, it was the younger one, the Commander with three stripes on his sleeve, the two rows of brass buttons on his jacket twinkling in the light of the afternoon sun, who spoke most and attracted Rod's attention. The questions were asked in a persuasive, drawling voice, and there was every evidence of friendliness in his face and expression—a fleshy "well-fed" face, clean shaven, full lips that formed easily into a smile, intelligent, knowing brown eyes, large nose, receding curly brown hair at the forehead, full-growing at the side.

"And did you hear any order to take in sail before the squall struck?" Lord Charles Beresford asked Rod.

"Yes, sir. But there wasn't time to comply. Some of us were up the mizzen topmast yard when we were called down."

"A bit of confusion—eh, laddie?" The Commander smiled confidentially, so that no one could have given other than a straight answer.

"Yes, sir." Rod recalled the screams, the struggle to get down, the raw panic of boys suddenly fearful for their lives. And when the Admiral asked if there had been disorder, Rod said, "Yes, sir. Especially when the Captain shouted, 'All hands for themselves!'"

Rod recounted how the cutter had been torn away, how the ship had heeled over so hard that six men at the wheel could not right the helm, that the water was suddenly over the lee netting, that . . .

Rod was in the Admiral's office for more than half an hour, a secretary taking notes of all that was said. The more he spoke, the better he was able to recall those fatal minutes —how he had watched the black cloud towering over the

Isle of Wight Downs, had remarked on it to his friend and fellow survivor, how they had both been surprised that no order had been forthcoming.

"Had she hauled the wind for Spithead when the squall struck?"

"Yes, sir," Rod said decisively.

"So the cloud might have been obscured to the watch?"

Rod paused. He had not thought of that. Then, "Yes, sir, that is possible. Though my friend Ben Cuddiford and I saw it well enough."

The questions at last ceased. Rod told of his own experiences in the water. At the end there was a moment of silence, the only sound the ticking of the big brass clock on the wall.

"Well, little Midge, you were lucky," said Beresford. "That should be your name now—'Lucky Midge.'"

Rod smiled. "Aye aye, sir."

The inquiry had been so relaxed, the two officers so human and friendly, that Rod found it easy to ask the question that had been nagging at him for the past days.

"Is the Navy going to salvage the *Eurydice*, sir?"

The Admiral looked up from his papers. "Yes, Maclewin. It is very important to find the truth."

Lord Charles Beresford was looking at Rod curiously. A short, almost frail-looking boy. But that might be deceptive. His name suggested he was a Scot, his expression, his straight answers, the firm lift of his chin suggested integrity. A real salt? He thought so. "Why do you ask?"

"Well, sir. I was interested, sir. My father being an engineer an' all."

"And your father? What is he doin' now?"

"He's dead, sir. He was killed by a burst gun."

The Commander questioned him further, clearly surprised at and interested in the tragedy. "And you want to specialize in gunnery?"

"Yes, sir."

Lord Charles Beresford turned to the Admiral, smiling and

glancing at Rod as he spoke. "Seems a likely lad. I'll take him, with your permission, sir." And when the Admiral nodded at once, Lord Charles turned back to Rod and said, "I'm involved in the salvage operations. They're going to be interestin'. She's a hazard to shipping, but we can't blow her up, not with all those bodies still in her. And we're lookin' for evidence of why it happened. We're goin' to use wire hawsers for the first time, and lighters. Like a young filly being broken in, they'll either snap or do as they're told. I hear you can write, and you seem to be interested. Do you want to come as my assistant, Lucky Midge?"

"Yes, please, sir."

"Don't know what I'll say to your Mama if a snappin' hawser gets you after you beat the sea, eh?"

The salvaging of the *Eurydice* was a long, complicated, and sometimes dangerous business. Rod learnèd much from it, but the chief benefit was his friendly association with the eccentric, impetuous-but-clever, warmhearted Anglo-Irish officer. By the end, they had developed a close master-pupil relationship. When at last they were separated by the demands of the service, they understood each other well.

But three and a half years passed before they met again. During this period, Rod served in a frigate on the North American station, cruised to the Far East by way of that recent wonder of engineering, the Suez Canal, returned a year later by way of the Cape, and completed a gunnery course at the shore establishment H.M.S. *Excellent*.

He was now Gunnery Able Seaman Roderick Maclewin, eighteen years old, with the emblem of a gun with a star above and an anchor on his sleeve, earning 1 shilling 3 pence a day (and sending half of it home to his mother). Physically, he was now very strong, with arm muscles like miniatures of the hawsers he had seen raise his old ship from the Channel. He could pull a whaler with the best and was in demand for races. He was also a first-rate boxer, quick on his feet, sharp in his reactions, and utterly courageous. He was in the bantamweight class. He had grown little in height over the years and had acquired the nickname Midge that Lord Charles Beresford had first given him. But one couldn't experience the daily life of a sailor in the 1880s, with drills and evolutions, polishing and scrubbing, without acquiring hard muscle. On the few occasions when he was able to come home on leave to Newcastle, Doris Maclewin recognized the broadening of his shoulders and chest.

His mother saw something else in her son. Petty Officers and officers alike who had served with Rod noted his qualities and reported on them. He was rated highly in his records. And he deserved it. But it had not all been easy for him. Rod had seen much cruelty and unhappiness in his short life as a sailor. Since that first birching, and many more, on board the three-decker at Devonport, he had witnessed much bullying—physical and mental bullying: bullying of boys by older boys, bullying of boys by police corporals and bo'suns, humiliation of officers by senior officers, of Petty Officers by junior officers.

Rod had seen young boys forced to submit to acts of indecency by veteran ratings, and had judged it was an insult to animals to give them that name. Sodomy was rife, especially on long voyages with many weeks between ports, even though it was a serious offense against Queen's Regulations—"The Captain is to suppress all dissolute or disorderly conduct . . ." He had been attacked several times but fought so tenaciously that his would-be seducer had given up.

Time and again when ashore he had seen his shipmates squander their money, drinking themselves almost unconscious—but remaining just conscious enough to lurch to the nearest brothel to be stripped of the remainder of their money. On board again, he had seen these same men laid out in their own vomit in the scuppers, and woe betide any who were not fit for watchkeeping the following morning.

Rod had been physically hardened by taking in sail in a rising gale, clutching the rigging with his feet alone—no hand for himself, both for his country. By holystoning decks for two hours with the tropical temperature in the 90s. By standing watch in the sub-Antarctic night wearing a Fearnought coat that might have been a single layer of cotton.

He had also learned to accept the cruelty of the sea, which he had seen at its most vicious and deceitful on that March afternoon when he had been only fifteen. He had seen men crippled for life from accidents, and three times had watched (his stomach suddenly like lead) a rating fall to his death from high up the rigging, turning over and over, arms reaching frantically for a rope, until the heavy thud as he smashed against the deck—a deck that would have to be scrubbed at that place more thoroughly then ever the next morning.

The cruelty of the sea was one thing. He could accept that, for there was no alternative. The cruelty of man was quite another thing. He remembered telling himself long ago, "My feet are getting hardened, and my hands—and my heart."

But subconsciously he knew, and his mother recognized, that his heart had not hardened. If only it had, he would not have suffered so much anguish. He may have learned to eat a full meal after witnessing a birching. His stomach needed the food; rations were short enough for the physical demands that had to be met. But for his heart it was different. From time to time, when he was at gun drill in a team, loading the big 110-pound shells, he wondered how he would feel if they had been destined for the enemy instead of a canvas target on a towed raft. How would he react to real killing? Not just a backside covered with bleeding weals or a shipmate crying with the pain from a broken hip, but men blown to pieces by the shell he had helped to load or he had fired with the lanyard. Would he be any good if it came to war?

War with Russia had seemed possible for most of the time Rod had served at sea, and there had been war in Africa against first the Zulus and then the Boers. But these had been land campaigns that had not directly involved the Royal Navy. As the year 1881 ran out, however, as the chance of war against Russia diminished, another war—a war which must involve the Navy—seemed to threaten.

And it was at this time that Rod, as he completed his course at H.M.S. *Excellent*, heard again from Lord Charles Beresford.

"We have received a telegram," Rod was informed by the Chief Petty Officer in a voice that suggested that he was being honoured far beyond his deserts, "from the drafting officer instructing Able Seaman Roderick Maclewin to report on board H.M.S. *Condor*, Commander Lord Charles Beresford. Immediately," he added.

"Yes, sir."

"Well, don't just 'Yes, sir' me. Move. Look smart!"

"Aye aye, sir."

Rod packed his ditty box and seabag with his kit—his white duck trousers, spare shirt, the nightshirt his mother had made for him (an object of mockery and Rod did not care), boots, socks, and cap; and his personal possessions, including a Bible and a Prayer Book, *Robinson Crusoe* (one day he would sail to Juan Fernandez), tin plate, fork, and spoon. Then he said good-bye to the friends he had made on board the *Excellent* and made his way to the railway station, his canvas seabag over his shoulder.

"Maclewin. Lucky Midge. Able seaman now. Not much bigger than I remember you," said Lord Charles Beresford as he glanced up from the record papers lying on his desk.

Rod looked squarely into the brown eyes and said nothing. His new commanding officer smiled, his head slightly tilted. Rod saw that his hair had further receded, that he seemed a shade plumper in the face. Otherwise he was little changed. As friendly a face as he had remembered it. Steadier? Who could tell? He still looked as if he might suddenly be hell-bent on something, even if it was only a seven-foot hedge while out with the Waterford pack.

"Last ship we were on board together was the poor old *Eurydice*. You shouldn't have been there. Nasty sight. Nasty business identifyin' 'em, too, I'll have you know. And buryin' 'em.

"See you've had some foreign service. Now you're goin' to

have some more. Maybe some fun, too. Need it, too, after the *Osborne*. Soft livin'." He was referring to his time as Commander of the Prince of Wales's yacht. "Things are warmin' up in the Med. You've heard we're sailin' to the Med?"

"Yes, sir."

"Admiral Sir Beauchamp Seymour. Flagship the *Alexandra*, named after the Princess of Wales, of course. Nine thousand five hundred tons. *Condor*'s less than a tenth of her displacement. But size is nothin'. Think of Nelson with his barge and thirteen men off Cadiz, capturing a Spanish gunboat. Killed more than half her crew of thirty."

Lord Charles got up from his desk and walked across his cabin to stand in front of a reproduction of a painting of that action in 1797, Nelson lunging at a Spaniard with his sword. "Come here, little Midge. Now there's a man. Not for nothin' was he called 'The Hero.' But he wouldn't have survived but for his cockswain, that man there, see? He put his arm in the way of a cutlass stroke that would have killed Nelson on the spot. Nearly died himself, too. No Nile, no Copenhagen, no Battle of Trafalgar."

Beresford chuckled. "You're goin' to be my cox. Did you know that, Maclewin? My cox. And if the need arises, you'll save my life for my Trafalgar." He chuckled again and then burst into laughter—deep rumbling laughter. He turned and looked down at Rod. "Well?"

"Aye, aye, sir."

Yes, Rod decided he would like that. Life might be interesting with this Commander who could break into booming laughter while talking to a mere rating. And if there was to be war there could be no doubt about how he must perform alongside this officer who remembered him after all these years, and trusted him. Yes, he would be prepared to risk his life for Commander Lord Charles Beresford, like Nelson's cox.

Approaching the sleek, shining white *Condor* at her buoy in Portsmouth harbour, Rod had admired her lines, her curved yacht prow, her compactness, her purposefulness. She was a barque-rigged gunvessel, 780 tons and smaller than the *Eurydice* even, rigged with square sails on the foremasts and the mainmasts, fore-and-aft sails on the mizzen. A single tall funnel stood forward of amidships between the foremast and the mainmast, ventilators sprouted from the upper deck like swans with necks extended. Close to the funnel was the *Condor*'s sting, a seven-inch muzzle-loading gun which could be traversed to fire on either quarter, and this weapon was supported by 64-pounders fore and aft which fired through ports. Rod had worked both these guns at the *Excellent* and knew their hitting power, merits, and demerits.

The *Condor*, he decided, was a vessel he could become proud of—small, handy, and powerful for her size. In an iron-clad battleship of the line like the *Alexandra* or *Inflexible*, you could feel lost as one of hundreds, knowing the names of only the officers and the men on your watch.

And it was good to be at sea again, to feel the first lift of the deck as they struck the Channel at the Needles, beating into a strong south-westerly in sharp January sunshine. Many ships' Captains used engines only in an emergency and regarded it as a sign of weakness if not failure to have to order the Engineer Officer—a despised being with his own quarters and accommodation because of his inferior social class, his supposed oil-stained hands and uniform—to start engines. Moreover, these Captains contended, with greater truth, coal and coal smoke were filthy, got into every nook and cranny, stained polished woodwork and brightwork. God rot the fiend incarnate who invented the damned marine engine!

Beresford was not one of these. During the first days of this commission, he showed his ship's company that engines spelled efficiency and that efficiency (and especially fighting efficiency) was his first concern. The watch went aloft and made sail whenever it was beneficial to do so—and that was not when beating down-Channel into a 25-knot wind.

So the engines—those vertical triple-expansion engines—did all the work during those first three days at sea, to the joy of the Engineer Officer and the relief of all the ship's company except the stokers, who sweated shovelling coal into the fire-boxes in the heat of the boiler room, while the watch on deck huddled in any shelter, clutching their Fearnought coats about them.

Ushant, a familiar rocky island seen through a light snow-storm; the bay living up to its reputation, and the little *Condor* biting deep into the waves, rising from the troughs to the dizzy heights with the water pouring off her forecastle, hot soup a lifesaver when coming off watch; Cape Finisterre off the port beam, low-lying, unlike St. Vincent seen at dawn thirty-six hours later; then, late in the afternoon, Trafalgar, these last two capes immortalized by two of Nelson's greatest battles. And suddenly, the wind favourable, a balminess in the air, the *Condor* slipped between Africa and Europe through the Pillars of Hercules into the Mediterranean, Gibraltar to port, the mighty rock like a crouching lion, symbol of British Imperial power, scene of siege and bloody combat . . .

Rod stood by the Captain's gig as the *Condor* headed for the anchorage under a full spread of sail, both watches standing by to shorten as they prepared to pick up their buoy. It was a tense moment for everyone though few much showed it, and the Captain not at all. At Gibraltar, there would be many eyes, many experienced and critical eyes, watching the little gunvessel coming to her buoy. It was the first port for Beresford's first fighting ship, and the ship's company was anxious to put on a good performance. As soon as they were hove to, it was Rod's duty to ensure that the Captain's gig was properly lowered, the falls let go, while the boat came down with a run from the heads of the davits into the sea. Now the Captain himself must be properly received and rowed ashore, all in conformity with hallowed tradition. After four years as a sailor, Rod knew the orders as well as the words of The Lord's Prayer intoned every morning on board H.M. ships; and when the time came:

"Get your oars to pass."

"Give way together."

Rod was at the stern, behind the Captain on his polished

mahogany seat, dressed in white tropical kit and white topee; Rod watched the stroke, making small adjustments to the tiller. A sea of faces on the jetty, many more about the town, leaned from windows in the sun, many more again on the men-o'-war and merchantmen, the tugs and fishing boats, anchored or alongside. Ignore them all, concentrate on the job in hand. . . .

"Oars!" And the galley's crew lifted them in unison, holding them horizontally in their rowlocks, until—

"Toss oars!" And up they went to the vertical as one. The galley came alongside the Ragged Staff Steps; the crewman with the painter jumped deftly.

"Thank you, Cox."

"Sir."

Life on board the *Condor* became softer after Gibraltar. The passage to Crete to join Admiral Seymour's fleet was an easy one; and as so often at sea, when they had more time on their hands and less work to occupy them, relations that had been forged in cold and storm and adverse winds did not further improve in the calm seas and early spring sunshine of the Mediterranean.

Rod had been aware from the beginning of a feeling of hostility towards him among a small group of ratings of the port watch. Not until the second day out of Gibraltar did he recognize it more clearly, and the reason for it, and its leader. Rod had been the last rating to join the *Condor* at Portsmouth, when the company thought they were complete. Then this small, eighteen-year-old leading seaman had joined the ship, and was at once offered the sought-after duties as Captain's cox.

"Masters's goin' t'get yer. You watch."

Rod heard the soft voice of his cockney neighbour as they swung in their hammocks late in the evening after being piped down for the night.

"What for?"

"Never yer mind. 'e's a rough one—you watch."

The *Condor* had all sail set, with a light breeze from the nor-nor-west, and the engines and boilers were shut down. The ship's timbers creaked gently, the only sound the swish of the water against the hull, distant footsteps and voices, a snore, a light groan. The *Condor* was at peace but there were currents of hostility coursing through her company.

Ordinary Seaman Masters was a tall, dark, cadaverous rating from Hull, a man who had seen much of the world, and the rougher end of it at that, as the scars—especially a deep blue scar on the back of his neck—testified. He had ten years of service behind him and an air of authority to which his rank did not strictly entitle him. He was a man who attracted satellites, again for no immediate apparent reason, and his influence on the mess deck was always in evidence— organizing a game of cards for stakes higher than anyone really wanted, or a booze-up with grog extracted from non-drinkers or brandy purloined from the wardroom.

Rod had overheard him only a few hours earlier, showing off knowledge he had picked up ashore at Gib. "Our Charlie boy's in trouble again," he was telling an awed audience. "Now he's out of Parliament, he can't stop. Writing to his high-and-mightyship the Prince of Wales and the newspapers, telling them the Prime Minister's soft and the only way to get order in Egypt is a show of power, not this soft Liberal way. 'All persons belonging to the Fleet are forbidden to write for any newspaper on subjects connected with the Naval Service.' Article 637, Queen's Regulations. I looked it up. And 'sack the French as Allies,' he says. 'They can't be trusted neither.'"

He looked around at his audience; it was as impressed as he intended it to be. "And their Lordships at the Admiralty have found out. Shouldn't wonder if our Charlie boy isn't relieved of his command. Then we may get a real Captain— what about that?"

Later, Rod wondered how Masters got his information, for Rod knew that there was some truth in what he had divulged. As Captain's cox, he was almost as privy to his Captain's private opinions as his personal servant was, and there were other hints that he could not ignore of his activities outside his duties as Captain—the heavy sealed envelope with the Prince of Wales's coat of arms embossed on the back, which he had delivered to him in his cabin, magazines like *Vanity Fair* and *The Army and Navy Gazette* and copies of *The Times* newspaper, with passages circled or underlined, lying about in the day cabin.

Rod would hear sudden explosions of wrath when his Captain was reading, or exclamations like "Impudent puppy!" or "The country's going to the dogs under this damned Gladstone!" There could be no doubt that Commander Beresford had not left politics behind in the Palace of Westminster, and that he was playing a dangerous game.

But Rod was also becoming increasingly admiring of his Captain. He liked the way he spoke his mind, however outrageous his thoughts were. He liked the warmth and spontaneity of the man, the way he loved or hated so passionately, his eccentric outbursts, his guffaws of deep laughter at some absurdity.

"Why does Masters seem to hate him so much?" Rod asked himself, for most of the lower deck admired their Captain. But almost every ship had its small minority of dissidents, forever in search of trouble; resentful sailors who never got promotion because they always set themselves against authority and suspected all those senior to themselves. In their jaundiced eyes, promotion meant treachery to the cause of antiauthority.

Rod was one of a number of enemies of Masters and his cronies. As Captain's flunkey, called "Lucky Midge" by him, sharer of secret jokes, he was a frequent target of their attacks, which became more bitter as the weather grew warmer and time hung heavily.

So far, Masters had not physically attacked Rod, although he had often come close to it. There seemed to be something in Rod's air of steady defiance that discouraged Masters from striking him. Besides, the Captain's servant, a nice and efficient young ordinary seaman, but with a cringing manner that invited the bully, was a softer target.

He was called Thomas—Ordinary Seaman William Thomas from Swansea in South Wales. Thomas the Drudge was his nickname. A dark, short twenty-five-year-old who, by his hangdog stance, tended to make himself appear smaller than he really was. He had large, frightened brown eyes, like those of a deer who has scented danger. Kind ratings and Petty Officers were sorry for him and concerned for his innocence; those who were more belligerent tended to take it out on him.

Rod saw a lot of him and liked him but wished he had more spine. Once, Rod had told him to stand up for himself —"There's no greater coward than a bully." But it was no good. Thomas the Drudge continued to get knocked about and to find himself pushed to the end of any queue, and was rarely without some scar or bruise as evidence of rough handling on the lower deck.

Malta was five days out from Gibraltar at 240 miles a day, all under sail, and all the time with royals set. A great rock set in the blue Mediterranean, as if hurled by some African giant, followed by a smaller missile, Gozo, to the northwest. And there was Valetta harbour again, the perfect anchorage for a priceless fortress island, the white Moorish buildings rising tier upon tier, the castle solid and resolute, a bastion of the Knights of St. John for centuries. Besides the dghaisas—their Arab oarsmen forever chanting—the sailing yawls and dinghies, several merchantmen, an Indian troopship, and two P & O liners, white and rich-looking as wedding cakes, there were numerous men-o'-war in the harbour: two protected cruisers, a second-class cruiser, and a new turret ironclad with topmast struck and the white ensign flying from the ensign staff astern. Steam ferryboats and a single paddle tug slowly etched the still waters with their wake and the sky with their smoke trail.

The arrival in a busy harbour always excited Rod, especially after a long passage, and the fascination of identifying vessels and speculating on their destination and port of origin never diminished. Every harbour had its special character and smell: steamy hot with the stench of bodies and rotting fruit at Madras; sharp with the mixed smell of heather and fish up the Hamoaze; clamorous, stirring, and bitter cold in winter at New York.

And now Malta again, part European, part African, part Oriental; milestone to the East, its narrow streets and alleyways swarming with dark figures in white shawls and cloaks and turbans, even in the heat of the day, like alarmed termites streaming from an old log.

Rod's starboard watch was lined up on deck, facing the Governor's palace as the *Condor* drifted past under shortened sail; and the brass signalling guns cracked out seventeen times and were answered from the fort.

Commander Beresford was of the old school, originating in the days of scurvy, that believed in getting as many of the ship's company ashore as soon as possible, and boats were lowered within five minutes of the *Condor*'s coming to her buoy. Rod was in the first shore party. He planned to revisit a shop in which he had seen a beautiful model of a schooner in a bottle which he was going to bring home as a present for his mother. He had seen it on his last visit and now had saved up the money and was going to buy it if it was still there. A friend he had made since joining the *Condor*, a fellow Geordie named George ("Ginger" inevitably for his hair and high colouring) O'Sullivan, came with him. They would make their purchases, have a few drinks, go to the market for fresh fruit, have a meal out of doors at one of the many cafes down near the harbour, and return on board well before "Pipe down." That was the plan.

It did not work out like that. Not at all. For a start, the two seamen saw Thomas hanging about disconsolately on the quayside, obviously at a loss to know what to do and unable to cope with the beggars who clustered around, hands outstretched. After a word with O'Sullivan, Rod called out to him, "Will you join us, William?"

Thomas did so with pathetic eagerness. It was his first visit to Malta, he told them, and he found the place alarming. The bottle boat had been sold, but Rod bought another, a beautiful red-painted brig, for little more money. They stayed longer than they had intended, and it was almost dark when they made their way down a steep alleyway to the quay. There were women in the doorways, many of them young prostitutes who called out to them as they passed, others wives and mothers with their children about their knees or in their arms, just as if they were in Groom Road, Newcastle-upon-Tyne.

There were other Maltese at upper-floor windows, open to catch the evening breeze, and men were drinking or eating plates of oily fish at the cafes. There were many other sailors about, ratings and Petty Officers and Royal Marines and a few soldiers from the troopship, as there always were in Valetta.

The lights of the quay were in sight when a party of sailors emerged noisily from a bar in front of them, sennit hats askew, arms linked, and singing loudly. One of them turned and stared at the party of three carrying their purchases. It was Masters, very drunk, his dark face towards them, black eyes focussing slowly. Then: "Look who we have here! The Captain's little boys, with their shopping. Charlie's darlin's!"

"Ginger an' little Drudge!" another voice cried out. "Little innocent."

"Time he had a woman." It was Masters again, lurching towards them, the others blocking the way.

'Let's find him a woman."

The attack was uncoordinated, wild, and spontaneous. There were ten of them in all, ten against three, and the little Welsh boy was picked up at once, fearful and shouting. Rod fought back with one hand, holding his bottle protectively high. He was hit twice on the head. "He's fighting with a broken bottle!" "The coward! Get snivelling Midge!"

The ship bottle was wrenched from his hand and hurled

to the stone cobbles, and Rod was knocked down, cutting his wrist on the broken glass.

Now only confusion, noise, and pain. He saw O'Sullivan go down just as he got to his feet again, struggling to rescue Thomas, who was being held high, his trousers already off. They were in a bar, rich with the smell of aniseed and sweat. Rod smashed his fist into Masters's face and fought to get at the four sailors who were dragging Thomas towards a stairway. There were women about, half a dozen or more, screaming half-hysterically or just laughing.

"Who's going to have him? He can do two at once."

A hand held up, clutching Maltese coins, and now it was the women struggling to get Thomas upstairs. One was stark naked, two more bare-breasted and wearing only a flimsy skirt, shouting and giggling. One of them grabbed the money, another tore at Thomas's shirt, and they all disappeared up the dark winding staircase, the screaming, the laughing, the shouting, becoming muffled.

It was like a scene out of an illustrated Dante's *Inferno* Rod had once seen in the Armstrong Library, and through the pain, Rod felt close to tears of anger. But he was held back by a dozen arms, helpless, the blood dripping from his arm. Masters, bleeding at the mouth, was before him, three inches taller, an expression of wild hatred on his cadaverous face. Without a word he struck with his fist, hitting Rod on the nose, so that he sank to the floor, the arms letting him go, and he recalled nothing more.

Nothing. Then, very slowly, Rod became aware of an aching back, a pulsating pain in his arm, a throbbing head. A faint, grey light, seen through metal bars. A moaning sound. From himself? From someone else? He tried to move, and this time it was for certain his own moan that he heard. Voices, first distant, then near, distant again. "We'll have that one over there." Pause. "And that one."

There were arms under his shoulders, and he was being carried. But not for long, and not gently. When he was dropped, and a voice called out, "Any more, Jack?" the pain brought him fully back to consciousness. He had been in the Guardroom, along with the habitual drunks, and treated as one. The voice belonged to one of the *Condor*'s marines, a corporal; the higher-pitched voice was Midshipman Connolly's, no doubt duty Midshipman of the dinghy, and not pleased at being roused to fetch on board these reprobates.

From the bottom of the cart, Rod tried to raise his head to see if Ginger O'Sullivan or little Thomas was among the limp bodies lying beside him. There was no sign of either, just half a dozen of the *Condor*'s lower deck and a marine, grey-faced, unconscious, breathing stertorously. Rod slipped into unconsciousness again and came to when someone was bending over him. It was the Midshipman again, and he was saying, "Cox here—Captain won't be pleased. Not like Maclewin to get mixed up with this dreadful crew. Been fighting, too." He bent down and pulled at Rod's arm, causing him acute pain. "This doesn't look too good. Will you tell two men to take him to the sick bay?"

"Aye aye, sir."

The ship's surgeon was questioning him. How did he cut his wrist? And his nose?

Rod's voice came croakily. "Got in a bit of a fight, sir."

"You can tell the Captain all about that later. But you haven't improved your looks. Your mother wouldn't recognize her boy." The surgeon was a good-humoured man, smelling of drink himself, and chuckled as he applied antiseptic to Rod's nose and swabbed it gently. "I'm afraid that's broken, son, and there's nothing even Harley Street could do."

Arm in sling, and wearing fresh white drill, Rod was escorted to the Captain's cabin at defaulters by two ratings with police badges on their left cuffs. His head still ached, his face was sore and looked worse, with two black eyes and split skin across his nose, which had assumed a new flat shape. It scared him when he had first looked in a mirror. But he felt stronger and ready to take any punishment meted out to him.

Beresford remained reading papers on his desk when they entered, all three at attention. Then he looked up, staring curiously at Rod's face, his eyes flicking down to the sling. He dismissed the escort and stood Rod at ease.

"What went on last night?"

"There was a fight, sir."

"I can see that." The voice was impatient. "What was it about? Who with?"

"I'd rather not say, sir."

Silence. "This can lead to disratin'. You had better tell me. I have seen O'Sullivan and Thomas."

Rod was thankful to hear the names. "How is Thomas, sir?"

"Not good. Awful. Not much hurt—not physically. But bad. I know some of the story. I want the rest of it—from you."

Rod remained silent, staring in front of him. There was a picture of the Royal Yacht *Osborne* on the wall behind the desk, and he kept his eyes on it—a pretty vessel sailing close inshore, mountains behind.

"I know the names already. I want more details."

There was a long silence. Rod lowered his gaze and saw Beresford's clear brown eyes staring at him, willing him to speak.

At length the Captain said, "Very well. You are dismissed." His voice was harsh with irritation. "It was a despicable crime and their punishment will be harsh."

Tea on the mess deck. The clatter of tin plates and mugs. About thirty ratings drinking and eating, and not a word being exchanged. The ports were open, and the only sound was of far distant voices in Valetta and the mournful chanting from the dghaisas. A faint breeze came in through the ports but hardly enough to stir the hot air.

As he walked over to the mess table, his mug and plate and spoon awkwardly held in his right hand, no one greeted him or looked up. Every sailor knew every detail of what had happened in the fracas the previous night. They also knew that Rod had been with the Captain. All they did not know was what he had said. But even that they would find out later. Nothing remained a mystery for long in a man-o'-war as small as the *Condor*.

One rating did, however, get up from his seat. Ordinary Seaman Thomas, pale and somehow shrivelled, rose silently and took Rod's mug, placed a slice of bread on his plate, added jam, scooped the mug into the barrel of tepid tea and condensed milk; and, still without saying a word, sat down beside him. He used his own knife to cut up the bread.

A month was a long time to spend in the punishment cells of a small warship in the heat of the eastern Mediterranean. Masters and the two others sentenced with him were released at Suda Bay, Crete, where the *Condor* joined Admiral Seymour's Fleet. Rod had taken Beresford, his navigating lieutenant, and four other officers ashore for a shoot. All day long the guns cracked, sometimes in volleys like a Gatling gun, as the parties from many ships of the Fleet worked their way inland. Rod played football on the beach with other ratings and Petty Officers, and the *Condor*'s party came back shortly before four o'clock, laden with a bag of woodcock, snipe, and duck—enough so that there would be a Sunday feast for the lower deck as well as the wardroom and Warrant Officers' mess.

Beresford was in jovial form as Rod coxed the gig back to his ship. It was a hot, sunny afternoon and all the anchored Fleet had white awnings spread, from the mighty new *Inflexible*, *Temeraire*, and *Sultan* and other ironclads to the smallest of the gunvessels, the little *Decoy*.

Beresford was holding up a duck, its wings spread. "That's where you winged it, Pilot. Lucky I got my shot in time." And he roared with laughter.

"Beggin' your pardon, sir, it was the other way round. Wasn't it, Arthur? The Captain winged it after she was a goner. Waste of good ammunition, what?"

Rod brought the boat alongside the ladder, and in accordance with custom, the Captain disembarked first, and the other officers followed him, briefly silent as the ceremony of coming on board was performed.

Rod supervised the securing of the galley and, with his duties completed, made for the mess deck. He almost bumped into Masters as he turned a corner in the pasageway leading aft. So he was out.

The two seamen stood looking at each other for a fraction of a second, Masters appearing to tower over Rod, pale-faced from his long confinement and punishment diet, angry, piercing eyes staring at Rod's brown face. Rod held the black eyes, recognizing the malevolence and hostility that seemed to shine from them like two of the *Inflexible*'s new electric searchlights, and fighting against the rising fear.

Rod said nothing, moved a little so that they could pass each other. Masters remained still. The black mat of hair on his chest reached almost to his neck. There was a tattoo of an anchor on one white arm, and one of a plump naked woman on the other.

"Ye'll pay for it, little 'un," Masters said in an even voice. "Ye'll pay, ye and that Ginger mate o'yourn." Then interrogatively, "Ye know that?"

Rod said nothing. There was nothing to say. The evil had been done, the price paid. Rod would never be the same again. It was not only the shape of his nose that had been changed. But there was nothing to say, and he walked on without a word, thrusting from his mind the premonitions of disaster that had suddenly all but overwhelmed him.

On that same evening, the yardarms became busy, signals being rapidly hoisted on the Flagship, and the rest of the Fleet answering, confirming, lowering, only for fresh messages to pass. Rod was on watch, delighting as always in the speed of the *Condor*'s Yeoman of Signals, a sailor of immense experience and skill. With a glass to his eye trained on the Flagship's signalling platform, the Yeoman could sometimes identify and anticipate flags while they were still rolled, rattling out the message to the Lieutenant, who transmitted it instantly to the Captain, and hoisting the confirm even before the flags fluttered out.

"Admiral will be shifting his flag and squadron will weigh anchors at . . ."

The situation in Egypt had suddenly become critical. The lives of British citizens and of other Europeans were in danger from the Army under the usurper and dictator Arabi Pasha, who ("Egypt for the Egyptians") was seeking to kill or throw all foreigners out of his bankrupt and corrupt country. This was dangerous for Britain and France especially, for not only had they financed the recently completed Suez Canal, but their trade to the East passed through it. Above all, the free passage of commerce and the security of the Near East depended on a stable Egypt. Always there remained the threat from Russia with her eyes on the canal, on Turkey and Egypt, and like the predatory bear she was, on the whole Middle East, and eventually the supreme prize of India.

The port of Alexandria was the heart of the crisis. Here many British, American, French, and Italian subjects lived and worked. Now their lives were threatened, along with the lives of thousands more Europeans and their families. Arabi Pasha was in control, his hordes of undisciplined troops were roaming the streets, the fortifications were being strengthened. Every officer in the Mediterranean Fleet knew how dangerous these developments were.

The *Condor* was one of the two gunboats ordered to Alexandria, in company with Admiral Seymour's new Flagship *Invincible*, chosen for her shallow draught.

Beresford was overjoyed at the news. Rod took him for consultations on board the *Invincible* and brought him back again before sundown. Beresford took his hat off as soon as they were clear of the Flagship, wiping his damp forehead with an enormous silk handkerchief.

"Well, little Midge, it looks like war." He was smiling broadly as he looked up from his seat. "What do you think of that?"

"Excited, sir. Like all of us, sir."

"Scared? Stomach uneasy, eh?"

"I expect we'll be too busy for that, sir."

" 'Off to hell, with shot and shell,' " the Captain quoted. "Eh? You know what Nelson said at Copenhagen, Lucky Midge? When it was really what he called 'warm work'? He said, 'This day may be the last to any of us at a moment. But, mark you! I would not be elsewhere for thousands.' What d'you think of that, Midge?"

"I hope I'll feel the same, sir. But I couldn't have thought that up, quick like that, in the middle of a battle."

"That's right. Clever *and* brave, The Hero."

The flames of petty quarrels and controversies were doused by the urgent demands for a rapid departure, for speed, for preparation. War. What they had spent all these years preparing for. What this fighting ship was built for, its guns for firing at a real enemy.

That night, the *Invincible*, with her ten 12-ton guns and flanked by her two minions, sped south towards Egypt. Rod, on the middle watch with O'Sullivan, pointed at the phosphorescent sparkle in the wake of the Flagship on their port beam. It was a clear, still, moonlight night, and the funnel smoke marked the sky black in three lines like charcoal on a silver sheet.

"What d'you think of a night action?" he asked O'Sullivan.

"That's all right. Any action. A night battle must be the most exciting of all."

"If the Captain were here, he'd be telling us of the Battle of the Nile, for that's where we're heading, isn't it? Eighty-four years ago. And that was a night battle."

They raised the Egyptian coast shortly before dawn on June 11. Rod recalled the low, flat coastline from his first passage through the Suez Canal two years earlier. The brown of the desert in the west blended into the greener line of Arab's Bay and the approach to the Nile estuary. Alexandria itself was marked by the blur of buildings, an irregular spread of white on the horizon broken by the minarets of mosques, the forts south of the city dominated by the ocher finger of Pompey's Pillar in the distance, contrasting with the nearby white finger of the Ras-el-tin lighthouse.

In another twenty minutes at their 8 knots, the six-vaned windmills of Meks were discernible beyond the breakwater, unique as a distinguishing feature of this harbour, and innocent by contrast with the forts and gun batteries that stretched as far west as the island of Marabout to the mighty Pharos Castle in the east. There on the peninsula that spread out east and west from the heart of the city, like an inverted boot with a spurred heel, were the Royal Palace and the arsenal and other great buildings, certain targets for any bombardment.

There was shipping in the main harbour as well as in the new harbour in the eastern cup formed by the peninsula, warships of many nations—Greek, French, Italian, and American—sent to protect their nationals, merchantmen and troopships from the East or destined for the Orient, down to countless little feluccas, their white lateen sails bright in the rising sun.

It appeared a peaceful scene, with thin fingers of smoke rising over the city and from the funnels of several of the larger anchored vessels. But Rod knew that there were enough guns amassed among the warships to blow the city to pieces, and enough guns in the protecting batteries along the shore to sink every ship within range. All that was needed was the spark, and it would be like the explosion of a great magazine . . .

The *Invincible*, with the two gunvessels in line astern, at the rear, steamed slowly through the larger men-o'-war anchored outside the harbour, exchanged courtesy signals, rounded the breakwater, and dropped anchor within the harbour. The gun crews were standing to beside their weapons in case of emergency, but none of the British ships was cleared for action, in case this would be regarded as provocative.

A signal from the *Invincible* ordered Beresford on board

for further consultations with the Admiral, and Rod coxed the gig over to the Flagship. The sights and sounds and smells of every harbour were always different and here at Alexandria Rod scented a pungency in the still air reminiscent of a crowded bazaar, as well as the more subtle scent of danger.

They were taking the strokes slowly in this temperature already high and rising in the early morning. With a brief tremor of excitement, Rod realized that at any moment the nearest fort could open fire, blowing this boat to pieces, a valuable target disposed of by sudden treachery.

From the city there came faint echoes of shouting and the occasional crack of firearms. The trouble, it seemed, had already begun.

Captain Molyneux was at the *Invincible*'s gangway to greet Beresford as he was piped on board and strode off to call on the Admiral. It was a brief visit, and ten minutes later, Rod ordered the boat's crew to toss oars. Their Captain was at the head of the gangway again, shaking hands with Admiral Seymour—grey-bearded, stout, stiff, and serious in demeanour—and saluting him. Beresford, too, was unsmiling. Swiftly, purposefully, he trotted down the Flagship's companion ladder and jumped back into his boat. The sounds from the city were rising: ugly, fearful, hysterical cries; and there was smoke to be seen, and the faint crackle of flames.

"The mob's at work. No time to waste. Speed up the stroke-oar, Cox." The crew dipped in their oars more swiftly, and the gig cut rapidly through the harbour water. Glancing astern, Rod could see the crews at the bow 64-pounders alert for trouble, and no doubt the heavy guns in the central battery would be manned, too.

"We're going ashore, you and me," Beresford said. "As soon as we get on board, draw side arms from the armoury. Better draw some iron rations, too. Just in case."

"Aye aye, sir."

Within half an hour, their boat was alongside the harbour steps, and Beresford, like Rod armed with a revolver with spare rounds in pouches, was climbing the steps of the quay. "Just a reconnaissance, Midge. We're not lookin' for trouble. But if we meet some, don't you hesitate to use that gun. These Gippos hate bullets, especially British bullets, which usually hit—unlike their own." The Captain chuckled and began to walk rapidly across the empty paved quay in his eagerness. "We'll have a word with the harbour master first. He's an old chum of mine. Captain Blomfield."

The harbour master was too distraught with anxiety about his wife, who had gone into the city earlier in the morning and had not returned, to be able to offer advice or information.

"Any chance of a shore party, Charlie?" he appealed. "The sight of a few British bayonets and uniforms would scatter them."

" 'Few' it would be. We couldn't find two hundred men to land. Good men, but not enough for the mob of Alexandria and probably half the Egyptian Army." Beresford laughed bitterly. "There are people dying there in the streets because of the Prime Minister's cowardice. Damned Liberal swine. Wouldn't send any more ships in case it provoked the Khedive. Gladstone's a murderer, and I'll write to *The Times* and tell the editor just that."

The sounds of the mob were louder than ever. Rod glanced out of the harbour master's window. How steady and impressive and well ordered were the white anchored warships in the harbour by contrast with the anarchy ashore!

"I'm sure your good lady will be all right," Beresford said soothingly. "But if we can borrow your carriage, my cox and I'll have a look-see. The Admiral wants a report on the situation in any case."

The carriage was a little, light, open four-wheeler, and the two horses were small Arabs. Beresford said, "Hop up, Midge. And loosen your holster."

Rod had never seen him so elated, almost as if he were drunk with the excitement of imminent action. "Thor and Woden—those are your names," he said, brushing his hand over the two Arabs' necks. "God of war and his son—and to war we go!"

Beresford leapt up beside Rod and seized the reins. The horses responded at once, as if recognizing the Irishman's command and understanding, and the carriage bowled rapidly along the quayside of Anchorage Port and headed towards Lazanetto. They were making for the English Consulate on the eastern side of the peninsula where they hoped to gather news. It was ten o'clock in the morning and the streets would normally have been crowded with shoppers, merchants, children, and beggars. Now they were quite empty. Only a few mangy dogs scavenged among the piles of stinking rubbish, breaking into a fight over a morsel.

Beresford drove the carriage round a sharp corner on two wheels, and Rod saw ahead the first signs of looting—the shutters of a small store smashed in, broken furniture lying in the street; a street stall overturned, fruit lying in the gutter; the lower-floor windows of a house smashed in, torn curtains hanging in tatters, a discarded rug in the street.

Then, like a progression towards purgatory, the scenes became worse, with first a house blackened from arson, its contents thrown from windows; a pathetic pile of old clothes; then the first corpse, an old woman close against the wall, her throat cut and the blood pool beneath her head drying in the sun; another, a child of about ten, neck broken grotesquely.

"Not nice!" shouted Beresford. "Gladstone's corpses, every one. Remember that, Midge."

Still they had not seen a living soul. It was a city of the dead, or of the living mob. So it seemed until they came across the first living victims of the mob, a terrified party of Greeks, every one of them carrying the mark of recent wounds, running towards them, running past them without a glance, seeing salvation beyond, somewhere in the far distance. Only one of them fell in the rush, a young girl with a bleeding gash in her cheek, for whom the pace and her wounds were too much.

Rod wanted to stop to pick her up but he saw at once that the task of rescue was far beyond their power. For down the next street the scene was like that of a tattered army in retreat—Lebanese, Italians, Jews, more Greeks, and others who might have been British or French—all running or hobbling along, some carrying bundles, most showing the mark of the mob somewhere, women crying, men carrying babies.

Beresford had to haul on the reins to slow down the carriage and avoid running down these people in the narrow street. One man, waving his arms, shouted above the cries, "Don't go on, sir! Don't go on. They'll kill you!"

Past a gutted house, still smouldering, a Roman Catholic church, its doors smashed in and doubtless all its relics and valuables stolen. Then the mob, an ugly, menacing tidal wave of turbaned figures, some with torches, others with long sticks—*naboots*—all running, and with the gleam of insane destructiveness in their eyes. Here was the diseased heart of purgatory, whipped into a frenzy by zealots and the Army.

Beresford brought the carriage to a halt and drew his revolver. "Not much hope against this lot, Midge. Not much hope for Mrs. Blomfield either."

He took aim at the figures at the head of the crowd and fired a single shot. A man collapsed, and was swallowed up by those behind him even before he fell.

Rod held his big .36 Colt steadily. Always before it had been targets on board the *Implacable*, a canvas target towed alongside, a cast with weight and flag floating past, on the range at the *Excellent*. Innocent then, and he had shown himself above average, a good shot. Now it was flesh: men, figures running with murder in their faces, intent on his own death. How often had he wondered what it would be like? Now there was nothing to consider: no hesitation, no doubts. Just squeeze the trigger—once, again, and once more.

He could not fail to hit, and Beresford was firing again, too. But the momentum of the mob was too great, far too powerful to be halted by little lead missiles, even if those in the lead had wished to falter or retreat. The *naboots* were beating the horses, which were rearing and screaming, straining at the traces. Other blows were aimed at the side of the carriage, brown arms were rising and falling as the mob almost engulfed them. Beresford was hauling on the reins, trying to bring the horses round, inspiring them with desperation. A sudden gleam of a knife in the hand of a man who had climbed onto the hub of one of the leading wheels. Rod turned, felt a blow on his shoulder, fired at a range of six feet. The attacker fell back and was caught by his fellows.

The carriage was at right angles across the street, the horses prancing, forelegs high and beating the air, beating against Arab bodies, and crushing or knocking them aside. Beresford was shouting at the horses. Rod just heard the words—"That's it, me boys. C'mon, old Woden, God of war." At the same time, almost casually, he kicked in the groin an Arab who was on the step, sending him doubled up backwards.

They were almost round, and the horses, inspired with fear and the need for survival, beat down a passage as they gathered speed. Beresford fired his last round into a face only feet away, received in return a savage blow on the head.

Rod turned round as they broke clear. A single intrepid young man, burnous flying, had climbed up onto the back and was making his way forward, fast. Again the gleam of steel. Rod had one round left. He fired, missed, got up from the seat, threw himself at the man, the butt of his Colt a club. He caught him on the side of the head, and then was thrown down, kicking at his assailant as he fell on him.

The struggle was brief. The carriage jerked in sudden acceleration, throwing them both off balance. Then Rod, lying on his back, winded and with little strength to call upon, recognized the blurred figure of his Captain, felt the relief of weight from his body, saw in one dramatic briefly held picture Beresford, pith helmet long since lost, white uniform torn and stained with blood, holding the Arab high above his head. Then Beresford threw him out, unwanted rubbish, from the carriage.

Thor and Woden were doing well on their own. When Rod recovered himself and crawled forward to the seat, Beresford had seized the reins again, and they were making for the harbour at a full gallop, fast outpacing their pursuers.

There was still no one to be seen down at the quay. Only the harbour master, armed now with a rifle, standing outside his office.

"Glad to see you back. You look a bit the worse for wear, Charlie."

"Damn close-run thing—like Waterloo." He threw the reins over the horses' sweating backs and jumped down. "Couldn't see your wife anywhere."

But it was all right. Blomfield had just received a message. She had taken shelter in a hotel and was safe.

Beresford banged him on the back. "That's grand news. Now I must report back to me Flagship. Come on, Midge. Thank you for savin' my life, and you can thank me for savin' yours, eh?"

He had wiped the blood from his face and his sweating, receding hairline, and was laughing that great booming laugh. Rod had never seen his Captain enjoy himself so much, this fighter with the gleam of victory in his Irish eyes.

"Aye aye, sir."

The riots of June 11 were only the beginning of weeks of destruction and massacre in Alexandria. Supported by Arabi's soldiers, the citizens appeared hellbent on killing every foreigner remaining in the city and destroying all their property. Much of their own property also went up in flames as prowling incendiaries and looters worked their way from one end of Alexandria to the other.

The Royal Navy had instructions from home not to interfere in any way with this anarchy, but to rescue as many

Europeans as they could. Lord Charles Beresford was put in command of the evacuation, and Rod was constantly at his side as personal assistant. Day after day, and far into every night, they continued taking off the Greeks, Jews, Italians, Armenians, Turks, Italians, French, and British, many of whom had lived for years in Egypt and had no other home than the ruins they had left behind. Many had been wounded or were ill, and burial parties and surgeons were busy every day.

The sailors did what they could to make the refugees as comfortable as possible on board their ships. Communities gathered together setting up tents on deck, while the Armenian Jews, incorrigible traders to a man, set up stalls as if back in the bazaars. These were strange as well as tragic days. Royal Navy bluejackets, trained to cleanliness and polish, saw stalls piled high with vegetables on their ships' upper decks, goats breaking loose and found wandering on quarterdecks, little Levantine children playing down in the engine room or in the ships' kitchens.

"All hell would break loose if those damned forts opened fire on us now," Beresford said on one day of special chaos, with boatloads of excitable women being embarked on a small collier, and complaining about the coal dust.

It was on that same hot day, on the same collier anchored near the harbour entrance, that a young, very fat coloured woman broke away from her party and clutched Rod by the arm.

"Baby he come, sare, directly, sare, myself, sare!" she said in an urgent voice.

Rod turned and called out to Beresford, who was giving orders to a working party. "Woman here says she's giving birth, sir."

"Tell her she can't just now. We're too busy."

Rod passed on the message, and the woman answered by lying down and pulling up her numerous skirts. Rod felt close to panic. "It's no good, sir. She's having it."

Beresford hastened to the scene and ordered a canvas

screen to be rigged. She appeared to be the only coloured woman and none of the others would offer to act as midwife.

"We'll have to do it ourselves," said Beresford briskly. "Lend me your knife, Midge."

And so it was that, beneath the midday sun, on the deck of a collier thick in coal dust, with the help of a sharp sailor's knife and a bowl of tepid water, Rod learned the intimate secret of birth as the child, a tiny, wrinkled, shiny, damp object, as black as its mother, emerged.

"A damned gel!" exclaimed Beresford in sweeping condemnation of the sex. But he cut the cord with Rod's knife as if he were a trained midwife and held the baby up by her feet and slapped her on the back until she let out a pathetic howl.

"You look as if you've done this before, sir," said Rod in admiration.

"Damned fool of a woman had one out huntin' with the Quorn last year. No one else about so I had to deal with her." He wiped his hands on a towel—a grey, much used towel—which Rod had found. "At least she had the sense to have a boy. Half an hour old and he was takin' the fences like a man, me holdin' him of course—hounds got a scent and there was no stoppin' Black Boy. Should have a good seat when he's a bit older, that fellow."

All during the evacuating and the accommodating of the refugees on board the ships in the harbour, the tension as well as the destruction in the city was growing. Many more troops arrived from Cairo and elsewhere in Egypt, and every day those on board could observe teams of workmen dragging more guns into the forts and strengthening the defenses of the harbour.

The riots of June 11 had caused an outcry in England, and words stronger even than those Beresford used against the Prime Minister were heard in the streets and in the clubs of London, and written in the newspapers. Now, at last, the whole Mediterranean Fleet was ordered to Alexandria, the great ironclads *Alexander*, *Superb*, *Sultan*, *Temeraire*, and *Monarch*, and most modern and powerful of them all, *Inflexible*, commanded by the brilliant, eccentric Captain J. A. "Jackie" Fisher: fifteen men-o'-war in all, the towering masts and yards, the great gun muzzles in ports and turrets, making an intimidating and overpowering impression—and only a few miles from the scene of one of Britain's greatest victories over the French.

At one time the French, who were as concerned for their property and security of the Suez Canal as were the British, were committed to sending their Fleet, too. But there was a change of government and a change of policy to a less warlike stance.

"Trust the Frogs to back out," was an expression heard throughout the British Fleet. "Especially when there's likely to be any fighting."

As the defenses continued to be reinforced, the Egyptians working throughout every night until there were no fewer than 261 guns in place, Admiral Seymour sent protests to the authorities and then threats that if the forts were not disbanded and the guns removed, the British Fleet would attack and destroy them.

On July 10, Rod once again took his Captain over to the Flagship for a war council, as the last of the refugees were ferried out to safety in recently arrived merchantmen. On his return, Beresford gave orders to turn up all hands, and addressed them. "Tomorrow morning," he began, "war with Egypt begins. That mad Arabi Pasha has turned down all offers of peace, and in spite of promises to the contrary, continues—as you've all seen—to build up his forts. So we're goin' to knock 'em out."

He looked round at his ship's company, a smile of satisfaction on his face, his eyes dancing with excitement. "Now there's one fort the Admiral thinks cannot be attacked, the second largest fort of them all, the Marabout Fort. You've seen it, over there far to the west. An awkward bugger. He says he can't spare an ironclad for the job—and, of course, any little mite of a ship like the *Condor* would be blown out of the water if she got within range."

Beresford let forth a deep chuckle, smiling again at his men. "Now, me lads, if you'll rely upon me to find the opportunity, I will rely upon you to make the most of it when it occurs. All right?"

So war would come in a few hours, at dawn on Wednesday, July 11, 1882, and this harbour would be filled with smoke and fire and high explosive projectiles, and a thousand bullets would race towards their targets, ashore and afloat.

Chapter VII

Round the world. A circumnavigation. The word still had a magic ring to it although it had been 360 years since one of Magellan's caravels had completed the first ever. The Prince of Wales pronounced the word with a heavy German "r," just as he spoke "crruising."

"You have had some cruising, Georgie. But now we think you should have a long cruise, perhaps two years. A circumnavigation."

"I shall miss you and Mama dreadfully. And Louise and Vicky and Maud. And the dogs." It was not unexpected news; it was inevitable even, and Prince George had discussed it with Buller many times on the shorter cruise in the corvette *Bacchante* to the West Indies and the Mediterranean.

"Will Eddie be coming—and Archy? I would like Archy to come, too." Prince George glanced at Buller pleadingly, as if the decision rested with him. Buller observed with surprise that his friend had become pale.

The Prince of Wales turned to Buller, too. He was smiling, that charming confiding smile to which so many women—

and the English public, too—had succumbed. "Well? A circumnavigation. It will be a great experience but it will be hard work."

Buller nodded, and before he could thank the Prince, the Prince said, "Buller seems to want to come. Yes, Eddie will be with you; it will offer him the opportunity of catching up on his instruction—which is lamentably behindhand. So Mr. Lawless and Paymaster Sceales will be on the voyage, too," he added, referring to the mathematics and navigation tutor, and the French tutor.

It was late June 1880, a year since they had left the *Britannia*. The friendship between the two boys had deepened. The Queen and the Prince and Princess of Wales approved of it because it was considered suitable for Prince George to have friends outside his family, so long as the breeding and background were totally respectable—and no family could be more respectable and naval than the Bullers. No one could have been more pleased by the arrangement than the Bullers themselves.

Buller was staying at Sandringham and having a relaxed time riding and sailing, playing golf and lawn tennis, with no lessons to break up the day. The Prince of Wales was frequently in London at Marlborough House but had returned for the weekend. It was midday, and he had just descended from his rooms, dressed in breeches and Scotch tweed plaid jacket, gold chains crisscrossing his ample stomach. He was in a jovial mood, a glass of champagne in one hand, an enormous cigar in the other. He smelled strongly of tweed, expensive soap, and equally expensive cigar smoke.

"I saw your father the other evening at the Marlborough Club," he said, addressing Buller. "A guest of the Duke of Portland. He looked well. We must make him a member." He chuckled; and again the thick "r" as he added in a mock-mischievous voice, "He is rich enough. Asked after you, and I informed him you were capital—and as up to no good as my own son! Ha ha—eh, Georgie?"

"Well, Papa, I don't think that is quite fair. We have both

been extremely diligent and well behaved. You ask Mr. Dalton."

Prince Eddie would not have dared to speak to his father like that, Buller noted, but then the older boy seemed quite cowed by him.

On Sunday evening, Buller travelled to London for the first time in the Royal Train, in company with the Prince of Wales. It was extremely comfortable, but the Prince spent the journey reading Saturday's *Times*, *The Illustrated London News*, and *Vanity Fair* and scarcely spoke a word. The cigar smoke was so thick by the time they reached King's Cross station that Buller's eyes were streaming, and he was relieved to get out into the fresh air.

"Put this lad into a hansom for Paddington," the Prince ordered an equerry, and climbed into his carriage from the carpeted platform.

"Give my respects to your father," he said from the open window of his carriage. "And tell him he and Lady Buller will be losing you for a couple of years." He chuckled and raised his black Homburg hat. "They'll open a bottle of bubbly to celebrate, eh?"

Buller bowed and muttered, "Yes, Your Royal Highness." He was going to add his thanks for the Prince's hospitality, but the window had slammed up, and the coachman, who knew his master hated hanging about, had the horses moving.

Curious glances from the crowd followed Buller to the hansom cab, and he was glad of the anonymity of the dark interior. And Georgie was fated to experience this for all his life!

"Yes, Mama, Cape Horn and Chile, and the Galapagos Islands—you know, where Mr. Darwin got the idea for his book, *The Origin of Species*. And San Francisco and Vancouver, and then to the Hawaiian Islands."

"Shipwrecks at Cape Horn," said Guy threateningly.

"Very quick with the dagger in Hawaii—remember Captain Cook." Henry held the carving knife above his head and grimaced at his younger brother.

Buller inquired of his mother in tones of mock innocence, "Are those boys really older than me, Mama?"

"I sometimes wonder, dearest. But continue with your itinerary."

"Oh, Japan, China, Siam, Ceylon, and back through the Suez Canal," Archy continued grandly. "The Prince of Wales calls it a circumnavigation," and he imitated the guttural voice.

"A little respect for the Royal Family, please," said Lady Buller, unable to resist smiling. "The Royal Navy is for preventing wars. 'Peace through strength,' you know that motto, dear. If war comes as a result of the failure of politicians, then the Navy must fight, and you also know full well how wonderfully it has always fought." She gave a brief meaningful glance up at the portrait of Captain Cuthbert Buller who had lost an arm at Camperdown. "But don't. *hope* for war, Archy."

"I am hoping we'll see some action somewhere, Mama. There are so many jolly wars going on—the Zulus, and perhaps Russia. I should like to fight the Russians, Mama. Do you think there will be war with Russia? I do hope so. Do you know, Mama, I have not yet heard a shot fired in anger."

"I am very glad, Archy."

Weir Park seemed always to be Hullos and Good-byes nowadays, ever since Buller had left for his first term in the *Britannia*. He supposed it had been the same for his father and for his grandfather—right back to Captain Alastair Buller. But at least most of them went off to war, to a fight, to prize money.

This time there were just three days between arrival and departure to join the *Bacchante* at Spithead. Cecily Buller said that she was going for a hack after luncheon. "How many of you will be coming?"

"Oh, Mama, we know your hacks," said Guy, and yawned deeply. "An hour's trotting, an hour's cantering, half an hour's galloping, and back for tea, horse and rider worn out.

Henry and I shall have a little sit and then a gentle game of croquet. 'Home is rest, Home is best.' That is the motto I have hanging above my bed."

Lady Buller snorted in disgust and reappeared in a few minutes in her riding clothes—very creased they were, and mud-bespattered from yesterday's hunt, just as if Weir Park had no servants, no laundry. A ride with their mother was an energetic business, all the boys agreed, but Buller loved it. He had his father's hunter, Big Ben, saddled up, joined his mother outside the stables, and they cantered off side by side. Cecily Buller was considered rather eccentric in refusing to ride side-saddle, which she hated—"Always come off at the big jumps!"

"We'll go over to the Golden Valley and make Lady Speakman give us tea," she said.

It was a crisp July day with a strong westerly wind bringing squally showers intermittently, a perfect day for riding the country straight. They dipped down into sharp little valleys, galloped up winding bridle tracks again, jumped a couple of very high walls with toppers and drew up at another which had wire strung across the top. "Damn stuff—who owns this land, Archy? We must tell him to move it."

The sun was still high in the sky when they got back at six o'clock, both horses sweating and with much froth about their bits. Disregarding the mounting block—she always did—Cecily Buller swung out of her saddle and threw the reins at Clarke, who glanced disapprovingly at the condition of the horses, which had been hunted hard twice that week already.

Buller knew how he felt and apologized. "I shan't be riding Big Ben again for about two years, don't worry, Mr. Clarke."

"I did hear it was a long cruise you was going on, Master Archibald. But two years!" And he shook his head. Clarke found very little to approve of in life.

"I hope you come back safe and sound, sir."

"I am hoping for some fighting, Clarke. I'll come to say good-bye tomorrow."

Mother and son walked into the house together, using the main entrance into the servants' quarters. Cecily Buller carried her hat and veil and, in a characteristic gesture, ran her other hand as a comb through her hair.

"Lord Huntley's dining tonight. With his pestilential dogs and his daughter, Lady Clemmie, a jolly girl, I've heard." They were pacing through the main kitchen, and Lady Buller paused to lift a lid from a large pot on the range and sniff the contents. She turned to the cook, who gave a quick bob. "Can I have a touch more onion in it, Mrs. Budge? I do like onion."

"A pleasure, ma'm. Mrs. Franklyn says it'll be twelve for dinner."

They were passing through the green baize door into the main house before Archy could say, "But Admiral Huntley's commanding the Flying Squadron, Mama."

"That's why Papa invited him. A rum fellow, but it's as well for you to know him. And better still for him to know you. Oh, but those dogs, so I've heard! You had better lock up Junus and the others in the kennels."

Admiral the Earl of Huntley, or "Lord Tumblehome," was in his late fifties but looked a great deal older. He had married late in life and had one daughter, of Buller's age, whose birth had caused her mother's death. In a service noted for conservatism, Admiral Huntley was regarded as a traditionalist. And in a service notable for its unconventional officers, Admiral Huntley was regarded as eccentric. His three appalling dogs were only a start. He also took with him everywhere his Chinese laundryman, Ping, whom he had bought, when on the China Station, for a golden guinea in 1868 from a mandarin whose pirate junk he had just sunk. He declared that all laundries and laundrymen, except Ping, introduced a chemical into their water designed to cause him skin irritation.

Lord Huntley was a notable hypochondriac and firmly believed that walking destroyed the feet. In his own house, and about his vast estate in Wiltshire, he was carried everywhere in a sedan chair by two tolerant menservants called Thrush and Sparrow, who could not have been more ill-named as they were both muscular and elderly, at least ten years older than their master.

Archy had heard much of Lord Huntley and was curious to meet his Commander-in-Chief. The Admiral arrived exactly one hour early, as his clocks at home conformed with those in his ships, and these and the ship's chronometer were all set one hour ahead of the rest of the Navy, and of Greenwich. He claimed to have documentary evidence that the Astronomer Royal in 1727, in a drunken stupor, had advanced the hands of the great timepiece exactly sixty minutes instead of winding it, and his staff were too terrified to point out the mistake. "The time is out of joint," quoted Lord Huntley when anyone questioned his claim or complained of its inconvenience.

George Buller, who was visiting naval dockyards in the northeast at the time, failed to warn his family of the guest's practice, but this gave Buller, who had fortunately changed early, the opportunity of entertaining the Admiral. The footman opened the door to the guest's manservant, who was followed by Lord Huntley himself, a small man with flowing white beard to his chest, and sidewhiskers, like the bulging side of a First Rate three-decker, which had given him his nickname "Tumblehome." His daughter, no doubt accustomed to the awkward situation, disappeared discreetly and silently, except for the rustle of her long blue taffeta dress, towards the drawing room.

Buller was halfway down the stairs when he saw his future Commander-in-Chief bustling awkwardly on flat feet from the front door, allowing the footman to relieve him of his black velvet coat and deerstalker hat. His dress was otherwise orthodox for the occasion: gleaming white starched shirt, white tie, black trousers and tailcoat. Only the orders and the decorations, including the Victoria Cross, singled him out as a service officer. He shuffled across to the library, brushing aside apologies for the absence of his hostess. He was clearly accustomed to the rest of the world being an hour behindhand, and this comfortingly confirmed his opinion of the slackness rampant everywhere.

When Buller introduced himself, changed and on time, Admiral Huntley was, therefore, gratified and said in a gruff voice, "Glad to find an officer with some sense of time. Very rare."

"I'm not a real officer yet, sir. Only a Midshipman."

Admiral Huntley had settled himself into an armchair in front of the fire with *The Illustrated London News,* and a large brandy and soda syphon at his side. Buller, unsure whether or not he was wanted, stood awkwardly by the fireplace. The three Yorkshire terriers, which had burst in through the front door ahead of their master and ranged, yapping, throughout the house, up and down the stairs nipping at any passing ankles, had now concentrated on scratching at the closed library door.

"Shall I let them in, sir?" Buller asked tentatively.

"Yes, pipe 'em on board, boy." The terriers at once tore in dementedly, leaping up onto tables and chairs, knocking over ornaments and books, and eventually homing in on Buller's ankles.

"Kick 'em—hard. It's the only way," said the Admiral, hurling a copy of *Punch* at one of them. "PANSY!" The voice was like a bo'sun's mate's at defaulters' parade, and the terrier cringed and crawled under a sofa.

"So you're sailing round the world with me, eh, young man?" The Admiral took a long draft of brandy and for the first time gave his full attention to Buller, who saw clear blue eyes, a small nose, a rather small mouth among the abundance of whiskers and long white hair. "And I mean sailing. We're not having any truck with these engines they put in ships nowadays. Note that, young Buller. I wanted to call it the "Sailing Squadron" because that's what we'll be doing. But those fools at the Admiralty—all fools except your father—wouldn't have it."

The rest of the brandy went down, like water out of the

scuppers in a heavy sea, and the attentive footman whisked away the glass and replaced it with a fresh one. It crossed Buller's mind that to be one hour ahead of the world allowed for one hour of extra drinking time as a guest.

"In the *Bacchante*, eh? With the Wales boys, eh? Younger one's all right—bright little fellow. Older one's slow, so they're putting him in the Army. Quite right." Pansy emerged from under the sofa, and with the other two—Flos and Daisy —jumped quietly onto their master's lap, casting hair all over his black trousers.

For the next half hour, while the Admiral drank three more brandies, Buller listened to Lord Huntley's philosophy of sea power and beliefs on naval architecture and ordnance. They were rigid, convincing, and unanswerable—or unanswerable by a junior Midshipman about to sail round the world with this senior Admiral and Earl as his Commander-in-Chief.

Personnel: flogging, and keel-hauling in extreme cases, were the only means of keeping discipline. Diet: salt beef and pork were nourishing and what the men liked. Compulsory lime juice against the scurvy. Grog to keep them contented and as an occasional reward—"Always believed in the stuff. Nothing like splicing the mainbrace for a happy ship." (And he did just that with his third brandy.) Ordnance: nothing like smoothbore muzzle-loaders. Simple to load and fire; encourage a commander to lay his ship alongside the enemy where you can see the whites of his eyes. "That's what did for the Frogs and Dons!" And ships: back to "the wooden walls." Last forever. Sails keep the men busy, out of mischief. The rubbish they build today's out of date at the end of the first commission.

"Damn engines!" Lord Huntley spat out the words so vehemently that the terriers leapt from his lap as one and scuttled behind the brass coal hod. "Sulphurous fumes and dust ruin your brightwork, get in your lungs. Sparks set fire to your sails. Smoke shows the enemy your position, unsights your gunners. And what happens when you run out of the damn stuff?"

It was an accusation rather than a question, but Buller said obligingly, "Coal ship again, sir."

"And what if there's none left? Collier forgot to call at the coaling station, or sank? Then what, young man?"

"I'm afraid I don't know, sir."

"Nor would the Captain, eh." He beat his hands on his knees and recovered himself with another draft. "What would the *Thunderer* do—without sails *or* coal? What would Nelson have done with a coal-fired Fleet arriving in the West Indies chasing that Frog, Villeneuve, and finding no coal? No, young fellow, engines are the work of the devil. Just remember that. And engineers and stokers, with their coal-stained oil-stained hands and uniforms are the devil's disciples. Never speak to them myself. Never allow Engineer Officers in the wardroom in my ships. Devil's disciples," he repeated.

Lady Buller entered the library on those words, and the terriers exploded into activity again. "I'm *so* sorry, Lord Huntley," she said above the yapping. "It is quite unforgivable to be so late." She had Clementine beside her, rescued from the drawing room, a fair, well-developed girl of fifteen with hair cut short and drawn back in the fashionable style of the Princess of Wales.

"Papa likes to be in good time," said the girl, putting everything right firmly and quietening the dogs at the same time. But it was Pansy, Flos, and Daisy who led the way into the dining room and positioned themselves round their master's chair where they were fed almost continuously with scraps from every one of the seven courses, and especially from the Stilton cheese.

"Papa does so spoil them," said Clemmie at one point. Buller had been placed next to her, and although on principle he despised all girls, this one engaged his attention and even his approval by talking Navy throughout, and talking confidently and without restraint like his mother, of the great Admirals of the past, of great battles like Camperdown and

The Nile, and right back to the Armada.

Then she spoilt it all towards the end of the meal. The conversation went like this.

"Papa says Prince George is a special friend of yours."

"Well, yes, I suppose he is," said Buller cautiously.

"He and his brother and their parents stayed with us on the way to Dartmouth once. Before the Princes' third term. I thought Prince George was very jolly. Of course I could never marry him. He will marry some Princess, probably a German one, there are so many. I will marry some Lord or some Honourable like you."

Buller found himself turning scarlet, and was relieved when the girl turned to talk to the Bishop of Gloucester on her other side. Marry some Honourable like me! Buller was outraged and determined there and then never to marry, or if he did, not for ages, and then, if there were to be children, he would only have boys . . .

The Flying Squadron departed from Spithead on September 14, 1880, under the command of Admiral the Earl of Huntley. During the course of the leisurely world cruise, which took them to South Africa and then to Australia, there was plenty of time to forge new friendships and cement old friendships. Living on shipboard with the two Princes day after day and month after month, Buller got to know them even better, and to like Prince George especially more and more. Buller also formed a warm friendship with a tall, gangling Midshipman, a year senior to him, called Mark Holly—a young man who often acted the buffoon and never seemed to take himself seriously but who had a great love of life and a warm heart that Buller found very engaging.

Mark Holly was a comforting person to have around in dangerous moments, and there were several of these on the long voyage, including a ferocious hurricane in the roaring forties as they neared the western Australia coast. In Australia they were given a tumultuous welcome wherever they went, especially in Melbourne and Sydney. The cruise continued uneventfully until early in May 1882. Then, one day, an Admiralty telegram was received on board the *Inconstant*. Its contents flashed through the squadron as if by that new American invention, the telephone. The Flying Squadron was to cut short its cruise and head via the Cape for Gibraltar. Several units of the Mediterranean and Channel fleets required certain additional personnel.

That evening lists went up on the notice boards of all five men-o'-war. "The following officers, Midshipmen, Petty Officers, and ratings are to disembark forthwith and transfer to the troopship *Ocean Bay* for onward passage through the Canal to the Mediterranean where they will join H.M. ships as indicated at Suda Bay . . ."

And there, under cadets and Midshipmen, were the names in alphabetical order, Midshipman W. B. Basset—and, only second in the list of five, Midshipman the Honourable A. Buller. Third on the list was Holly; Buller and he were to joint the *Inflexible*, Captain J. A. Fisher.

"I say, is it really true?" Mark Holly, towering above the others clustered round the board, held on to Buller's shoulder. "We're both going! What luck!"

For a few moments, Buller said nothing, savouring the news in silence. So, his luck had turned at last. The Buller luck, which had escaped his father for so long, was his. It *must* be a major war, not like that affair in Natal, or the Zulu or Ashanti business. And Russia might be drawn into it—that old blundering bear had been spoiling for a fight for years . . .

"And the *Inflexible*, Archy!" Holly was saying. "Imagine it, old fellow. The newest, biggest, most powerful, most modern battleship in the world! Remember seeing her in the dockyard fitting out at Portsmouth?"

If it was a triumphant moment for Holly and Buller, it was no more than a hard pill for Prince George to swallow. They met him a few minutes later, on their way down to the gunroom, and both young men had to hold their excitement in check.

"Titch, I'm sorry. Jolly bad luck."

Prince George's nickname had become something of a misnomer on the voyage of the Flying Squadron. He had filled out, grown a couple of inches, and possessed now more the bearing of a man than that of a boy. He had also acquired a new self-confidence, a new dignity that hinted at the august station in life that he would soon occupy. But no pomposity—none at all. And he retained a capacity for fun and jokes as great as ever. Now he was making a gallant effort to be pleased for them and to conceal his own disappointment.

"I'm really fearfully excited for you. You will write, won't you? Tell me about the fighting, I mean?"

"If there is any," said Buller. "The whole thing will probably have blown over by the time we get there. Just like the Boer business. I mean, the Gippos haven't got a navy. But it would have been fun for the three of us to have stuck together."

"Can't be helped, old boy. I think if I could secretly get away somehow and perhaps distinguish myself in a fight, my Papa would be pleased about it. But Grandmama would have a fit—and anyway, that's all a dream, because everyone knows that Eddie and I are to be kept wrapped up in cotton wool for the rest of our lives."

The Prince was unable to conceal the bitter note in his voice. But, a second later, he was again smiling his slightly mischievous and confiding smile that he had inherited from his father.

"We've got to go now. So good-bye, Titch," said Buller. "And give my respects to your father when you see him," he added, the thought passing through his mind that he might never see the Prince of Wales or Georgie again.

It was indescribably hot and almost unbearably uncomfortable in the troopship *Ocean Bay*, with 850 Indian Army soldiers and a battalion of Sikhs on board, with their officers. The officers from the Flying Squadron bore it stoically, encouraged by the knowledge that the voyage could not last for long, and that most of those on board were suffering a great deal more than they were.

At Aden an Admiralty cutter put off with mails and telegrams. Buller had a letter from his mother, pages of rapidly and carelessly written local news and events rattled off just as if she were speaking, but asking affectionately after him, and telling him that Junus was well, and—a typical Cecily Buller touch—covering his paw with ink and making his mark at the end of the letter. There was another joint letter, full of buffoonery, from his twin brothers, who were serving in a Channel Fleet battleship at Gibraltar: "Guy challenged our Paymaster-Lieutenant to a horse race down the rock and came a fearful tumble. The girls here are spiffing . . ." And a rather formal, but affectionate one, from his father, under The Admiralty embossed letter heading.

There was something more important from another department of the Admiralty, which affected them all, and that was a telegram dated the previous day ordering them all to join their ships at Alexandria instead of at Suda Bay. And newspaper reports told of the growing crisis, of riots in Alexandria.

"It really does look like war, Holly. And I heard one of the engineers say, 'We've orders to squeeze out another couple of knots.' "

For three days and nights the *Ocean Bay* steamed up the Red Sea at 12 knots, vibrating like an old man with the palsy, adding to the discomfort caused by temperatures of more than 100 degrees. To port or starboard, they passed villages and towns with strange names like Wahla and Kabr e'Shekh, Khalis ed Daff and Ras Abu Dara—names with a sound that was to become familiar to their ears in the months that lay ahead in a prolonged and bitter war. Once, they caught a glimpse of distant hills, shimmering in the heat haze and as brown as the desert from which they arose.

But for most of the time all that was to be seen were their own dark stain of funnel smoke trailing astern, scavenging sea birds and high flying kites, and occasional shoals of flying fish that arose like shining bead curtains from the sea and were gone again.

Then the Gulf of Suez, a brown collar closing in on them, and Suez itself—low white buildings, slow-moving white figures, camels as final confirmation of their whereabouts, the heat of the land beating at them as if an oven door had been opened.

For nearly two years now, Buller had been travelling to strange and distant places about the world, from Montevideo to Yokohama, from Singapore to Brisbane. He had arrived in the *Bacchante* at ports where it was cold and raining, where it was so hot and dry it was hard to believe that it had ever rained, but always there had been a feeling of welcome and hospitality—often, at places like Sydney and Hong Kong, royal and ecstatic welcome.

The minarets and Pompey's Pillar, the Ras-el-tin light-house, rose out of the distant white blur that was Alexandria; and Buller could already sense the hostility in the air that was in such strong contrast to all the earlier places they had visited. And momentarily, as the *Ocean Bay* closed the shore, he felt the first pulse of adrenaline coursing through his veins and the lift of expectation of danger. Yes, there was no denying it, the taste of battle was there on his tongue, just briefly, but unmistakably.

Then Holly said, "There she is! Look at her! What an ironclad, Buller!"

The roadstead and harbour of Alexandria were crowded with warships of all sizes and many nations, feluccas and fishing boats, Navy cutters and gigs, native rowing and sail-ing craft, a few merchantment, all like satellites to the men-o'-war. There she was indeed, along with the *Invincible*, the *Alexandra*, the *Sultan*, and the *Superb*, and the other vessels of the Mediterranean Fleet. The *Inflexible* was at once distinguishable by her twin turrets, her four 16-inch guns, her twin funnels and twin masts complementing one another as a symbol of the transition from sail to steam—and her sheer size, almost 12,000 tons of glittering white upperwork and turrets.

"The ship of the future."

"The battleship of today."

A steam launch was putting off from the *Inflexible* even before the *Ocean Bay* had dropped anchor, and was making towards them.

"Not wasting any time, are they?"

" 'Jackie' Fisher's not a time-waster, so I've heard," said Buller.

The *Inflexible* had been commissioned just a year earlier, under the command of Captain John Arbuthnot Fisher, a fiery, fierce, impatient officer who had already made a name for himself in the Navy as a proponent of the torpedo, as an officer of unusual talent in the first-ever ironclad, the *Warrior*, and as a peerlessly brave fighter in the bloody China War of 1859 in which he had distinguished himself at the storming of the Taku Forts.

Everyone in the Navy knew of Jackie Fisher's reputation with the women, his love of dancing the night through, his stormy temper when thwarted, his boyish delight when he got his way, which was nearly always. War or no war, life in the *Inflexible* would not be dull. And war it was to be, so it seemed, from what Holly and Buller learned in the short trip from the troopship to the battleship.

"Shouldn't wonder if there isn't trouble tomorrow," the Petty Officer divulged in a low voice, and looking very knowing. "Shouldn't wonder at all. The Gippos have been building up those forts there. Look at 'em," he said, pointing along the shoreline where they could just see the circular black muzzles of heavy guns. "And they've been bringing in thousands of troops. And I reckon we're going to blow 'em up—the lot of 'em. Then put a landing party ashore."

It was July 9, 1882, and sunset was in half an hour . . .

❧ ⚜ ❧

Chapter VIII

Breakfast on the *Condor*'s mess deck was by shaded lamplight at 4:30 A.M., the men in working dress talking quietly among themselves. There was not a trace of light when Rod and Ginger O'Sullivan emerged on deck, still chewing their last mouthful of bread and jam, barefoot, bell-bottoms rolled up to just below the knee, a scarf under their caps tight across the head and over the ears as protection against the percussion and sound of the charge.

Although still Captain's cox, Rod's training as a gunner in H.M.S. *Excellent* qualified him to be one of the crew of a dozen serving the *Condor*'s four-and-one-half-ton gun. The rest of the gun crew joined them about the big seven-inch muzzle-loader one by one, their presence felt rather than seen. Silence on deck had been ordered, and the only sound was the steady beat of the *Condor*'s reciprocating engines deep below, turning over at minimum revolutions ready to provide power. Yards had been sent down and the bowsprit rigged the previous evening, and like every vessel in the Fleet, the little gunvessel was cleared for action.

Still nothing was to be seen; the predawn air was only warm, but it carried the certainty of heat and violence. Rod squatted on the wooden deck behind the breech of the gun, just able to discern the heavy, circular silhouette of the barrel against the eastern sky. One of the powder monkeys was standing beside him, probably young Sid Brewster, just fifteen years old, younger than Rod had been when the *Eurydice* had gone down. Nice boy, a cockney from Shoreditch, small for his age, as he needed to be for his job, nipping to and from the powder magazine and avoiding all obstructions with his lethal load.

"In the event of my not receiving a satisfactory answer," the Commander-in-Chief's General Order had begun. The Military Governor of Alexandria had been told that unless the newly constructed forts were surrendered to the British Fleet, they would be destroyed within twenty-four hours. Admiral Seymour's order had assigned targets to each battleship, but there were still too many forts and too few ships, and one fort in particular—the powerful Marabout, far to the west—would be able to fire unmolested. Because of their size, "The gunvessels and gunboats will remain outside and keep out of fire until a favourable opportunity offers itself . . ."

Knowing their Captain as well as they did, the crew of the *Condor* reckoned that this "favourable opportunity" would very quickly be found, and there was no fear that they might be out of the fight.

By 5:30, a grey light began to spread across the sky, brighter and with a touch of pink to the east, still dark to the west. Then the pink darkened in colour, brightened in intensity, and one could begin to call it dawn. More distant shapes were revealed, unchanged and familiar along the shoreline where the British had watched the batteries become more powerful day by day, and at night, too. The scene was less familiar in the harbour and the roadstead, for yesterday had seen the departure of all foreign shipping, warships and merchantmen alike, in anticipation of the bombardment. The Flagship's band had played out each vessel with its national anthem, making a fine long chorus of international music. Early in the afternoon, as the word of the ultimatum spread, the feluccas and dhows and all the local small boats had scurried for safety, too.

Now, as the ships emerged one by one in the faint grey light, Rod could make out the stark and purposeful silhouettes of the ironclads, the turret ironclad *Monarch* nearest, beyond her the *Temeraire*, the *Alexandra*, and the *Sultan*. Minutes later, much closer inshore and almost within the harbour breakwater, the upper works of the *Invincible* and the smaller *Penelope* revealed themselves, little more distant than half a mile from the Egyptian forts of Mex and Mex Lines, known to mount some thirty-five guns, a number of them heavy rifled guns of modern design.

Full daylight broke, fair and fine; it was already hot, the wind light and from the northwest. Every man in the *Condor* was at his station, talking little though it was now permitted. Rod's gun was loaded, ready to be traversed or elevated, Rod himself with firing lanyard in hand and standing to the left of the breech. The Captain was on the bridge, pacing to and fro with the Navigating Lieutenant at his side, both officers wearing white duck trousers and service coats, with pith helmets, a telescope under the arm. Beresford was pointing at something on the shore, and the Lieutenant trained his glass upon it.

Suddenly Beresford turned and called down to the gun crew, like a theater manager barely able to control his excitement, "Two minutes, lads, then watch for the fireworks!" His booming laughter was echoed by several of the men, and someone called out, "Aye, aye, sir. Especially ours." And from the nearby Gatling quick-firer crew, "We'll give 'em hell, sir."

Someone else started to give a shout, too, but no one heard what he had to say, for at that moment, at the stroke of seven o'clock, a heavy gun crashed out. Rod saw the puff of smoke from the *Alexandra*, and a second later the flash and spout of grey dust rising from the distant Fort Ada near the Pharos lighthouse. At the same time, the *Invincible* hoisted the signal for general action.

At once a dozen heavy guns from the fleet blasted out, and as if touched by a simultaneous fuse, the shore batteries replied, the sparkle of their muzzle flashes ripping along the coast from Fort Marabout to Pharos Fort six miles distant. The Egyptian gunners were as ready as the British gun crews, and it was at once evident that the despised enemy, who many thought might at once raise the white flag, was prepared to fight it out.

The massive sixteen-inch guns of the *Inflexible* spoke like the bass voices in a choir, the Flagship's ten-inch guns with the note of a tenor, then the chorus, a sudden mixed thunder of concussive sound that pounded the eardrums, the background chorus the ticker-tock of Nordenfelts and Gatlings. The powder smoke was already rising in a cloud from the ships, the gunsmoke and rubble dust from the forts joining it and then drifting away south over the city. Beneath this pall, which was already giving the gunlayers trouble, fountains of water spouted out from the sea from exploding Egyptian shells, some close about their targets, several registering hits with a brighter flash amidst the spray and drifting smoke.

Between the loudest crashes another sound could be heard, too—the sound of men's voices, perhaps in cheer, perhaps in agony. And then a louder, clearer voice, Beresford's voice: "Full speed ahead! We'll pass her a tow."

One of the crew was saying excitedly, "Look at the *Temeraire*—she's aground!"

"She's struck a shoal!"

The smoke cleared about the battleship, and Rod could see her, cable parted and close to the shore, and stationary, a sitting duck for the Egyptian gunlayers. The *Condor* was making for her, decks vibrating, engines at full speed, and a party had been formed to get the tow to her. A near miss from a shell from the Mex Lines fort sent up a fifty-foot tower of water into which they steamed, the water crashing down on the gunvessel's upper deck, drenching Rod and the rest of the crew.

"Why aren't we replying?" someone shouted, wiping the water off his face.

"We've enough to do," someone else said.

Their little ship was close to the high sides of the stranded vessel. The *Temeraire* was firing but her situation was a difficult one. Rod caught a glimpse, as they turned, of men on the *Temeraire*'s forecastle securing a cable. Both parties had acted with remarkable speed and skill, the fruit of long practice. And now the *Condor* was turning and taking up the strain, black smoke pouring from her single funnel, 700 horse-power and 800 tons straining to tow 7,500 tons of iron and steel. The battleship was not hard aground, that was soon clear, for almost at once she began to move off the shoal and a cheer rose from her upper deck, drowned by the crash of a shell exploding close alongside her. This time the whine and rattle of steel splinters added a lethal touch to the deluge of water that descended on the Condor.

"Cast loose!"

The roar of the combat had reached a new level. Every ship was firing as rapidly as the gunners could clean out and reload, and the return fire from the forts appeared to be keeping up as strongly as ever. Both the *Monarch* and the *Temeraire*, and more distantly the Flagship and the *Penelope*, who were seeking to get in closer within the breakwater, were taking a peppering from the most westerly of the forts, Marabout.

The *Condor*, released from her burden, was gathering speed. Someone—was it the Captain himself?—was shouting, "Stand by to fire!" At last. But what was the target?

Then Rod saw, and at the same time the Gunnery Officer behind him cried out, "We're making for the fort. Stand by to fire!" They were steaming full speed for Fort Marabout, with its seven heavy rifled guns, more than almost any other fort, and numerous smoothbores. One well-placed hit from a nine-inch gun could send them to the bottom within minutes, but the Captain was taking a chance, dodging the shoals that littered this stretch of water, and the shells that fell thick about them. If an ironclad could not be spared, then it was up to the little *Condor* to knock out these guns. This was Beresford's opportunity.

Frederic Villiers, the war artist who had shrewdly selected the *Condor* as the ship most likely to show him the action, was sketching the scene in swift strokes near Rod's gun. Rod had heard that *The Times*'s war correspondent was on board, though he had not yet seen him. So their little ship might be in the picture papers as well as in the august *Times* itself! If they survived.

The fire was getting hot now, the noise cacophonous. Shells were passing close overhead; a heavy shell burst in the water not fifty feet from the gun's muzzle, showering the upper deck and the bridge with a deluge of water. Wiping it from his own face, Rod saw the Captain and the Navigating Lieutenant and a man in civilian clothes—must be *The Times* man—bent double and shaking out their hats. The whine that followed the water indicated a ricochet over the ship. And it was at this moment that the Captain gave the order to anchor. *Anchor!* With the enemy shells bursting about them! Suicide! But then, as soon as the anchors were out, Rod saw that they were going to use one to warp to and fro before the fort, veering away and then heaving in cable.

Rod impatiently awaited the order to fire. The layer had the sights on the embrasures set into the stone of the fort, the big guns clearly visible at less than 300 yards, the sudden flash from one and then another indicating the intensity of the fire and the dangerous situation they were in. There was a concussive shock, and Rod realized that they had been hit. The whole ship shook like a struck animal. He felt the thud through his feet, and the sights shifted off target. Then again, more violently this time.

The first pangs of fear were like cold hands at Rod's throat; and then they were at once thrust aside, cast far distant, by the sound of a voice—a voice of command his years of training had taught him to obey. "Open FIRE!"

No elevation—gunshot range. Rod pulled on the lanyard, and the gun exploded into life with the click of the striker, the recoil hurling it back to be caught by the tackle. A blast of flame from the muzzle, slow-rising black smoke turning to grey. The gun was run in. O'Sullivan and his mate were already sponging down the barrel, the powder monkey standing by with his silk bags. The shell from the ready-ammunition stack, two men straining at its weight, slipped into the muzzle . . .

The routine that seemed so cumbersome and laboured in practice was now a swift natural sequence, a smooth routine almost: load, lay, fire! They were close to the fort, so close, Rod suddenly realized, that the Egyptian gunners were unable to depress the barrels of their rifled guns to bear on the *Condor*. They were in that exquisitely dangerous yet temporarily secure situation of being *below* the enemy muzzles!

"FIRE!"

And again, "FIRE!"

They were getting off three rounds a minute. The fore and aft 64-pounders were adding their weight, and now as they worked and sweated in the morning sun, coughing in the smoke and drifting dust, closing their ears to the concussive sound that beat at their heads from their own bursting charges, and the thunder of the fort's guns, and the whine of the shells overhead—and now as the gun crew worked in battle together for the first time, they became aware that they were winning. Slowly, minute by minute, the intensity of the Egyptian fire was diminishing.

Rod could see little, firing round after round with the same elevation and direction as the last, checking when the smoke momentarily cleared, and observing then some of the effects of the fire—the scarred earthworks, the stacked sandbags torn apart, the gun muzzles askew and silent or tilted forward as if in abasement.

"Cease fire!"

The silence was so sudden it came almost as an impact, and for a few seconds the buzz in Rod's ears drowned the more distant boom of the bombardment that still proceeded to the east, where a pall of smoke now arose thousands of feet into the air.

The gun crew collapsed onto the deck, exhausted by the strain of forty minutes of continuous firing. Rod was squatting, head between his knees, the sweat dripping from his forehead, when he felt a hand on his shoulder. It was the Chief Petty Officer, Rawlinson, Lord Charles Beresford at his side. The Captain had powder streaks across his face, and his uniform was stained dark by seawater and sweat. His eyes were blazing with the joy of danger and battle.

"Are you beat, Midge?"

Rod sprang to his feet and stood at attention, and Beresford repeated his question. "Are you beat? I've more work for you. I want you to cox the launch. We need your luck, Midge. Landin' party under Chief Petty Officer Rawlinson. Spike the damn guns. The Gippos seem to have run like scalded cats but they'll come back if the guns can still fire."

"Aye aye, sir."

"Look smart, then."

The *Condor* had been towing her boats astern since she had cleared for action the evening before, and Rawlinson had the launch alongside in minutes. There were fifteen men in the party, all armed, Able Seamen Chivers and Cartwright among them, and Ordinary Seamen Crowe and Masters and the rest, four Royal Marines, and the heavy equipment needed to destroy the guns. Rod sat in the stern, the men at the oars pulled the boat away, and the rest of the company sat alert,

Lee-Metford rifles at the ready, studying the battered facing of the fort.

Fort Marabout was on an island, and if there were any survivors they could escape only by boat to the next fort, Fort Adjemi on the mainland. A single shot rang out and the oarsmen ceased rowing and reached for their rifles, the marines raising their guns to their shoulders. But the sound was not repeated, and it appeared to be no more than an act of defiance.

"Give way together," Rod shouted, and the launch recovered her way.

They landed awkwardly among rocks, and as soon as they were ashore, clambering swiftly up the slope, avoiding shell holes, Rod ordered his crew to stand off a quarter cable (50 yards) so that they could get in again quickly when they returned. Meanwhile they dipped their oars as necessary in order to remain on station.

Rod had time to glance out to sea and across the bay. The *Condor*, looking proud of herself and of the wounds that had scarred the paintwork of her hull, was half a cable away. Beyond, across the bay, there was only smoke to be seen, a massive grey cloud that concealed minarets and the Ras-el-tin lighthouse and the ironclads. It moved steadily towards the shore and was fed anew by the guns whose fire could sometimes be identified by flashes in the murk, like ignited and suddenly doused matches. The thunderous boom was continuous, and it was evident that the big ships had not yet been as successful as the little *Condor*.

Then—"Crack! crack! crack!" from the battered fort. Rod spun round. One of the crew called out, "There's a fight—they're 'aving a fight . . ."

The rifle fire continued, intermittently, and they saw a figure leap from behind a big rifled gun askew on the mounting in its embrasure. He paused and turned, rifle at the firing position, bayonet fixed, and fired. Others joined him, and more figures were at the next embrasure, as if in ordered retreat. Then Rod spotted Rawlinson, who was waving an arm, signalling the launch to come in. Rod already had the boat speeding back to the rocky shore, observing as he did so the sailors and three of the marines climbing rapidly down the slope. One of the marines and three ratings remained sheltering behind a smoothbore gun above the parapet, firing from time to time. They were the rearguard party covering the rest, who in turn took up firing positions at the base of the slope while the others descended, jumping from rock to rock, guns in outstretched arms.

There was no panic, no shouting, and when they were near the bottom, one of the *Condor*'s 64-pounders fired a single shot which exploded right inside the embrasure, sending up a shower of rocks and limestone. A voice cried out, "Bull's-eye!"

Then Rod, with the launch's bows beating at the rocks on the water's edge, was taking in the party. Eight, nine, twelve, then two more, all panting, dusty, pouring with sweat. The rear guard, all four of them, one nursing an arm running in blood. But still one of the party was missing.

"Who's to come, Chief?" he asked Rawlinson.

The Chief Petty Officer looked round, counting heads. "Dawes was missing, but he turned up. There he is—in the stern. Where's Masters? He disappeared, but I thought I saw him again." He called out to the launch's complement, "Has anyone seen Masters?"

At the same moment a signal gun cracked out from the *Condor*, and Rod saw that she was flying the instant recall signal.

"We'll have to leave him," Rawlinson said.

"I'll go back for him," someone volunteered.

"No. Get under way, Maclewin. We're not risking more losses. The fire was pretty thick up there, I'm telling you. Must have been a hundred of them. And they didn't run like we expected. Plucky lot, seemed to me. And the dead all round their guns, like the bag after a big shoot. The kites are going to have the time of their lives . . ."

Rod should be obeying orders, getting the boat under way. Everyone's eyes were on the *Condor* now, their refuge, their home. They had done what they had been ordered to do. Rod was the only one to give a last glance back at the slopes of the fort, the only one to see a tall, dark figure running helter-skelter down the slope, tripping, falling, recovering himself at the cost of his hat and his rifle.

It was Masters all right. Masters was not lying on his back in the fort, black eyes staring upwards in death, unseeing as the birds of prey circled overhead, as Rod had imagined. He was racing for the boat, falling again, this time landing with a fearful crash, sending up a shower of stones and a cloud of dust. And at exactly that moment another figure emerged from behind a rock, long flintlock musket at his shoulder. The range was not a dozen yards. He could not miss.

So swift was Rod's reaction that no one in the boat turned until his shot rang out. Rod raised, aimed and fired the big Lee-Metford in one swift movement as if he were competing in the final round at a rifle competition. And he would have taken first prize, the silver cup—no doubt of that. For the Arab fell—wounded or dead, Rod would never know— and Masters was on his legs and five seconds later was wading out, arms raised, a wild look on his face, shouting, "Hold it—help!"

"Old 'Ocean Swell' reckons we're the dud ship of the Fleet," remarked Midshipman "Stuffy" Hadow. "That's because we're not the smartest at crossing topgallants and shifting topmasts. 'Damn,' says Jackie, 'this is a steel fightin' ship, not a show yacht.'"

"Is that really what the Captain says?" asked Buller.

"He doesn't mince his words, our Jackie—you'll see. And you'll hear his language. Like when we first commissioned. The electric light is dashed good now but at first it was all sparks and explosions. And you couldn't breathe below the main deck. Ratings passing out all over the place—no air. The designer forgot that even sailors *breathe*. And all the electric motors for the pumps—none of 'em *worked*."

Over gunroom supper of cocoa, ship's biscuit, rancid butter, and hard cheese from Crete, Buller and Holly were being introduced to the mysteries of the *Inflexible*. Farther down the table, two more Midshipmen were engaged in a race between two weevils tapped out of their biscuit and now "guided" by their sponsors from one side of the table to the other amid the cheers of their backers.

"Another thing. The designers didn't expect us to have to know where we were, or where we wanted to go to," continued Midshipman Hadow. "It was like Hampton Court maze. Every compartment, every passageway, on every deck was exactly the same. Then Jackie has this notion of putting up coloured arrows and signposts. So if you want to go down to the engine rooms, you follow orange arrows, to the port turret, white arrows."

The mighty *Inflexible* was as different from the little *Bacchante* as the *Britannia* from a paddle tug. The broad upper deck ran flush from stem to stern, well over 320 feet of it, with the two great funnels and two gun turrets amidships, signalling the new age of steam and ultimate firepower. Adding to her radical modernism was a torpedo-launching device on the forward superstructure right at the bows, and at the rear of the after superstructure deck were two sixty-foot torpedo boats for launching at an enemy in close action or for attacking him in the harbour.

Later, Buller and Holly were shown the citadel protecting the ship's vitals—her engines and magazines and the rotating turrets, an impregnable wall of iron two feet thick, the armour itself weighing as much as the *Bacchante*. Never had a man-o'-war better lived up to the name *ironclad*.

The *Inflexible*'s two new Midshipmen had just one day to familiarize themselves with their new ship; and only a few minutes to familiarize themselves with their Captain. They met Captain Jackie Fisher by chance as they were passing the wardroom door and crushed themselves against the wall, standing to attention and hoping they would not be seen.

The Captain had almost passed when he suddenly swung back and stared expressionlessly at them, as if observing dirty paintwork. Buller saw a face of dark complexion, cold, clear, brown, protruding eyes, full, sensuous lips. Fisher turned to his First Lieutenant standing behind him.

"And what are these?" he asked in distaste.

"These are our two new Midshipmen, sir. To replace the two we left behind at Malta with the fever."

The Captain looked at them more closely. "And your name?"

"Buller, sir."

Fisher's face at once lit up with pleasure and new interest, and his lips formed into a smile of great charm. "Ah, Buller. George Buller's boy—Matthews, this is the Third Sea Lord's boy, eh? How's your father? Great man. Served under him once. Fine officer."

"I haven't seen him for nearly two years, sir."

"Why not—eh? Ah"—that smile again—"you were with the Flying Squadron—Admiral Huntley. I'll warrant *you* did not burn much coal." He chuckled. "And you had those Princes. Younger one's going to make a fine sailor, so I'm told." He turned to the Lieutenant again. "What are these snotties' stations?"

"Both with the starboard aftermost twenty-pounder, sir."

"Well, you're going to see some action, lucky bounders."

The Captain resumed his progress, walking with short punchy steps, and Buller sensed the greatness of the man as he disappeared. Captain at the unusually early age of thirty-three, a passionate believer in innovation and reform, now commanding the newest and most powerful ship in the Royal Navy. But he had also heard from his father that Fisher's rapid promotion and dogmatic manner had made him enemies, who sought to discredit him by hinting at his doubtful parentage. That olive complexion? A touch of the tarbrush?

* * *

"I've only heard them fired once. And that was enough to lift off the top of my head."

"The blast made our first Gunnery Officer insane. Never recovered."

"Takes off all the paint for a hundred feet."

The subject of the *Inflexible*'s four giant guns was always a favourite one in the wardroom, the gunroom, and the battleship's messes. And now that they were to be fired at an enemy for the first time, there was a lot of "scare" speculation on the results of the forthcoming bombardment.

These guns, housed in rotating turrets protected by sixteen inches of iron armour plate and eighteen inches of teak, fired shells weighing 1700 pounds, which were supposed to be able to pierce armour as thick as the *Inflexible*'s own. The Navy had still not overcome its prejudice against breech-loading, and elaborate arrangements had to be constructed for depressing the guns' barrels into a glacis from which they were reloaded, the charge being hydraulically rammed home.

There was the breakwater, a thin, dark line less than half a mile distant. Beyond, the gold-domed mosques and towers rising above the white spread of Alexandria's buildings. The only sound was a distant one of waves breaking on the shore below the Mex Fort, and a train puffing laboriously out of the station. A dog barked once. All so peaceful, so tranquil. Thousands of families in their homes scarcely a mile away, waiting for sunrise to begin a new day . . . And yet, so near, hundreds of guns, all expectantly manned, facing one another across a narrow stretch of water . . .

Buller could just make out the shape of the all-white *Temeraire* no more than two cables to the west, the older single-funnel *Monarch* closer inshore.

"Gun fired in anger." As the four words went through Buller's mind like a liturgy dating back almost to the nursery, he could not help smiling to himself in the half-light. Now a hundred guns fired in anger. A private joke, and he would have rather died than have shared it with any of his shipmates. But Guy and Henry now—that would be different, and he would take the utmost satisfaction in deliberately not crowing to them about this battle when he next saw them. It would be more effective that way. The twins stuck peacefully in Malta while their younger brother took part in his first action 1,100 miles away.

The Chief Gunnery Officer had said, "It's your job to keep their heads down. And don't waste your ammunition."

Buller loved the little naval 20-pounder, a quick-firing gun with plenty of hitting power. He loved the feel of the hardened steel, the brass, the crisp, smooth movement of the breech, the precision of the sights, even the name "Armstrong" etched so beautifully into the metal.

The Egyptian military dictator had acquired a number of rough nicknames among the British sailors. " 'Orrible Pasha" was the most popular in the *Inflexible*, and Buller was just able to read those words scrawled across the heavy shell-box beside him—"These for 'Orrible Pasha."

It was broad daylight, already hot, and they were talking among themselves, impatient for action. The *Alexandra* fired her single shot, like a giant starting pistol. The *Inflexible*'s starboard turret had long since swung round on its axis under its near-silent hydraulic power, the twin white protruding sixteen-inch guns aimed, with no visible elevation, at their first target over the breakwater. This was one of the line of forts on the south side of the harbour, Dom el Kubebe—or "Hold My Baby" as the gunlayers called it. Clear to the naked eye were the scarps and counterscarps below the reinforced parapet, revetted with stone, the embrasures, and centrally within them the small black circles of the guns' muzzles.

Buller was looking at one of these, the words "cannon's mouth" passing through his mind, when the black of its muzzle was suddenly transformed into a vivid yellow splash, at once followed by a blast of black smoke. "It's firing!" he exclaimed. And, laughing at his own naïveté, "It's firing at ME!" Outrage. Someone trying to kill me.

Someone else shouted, just as futilely, "Look out!" They

could see the shell clearly, rising on its parabola of flight, a small, black object in the morning sky, lost to sight as it fell again, terminating its passage in a fountain of water thirty yards short of the battleship.

When the *Inflexible* fired her first shell the effect was like being struck by a huge chunk of air, air transformed into a solid mass by some superhuman pressure—and then *thrown*. The sound was overwhelming, but the real blow came from the concussion that seemed as if it might stave in your skull. The 12,000-ton man-o'-war shuddered from stem to stern, and the gun barrel emitted a gush of black smoke as if squeezed from her lungs under great pressure.

They all saw the 1700-pound shell explode. It struck the limestone face of the fort between one of the embrasures and the parapet, sending up a yellow cloud of rubble, and when the dust and smoke cleared, they saw a scar in the parapet like a gap in a set of teeth. The 20-pounder crew gave a great cheer, echoed by all those still above decks, but the cheer was drowned at once by the explosion of the second gun.

After that first shot, they never again saw clearly the effect of their fire. As the action became general, the gun-smoke and the effect of hits on the forts as well as on the ships filled the sky with a slow-moving dark cloud that rose ever higher into the sky. And soon Buller's 20-pounder was making its own contribution.

The *Inflexible* was moving in closer to the breakwater, and then eastwards. The Flagship and the *Penelope* had steamed slowly into the harbour and were now firing at their first target at very close range, while the *Inflexible* was concentrating its fire on the Ras-el- tin lighthouse fort, hurling shell after shell at this more easily identifiable target.

There was a spotter in the foretop shouting down reports and directions through a megaphone, his voice sometimes carried away by the thunder of battle, at other times distinct—"That was fifty yards over!" or "Short a hundred yards," or "On target." Then came the words, "Enemy on the parapet directing guns." And, only seconds later, the voice of the Gunnery Lieutenant, bearded Lieutenant Jackson, "Twenty-pounders—open FIRE!"

Targets of opportunity. How often Buller had practiced this. It was one of the delights of manning the lighter guns that you could choose your targets, shifting your line of fire in seconds. Momentarily, the smoke cleared, revealing a strip of the shore, waves breaking on rocks, piled rectangular stones like giant children's bricks, rising to the main line of the fort, rising again to the towering lighthouse, its top concealed by drifting smoke.

There was the parapet, less than a mile distant, the smaller smoothbore guns firing over it. And the spotter was right. There were white figures visible standing on it, a dozen or more, waving their arms either in defiance of, or encouragement to, the gunners, or directing their fire. The layer brought round the 20-pounder's barrel, checked the elevation, the gun cracked—a miniature echo of the sixteen-inch—and at once working with the smooth precision of the sliding breech itself, the team reloaded, closed up, and fired again, and again.

Buller was too busy to see the effects of the fire until the order to cease was called out. They had fired twenty rounds and the parapet was now clear of figures, who had been either blown off or sent scattering in retreat. He turned to Holly, who was sweating as much as he was. There were powder marks on his face, too, and his overeagerness had led to a cut on his hand which he had hastily bound up with his scarf.

Buller was about to say, "We've done for them . . ." But before he could speak the words, they were proved false. By no means had the *Inflexible*'s mighty guns knocked out the fort, nor had their own 20-pounder killed all the gunners. Egyptian fire had already done much damage to the rigging above them, hits which they had not noticed in the heat of the fight. Now the ship gave a sudden shudder, a twitch as if she were a kicked dog, a quite different effect from the recoil of her heavy guns.

A heavy shell had struck her side, and the shouts from below that followed it suggested that it had caused damage if not death. Almost at once there was a second crash, much louder than the first. Buller felt the deck beneath his feet shiver so violently that they were all thrown down. A blast of hot air passed over them, there was an ear-ripping sound, a crash, and sudden silence as if the bombardment had ceased out of respect for the dead. And dead there were. When Buller got to his feet again and looked about him dazedly, he saw Holly and the rest of the crew standing about the gun. But one man had not risen. Six feet away, Lieutenant Jackson lay still beside a wide hole torn in the deck, edge turned up jaggedly, smoke like a volcano's rising slowly from it.

Lieutenant Jackson would not be getting to his feet again to issue orders. His right shoulder and arm and a good deal of the right side of his head had all been carried away by a ten-inch rifled shell which had failed to explode: if it had, they would all have been dead, and many more besides the gun crew.

The officer was lying on his face, and Buller bent down to turn him over, gently—as if it mattered—onto his back. Most of the face was intact, the dark beard unstained by blood, the eyes closed in seeming contentment. There had been no suffering. A quick death in action; it was the right way to go. It was an untidy sight, with parts of the brain scattered about the deck, and the blood stain spreading widely. But Buller felt curiously objective about it. He had seen corpses before, several times—a gunnery accident, falls from the rigging.

The Petty Officer said, "Leave him be, Mr. Buller." Then, "Prepare to commence firing."

The surgeon and two of his assistants arrived and quickly bore off the corpse. "Carpenter Shannon's a goner, too," one of the assistants told them. "And you should see the Captain's cabin—'e won't be pleased. It were a richochet upwards."

Then they began firing. And it was all sound and fury again, and stench of powder and hot grease; they worked faster than before as if in unspoken pledge to avenge the deaths.

They were firing now at Fort Ada, near Pharos. The Flagship was signalling, "Go as close to forts as water will permit." The *Superb* was firing at the same target, and suddenly there appeared an enormous gush of flame and smoke which pierced the cloud hanging over the harbour and city, causing the cloud to swirl and boil under the pressure of the explosion. They had got one of the enemy magazines, and the gunners of both battleships let out a cheer, each crew claiming it as their own strike.

Still the Egyptian firing continued, and Buller could not help admiring the pluck of the Egyptians continuing to man their guns against this continued onslaught of modern heavy and light guns. It was not until well after noon, with their own ammunition running short, and their weariness further slowing up the rate of fire, that they became aware of the reduction of the enemy fire. First one, and then another, from Fort Marabout in the extreme west, to the nearby Pharos, were silenced; and the thunder faded from Alexandria like a storm borne away on a wind.

"Look at that gun, Archy," Holly exclaimed in a lull. The blood on his hand had hardened, the blood on the deck had been swabbed, the battle was nearly over, and their own gun was silent. He was pointing at one of the nearest embrasures where a heavy-caliber gun had been hurled from its mounting by a direct hit, the barrel hanging like a giant corpse from a window. "D'you think that's the one that got us?"

The flag of truce flying from Fort Pharos, the silence from the guns, and beyond, the rising pall of smoke from the European quarter of Alexandria, told all that they needed to know about the situation. After admitting defeat in the gunnery duel, the Egyptians had retreated into the city, and there, with the mob and more of Arabi's troops, were looting and burning and no doubt raping and killing. The sounds confirmed this conclusion—the crackle of flames, the shouts and screams, the intermittent bursts of rifle fire, all on a vastly greater scale than that of a month earlier.

"Heaven help any of our people still ashore," Holly said.

"It looks as if we're going to help them if they are." Buller was reading the flags just hoisted by the *Invincible*. "Flag to *Inflexible*," he read out, glass to his eye, "send reconnaissance party ashore and report on situation."

Almost at once the order went round that twenty-eight of the starboard watch were to make up the shore party, and among those included was Buller.

The battleship was still stripped for action, the paint on the guns scorched and peeling, the rigging still a shambles of severed and twisted rope, and the damage to the fabric of the ship unrepaired. The brightwork was no longer bright, and the decks lacked that peacetime white gleam. The *Inflexible* was for the first time a fighting ship, and Buller was proud of her scars and vastly satisfied that he had experienced his baptism of fire.

Now he was to be one of a shore party that must be facing new risks, and, likely enough, be facing the enemy at close hand this afternoon. He was experiencing a new and wonderful sense of elation, more satisfying by far than the anticipation of taking a high Cotswold wall in a downhill gallop when the hounds had the scent: a long ache for success and glory.

And then he remembered Holly, frustrated and disappointed. "I'm sorry, old man. I really am. I'd have so liked us to be fighting together."

"Don't let yourself be killed," said Holly. He helped Buller on with his revolver holster and belt and checked that the ammunition pouches were all full. Buller had changed out of the drill he had worn during the bombardment and had dressed smartly in number. 8 white undress uniform.

Buller laughed. "Killed? Not at the hands of a few Gippos," and he ran along the superstructure and down the steps leading to the upper deck amidships where the shore party was quickly assembling. The ratings carried Lee-Metford rifles and bayonets and wore puttees and boots. There were a dozen Royal Marines under a Sergeant and a Lieutenant, similarly armed and wearing pith helmets instead of the ratings' sennit hats.

Captain Fisher appeared with his Commander when they were all lined up and to their astonishment told them that he would be leading them. "The Admiral," he told them, "has ordered a shore party of as many men as can be spared from all ships tomorrow, and I will be commanding them." He looked at them in satisfaction, a mischievous smile on his full lips. His voice, Buller noticed, was rather high-pitched, but it was a pleasing, persuasive voice. And how dark his skin looked, even darker out here on deck, as if he had spent his whole life in tropical sun. "And you are what is called in military parlance the spearhead." He turned to the officer at his side. "Carry on, Mr. Brewer.'

It was naval custom for the senior officer to be last into a boat, and they had all clattered down the ladder and climbed into the ship's big sixty-foot torpedo boat before Jackie Fisher trotted rapidly down the companion ladder and jumped into the stern.

A small jetty projected from the rock at the base of Fort Ada, the next fort to Pharos with its shell-damaged minaret, and the cox brought the steam launch alongside it while two ratings jumped ashore to secure the vessel. Buller noticed for the first time, as Fisher jumped ashore, that the Captain carried no arms; only an English walking stick, which he used to help himself up the steep track to the parapet high above.

The path had been struck several times by smaller-caliber shells, and they had to climb over dislodged boulders and round craters and piles of limestone rubble. The Captain led them in silence but without special caution, as demonstrated when Buller saw him against the sky, standing on the parapet and waving his stick for all on board his ship to see.

"Only ghosts here," he called down to them in a loud voice. "And they're all lying down." And, more formally, as they assembled beside a dismounted ten-inch smoothbore gun, "Quartermaster, signal my ship, 'Deserted by all but the dead.'"

It was a sight Buller would never forget. One ten-inch gun had been hurled onto its side fifteen feet away from its slide and the parapet over which it had been firing. This parapet had been torn apart, fitting testimony to the power of the *Inflexible*'s big shells. Another gun, a short distance away, had also been dismounted, its massive barrel thrown a greater distance, as if it had been no heavier than a lawn tennis ball. Two more had been knocked out by direct hits, which was proof of the accuracy of the *Inflexible*'s gunlayers, for the muzzle of even the largest gun makes a poor target at 1,500 yards.

Everywhere lay rocks and rubble, spent ammunition cases, shells from ten-inch to 20-pounder guns, military equipment of all kinds. Where the magazine had once been, there was a crater like the mouth of a volcano, and about it and as far as the massive gates to the fort, now lying open like some signal of submission, lay numberless stones and lengths of scorched timber and broken shells.

It was a scene of utter destruction, the last and terrible and grotesque touch being the corpses and part-corpses that lay everywhere—a leg here, a torso there in uniform, a bare arm and shoulder, a complete body in smart uniform seemingly uninjured. The awful detritus of battle, already giving off a vile stench, already attracting scores of kites scavenging for flesh, tearing at the flesh, slow to hop or fly away when approached.

Buller glanced away for a moment, out to sea, where his ship lay at anchor, black and white, smart as ever at this distance with her scars invisible, huge and squat and purposeful, her sixteen-inch guns pointing directly at him and at the death and destruction they had recently caused.

"Signal my ship for a burial party, Quartermaster," called out Captain Fisher, his voice now harsh. "We don't want an outbreak of fever on top of our problems."

He turned and began walking to the gate, a handkerchief to his nose, and then called back, "Mr. Brewer, we shall now march in open order into the town. Keep your eyes open."

Chapter IX

━━━━━━━

Lasting friendships are made at school, or in clubs or in pubs; in the Royal Navy on messdecks and in wardrooms and in gunrooms. The friendship between Midshipman Buller and Leading Seaman Maclewin was made in a railway station— a beleaguered railway station; and, like the wrought-iron wire of an Armstrong gun, it was to be tested again and again in the thunder of battle.

Two days after the bombardment of the Alexandria forts, and twelve hours after the return safely on board of the *Inflexible*'s reconnaissance expedition, a full-scale landing party of 800 Royal Marines, bluejackets, and officers from every warship present was put ashore. Their commander was Captain Fisher, who in turn appointed Lord Charles Beresford as Provost Marshal and Chief of Police. The task of the main body of armed sailors and marines was to clear the city of Arabi's troops and secure the defenses, while Beresford's small force was deputed to halt the incendiarism, looting, murder, and rape in the European sector of the city, restore order, punish the guilty, and bury the dead. Both operations were appallingly difficult and dangerous to accomplish with the number of men available. They were assisted by the presence of a small number of loyal Egyptian troops who were guarding the palace of the Sultan of Turkey's viceroy, the Khedive of Egypt. But this advantage was more than off-set by the release from the city's jail of hundreds of criminals who were more desperately wild and ruthless than any of the mobs that roamed the streets.

After the return of the spiking party on board the *Condor*, Rod had been summoned to the bridge.

"Well, Midge, I hear you nearly lost Ordinary Seaman Masters," said the Captain.

"Yes, sir."

"I don't like to lose men. But we wouldn't have missed that troublemaker." Lord Charles studied the scarred face of Marabout Fort. Lord Charles, three inches taller than Rod, looked down at him, smiling confidingly. "You know what, Midge?"

"Sir?"

"I think you bring me luck. No, I *know* you bring me luck. That's one reason I made you my cox. I reckon you're a lucky sailor. Some sailors have luck stamped all over their faces. Look at that Duke—what's his name?—Medina Sidonia. He couldn't win the Armada battle with a face like that. No luck in it. Then look at Drake. Luck never left him—not till he pushed it too hard. Nor Nelson. And it was even lucky *he* died when he did—the nation's Hero."

"Why was that, sir?"

"That woman!" Lord Charles spat the words. "That woman would've made him look an even bigger chump. And all his debts, that's what he would have returned to. Never run up debts, Midge. I've learnt my lesson there. And watch your choice of a lady. But you'll be all right. Mark my words. Leading Seaman Lucky Maclewin, Lucky Midge. Which is why I wanted to talk to you—not history or women's morals—eh?" The laughter rumbled. "The trouble here's only just started. We've a ripe big war on our hands and no mistake. And wars need luck. So, as my cox, you're to stick by my side. We've busy days ahead."

The *Condor* had been steaming at 3 knots back towards the main body of the Fleet, her task accomplished and awaiting further orders. Instead of orders, another set of flags fluttered from the Flagship, and the Yeoman of Signals called out, "Flag signals 'Well done, *Condor*,' sir."

At the same time, a burst of cheering rang out from the *Invincible*, which had now ceased firing from her position within the harbour.

"Flag signals, 'Captain of *Condor* to repair on board,' sir," reported the Yeoman.

Lord Charles showed no sign of the pleasure he must have been experiencing at these messages. All informality gone, he turned to his Navigating Lieutenant and ordered the gig. When Rod took him to the *Invincible*, Beresford was dressed in immaculate white drill trousers, frock coat and tricorn hat, and was wearing his sword. Another Lord Charles Beresford, this—formal and distant, preparing to take the praise and honours he had earned.

Beresford was on his way to the city, for the second time and again with Rod at his side. Smoke was still rising from the fires of the past two days. Reports spoke of Arabi's troops in firm occupation of the southern end of the city and of the railway station, encouraging the mob to complete its work of destruction. Bedouin tribesmen, it was said, were also making looting raids into the city.

Rod had seen his Captain's orders "to restore law and order as soon as possible, put out fires, bury the dead, and clear the streets." Later, he read Lord Charles's informal report on the state of the city they were about "to clean up."

I never saw anything so awful as the town on that Friday [July 14]. Streets, squares, and blocks of buildings all on fire, roaring and crackling and tumbling about like a hell let loose, Arabs murdering each other for loot under my nose, wretches running about with fire-balls and torches to light up new places, all the main thoroughfares impassable from burning fallen houses, streets with many corpses in them, mostly murdered by the Arab soldiers for loot. A pandemonium of hell and its devils.

There was a small party of Royal Marines on the jetty awaiting them as preliminary escort. Bringing the gig alongside, Rod asked, "Is this all we shall have, sir?"

"We were only two last time, Midge." Then he added, "Yes, we'll have one hundred forty altogether when we start patrolling. With your luck, that should be enough . . ."

July 17, 1882. A Saturday, the temperature in the upper 90s. The fires almost out, just a few of the bigger ones in the Rosetta Road still smouldering and occasionally bursting out with renewed flames that were rapidly doused by the firemen standing by. The stench of rotting flesh was still heavy in the streets, oppressive and worst in the narrow alleyways. They had buried hundreds of bodies in mass graves near Ramleh Gate, but it would take weeks to find all those lost in the rubble of buildings. The main thoroughfares had been cleared; drumhead courts-martial set up on the first day had sent murderers and rapists to the firing squads, whose measured volleys contrasted with the scattered firing of the days of anarchy. Proclamations had been posted at street corners, a curfew strictly enforced.

Only once, in a storm in the Indian Ocean, had Rod been longer without sleep. But he had scarcely had time to think about it. Like Lord Charles, he was on horseback almost all the time, passing on orders, giving instructions through an interpreter to hired gangs of Egyptians for the clearance of wreckage and rubble, and with the help of another rating from the *Condor*, nailing the proclamations to posts and doors.

This unremitting work had brought them frequently in touch with Captain Fisher's armed forces of marines and bluejackets who had the equally risky and difficult task of driving Arabi Pasha's forces from the outskirts of the city. It was not the first time that a party of Fisher's Royal Marines had called for assistance from the Provost Marshal's men when, at seven o'clock that Monday evening as the last of scarlet light was leaving the sky, a Lieutenant of the Royal Marines arrived on horseback at Beresford's H.Q. at the Arsenal.

"We are attempting to drive Arabi's men out of the railway station tonight, sir, and Major Hoskyns would like fifty of your men if you can spare them."

Beresford, as always in the saddle, was drinking from a bottle of wine and chewing at some cheese. They were due to check the curfew patrols in ten minutes. His uniform was filthy and he had not shaved for two days.

"Can't spare you anyone, Lieutenant," said Lord Charles between mouthfuls. "We're at full stretch and my men are pretty well done." He turned to Rod. "Eh, Midge?"

"I'm all right, sir."

"But we'll have to, I suppose. At least some action may keep them awake. You can have twenty-five." He glanced at Rod. "Maclewin, will you present my compliments to Major Arkshaw and ask him if he will be good enough to make the necessary arrangements."

"May I go, sir, please?"

Beresford looked at him bleakly. "If you swear not to get killed." He laughed and turned back to the Lieutenant. "This lad's my good luck token. See you bring him back undamaged."

This, then, was how it came about that Leading Seaman Maclewin, his old adversary Masters—who still had no idea that he owed his life to Rod—together with ten more ratings and the same number of marines, all equipped with rifles and 200 rounds of ammunition, marched through the darkened streets of battered Alexandria towards the sound of firing at Moharem Bey Railway Station.

Many of the city walls of Alexandria followed a northeast

to southwest line. The station itself was set into the wall and the dry ditch outside it. It was a long, narrow building, in the style of the period, with much wrought iron, a curved glass roof, four main platforms with two additional sidings and more sidings outside the main structure for spare rolling stock and locomotives. At one end were the booking offices, waiting rooms, and administrative offices, the eastern end being open, and the lines continuing east and parallel with the Mahmudiya Canal before turning sharply right and south in the direction of Cairo.

Arabi's troops had been in firm control of Fort Kum el Dik, the city walls about the station, and the station itself since the bombardment and the subsequent landing. It was the enemy's last toehold in the rubble-strewn city, the rest of the Egyptian Army now being encamped out in the desert, gathering ever greater forces to drive the infidels into the sea. To reopen the railway line to Cairo would confirm British control of Alexandria and establish them in a position to protect the vital Suez Canal from Arabi's Army.

With a force of fewer than a thousand men against Arabi's tens of thousands, it was a formidable task for Captain Fisher and the Colonel of Marines who shared the command. What they missed most of all was any Intelligence on the strength and position of Arabi. Any reconnaissance patrol into the desert would meet with immediate annihilation.

But the immediate military situation was as clear as the moonlight, which revealed the long black length of the railway station, the city wall towering above it on the northern side. The station was like an iron battering ram inserted into the defenses; and it was occupied by Egyptian troops. The British besieging force, under the command of Major Eric Hoskyns, was entrenched on a slope below to the south of the station: 200 marines and bluejackets equipped with two Nordenfelts and a Gatling gun, and protected by railway storage huts, some makeshift piles of rock, and sundry other forms of shelter.

Major Hoskyns emerged from the darkness when the reinforcing party halted some fifty yards behind the British line. He was a heavy man with a bristling moustache and side-whiskers. Rod heard the Lieutenant who had led them here ask, "Any change in the situation, sir?"

"Sent out a couple of parties. Got beaten back. Not easy. They've occupied that pillared portico above the steps along the side of the station. Deuced difficult to winkle 'em out."

The discussion continued, and Rod took advantage of this time spent awaiting orders in sizing up the situation. Immediately ahead were a number of lines terminating in buffers, shunting lines on man-made slopes, glinting in the moonlight, half a dozen or so in all. There were scattered trucks, a single ancient locomotive with a tall stack, and two open passenger carriages. Beyond and above lay the long dark shape of the terminus building, most of the glass in the curved roof now smashed, a few surviving panes reflecting the moon. The city wall and the ditch beyond were obscured by this building, but the wall, Rod knew, was strongly occupied by Arabi's men, probably as many there as in the whole of the British force.

Rod heard the Major saying, "A charge—that's the answer. Bayonets fixed. That'll do the trick. Gippos don't like cold steel."

Even Rod, with no formal military training beyond the use of weapons, could see that this would be suicidal. It was hard to make out the portico in the side of the station because the moon was in the northeast. But there was just enough light to reveal the white columns flanking the wide entrance, the sweep of steps leading up to it, and the formidable barricades thrown up across it at the top of the steps: a clever piece of defensive construction, Rod recognized. Intermittently, and seemingly haphazardly, a shot came from one or other point of this makeshift emplacement, and a ricochet passed over their heads while they were standing there, the Major and the Lieutenant still in conversation.

A sailor next to Rod spoke out of the corner of his mouth.

"Why don't they bleedin' well stop talkin' an' let's get on with it?"

A sudden volley from the enemy position decided the issue. For the present, it seemed, there was to be no frontal assault, and the reinforcing party was formed by a Petty Officer into various groups of sailors and Royal Marines who were scattered in concealed defensive positions about the approaches to the sidings.

Rod found himself with a party of six bluejackets under the command of a Midshipman. The group was lying behind a mysterious piece of iron machinery which might once have been the base of a crane. Voices in the dark:

"Where're you from?"

"*Inflexible.*"

A groan. "It was your Captain got us into this mess."

"What mess? We're going to take the station. You watch."

"Jackie's all right. It's old Ocean Swell wot never makes up 'is mind." The voice lowered: "As for Major 'Oskyns . . ."

"Can't make up their mind 'ere, neither. First it's charge, then it's stay."

Rod: "Why don't we use those trucks for cover?"

Before anyone could answer there came the deafening sound of a Gatling, no farther than a dozen yards away, a tearing sound like someone wrenching a sheet of calico apart. The muzzle flash of its fast rotating barrels momentarily illuminated its site between two piles of rocks, and when it ceased firing it was answered by bursts from the barricade, accompanied by shouts of abuse or challenge.

A new voice in their party spoke. It was the Midshipman. He was lying on his stomach, Rod saw, his monkey jacket undone, his cap on the back of his head, and he was wearing bluejacket's bell-bottoms over his white trousers in order—Rod assumed—to be less conspicuous.

"I want a volunteer to come with me. If we get through safely, the rest of you follow." The Midshipman rolled over and sat up, protected now from the Egyptian line of fire. He pointed at one of the trucks on the rails fifty yards away obliquely from them and on the same line as the old locomotive.

Rod was surprised and flattered that his suggestion had been accepted immediately and without question. "I'll come, sir," he said, "seeing as it was my idea."

"Right. You're the new boy?"

"That's right, sir."

The Midshipman said, "What's your name?"

"Maclewin, sir. Leading Seaman. *Condor*, sir."

The Midshipman laughed. "You'll need a condor's wings if you're going to keep up with me."

For most of the afternoon, through the sunset and the rise of the moon at 9:15 P.M., Buller had felt the indignation coursing through him, a tidal flow of anger at the incompetency of all those in command of this operation. At the vacillation, at the contradiction of orders and the issuing of counterorders. At the way lives had been unnecessarily lost. At the failure to strike at the station at once, taking the enemy by surprise. And at the present disposition where the greatest fool in the Navy could see that they were bound to be pinned down. Outnumbered five to one. More like ten to one.

Major Hoskyns was a fool. A damn fool. He did not lack courage. Buller conceded him that. But what was the point of striding about in the open, risking the enemy fire, when you had no idea what you were going to do? No plan. Nothing. If only it had been Jackie in command here!

"At least give us some orders before you get shot," Buller wanted to shout at him. "And you deserve to be!"

So far, Buller had managed to conceal his anger from his men. As a junior Midshipman, he was highly conscious of his responsibility for his party. It was only because of a lack of officers that he had been given this tiny command. But having got it, he was going to see that they excelled. And it was no good if his men thought they were poorly led from above, although, judging from what he had overheard, some of them knew only too well.

"Grasp the nettle," "Seize the opportunity," "Take advantage . . ." The old sayings raced through Buller's mind, to be followed at once by words counselling caution. "That temper of yours, Archy. It'll be the death of you." He had heard that many times. And what about the death of his men? And yet . . . "Ah, dreams of glory!"

The last he had heard was that they were going to wait for daylight and for the arrival of some 12-pounders. But would they arrive? And, if they did, would they be effective? Buller knew that the men's morale was sinking with the passing of the night, the draining of the last drops from their water bottles, and, equally, the growing pangs of hunger and of weariness. The idea of using the wagons for cover had crossed his mind. It was the obvious means of getting closer to the enemy and breaking the deadlock.

And then this young bluejacket had been sent up, a single reinforcement, a little fellow with a Geordie accent; and almost at once Buller had heard him ask, "Why don't we use those trucks for cover?" This had caused Buller to develop the idea. It was not a great idea, not an inspiration. But it was worth thinking about.

If two or three of them could get there, in spite of the bright moonlight—and the moon was not due to set until shortly before dawn—and the Egyptian fire. If they could get there, and then, using the wheels as partial cover, provide covering fire for the others to follow. Then, Buller calculated, they would have enough joint muscle to tip the trucks over. And while the wooden sides could be penetrated by rifle fire, the steel or iron floor would likely not . . .

Buller gave instructions to the rest of his party to follow after them when he waved a white handkerchief, and then turned to Rod. "Boots off," he told him, unlacing his own. "And *crawl*—understand? None of that open-order nonsense. Right? You're to keep close behind me. If they open fire before we're halfway there, lie flat. After halfway, run for it—but keep behind me."

Unlike his own figure when he stood up in the moonlight, fear cast no shadow for Buller. A sharpening of his senses, a feeling of warmth coursing through his body as if his blood temperature had risen, a sense of exhilaration, a throb in his groin not unlike that caused by the sight of a woman's well-formed breast or well-turned ankle. But not fear. His death or injury was not a consideration; only a determination to succeed and a resolve not to see this bluejacket shot.

It was rough ground at first, strewn rocks, anonymous old lengths of metal, rubbish of all kinds. They could not avoid making some noise. Buller moved fast, disregarding the scraping of his elbows and knees, pausing only once to check that Rod was close behind and partially protected by Buller.

Then they were on granite chippings, signifying the proximity of the first rails. The moonlight seemed brighter than ever out here. When he turned he saw clearly the silhouette of the huts and other points of concealment of the besieging force. A figure moved close to the Gatling emplacement. Better than ever, he could see that a charge would have been suicidal, and he wondered again why they had not yet been seen.

Buller pulled himself over the wooden sleeper, over the rail tie and the rail, his feet shifting the granite chips noisily. The truck was fifty yards distant and appearing to offer even sketchier shelter now that he was closer to it. The track was raised to accommodate the rails and the sleepers; not much, maybe a foot or eighteen inches, but enough to give some Egyptian trooper a brief glimpse of his silhouette. A single shot rang out, an accurate one, too. Buller heard it thud into the granite and whine away over the British line.

A second followed it, and a third. From the barricade there came a shout. Buller could see clear through the station now that he was directly facing it, through the portico and out through its more distant matching portico on the other side. Now the fire was coming rapidly, not all of it aimed at them, and it was answered by a burst of Gatling fire. But too much of it was coming their way.

"Run!" he called out to Rod, still keeping protectively ahead of him, crouching but making good speed. "Run!"

Buller felt a sharp nick in his calf but it did not slow him. Over the next set of rails in one bound, and the next. And there was the truck, comforting in its dark shadow and size. He flung himself down behind one of the wheels and Rod almost fell on him. They lay there panting for a while, in intimate closeness. The firing had ceased, as if the soldiers had expected them to reemerge on the other side and were puzzled by their disappearance.

"All right?" Buller whispered into Rod's ear.

"Yes, sir."

Buller felt confidence in this young man. He had only caught a glimpse of his face in the moonlight—a square face, flat, broken nose, rumpled hair with his hat off, as now, lying here beside him, his breath steadier, like his own. All he had noted—his Geordie voice, and his eagerness to come forward —he approved. Small and tough.

"Move over and be ready to fire into the emplacement." Rocks had been piled up some six feet clear across the portico. He could see it in more detail from here, the uneven top providing secure firing .points—dozens of them. A clever piece of construction.

Buller drew the handkerchief out of his pocket and held it up, waving it slowly from side to side in the direction of his men. There was an answering wave, and he watched the first and then the second of the remaining four men emerge from cover, terrifyingly clear and easy to pick out. How in Heaven's name had *they* survived?

Then he swung back, elbows on the ground, holding his Lee-Metford's barrel close to the flange of the steel wheel, its butt tight against his shoulder, his finger curled round the trigger. His men would be running, every second that passed increasing their chances of crossing the tracks safely. Two of them from the *Inflexible*, Ordinary Seaman Smith and Able

Seaman Trotter. Then the stout bluejacket from the *Alexandra* and his opposite number whose name Buller had forgotten. And Boy Sainsbury, a likely lad, from the Flagship. They had been under his command for only a matter of hours, and now—under his orders—they could be running the gantlet of Egyptian fire. At any second . . .

Now! Yes, here it came, muzzle flashes like lethal will-o'-the-wisps, the detonations like an amplified riffle of drums. Open the cut-off, raise the bolt, pull back, push in. Now one up the spout, and five more in the magazine. As he fired, Buller felt the kick of the recoil against his shoulder, comforting rather than painful, an emphasis of his intention to kill, without conscience or hesitation. The round steel bolt in his hand, a wrench to the left and draw it back for the next round. He had been very fast on his small arms course, the fastest in his group, and his second shot came less than two seconds after his first. Then the next. And another clip from the pouch.

He and Rod were at a good enfilading angle, and their joint fire was telling, surprising the Egyptian troops, causing them to hesitate. They were only thirty yards distant. Good killing range. He saw one figure standing up defiantly. Why did they stand up, these Gippos? They had done the same thing during the bombardment, standing up defiantly on the earthworks, waving a flag, or making gestures of defiance. Either he or Leading Seaman Maclewin got him at once. Buller saw his body bend forward at an unnatural angle, remain for a second poised like the letter C, and disappear from view.

Another clip. Some of the fire was coming their way now, either because they had been seen or the rest of the party had almost completed the distance. And there was a lot of shouting from both lines, and firing had become general so that their party was not the only target any longer.

A figure fell beside Buller. The stout man had proved fastest, and he was quick at commencing to fire, too. Buller shouted, "Well done!" as if he had won a pulling race for his ship. It was amazing how much shouting was going on, maybe an antidote to fear, or an expression of defiance or triumph. "Hooray!" someone else was shouting. Another body collapsed behind the wheel. Buller could not see who it was. He did not fire, not at once—or at all. Instead, he groaned and said, "Oh Christ have mercy. . . !" Hit.

Buller sat up and swung round. The shooting was general again, a lot of it coming at them. How many had survived the journey? All it seemed, though one casualty. They were clustered close together in the partial protection. But they could not last long like this. So.

"Over with it, lads!" Buller shouted. "Over with it now!" Hands clutching the iron edge of the truck's base, crotch high. Four others spread out, Maclewin small at the end, the most exposed. Enough muscle?

"One, two, three—heave!"

There was no feel of movement. They were not going to do it. He had brought them all this way from safety to exposure. And they did not have the strength.

"Again . . ."

It might as well have been an ironclad in drydock. He had grossly miscalculated. No, he had not. No, there was a faint lift.

"Everything you've got, lads."

A ricochet sang overhead, a spur, like a galley-master's whiplash. The truck was rising, steadily, as if under a jack. Ten degrees, twenty . . . Easier all the time as the balance began to favour them. Then at the very point of the fulcrum . . .

"A last push!"

The truck was at 45 degrees. Buller at six foot two was at full stretch and only one other of the party was able to reach it. Forty-five degrees, and she was going. Already it was offering them protection. None of the enemy could bring a line of fire to bear on them.

The truck fell on its side with a crash that momentarily killed all other sound, and at once, like a gesture of celebration, the Gatling and one of the Nordenfelts opened fire.

There was more shouting. Figures were running, more figures from several parts of the line, encouraged to leave the security of their positions by Buller's success. The dust was still rising from about the truck when the first arrived. Then more and more, amidst the most tremendous of fire, stronger and more deadly than they had so far experienced. But the distance was not great, and the machine guns were helping to keep enemy heads down.

In five minutes the fallen wagon looked like the giant victim of massed, voracious ants that clung round it in hungry triumph. There must have been fifty, and there was scarcely room for that number. What had he started? Buller asked himself as he looked about him. Some bluejackets had climbed into the horizontal side and were lying outstretched, firing fast into the nearest emplacement. Others peered round the iron base, and when one of them ducked back to reload, another took his place. "What a party!" Buller shouted aloud. "What a great party!"

Buller could see three marines and a bluejacket lying dead or wounded in the open, stretched across the rails. And he now recognized his wounded man as Ordinary Seaman Smith. Buller bent over him. The man was in pain. "Where is it?" Eyes turned towards him. Was the expression accusatory? Not the voice—that was pleading. "It's me stomach, sir. They got me in the stomach."

"We'll have you back. I'll get the stretcher-bearers."

He could try hailing them. Or he could send someone back over the exposed ground. But stretcher-bearers were likely to come, anyway, under the white flag, to collect the other wounded. Buller rebuked himself for his hesitation. He bent down again and raised the man's shirt, the skin false white in the light of the moon, the blood like spreading storm clouds on a clear summer's day.

As if touched off by this sight of injury, Buller felt for the first time the throb of pain in his own calf, and the dampness of fresh blood beneath his trouser leg.

* * *

Within the shelter of the toppled wagon the air was hot and heavy with powder fumes. Rod, back resting against the rusting iron of the wagon's base, slipped another clip into the magazine of his Lee-Metford, wiped his shirt sleeve across his sweating and dirty face, and closed his eyes for a moment. He was done, quite done, and could have fallen off into a deep sleep with the rattle of rifle fire close about him. Then he pulled himself to his feet again, impelled by the esprit de corps and the discipline instilled into him after almost five years in the service.

The area behind the wagon was packed with bluejackets and marines, some, like himself, pausing to reload and at the same time giving someone else firing space. One of his party had been badly wounded in the rush across the rails, and he was lying on the ground, the Midshipman bending over and talking to him.

Men were being hoisted onto the top of the truck, and two sailors seized Rod's legs and lifted him as if he were a child. "There you go, Midge," shouted one of them. "Keep your midgey head down."

There was a lull in the firing, as if both the naval party and the Egyptian soldiers required a rest for their ears and their hot weapons. But not for long. The Gatling gun reopened fire first, like a crashing chorus at the opening of an opera's last act. It had been moved to a new position where its thousand bullets a minute provided lateral cross fire.

Lying on the wood slats of the side of the wagon with a dozen more bluejackets, Rod could just make out one or two heads moving behind the Egyptian barricade. Two further English parties had braved the storm of Egyptian fire and emulated them by occupying lone wagons and tipping them over. As the firing became general again, Rod was able to see the advantage they had gained by occupying these forward positions. But the general situation had not materially altered. Arabi's men were still in firm occupation of the station, and only a frontal assault could winkle them out. And that, besides causing appalling casualties, would not be possible with their limited numbers. Stalemate, in fact.

He raised the big rifle, holding the stock easily in his left palm, tucking the butt firmly against his shoulder. They had laughed at him in the early days in the *Implacable* at rifle drill. "Get a popgun for little Midge—he carn't 'old that gun . . ."

And he had scored a bull on his second shot and finished the course with top marks. That kept them quiet. And today he wore above his right cuff the crossed rifles with star above of a first class marksman.

Rod held the sights steady. The moon was as bright as ever and he had no difficulty in taking aim. In another hour it would be different, with the moon beginning to set, and then cutting off all light for an hour or more before dawn. He squeezed the trigger, took the recoil, slid the bolt. This time his target was a rock on the top of the barrier. Or a head? It was a head all right, for it fell back, for a moment exposing the shoulders of the man he had certainly killed.

So he was killing now, without compunction, without regrets. Some wretched peasant, no doubt, conscripted into Arabi's army, perhaps with a wife and children. But perhaps it was the dead man's bullet that had earlier caught that sailor in the stomach . . .

One fewer in Arabi's army. But however well he shot, neither Rod Maclewin nor any other crack shot could alter the state of this siege. Or . . . ?

It was the sight of the old locomotive with its tender just 100 yards distant that gave Rod the idea. He might have been back in Newcastle as a boy, out of work. Surely it was a Stephenson? With luck—a great deal of luck—and with the right timing, it could work. A hundred to one against, but what else except a gamble could break this stalemate?

"Yes," said Buller. And again, "Yes—yes," as Rod outlined his plan. He said it eagerly, too, nodding his head. Not like Major Hoskyns. Rod could imagine that fat Major pooh-

poohing the idea before he had begun to explain. A mere lead-ing seaman, not even a Petty Officer, telling him his job!

"But how do we know how to operate the thing? Even if it does work. I've never driven a locomotive."

"I have, sir. When I was fourteen."

"Good man. Worth a try—eh?" And he had laughed.

One hour later, the moon set to the northeast over the city. Rod, half-dead with weariness, watched it touch the tip of the highest mosque, its full circle contrasting with the half moon on top of the minaret, a sight for the opening of some Eastern fable. The light left the sky rapidly after that, and to add to the sense of unreality, thin yellow pencil-beams pierced the new darkness from the direction of the harbour, crossing over to form an X, then an inverted V. Of course. The *Inflexible*. She had electric light, he had heard, and searchlights, the first fitted to any ship in the world . . .

It was the Midshipman's original party again, less the wounded sailor who had been taken back on a stretcher. Five of them. In the darkness before the dawn, the Egyptians had begun to hurl torches, which burnt noisily on the ground, from their position. Each lasted a minute or two, illuminating the sidings sufficiently to prevent a surprise assault. But the route to the locomotive would soon take them outside the range of their light.

The engine was easier to set into motion than the wagon had been to tip over. It was a downhill run on the shunting slope, and soon it was going so fast that the Midshipman called out to Rod, "Get onto the footplate, Maclewin, we'll need to brake."

Rod climbed onto one of the tender's buffers and hoisted himself onto the stacked coal. The locomotive was travelling at running speed by the time he had felt his way onto the foot-plate.

Regulator, accelerator, brake, pressure control. It *was* the same Stephenson locomotive that he had helped to drive all those years ago. The brake lever was here, on the right, a long lever operating on a ratchet, crude in operation, merely bringing a steel shoe directly against the rear set of wheels. There was a squeal like a beaten dog's, but engine and tender began to slow at once.

"It's still warm, sir. You feel."

The locomotive had come to rest behind an engine shed, concealed from the station and from the city walls. Buller put his hand into the firebox and withdrew it rapidly. "The Gippos must have been using it until just before the siege."

"Perhaps for bringing up the rock for the barrier, sir."

Buller watched Rod shaking out the clinkers. Sparks rose from the firebox, and when he placed a shovelful of small coal carefully onto the embers, there was first a faint crackling sound, and soon after, the lick of yellow flames.

"How soon to get up steam?" Buller asked.

"About half an hour, sir. Perhaps sooner."

Boy Sainsbury and the fat bluejacket who had been so quick on his feet were on the footplate, too, ready to help. Able Seaman Trotter was keeping watch. There was occasional firing—"To keep their bleedin' 'eads down," as Trotter had expressed it. But nothing more serious, the stalemate apparently accepted by both sides.

There was light in the sky to the east, a faint pink glow that would soon turn to scarlet. Buller knew these Eastern dawns now, their speed, the coming of shadows, ghostly at first, then clear-etched as the bright red orb—twice the size of England's sun, surely—heaved above the horizon, bringing at once the heat that in less than a minute would cause prickling of the skin, and then dampness under the arms.

Buller awaited the arrival of the Gatling anxiously. Would the Major comply with Buller's appeal? He had worded the message the Petty Officer had taken back as tactfully as he could. "With utmost respect . . ." Or would the Major's pride be too great? A mere Midshipman. Yet even that fool Hoskyns must accept that something positive had to be done to break the deadlock, and if it later came out that he had frustrated the enterprising plans of a Royal Navy Midshipman . . . well.

Then, with growing excitement, and while Rod was bringing the fire to a heat that was now registering on the circular dial, Buller observed the first signs that he might be getting the Gatling after all. There were men moving behind sheds to the southwest, 100 yards away. The party paused before an open stretch of ground leading to the sidings. Then, perhaps a dozen of them in all, sleeves rolled up, sennit hats tipped back, emerged and in a steady trot and close together began to move towards them. They were spotted at once by the Egyptians, but the range was too great for accurate rifle fire and the spurts of earth were far short.

Yes, they had it. Buller could see the prized weapon held by six men on each side, its round barrel glinting faintly in the half light. He had seen it earlier, a new type .45 with the flexible yoke, and tripod mounted. The ideal light field-weapon, together with a 400-round Broadwell drum and two spares, enough for more than a minute's continuous firing.

And sleepers, railway sleepers. That's what they needed. Rod and the boy had excavated the coal from the center of the pile in the tender, providing a concealed base for the Gatling's mounting. A wall of stout wooden sleepers, each more than a foot thick, would provide the added protection they would need to survive.

The Petty Officer in command of the delivery party took his men off in search, and they were back in five minutes with six disused pinewood sleepers. Buller helped stack them up on each side of the tender, and three more at the end.

"Makes a handy fort." The Petty Officer was delighted with their effort and asked to come on the ride. "I've had a lot of experience with the Gatling, sir."

Buller agreed. Able Seaman Trotter; Leading Seaman Maclewin as driver; Boy Sainsbury, fireman; the fat bluejacket from the *Alexandra* who was a tireless worker and handy with a rifle, too; the Petty Officer; and himself. That would make up his crew, the company of H.M.S. *Stephenson*, the world's first armoured train, more a woodclad than an ironclad.

"How's the pressure?"

"Enough, sir."

The sun was rising over the city walls and the Rosetta Gate, the temperature with it. The sooner they went into action the better. Buller cast his eye over the locomotive and its tender, viewing it objectively for the first time: the ridiculously tall smokestack, like Puffing Billy's, the big brass steam valve and brass boiler rails (all unpolished for weeks), the six driving wheels, and only part-roofed footplate. Then the Gatling, its tripod legs set deep in the coal, spare drums beside it, barrel poised over a makeshift embrasure in the stacked sleepers.

It was all Buller could do to prevent himself from laughing —that might have damaged the self-confidence of his men. And he was utterly self-confident himself. He *knew* this operation was going to be successful, and he was enjoying himself as he had never enjoyed himself before. Better than a really good run with the Cirencester pack on a perfect autumn day. Better than standing on the *Britannia*'s main truck on that evening four years ago.

Someone had scrawled "H.M.S. Stephenson" along the side of the boiler, and the bluejackets who had brought the Gatling safely to them gave a cheer when Rod opened the throttle and the locomotive's driving wheels began to turn. They skidded once on the rails, with a sharp escape of steam, and then Rod eased the throttle open very slowly, and with a healthy and regular beat, they gathered speed down the line, out of the shelter of the engine shed. To the right was the Mahmudiya Canal, and beyond, the dry Lake Mariout. To the left were the city walls; the damaged Pharos lighthouse rose in the far distance over the city's sprinkling of towers and minarets, and behind, beyond the dark shape of the railway station, stood the column of Pompey's Pillar.

They were clanking over points onto the main line when the shelling started. Buller had known it was bound to come. A half-blind Egyptian gunner could not fail to see them and the rising cloud of black smoke they were making, from the city walls. The questions were: how accurate were they? How soon would they get the range? Would H.M.S. *Stephenson* make harbour undamaged, or would she be sunk?

The gouts of red soil and dust rose fifteen feet. Probably 12-pounders. One exploded quite close, no more than twenty yards away, and Buller, standing legs well apart on the coal, one hand on the Gatling's bronze barrel housing, felt the brush of its blast. It had fallen ahead of them, almost on the line, and they passed through the dust before it settled.

He could see Rod's hands on the long brake lever, and the locomotive skidded to a halt. Buller jumped down and, with the help of the Petty Officer, switched the points without difficulty; and Rod had the locomotive in reverse and already gathering speed when they jumped back onto the footplate.

Buller warned him, "There'll be a lot of lead flying about when we reach the station, Maclewin, so keep your head down. Begin to brake at a hundred yards from the entrance."

They were half a mile from the station. The shelling had increased, the sound of the 12-pounders echoing across the desert like summer thunder, the flashes on the top of the wall pinpointing the gunsites. But there was still no sign of hostility from the station itself, and they might have been the 3:18 from Cairo approaching on time with 500 passengers. Platform 1 was it? No, Platform 2, that was where the line was taking them, smack into the center of the station. Just right.

"We'll give those gunners a few rounds," Buller shouted to the Petty Officer; and he swung the barrel round on its yoke so that it pointed over the protecting wooden sleepers towards the grey line of stone wall. Already, ten minutes after sunrise, there was heat shimmer above the city. The smoke from the guns rose slowly in the still, hot air.

This Bulldog Gatling had a range of nearly two miles. Buller set the range at 650 yards by adjusting the jackscrew in the base of the yoke. The trunnions and the front sight were on the right, the crank with direct drive at the rear on this model. The Petty Officer held the crank. Buller shouted, his voice clear above the rattle of the locomotive's pistons and wheels, the gasp of steam, the crunch of the shovel against coal, the whistle of a passing shell, the c-r-u-n-c-h of another which landed very close behind them, turning the rails to twisted lengths of steel—above all these sounds was Buller's order, "Four turns—FIRE!"

The main shaft turned with the crank—no gear train to slow the rate of fire on this Bulldog—bringing the ten barrels into immediate motion, cartridges feeding from the magazine, bolts pushing them through the troughs and into the chambers. All in a split second.

The noise tore at Buller's eardrums—a continuous, annihilating noise, the individual explosions scarcely distinguishable, the tumble of empty cases bearing witness to the incredible rate of fire.

Forty rounds, three seconds. Buller traversed the top of the wall, maybe a hundred yards of it. He must have killed or knocked out a few of the gunners. But the shock effect was far more stunning. They were almost at the station entrance before the Egyptian guns opened fire again, and by then it was too late. Instead, it was rifle fire that they met.

With the Gatling's barrel back in its embrasure on the left side of the tender, its angle of traverse was limited. Buller at first saw only the British besieging positions, the huts behind which they had been sheltering all night, the overturned wagons, including their own. There were figures moving there, ready to advance at the sound of the bugle, and Buller felt like giving them a cheer.

Then the tall column at the left-hand side of the station

entrance came into his sights. Trotter and Sainsbury were crouching beside the gun, each with a spare drum of ammunition, the Petty Officer with both hands on the crank.

"Slow down—too fast!" Buller yelled at Rod. Rod had anticipated the order, and H.M.S. *Stephenson* was losing way as she entered port.

The Egyptian fire drove at them like a hailstorm. Every trooper defending that station had turned at their approach, like marksmen at an Indian elephant hunt, shooting as fast as they could work the bolts of their Mauser rifles, unable to miss this charging beast of iron and wood. White steam already spurted from a hundred holes in the boiler; the brass valve and the tall smokestack were peppered through and through, the front lantern disappearing in the steel onslaught.

But, like the charge of an elephant, it was impossible to halt the momentum immediately, and, though its machinery and motive power were destroyed, the locomotive continued down the track towards the buffers, its crew crouched behind their impenetrable protection of iron and wood and coal . . .

Buller raised his left hand, and the Gatling fire broke out the moment he had the sights on the inside of the portico, barrels rotating at the speed the Petty Officer wound the crank. Two hundred men there were—at least 200, he reckoned, every one until now secure behind the heaped rock and stone and rubble of their barricade. Then, the next moment, they were fatally exposed, from the reverse direction, to the world's fastest-firing machine gun.

Almost every one of the first 400 rounds from the drum killed or wounded. It was a holocaust. A terrible holocaust. The locomotive was down to walking pace, no more, and Rod had his hand off the brake. He was crouched, with his head low and between his knees against ricochets from the cab roof. The used brass cases from the Gatling were flying everywhere, as if given life by the pace of the firing.

The first drum expended. The haunting note of a dozen bugles. To Buller it was the music of hope and expectation.

Not yet triumph, but not too far distant from it. The bugles sounded above the crackle of Egyptian rifle fire, which was less than half its earlier volume. Many Mausers lay silent beside dead or wounded men. But already many more had been cast aside by troopers with no more fight left in them.

The second drum was clipped on, and Buller could now traverse the Gatling for the length of the station and to the passengers' entrance; the sandbagged ticket offices; the waiting rooms with their broken glass and signs in Egyptian, French, and English; the piled porters' trolleys. He began firing again, making that terrible riffle, that lethal crackling sound of death from the ten barrels. And, almost at once, he knocked up the Petty Officer's arm. There was no need for more killing. Everywhere, the helpless, exposed soldiers were surrendering, rifles cast aside, hands held high in supplication, many on their knees or lying flat with arms outstretched. One aged soldier, some fellah wrenched from his plot of land, stood in his Army uniform as if crucified, staring at them with an agonized expression on his face.

And now the besiegers broke through, bluejackets and marines with bayonets fixed, leaping over the barricades, carried forward on the momentum of their charge. Buller watched them come with a feeling of mixed horror and elation. For, inevitably, there was killing. A dozen or more Egyptians fell screaming, bayoneted or shot in the back, before the awareness spread through the attackers that they were fighting the already defeated, the already surrendering.

The station had been won, conquered by a single Gatling gun mounted on the world's first armoured train. The Stephenson locomotive thudded, not very hard, against the buffers, itself mortally wounded but still defiantly spurting steam and smoke from its first and last military action.

Buller leapt down from the footplate, savouring the hot mixed scents of oil and steam and expended gunpowder and the sweet smell of success. They had won. Against all the odds, they had taken the station. The tumultuous scene of combat was settling, the sounds of battle dying, the Royal Navy with its training and instinct for order, sorting things out, herding the prisoners.

Buller turned, searching the milling crowds of victors and vanquished for a senior officer to whom to report. A shot rang out, like the last death rattle of the battle of the station. Then there came the crack of another shot, close by. Buller turned again, suspecting an attack by an Arab trooper who had refused to surrender. Instead, he caught a fleeting glimpse of a barrel above the rocks and rubble of the barricade, a flash from it, the whine of a ricochet, the swift movement of a disappearing naval sennit hat.

A bluejacket having sport with surrendered Gippos? Buller was outraged at this un-British behaviour and began to run towards the hidden marksman. The distance was nothing, a dozen, fifteen yards, no more. But the milling crowd of scared Egyptian troopers being herded together like cattle by the British sailors, and the piled-up corpses from the closing stages of the battle, made progress difficult. By the time he reached the barricade, the sailor who had been firing was lost in the crowd.

"They got 'im—look, sir, they got our Rod."

Buller looked down into the angry face of the sailor who was pointing back towards the locomotive. "We ought to line 'em up and shoot 'em like dogs—that's all they are. The white flag one minute, then . . ."

Buller raced back towards H.M.S. *Stephenson*, standing at the buffers, steam still belching from a hundred boiler holes. He caught a glimpse of a sprawled figure on the platform which was at once obscured by men gathering anxiously about it.

Rod saw and instantly recognized the dark sailor kneeling on the parapet. He picked out and identified Masters as if he were observing him through a Barr & Stroud naval telescope. When Masters raised the Lee-Metford to his shoulder

Rod felt no disquiet, let alone fear. He did not even speculate in his mind what the man was doing, even when the barrel came swiftly round and steadied upon himself as the target. It was simply not credible that the man whose life he had saved only days earlier was now about to murder him.

No more than two seconds passed between Rod's identification of Masters and the instant that the bullet struck him on the left side. It was like a hard punch from a man wearing a sharp ring, very much as he had imagined it might be when he had contemplated the idea of being shot in battle.

"Death"—the one word passed through his mind as swiftly as the bullet passed through his body—"death is a painful thing" was the single thought. Not noble or full of singing angels, no white-bearded, kindly St. Paul to greet you, as the Minister had suggested. Just pain. And then he was tumbling into the ever deeper grey mists of unconsciousness, over and over, just aware, with his strong nonconformist conscience, that justice had after all been done, that he deserved to join all those others for whose death he had been responsible . . .

Masters saw and cursed the tall, burly figure of Midshipman Buller as he turned in his direction, obscuring his line of sight and forcing him to drop down behind the barricade, where he fired twice more, without effect before, unseen, quickly joining a mixed rearguard party of Royal Marines and blue-jackets who were running into the station.

Masters's one shot from his Lee-Metford had struck Rod fractionally below the liver and even closer to the gall bladder, passing out again below the waist on his right side. It did massive damage to flesh, muscle, and tissue on the way, and the puncturing—minute though it was—of the stomach wall was to give him trouble for the rest of his life. But Surgeon-Lieutenant Redgrave discovered also that it was a clean wound, and of course the fact that the bullet had passed through the body simplified things for him and for Rod.

Rod was unconscious for about half an hour and came to briefly on a stretcher. He caught the scent of dust and heard the deep boom of heavy guns. The Fleet was finishing off Arabi's guns, which had nearly done for the train, on the city walls. The rocking motion of the stretcher sent him off to sleep. He felt little pain again until the surgeon examined him in the sick bay of the Fleet Flagship. He remembered asking, quite calmly, he thought, if he was going to die.

"No, you'll be all right, lad."

And Rod thought for a second, "That'll please Ma." He remembered little more until he heard a familiar booming voice, which fell in volume when another voice asked for quiet.

"Well, Midge, what did I say? Though you nearly pushed your luck too far this time, eh?" He laughed and Rod felt a hand that was unexpectedly soft and cool on his forehead. "You dodge all those bullets from Arabi, then get shot by some lunatic on your own side. And survive that."

Lord Charles Beresford stayed for only a few minutes, and Rod was astonished that he had visited him at all considering the weight of responsibility he was carrying in the city.

When Buller came the next day, smart in white drill by contrast with Rod's last sight of him, one of the battleships was firing at a shore target at two-minute intervals. Every shot was like a sharp nudge at Rod's stomach, but he managed to conceal the pain from Buller.

"That'll be the *Inflexible*, won't it, sir?" were his first words.

"You can't mistake that boom."

There was another crash, and even down here, on the orlop deck of the *Invincible*, it was as if the hot air were being torn apart.

"I hope they're shooting well, sir."

Buller sat down in a hammock beside him, long legs swinging. "They always do, Midge. She's my ship."

This friendly, smiling Midshipman had taken the trouble to learn his nickname.

"You're in the *Condor*, is that right?"

Rod nodded, and Buller said, "Ah, 'Well done, *Condor*.' That's what the Admiral signalled. You did for that Fort Marabout, and no mistake. And you were the smallest ship in the bombardment."

"Nearly, sir. And yours the biggest."

Buller helped him to a sip of water. It tasted as warm as the air. "When did you learn to drive an engine, Midge?"

"Up in Newcastle, sir. I was just a boy, out of school. Work was hard to get, and I had a month as an apprentice."

"Why did you give it up?"

"I didn't, sir. It gave me up. The supervisor sacked me. Said I was undersized and not strong enough."

Buller laughed at that. "He should have seen you yesterday—working overtime, eh? Your own fireman. So you joined the Navy."

"Not long after, sir."

"Near enough the same time as me, I'd guess. How old are you?"

"Nineteen, sir."

"A bit older than me."

The *Inflexible* fired another round. After the distant sound of the bursting shell had faded, Rod said, "The sick bay attendant said you saved my life, sir. He said you got in front of the man who was firing at me and stopped him hitting me again. So that's one up to you, sir."

Buller laughed. "That was just luck, Midge. If I'd known he was firing at you I'd have dropped to the ground." Buller took off his pith helmet, revealing sweat-soaked brown hair, and scratched his head. "You can't have any enemies, Midge. Who'd want to shoot you? Someone gone mad with the heat and excitement, I suppose."

"I don't know, sir," Rod said hesitantly. "I don't think I want to know, either."

In the hot cabin after Buller had left, with the intermittent sound in his ears of the *Inflexible*'s great guns firing at their target, Rod determined never to tell anyone that he had recognized his assailant. No, it was against the traditions of the service to inform on a shipmate, and in this case, deadly dangerous, too. It would be a secret for all time.

As for his family, they must never even learn that his wound was inflicted by a fellow sailor, for that would be like marking a cross of shame against the Royal Navy itself.

Chapter X

The Prince of Wales said, "The Royal Navy has always been slow to accept anything new. It's part of the tradition. They were slow to accept me." He gave forth a deep laugh which turned into a cough. When he could breathe normally again, though wheezily, he glanced provocatively at Buller.

Dutifully, Buller asked the obvious question: "How do you mean they were slow, sir?"

Speaking with the long German *r*'s to which Buller was now accustomed, and with a note of lingering resentment, the Prince said, "I am surprised that you don't know, young man." Then, turning to Buller's father: "George, haven't you ever told this son of yours how the Queen wanted me to be made an Admiral of the Fleet and their Lordships thought fit to refuse—because I was not an old salt? So, to snub the Royal Navy in return, she refused when they wanted to make me one."

Admiral Buller commented cautiously, "How disgraceful, sir! And how correct of Her Majesty!"

"No, the Navy hates change. Look . . ." and he spread

his arms wide, "look at all these masts and yards in this year 1887. Just as if Mr. Fulton had never invented the steamship before the Queen was even born."

Certainly Buller for one had never seen so many masts in all his naval life, and most of them were rigged for sail. He was one of the party on the bridge of the Prince's Royal Yacht *Osborne*, steaming slowly between the columns of men-o'-war drawn up at Spithead for Queen Victoria's Golden Jubilee Review on July 23, for which this Royal inspection could be said to be an overture.

It was a fresh day of gusty winds, of flashing sunshine and cloud shadows racing across choppy water. For as far as the eye could see there stretched stately ironclads, purposeful cruisers, sloops, gunvessels, diminutive torpedo boats, auxiliary vessels, little paddle tugs, and 135 men-o'-war gleaming black and white in shimmering new paint and brightwork. Every yard—and the number was countless—was manned by bluejackets, who also linked hands along the lengths of the upper decks, and every ship was dressed overall with flags and bunting.

It was the bravest, noblest, most spectacular and impressive sight Buller had ever witnessed, the material manifestation of the romantic dreams of his boyhood. The world's greatest Navy had been assembled from the corners of the earth to demonstrate its loyalty to the Queen and its strength to the world: *Minotaur*, *Agincourt*, *Sultan*, *Monarch*, and *Iron Duke*, battleships from the Channel Squadron. *Hercules*, *Invincible*, *Hotspur*, *Devastation*, *Ajax*, and Buller's old ship *Inflexible*—a roll call of British might and achievement.

But no one on the *Osborne*'s bridge, itself a-glitter with gold braid, orders, and decorations, appeared to be impressed by the sight except Buller. His father, now Second Naval Lord, was deep in conversation with the First Lord of the Admiralty. Two ancient retired Admirals of the Fleet, who had been almost past their prime in the Crimean War, were reminiscing away while the breeze blew through their long white beards.

Commander Prothero "the Bad" was arguing crossly with Admiral Sir Keith Rawlings, seniority in rank in no way tempering his language. But it was the Prince of Wales himself who had sparked off the loudest argument, while leaving the impression (like all the officers present) that he was giving his full attention to the ships he was passing and from time to time saluting.

Buller, present with his twin brothers at the invitation of his father, listened in awe to the outspoken and even disrespectful language. Admiral the Earl of Huntley did not even bother to call the Prince "sir," let alone "Your Royal Highness." As the seventeenth Earl, he properly regarded the Hanovers as upstarts, and German upstarts at that.

"Rubbish, Wales," he grunted. "You don't know what you're talking about. You may know something about backgammon and a pretty turn of ankle, but the Navy's a closed book to you and your lot." And he repeated the arguments against steam which Buller had been treated to at Weir Park more than five years ago. For the present his dogs were quiet, Pansy, Flos, and Daisy being poor sailors and now lying in a forlorn heap on the starboard side of the *Osborne*'s bridge. "Only a few years ago I took those boys of yours to Australia and back without raising steam once," he continued in ample exaggeration, which caused Prince George to wink at Buller.

"I agree with His Royal Highness." It was more like a bark than a statement. Jackie Fisher, an Admiral now, recently appointed Director of Naval Ordnance and Third Naval Lord in succession to George Buller, was known as the Board's arch-reformer and revelled in it. He saluted the mighty *Devastation* as they passed the battleship, which by unfortunate chance was the first Royal Navy battleship not to carry sail; and then swept his right arm like Moses before the Sea of Galilee. "I would burn the lot—every mast and yard. Use the canvas for making hammocks in our new submersibles."

The Prince of Wales laughed again. "I am flattered to have

your support, Fisher. But I don't quite follow you. Submersibles?"

"Yes, sir. Undersea men-o'-war. Cheap, invisible, deadly with their torpedoes. Will soon make the battleship obsolete, you mark my words, sir." Fisher's decorations winked in the sunlight like a signalling lamp with a confidential message. "We could build a hundred of 'em for the price of a battleship, and imagine a hundred unseen killers let loose like black mamba snakes in the night amongst this lot."

Fisher's old friend and fellow reformer, as well as close friend of the Prince's, chipped in with his support. "Your Royal Highness may have seen what *The Times* wrote the other day," said Lord Charles Beresford. "Referring to Mr. Nordenfelt's submersible, which I was studyin' myself at Barrow the other day. It said, 'There is nothin' impractical in the idea of constructin' a vessel which should rise and sink, propel itself beneath the surface, and skim upon the surface.' And that's just what it does, sir."

Admiral "Tumblehome" Huntley could remain silent no longer. His cheeks scarlet beneath his side-whiskers, like a setting sun seen through thin cirrus cloud, he exploded, "These so-called officers, Wales, would give the Royal Navy to the Frogs. I'd string 'em both from the highest yardarm for treason. How'd you like young Georgie here incarcerated in a stinking steel cigar and dropped overboard?"

The word "cigar" proved too much for the Prince of Wales, who brought the conversation to an end by ducking into the wheelhouse to attend to a battleship-size Havana Corona-Corona burning away in an ashtray. There were enough Admirals on the bridge already to satisfy the Fleet for a few minutes while he indulged in the delicious aroma and downed a modest glass of champagne.

The lines of warships did have an end after all, and the *Osborne* was nearing it, the New Forest (which in the past had supplied so much of the good oak for "the wooden walls" of old England) cutting a fine green line in the distance.

Prince George moved alongside Buller. "I wonder if they'll continue this argument tomorrow night."

"How do you mean?"

"The Huntleys are having a Jubilee Ball, and Jackie Fisher and Charlie B. and the rest'll all be there." He glanced questioningly at Buller. "You'll be there, won't you?"

Yes, he would be there. But he would not be listening to arguments about modernization of the Navy, nor would he take much notice of who else was there. Except, of course, the host's daughter, with whom he would endeavour to have every single dance. For Archy Buller was madly in love with Clemmie Huntley, and for the moment could care nothing for the latest ironclad, or for Mr. Nordenfelt's submersible for that matter.

Except for the Buckingham Palace Ball, no ball could match the Earl of Huntley's during the Jubilee festivities for size and for grandeur and for the eminence of the guests. Among the Princes were the Crown Prince of Germany, the Prince of Wales, Prince William of Prussia, Prince Christian of Schleswig-Holstein, and Prince Albert Victor and his younger brother, Prince George of Wales. The Dukes included the Duke of Edinburgh, the Duke of Connaught, the Grand Duke of Hesse, and the Grand Duke Serge of Russia.

The Maharajahs arrived like a tidal flow of ebony and diamonds from the East, His Royal Highness the Rao of Kutch, His Royal Highness the Thakore Sahib of Morvi, and others in glittering turbans worth more than the gross capital of a European city. Peers of every rank, Barons and Baronets, upon whom the orders of Thistle and Bath sat as easily as a Regimental tie upon a junior officer. In the ballroom the dark-blue ribbons of the Garter were like the night sky, the twinkling decorations like the Milky Way. No fewer than fifteen Victoria Crosses could be counted, nine on Generals and six on Admirals. But paradoxically, to be without titles or decoration was perhaps to figure in the most exclusive rank of all, hinting as it did at achievement or wealth beyond all honours or decorations.

The Prince and Princess of Wales arrived at their usual late hour, but for once scarcely a head turned in their direction. The Earl of Huntley himself sat moodily in a corner beneath a potted palm taking not the slightest interest in his guests, feeding his repulsive dogs caviar sandwiches and drinking endless brandy and sodas. He went to bed, without a glance to right or left, on the stroke of midnight by his clocks, which had already led to a number of eminent guests' adjusting their pocket watches, in puzzlement, to the exclusive mean time of Huntley House.

There were two Royal Marines' bands, one in the ballroom itself, the other at the head of the main staircase. At 2:00 A.M. Lillie Langtry, who had been the mistress of at least two of the Princes and others of lower rank present, recited Lady Macbeth's "Dagger" speech to unstinted applause. By 3 A.M. more than 3,000 bottles of champagne had been drunk, and an elderly backwoods Peer had completed his third seduction in one of the bedrooms freely available for such purposes. At 3:30 A.M. Lady Randolph Churchill at last succeeded in persuading her schoolboy son, Winston, to go home.

On Lady Clementine Huntley's dance card, the Honourable Archibald Buller's name appeared fifteen times, all that she thought proper, although she was quite as much in love with him as he was with her. Clemmie had none of the eccentricity of her father, whom she adored. She was a practical, sensible girl, interested in things, in events, liked hunting and dogs but also reading poetry, Lord Byron being her hero. She loved to hear about the Navy and encouraged Buller to talk about his life at sea, about his encounters with Chinese pirate junks when he had commanded a gunboat in the Far East, and about his adventures in the Egyptian War five years earlier.

During one waltz, Buller held her tightly to him as they whirled about the crowded floor. She was a tall girl and her fair hair brushed against his cheek, and he could feel the exciting shape of her body in spite of her stays and corsets. She smelled fresh and clean as if she had brought the air and the garden scents of the Huntley estate in Wiltshire with her to London.

She did not resist his pressure, and when the dance was over she smiled at him with special warmth and intimacy. On the great balcony overlooking Park Lane and Hyde Park, bold with champagne, Buller proposed to her. Characteristically, he put it quite simply, without any preliminary lead-up: "Will you marry me, Clemmie?"

"We're much too young." She was almost, but not quite, firm in her tone.

He slipped his hand over hers. "The younger we are the longer we'll be married."

She laughed and turned to look at him. "You are an ass, Archy. Do you really love me?"

"Deeply, passionately, totally. I want you to be my wife." He squeezed her hand. "I would like to talk to your father."

She laughed again. "I've never heard anyone say that before."

"Why?"

"Because everyone's supposed to be so frightened of him." Buller considered this for a moment. "Even if I was I wouldn't hesitate—for you. How could I? But actually I don't find him frightening. I like him, and he makes me laugh."

She said she was glad of that, and then tried to turn the conversation. "Father wouldn't come to the Abbey Jubilee ceremony. 'Not for that upstart,' he said. So we were in the country. And, do you know, we could count eighteen beacons from our lawn on Jubilee night. Wasn't that a marvellous day?"

"The only marvellous day will be when you agree to marry me."

She remained silent for a moment. Then speaking in a low voice and not looking at him, she said, "Let me think. I do love you, Archy, but I would like a little time. I will write to you, I promise."

Before the ball began to break up, long after sunrise, a middle-aged woman came up to Buller and introduced herself as Lady Rawlings. She was the wife of the Admiral who had been among those on the *Osborne*'s bridge during the Prince of Wales's review of the Fleet. She was a rather plump, heavily scented woman with a bright smile and a husky voice that Buller found attractive.

"Well, young man, you two made a nice pair on the floor. And I have no doubt you are madly in love."

Buller felt himself blushing. "Well, ma'm, I . . ."

She cut him short. "Never mind. I know the asnwer. You will be married within the year. So I must grab you quickly. In short, young man, will you come to my house party the weekend after next? Stoner Hall, you know." She added coyly, "And who knows who might be there."

Buller did not much care for weekend house parties, which tended to be boring with a lot of stiff conversation or silly giggling games and left you with a bad head and an overfull stomach. But the hint that Clemmie would be there made the sound of this one irresistible.

"Thank you very much, Lady Rawlings. I would like to."

Admiral Sir Keith Rawlings Bart was another one of those "odd admirals," as Buller liked to describe them. The range of eccentricity in the Royal Navy was wide. In the case of "Soapy" Rawlings, it ran to ultrafastidiousness. He was a tall, grey-haired, haughty- and austere-looking officer, who talked very little and when he did, in the tones of a priest incanting a psalm. Nor could he ever remember people's names. He had even been known to forget his own and to ask sharply of his Flag-Lieutenant who this fellow Rawlings was who presumed to be on his dinner list.

Rawlings preferred silence at all times. If it was necessary to speak, words had to be used economically. Above all, he would not countenance obscenities. If he heard the mildest expletive in his Flagship, he invariably requested his Flag-Captain to muster the entire ship's company and have them wash out their mouths in soapy water, always kept available in ship's casks for that purpose. Hence his nickname.

Admiral Rawlings shaved twice a day with a cut-throat razor presented to him by the Sultan of Zanzibar for saving his brother from hanging as a slave-trader. It had an ivory handle embellished with sunken diamonds and was said to have been used to cut the throats of five concubines who had in some way displeased His Majesty. He invariably wore snow-write piqué shirts, which he changed twice daily. He also wore lavender kid gloves, which were changed as frequently as he found dust in some recess of his Flagship, and the officer-of-the-watch received a roasting.

Admiral Rawlings was utterly unloved, even by his family, and especially by his wife. He had not a friend in the world. But he was a superb seaman. As a junior Post-Captain, he had been known to tack and wear a 100-gun ship of the line under plain sail and in a gusty, uncertain wind into Hong Kong harbour, packed with shipping and junks. Now as a senior Admiral in the new age of steel, his fleet invariably won at war games and his Flagship's gunnery was unsurpassed by any other man-o'-war.

Archy Buller at twenty-two made an attractive figure: light-brown hair grown longer than was suitable, with the high gloss of good health and parted in the center; the characteristic big Buller nose, brown eyes set wide apart. He had a generous covering of freckles in the summer and in tropical climes, which considerably embarrassed him; a full mouth that could as easily have been Augustus Buller's of the 1723 portrait, though with a less jutting chin beneath it. He had grown now to his full height of six feet two, possessed broad shoulders, a deep chest, and no-nonsense hands, as hard-skinned from his naval service as any veteran bluejacket's.

The guests at the Rawlings' house party at Stoner Hall, Somerset, remarked on how favourably the youngest Buller boy had matured. They approved of his courteous style, his directness and frankness and modesty. Mothers regarded all Bullers as good studs and steady husbands. The girls loved his looks and his manners, and all had heard of his fearlessness in the Egyptian War. The more discerning women recognized in his eyes an exciting strain of darkness that suggested an easily aroused temper as well as a passionate temperament.

During the course of that long weekend, a number of hearts beat faster when he turned towards them on the croquet lawn or on the lawn tennis courts, at the badminton net or on the ballroom floor. Buller was accomplished at most physical activities and sports but—again like his ancestors and his father—could not swim; a fact which worried him not at all.

Almost the first person he met after the dog cart from the railway station dropped him at the front door of Stoner Hall was Mark Holly. They fell into each other's arms, Holly's new beard rough against Buller's cheek.

"Well, look at you!" Buller exclaimed. "A great growth. Didn't know you could do it, old boy. Holly's holly bush, how do you like that," he said, rubbing his own smooth cheek.

Mark Holly, Lieutenant R.N., had filled out somewhat since Buller had last seen him, but he still gave the impression that he might fall out of his suit if he ran fast. The long voyage in the *Bacchante* had sealed their friendship, and Buller loved the rather simple, thoroughly nice young man who was so clumsy with his fingers that he could just about tie a reef knot and no more, and had finally been excused duties aloft because he was always falling out of the *Bacchante*'s ratlines and holding up everyone else.

"My, but I'm glad to see you," Holly said now. He lowered his voice. "To tell you the truth, I was rather dreading this weekend—all girls and their mothers eyeing you, and not many chaps."

"The last time I saw you was at Sandy Point in the Magellan Straits—remember, two years ago? You were coming back from the China Station, and I was on my way out in the *Albacore*. The only time I've been cold coaling . . ."

The reminiscing was broken up only by the demands of courtesy as their hostess approached them and invited them to take tea on the terrace. "I'm afraid your Clemmie has had to cry off—I'm so sorry."

Buller felt a jolt of disappointment. Worse still, it was a big house-party, he recognized at once; some fifty in all, several elderly military-looking men, some local squires, the Bishop of Salisbury, and as Holly had indicated, a great number of mothers with their unmarried daughters.

Tea, croquet, with modest claims of inadequacy mixing with exclamations of outrage, a turn about the lake, and, while the sun was still high in the sky, a retirement to bedrooms where jugs of hot water and hip baths awaited all but the privileged few with a new bathroom *en suite*. Champagne, the formal ritual of proceeding into dinner in pairs, and the seven-course dinner itself: soup, delicate little Weymouth sprats, roast partridge, a giant sirloin of beef which required the services of three footmen as well as those of the butler and the chef, who did the carving, followed by fresh raspberries and cream, a Stilton cheese almost as large as the sirloin, and fresh fruit from the hothouse.

Later in the evening, after several games of whist and an impromptu recital, Buller caught Holly's eye. "I must take a walk or I'll burst from food *and* boredom," said Buller quietly. "I suppose we'd get fat, too, if we weren't at sea most of the time." There had been supper at eleven o'clock: cake and smoked salmon sandwiches, crystallized fruit and iced hock.

They slipped out of the drawing room where someone was playing the piano and walked in the moonlight under the cedar trees and across the lawns to the river. It was a perfect late July night, and Buller experienced a feeling of total contentment, which he expressed to his old friend.

"We're damnably lucky, Holly, do you know that? We

live in the best country in the world which governs half the world. It's the most beautiful country in the world, too—look at this," and he swept his arm towards the river lapping past, the distant spire of the church, the noble cedars casting shadows on the grass, the great stone pile of Stoner Hall glittering with lights from its hundred windows. "We don't have to worry about money, we like our work, and—did I tell you? —I'm madly in love. She was supposed to be here this weekend. Such a glorious girl, and I think she will marry me."

Holly said, "Congratulations. Isn't there anything you want in the world? Sounds almost too good to be true."

They were both smoking cigars, a practice Buller had only recently taken up. He examined the glowing tip of his for a moment in silence. "Yes, there is," he said at length. "I expect you were the same when you were younger. I wanted to fight and prove my courage. 'I want to hear a gun fired in anger,' I used to say. But with all these years of peace, I think we're going soft. Not just you and me; the whole country. We need testing again, like in the Napoleonic days. Look at our ancestors, lean and hard from fighting wars to save their country. We haven't had a proper war for seventy years."

"Do we have to have a war to keep lean and hard?" asked Holly. "They're damn nasty things, you know. Even Wellington thought that."

"Seems so," said Buller, whose puritanical conscience was likely to reveal itself at the most inappropriate times. He belched. "I feel as if I've eaten an ox and drunk a cask of Navy rum. Let's work it off with a ride."

So the two Lieutenants made their way to the stables, found themselves a couple of likely hunters, saddled them up, and went for an hour's hack along the local lanes, breaking into a long gallop across the village green on the way back.

It was 4:00 A.M. when they returned; the moon had set and they had some difficulty in finding their horses' stalls and giving them a rubdown before leaving them. Holly was sleeping in the east wing, and Buller made his way alone up the stairs and along the wide corridor, lit by a single oil lamp, to his room. He was feeling fresh and wide awake after the night ride and the taste of fresh air.

When he let himself into his room, he became immediately aware of someone else's being there. The curtains were drawn back, and there was a figure before the window, just discernible against the dark grey of the predawn light. Thinking that he must have mistaken his room, he began to back towards the door.

A voice said, "Don't go. I've been waiting for such a long time. What have you been doing, Archy?"

It was the voice of his hostess, the same husky voice which had said at the ball, "So I must grab you quickly," and had more recently explained Clemmie's absence. And it was the same scent, too, unmistakable with its sharp, pungent, musk flavour.

Buller continued to walk backwards towards the door, repeating his apologies. Lady Rawlings stepped quickly towards him. He heard the swish of her silk dressing gown, and her voice, softer now, saying, "Polite guests always do their hostess's bidding. It is all right, this is your room. And it is quite time you went to bed."

She was very close to him. Buller could feel the warmth of her body though they were not touching. She sniffed his evening jacket and said, "Good gracious, you've been riding! How exciting!"

Now she reached upwards and put her arms round his neck. "Let's go to bed. It is really very late."

"But, Lady Rawlings . . ." Buller was suddenly confused and startled into awareness of what was happening. She was undoing the buttons of his jacket and talking at the same time as if she had not heard his protests. "You have the look of a virgin in your handsome eyes, and I am always right about that sort of thing. Come along now, you must do some of the undressing." She laughed softly. "If you are going to marry that pretty Huntley girl—and I think she is a very good choice—you don't want to take her to bed without knowing anything at all."

Buller found his hand being held against her breast, a full, heavy breast, which he found tinglingly interesting. Now she was saying, "My daughter Clarissa married a virgin and she said after the honeymoon, 'Mama, it was sheer hell. What shall I do? He just pummels me about and I can't bear it.' You don't want that to happen to your darling Clemmie . . ."

Buller found himself saying, "No," but he was not sure what it referred to. If it meant should he be caressing the thighs and the breasts of his hostess with whom he had exchanged no more than a few words, then the answer appeared to be, "Yes." But he was still puzzled by what was happening to him. Only that Lady Rawlings, perhaps forty-seven years old, was very insistent that they should remain close together as she helped to take his clothes off, and that this was uncommonly pleasant.

Buller was aware that he was breathing fast, and that this woman with the soft and altogether deliciously rounded body had her lips close to his ear and was breathing as rapidly as he was between the most intimate endearments. "Oh, how beautifully big you are . . ." Then, "Come along, now, you lovely boy. It's so much more convenient lying down."

They were both naked under the soft Irish linen sheet, and he was no longer capable of speech. She was talking all the time, though. "It is nice to talk when you make love. Women like it. So do you, now. That's right, put your hand there and move it about gently like that. Your Clemmie will like that, I promise. Just as I do now." And her voice broke into a groan.

But Lady Rawlings continued to remain in command, though obviously acutely enjoying herself at the same time. "Now, that's right, darling boy. You should kiss my breast, just as if you were feeding from your dear Mama again. That's nice for you. And this is nice for me. Now come and lie your lovely young body on me . . ."

Stage by stage, this comely woman, who seemed so greedy

for pleasure, brought Buller towards the agonizing culmination, until he found himself moving naturally and with ever growing need so that he hardly heard the voice close to his ear, "That's my lovely boy, now let it come. And so will I . . ." But the tight scream that followed might have come from his own lips or from hers. He did not know or care.

Their breathing slowly returned to normal, and her voice was quite normal, too, when she spoke again. "That was quite good for first time. What a nice boy!" And she eased him off, kissed him lightly on the cheek, and was gone, leaving behind her rich musk scent now faintly blended with sweet perspiration that Buller found totally agreeable.

Buller did not see or hear her go, though daylight was now creeping into the room. He was fleetingly aware of a tingling sense of satisfaction and well-being that spread out slowly to the extremities of his limbs, and in his mind a confused sense of guilt and bewilderment. "I wanted Clemmie to be first—and now she's not. But, my goodness, so *that* is what it is all about! Well . . . !"

And then, utterly exhausted, he was asleep.

Lady Clementine Huntley wrote to Buller as she had promised. It was a short, simple letter. "Yes, darling Archy, I will marry you if you still want me to, and if dear Papa approves." Not much more than that; written in her schoolgirlish, rounded hand in lavender ink, on writing paper embossed with "Huntley Hall, Wiltshire" in Gothic script.

It was waiting for Buller when he arrived home, and he slipped it into his pocket and said nothing to anyone. But it had been sitting for too long on the silver tray in the hall for its receipt to be a private affair, not with his brothers in the house. At luncheon, Henry said, "Smelt very nice, that missive of yours, Archy. Very ladylike, very lavender."

Guy addressed his mother. "That letter of Archy's—it did not look like an official communication from Their Lordships, did it, Mama?"

The twins had engaged for a number of years now in brief

and somewhat scandalous affairs and showed no signs of getting married. That their younger brother might be contemplating marriage never crossed their minds. They concluded that he must be in love at last, and the teasing continued on those lines, until Lady Buller shut them up, just as if they were eleven years old instead of twenty-nine. But, out hunting the next day, when the hounds lost the scent and Lady Buller found herself alone with her son in the corner of a field, the rest of the hunt circling restlessly some distance away, she said, "You're looking like a man suddenly, Archy. I'm not much of a one for intuition, but my guess is that you've either got a mistress or you're engaged."

Buller looked at her in surprise. She was on Cobbler, a stallion of vast size and strength which she loved controlling. He was sweating from a long run, and his mother's face—without veil as always—was shining, too, with straggling lengths of hair escaping from under her hat. Was it possible that so much could show in his face? And what would she say if he answered, "Both!"?

Instead, he said, "Well, Mama, I have actually asked a girl to marry me. An awfully nice girl. She was here once, with her father. Clemmie Huntley."

"Well, I hope that she is not as peculiar as her father. She seemed normal enough—a nice girl—the only time I met her. Have you told Papa?"

"Not yet. I was going to ask Lord Huntley first."

Until the engagement was announced a month later, Buller in London found himself in almost overwhelming demand by Society hostesses. He could not be certain in his own mind whether it was his experience with Lady Rawlings, or his forthcoming engagement and the imminence of marriage, but he was now finding the company of women much more attractive, and he went out evening after evening, sometimes with his brothers, sometimes alone, returning tired but elated in the small hours, and sleeping for most of the morning. The invitations came from Buckingham Palace and from Marlborough House at one end of the scale, to houses in Belgravia where some of the oldest and most select but less extravagant County people kept modest town houses and had balls sometimes with as few as fifty guests.

Clemmie Huntley was at none of them. For the month of August, her father invariably moved to Castle Cairnfeggus in Ireland where he fished fourteen hours a day in the several salmon rivers that ran through his 4,000 acres. Buller missed her and wrote to her daily. Then, at one of the smaller balls in mid-August, shortly after the yacht racing and social life of Cowes Week, he met Lady Rawlings again.

"When is your engagement to be announced?" she asked at once, appraising him favourably in his daring new deep-blue velvet dinner jacket with six brass buttons which was about to come into fashion.

He told her, and she invited him to tea the following afternoon. Still innocent, he thought it was a tea party. Instead, it was *à deux* in the small sitting room adjoining her bedroom. She was gently teasing but kind, and gave the impression that she was wholly concerned with his life and happiness. Later, she asked, "Do you feel less innocent now, my sweet?"

"I suppose I do. You were very kind."

"Nonsense. Purely selfish. I enjoyed it." She got up, came round to the back of his chair, and put her cheek against his, her arms round his chest. The musk scent was stronger than ever, evoking that curious and wonderful night when he was galloping in the moonlight one moment, and lying naked in this delicious woman's arms the next. So that when she said, "It is time for lesson two, Archy," he followed her into the darkened bedroom, where, this time swiftly and less shyly, he undressed and slipped between the silk sheets.

"That's right—that's much better," she said in her husky voice. And later, "Now we'll try it like this. Oh, that is lovely —admit it, you lovely boy . . ."

So Lady Rawlings became Buller's mistress for nearly three weeks, and they made love with fervour and increasing refinement every afternoon; so that the butler (who was well used to these arrangements, and very discreet) welcomed him with a butler's invariable reserve, but almost as an old friend.

Buller's search of his conscience became increasingly painful as the day of Clemmie's return from Ireland and the simultaneous announcement of their engagement approached.

But it was all right. On the afternoon she came back he did not visit Lady Rawlings but instead played baccarat at the Marlborough Club until five o'clock and took a hansom from there to Huntley House. Clemmie had changed into a walking costume—close-fitting black coat and bright-blue overskirt, long *tablier* in front and large bustle—and the sight of her, so fresh and innocent and springlike on this late summer day, filled him with tenderness. This was real, Lady Rawlings a fantasy who would now rapidly fade, and he would keep himself entirely for Clemmie.

They fell into each other's arms and remained close and silent for a while. Yes, it was all right, and Buller vowed that he would forever be tender and kind to this sweet girl who was to be his wife.

Chapter XI

For a moment after Rod woke up, he thought that he was still in Egypt. The eternal smoke of Tyneside might have been the smoke of the bombardment and fires of Alexandria, the red glow of the sun, the tropical sun rising above the desert on that July morning. The sounds, too, of rivetting, the crash of steam hammers, the beat of donkey engines, and the groans from the shipyard cranes could have been the sounds of war as Rod had known it three months earlier.

But there was little heat in this northern autumn sun, and soon the sound would be cut short by the Armstrong sirens blowing throughout the yards and workshops of Elswick, to be succeeded by the clatter of clogs on the cobbled streets and the deep chorus of voices as the men returned to pubs and homes.

From his bed, Rod could see the stacks that belched the smoke into the sky, the tops of the shipyard cranes moving restlessly to and fro all day with their loads of steel plates and girders, and dimly through the smoke, the highest rows of the little back-to-back houses on the southern bank of the Tyne, all as identical with one another as the Elswick houses, and with this house, number 19D Groom Road.

Hundreds and hundreds of back-to-backs, housing thousands of men and their families, some out of work and out on their luck, some working their ten-hour day for their 17 shillings 6 pence a week, to spend nearly that amount on "booze and baccy," or just to make ends meet on their wages by strict frugality, and that meant no butter ever, and meat—lights or a bit of shin of beef—once a week.

And probably not one person in all these working people's homes possessed enough savings to pay a week's butcher's bill for a small house in Eaton Square, London.

Doris Maclewin was one of the luckier ones; her daughter Kate was a senior parlourmaid at Cragside, and her son, a leading seaman in the Navy. Both sent enough money home to keep her in comparative comfort and to allow her to do what she most enjoyed: cook a great vegetable stew, with some bones and some scraps of meat in it, for the hungrier children at her end of Groom Road.

Worry was Mrs. Maclewin's enemy: worry about the children of out-of-work fathers or of drunken homes, worry about some of the old folk who lived on precarious charity, and worry above all about Rod. The shock of the *Eurydice* tragedy had left its mark. Never again, pray though she might, could she expect her son to be a one-hundred-to-one-chance survivor of a shipwreck like that. And then came the news of the war in Egypt, and Rod serving in the Mediterranean Fleet. While reading the newspapers in the Armstrong Library in late June, she had had a premonition that her son would be in the thick of the fighting.

And she had later been proved right. The *Condor* had been mentioned in all the reports—her gallant Captain, Lord Charles Beresford (Rod had written that he was his cox), the signal from the Admiral, "Well done, *Condor*!" The premonition remained after the bombardment. Then the telegram, like a physical blow at her stomach. ". . . GRAVELY WOUNDED . . ." Her appeal for more news. Nothing. At last another telegram. "YOUR SON RETURNING ENGLAND HOSPITAL

SHIP ORPHEUS." And three weeks later, Rod's first letter; cheerful, reassuring. He would be in Haslar hospital for some time. Had suffered a fever while recovering from a small wound. Would be well soon and returning home to convalesce. Everyone very kind.

In fact Rod had been so close to death on board the *Orpheus* that the ship's chaplain had sat all one hot night at his bunkside praying for his recovery, and the climax of the fever had lasted almost a week. At Malta the fever was raging at its worst and he was in a state of delirium as he lay tossing and turning, looking out through the open port at the white buildings of Valetta and reliving, on a worse-than-ever scale, that terrible evening with William Thomas and Ginger O'Sullivan in the brothel.

The evil, gaunt face of Masters haunted his nightmares all through the fever, and even now he would see that figure again, kneeling on the rocky parapet, rifle steady against his shoulder, and hear the voice on that day in the *Condor*, "Ye'll pay for it, little 'un . . . Ye know that?"

And he had paid for it, in full, from the moment that the bullet that had been intended to kill him had laid him low and, by some miracle—thanks be to God (and to Lieutenant Buller)—had brought him back to his mother and home . . .

His return and his long convalescence had brought new friends into Rod's life. Kate had become engaged to one of the footmen at Cragside, a young Scot called William, beefy, tough, and reliable. William's sister, Rosie, had been trained as a nurse and for three weeks had been coming in every day to help Doris Maclewin with her patient, washing him, and more recently helping him onto his legs again and about the room. Rosie, by contrast with her brother, was small, like Rod, though with William's fresh complexion and freckles on her face and on the backs of her hands.

Then there was O'Sullivan. He had transferred to another ship after the bombardment, and it had returned to its home port and paid off soon after Rod's return. O'Sullivan was on a month's leave and on the second day had travelled from

Tynemouth where he lived to look up Rod.

With attention and kindness and the daily cheer of Rosie's visits, Rod was recovering fast. But every stage of physical recovery brought with it an increasing sense of unease about the future. Unlike Buller, Rod had felt the full chill of physical fear during the fighting in Alexandria. There had never been any risk of his showing it or shrinking back from his duties, and in the heat of battle he had been oblivious to anything but the need to fight and to win. But it had been there, always, like some dark shadow.

Looking back on it now, with all the time in the world for brooding, Rod worried that, after his wounding, he might not be able to conceal his fear if the same thing should happen again. "Am I fit for the Navy?" he kept asking himself. "I only joined because there was no other work. Perhaps I haven't got the right sort of courage?" In his present weak condition, the nightmare of letting down his shipmates in a crisis kept reappearing in his mind; and with it, the evil face of Masters.

And there was no one, absolutely no one, in whom he could confide these fears; least of all his mother, who worried about him enough already.

Then two incidents added to his fears at two different levels, one more critical and imminent than the other. A letter arrived from the Admiralty in London informing him that a Surgeon-Lieutenant of the Royal Navy would shortly be visiting him to check on what they called his "fitness for further duties." The doctor duly appeared three days later, in uniform, which caused something of a stir in Groom Road, and some mocking cries from the barefoot urchins in the alley.

The bullet wound had healed well. There was stiffness about the scar on his stomach and sometimes a burning feeling after he had eaten. The Lieutenant examined the wound carefully, warned him off highly seasoned food, and informed him that he would be classified as fit to serve again in four weeks' time, limited at first to light duties.

Rosie was downstairs when the Lieutenant left in the hansom cab that had waited for him. She looked crestfallen when Rod gave her the news. Rod touched her cheek lightly with the back of his hand. It was the first time they had touched, beyond the needs of nursing, and she looked startled.

Rod said quickly, "I'm sorry. I wanted to tell you—tell you I won't be going away forever. They may even give me a shore job."

"I hope so." She reached for his hand and put it back against her cheek. "But I shall miss you."

"I shall miss you, too."

The next day was Saturday, a dour day of rain squalls and high winds that whipped down the steep streets and set the litter flying and made the fingers raw with cold. With her new modest wealth, Doris Maclewin now rented the rooms downstairs, and Rod made his first descent of the stairs in the evening to the fire his mother had lit. Later, Kate and William arrived. It was their turn for Sunday off, and they had taken the train from Cragside.

The five of them had tea together, tea of baps and jam, kippers and lots of strong tea; and they talked of their plans.

Kate said, "Ma, I would like to get you out of Newcastle. It's so unhealthy and noisy."

"But I like it. I like the people, and I like helping them when I can."

"We've been offered a cottage in the grounds when we are married. Come and live with us there, Ma. That would be nice."

"No one lives in Newcastle who can live outside in the country," William said. "It's a terrible place. Full of criminals."

Doris Maclewin laughed. "I don't know any criminals. There's nothing for anyone to steal round these parts."

"One of the footmen," William continued, "was telling me yesterday that he was in a pub and overheard a man—he was drunk of course—say he had come thousands of miles to exact revenge for a terrible wrong. My friend said, 'What sort of revenge do you mean?' And this man lurched about and pulled out a great long knife—a terrible-looking weapon, my friend said. Then this man said, 'I'm going to finish one off with this, and do for the other.' Newcastle's full of criminals like that," William continued earnestly. "They're always finding bodies in the Tyne. And anyway, all this smoke and dirt. You come and live with us, Mrs. Maclewin."

There was a pause. William put another knob of coal on the fire. Rod said shakily, "I'll go up again now, Ma."

Rosie got to her feet and helped him up; and Doris Maclewin said, "Yes, that's long enough for first time."

Lying in his bed in the darkness, Rod told himself over and over again, "It can't be—it can't be . . ."

But how could he ever be sure? What had the man looked like? He could not ask William to find out. William would say, "Why do you want to know?" And the footman would have forgotten, or it had been too dark—or he had made the story up, just to impress . . .

But he must warn Ginger, must tell him the truth about the shot that had nearly killed him, something he had divulged to no one. Ginger might scoff at William's tale, but Rod ought to warn him. He would, the next day, when Ginger would call and take him for his first walk.

O'Sullivan did not turn up at 19D Groom Road the following day. Nor the next day. "He's not well," Rod tried to convince himself. Or, "I must have mistaken the day his leave ended." But he knew that Ginger would at least have come to say good-bye before rejoining his ship.

Rod ventured out by himself for the first time. He felt quite strong on his legs, though the muscles had wasted from weeks of inactivity. He reached the station without too much trouble and took a train to Tynemouth, then a hansom at the other end. He had never been to O'Sullivan's house. It was very much like his own, the same red brick back-to-back with slate roof. The only difference was that here you could smell the sea, and that reminded Rod again of his imminent return to the Navy.

Ginger's mother answered the door at once. She was a stout, red-haired woman. She answered Rod's inquiry. "No, George is not in."

Now Rod could see how pale the woman was—pale and pinched with anxiety. "He left to come and see you," she continued. "He likes you. He likes his visits to you. But I thought he had stayed a long time. He wouldn't stay the night without telling me. He's thoughtful like that. But if he's not with you . . ."

Mrs. O'Sullivan's face crumpled, and she began to sob. Rod did what he could to comfort her and then left when she reassured him that her husband would soon be home. Then they would go to the police.

Twenty-four hours passed and there was still no news or sign of Ginger O'Sullivan. Then a policeman called at 19D. Rod saw the staring children first, suddenly silent and struck with awe. He was downstairs, and he pulled aside the net curtain and saw the tall, striding figure. He knew that the policeman was going to stop at their door.

"Sorry to trouble you . . . a question of identity . . . parents very upset . . . only son . . . I wonder if you could oblige . . . understand you were a shipmate and friend . . ."

Rod accompanied him to the police morgue. Yes, his body had been fished out of the river. Some children had found it at low tide. Thought it was natural causes at first. An accident. Drunk, fallen off the bridge. Happens sometimes. Then the knife wound. One blow. Fatal. "Yes, sir, we are treating it as murder."

The sheet was pulled back. Rod said flatly, "Yes, that's Ginger."

"Mr. George O'Sullivan, sir?"

"Yes—that's right."

The familiar, once cheerful face, sort of flat now in death, the hair carefully brushed but without its red shine. Eyes shut, and no sign of pain or suffering. Rod wondered if Ginger had known, in the last split second, that he was going to be attacked. Perhaps he even recognized his assailant?

Would he have thought, quickly, "I must tell Rod," just as Rod had felt at once, "I must tell Ginger." And he never had.

Outside, there was winter sunshine, and it was as cold as the morgue and the corpse of Leading Seaman George O'Sullivan. No matter how hard he tried to thrust it away, there was no denying that the fear had its grip now, a hard, implacable grip round the stomach, worst where Masters's bullet had smashed his flesh but failed to kill him.

The police were suspicious at first, and Rod could not blame them. Why had he not informed the naval authorities before? they wanted to know. This murder might have been prevented if he had. Why had Masters not been arrested for attempted murder in Alexandria? And O'Sullivan? If he knew that he was threatened, why . . .

Rod gave the answers as clearly and simply as he could, but it was difficult for those not in the service to understand the conflict of loyalties in a case like this. The Admiralty in London must be informed. This was a part civil, part Royal Navy case, both services combining to hunt down the murderer.

The fear of death at Masters's hands lasted for nearly six days, the period the police took to arrest him. He had identified the body late on a Friday morning. They caught Masters on Wednesday evening in a pub off Jarrow Road. He had fought furiously, breaking a bottle over one policeman's head, and it had required four of them to take him away. For the last two nights, the police had kept a watch on the Maclewin house. At 9:00 P.M. on Wednesday, there was a knock on the door, and the policeman told Mrs. Maclewin of the arrest. Rod had been unable to keep from her the story of Masters's vendetta against O'Sullivan and him; and now she broke down and cried with relief.

Rod's second fear, which had been screened from his mind for the past days, began to reassert itself as the last period of sick leave slipped away. There was a letter from Lord Charles Beresford, who wrote to congratulate him on his recovery, and on the arrest of Masters ("I hope they give him a hundred lashes and keelhaul him before they hang the skunk!").

The Navy don't seem to have any use for me any longer so I'll go back into Parliament and blast 'em from there. But, little Midge, if I get another ship I want you as my cox again. We'll get some more scraps together yet—perhaps the Frenchies next time—and I'll need you for the good luck you bring

YOUR OLD CAPTAIN
(*signed*)
Beresford

"More scraps?" Rod recalled that first ride into Alexandria and the desperate struggle. He wondered now that he had not succumbed to the fear that must have seized him when the mob closed in. Surely he could never face that again, or that ride on the footplate with Arabi's bullets like hailstones? Holding the letter with Beresford's embossed coat of arms on it, Rod answered it in a whisper to himself: "No, sir, you won't want me—not next time; my nerve's broken—broken by Arabi Pasha, military dictator of Egypt, and Ordinary Seaman Masters.

Finally, it was Rosie who put new heart into him so that, when the time came, he was able to face the Navy more or less cheerfully although he still felt that he would be no use to his shipmates if it came to war again.

Kind, understanding Rosie had winkled out of Rod the reason for his depression and evident anxiety. "It's nothing—it's just that I feel weak and useless after all these weeks."

"No, it's something more than that." She had a soft voice, with a Scottish accent, and strongly persuasive now, too. "You must tell me what's troubling you. Just talk your mind, Roddy. It doesn't matter what you say."

At length he had given in and told her of his fears—his fears for others who might die because of him—because he failed them at a critical moment.

"I believe your trouble is that you are too sensitive—that you have a conscience that's aroused too easily." She held his hand in both of hers. They were in the parlour, and Doris Maclewin was cooking in the kitchen, out of earshot. "That's what makes you so nice."

She smiled, and Rod said, "I'm not nice—I'm just frightened. I wake up frightened. My Captain used to call me 'Lucky Midge.' I think I've used up all my luck now."

"That's silly and superstitious. It's not luck, it's God who decides. He decides everything. And I should think He's now deciding about you."

Rod asked what she meant.

"I mean, He's deciding it's time you pulled yourself together. He might also be deciding that you're a wee bit ungrateful." She smiled again, sympathetically, but there was no doubt of her firmness; and while Rod had been taken aback by her tone and her message, he was forced to accept the truth in what she was saying.

She added, "You mustn't mind."

"I don't mind. I am pleased that you care."

"Of course I care. I wouldn't spend so much time here if I didn't." She laughed softly. "Now that you can wash yourself."

He felt a great deal better after that and was sensible enough to know that he had had too much time to think over the past months, and that it was time he was busy again.

Rod did not have Christmas with his family as he had hoped. On the morning of December 11, 1882, he dressed in his bell-bottoms, frock tucked in and buttoned, regulation boots, heavy overcoat and cap; and kissed his mother good-bye on the doorstep of 19D.

Kate and William had said good-bye the night before, and Rosie walked to the station with him, Rod with his kitbag on his shoulder, and a trail of little children behind him singing "The Merry Maiden and the Tar" from *H.M.S. Pinafore.*

The station at Newcastle was like the city it served in miniature—all smoke and noisy bustle. Amid the sounds of escaping steam and clanking cranks and pistons, the shouts of guards and porters and passengers, Rod and Rosie kissed for the first time. Nowhere in Newcastle could have been more public, and more private.

Rod said, "Dear Rosie, I think we should get married."

"We could think about it." She looked into his eyes, almost exactly on a level with her own. "Then when you are next home, we could talk about it."

"All right. Good-bye Rosie." He lifted his kitbag onto his shoulder again, and he saw her waving before she was lost in the crowd.

One brief nightmare still had to be endured. Masters would not be flogged (although that was still legal in the Navy), and he certainly would not be keelhauled, as Lord Charles Beresford had wished for him. But he would be hanged; of that there was no doubt.

First, though, there was to be a court-martial, and, inevitably, Rod was called as a witness. It took place on board the hulk *Bellona* in Portsmouth harbour.

Rod was determined that he would not look at Masters. It was not only the fear of the man, the fear of the evil he emanated, that caused him to keep his eyes on the President and the officials of the proceedings.

The footman from Cragside was called: "Yes, your honour. That is the man . . . Yes, sir. He said, 'I've come thousands of miles to exact revenge . . .'"

When it was Rod's turn, he told his story from the beginning, of the events in Malta, the first threat of retribution. And then, for the first time: "Yes, sir, I saw clearly who it was shot at me . . . Yes, sir, it was the accused. There was that much going on, no one else saw. No, not even Midshipman Buller. He thought it was one of our men still shooting at the enemy, sir . . . No, sir, I wasn't afraid of telling. But you don't split on your own shipmates, sir . . . No, not even if they're trying to kill you, though I know I should have done—seeing what he did to Ginger."

Rod continued to stare ahead as he spoke, but he became increasingly aware of the presence of the man in the dock a mere twenty feet away. He knew exactly where he was, as if searchlight beams shone out from him, illuminating Rod. And, like a trapped animal, Rod felt magnetically impelled to look at his one-time assailant.

His glance was a brief one, a mere fraction of a second; and it was a fraction of a second too long. Masters's hair had been dyed, or had turned grey. The deep cadaverous cheeks, the thin, cruel line of mouth were concealed beneath a full beard, so that at first sight this seaman did not resemble the wicked, ruthless Masters the crew of the *Condor* had served with. But no camouflage could diminish the malevolence in the man's black eyes, which stared at Rod as if he were about to transfix him with some unseen mystical weapon.

Rod broke off from what he was saying, stumbled over his words, and fell silent. There was not a sound in the *Bellona*'s great cabin for several seconds, as if the black influence of Masters had momentarily paralyzed the proceedings. Rod tore his eyes away from the figure in the dock. Haltingly, then more fluently, he continued his evidence. "Then, sir, I heard from a friend of the earlier witness . . ."

They hanged Masters two days later, on December 23, 1882. Not at the highest yardarm, which no doubt was what Lord Charles Beresford would have wished for him, but in the white-painted cell in the punishment block of the Royal Navy Prison in Portsmouth dockyard. Rod was stationed in the nearby barracks. He knew the day and the time of the execution, and was awake long before it took place, awaiting with feelings of mixed horror and excitement the moment of the release of the trap that would break Masters's neck and release Rod himself from the threat that had hung about his own neck for so long.

❧ ❀ ❧

PART TWO

Chapter XII

═══════════════

In a great Navy with stations as widely separated as China and South Africa, the Mediterranean and the Indian Ocean, with hundreds of men-o'-war in commission on their appointed task of "policing the seas," friendships made in one year might not be renewed for decades, perhaps never. Two ratings might serve together in a battleship in the Channel Fleet, and with the ship paid off, one could proceed on a four-year commission on the China Station, the other on the North American Station; and for a further ten years be as widely separated. Then, by the chances of fate and the movements of ships, they might bump into one another in Trincomalee.

The friendship between Rod Maclewin and Archy Buller lay fallow for ten years after the railway station battle in Alexandria. When they met again in Valetta, Malta, in the autumn of 1892, Buller was serving in the Flagship of the Mediterranean Fleet, the new battleship H.M.S. *Victoria*. Rod was now a Chief Petty Officer in the cruiser H.M.S. *Undaunted*. He also had continued to specialize in gunnery.

Both had been married, and they talked of their wives and

children. But only briefly, and in Rod's case, shyly. They talked most about the Royal Navy—its ships, its politics, its conditions, its officers and men; above all, of the Flag Officers, the Admirals who governed their lives and the conduct of the Navy.

They talked, too, of the officers under whom they had served in Egypt: Lord Charles Beresford, still a Captain— Captain of Rod's ship, as he had been in 1882; and Jackie Fisher, now a Rear Admiral.

After the last of Arabi's troops had been thrown out of Alexandria, General Sir Garnet Wolseley had landed with a large force of British and Indian troops and had routed Arabi's 30,000 men at negligible cost to themselves. The General entered Cairo, the Suez Canal was secured, and Arabi Pasha was captured, court-martialled, and condemned to death. The sentence was not carried out, however, and he was exiled to Ceylon instead.

After reinstating law and order in devastated Alexandria, Lord Charles Beresford came home to a hero's welcome, the Queen, the Prime Minister, and the Admiralty all sending him their congratulations. "Well done, *Condor*!" became a national catch-phrase of heroism. Never a modest man, Beresford complained that his services deserved a decoration. The Admiralty said promotion to Captain was enough. Beresford threatened to resign, attacked the Government over its Egyptian policy, and went onto half pay.

The Prince of Wales, not for the first or the last time, tried to cool the passions of his friend. "Take my advice, my dear Charlie," he wrote, "and leave Egyptian affairs alone." And then, "Having been promoted for the bombardment of Alexandria, it would be perhaps better if you did not criticize the action of the Government."

The Prince of Wales was one of the few people who could restrain Lord Charles Beresford; and then only partly and temporarily. As the years passed, this rich, spoilt, excitable, fearless, indiscreet and in many ways brilliant officer became more wild in his political and naval campaigns as well as in his personal life. His friendships and loves were passionate, his hates violent and bitter. His patriotism and his loyalty to the Royal Navy remained limitless.

In lectures and letters to the newspapers and in outspoken conversation at the Marlborough Club, Beresford denounced Admirals and politicians by the score, condemned ship design and naval policy. Many officers would have been sacked for less. But Charlie B had friends in high places—not only the Prince of Wales—and was powerful in Society.

In January 1890, no doubt to get him out of the way, Their Lordships offered Beresford command of the cruiser *Undaunted*, which that month was due to join the Mediterranean Fleet, whose Commander-in-Chief was an old friend, the much-admired but much-feared Admiral Sir George Tryon.

Two years later, on Chief Petty Officer Roderick Maclewin's return from the China Station, where he had served since the year after the Queen's Jubilee Review of her Fleet, Beresford applied for him as Chief Gunner in his ship. And so, once again, the colourful, masterful patron and his "lucky" protégé came together.

"Prince George lost his first class at pilotage by only twenty marks. The yarn is that one of his examiners, an old salt-horse sailor, didn't think it would do to let him fancy he knew all about it." Thus wrote Rear Admiral John Fisher to the Queen's secretary about her grandson—and Archy Buller's old friend and shipmate.

Prince George passed out of H.M.S. *Excellent*, the Navy's gunnery school, commanded by Jackie Fisher, in 1885 and was promoted Lieutenant in the same month as Buller. The Prince's first command was the little gunboat *Thrush*, which he sailed across the North Atlantic in the summer of 1890. A year later, he was promoted Commander. But his naval career was already almost over. His elder brother, Eddie, never very fit and never very satisfactory in temperament or achievement, caught pneumonia in January 1892; and died from it on the fourteenth.

As heir apparent to the throne after his father (who was already in his fifties and did not lead a healthful life), service at sea was considered too risky for him. This compounded Prince George's grief at the loss of his elder brother, whom he had dearly loved.

The connection between the monarchy and the Royal Navy had always been a close one, right back to King Alfred and Henry VIII and forward to Queen Victoria's uncle, King William, who had served in Nelson's time. The loss of Prince George was greatly regretted by the entire Board. Both Fisher and Beresford declared that he would be missed. George Buller, now retired, wrote to him and his father from Weir Park. "What a loss!" he began both letters. Old Huntley, also now retired, sent a four-page telegram to Marlborough House, quoting passages from the Old Testament, including The Song of Solomon: "Return, return O Shulamite; return, return, that we may look upon thee." The Prince of Wales was believed to have chuckled and noted to his wife that "the dotty old drunkard had become a monarchist—it's like the Archbishop of Canterbury going over to Rome."

The Prince's old Commander of H.M.S. *Excellent*, and Buller's old Captain at the bombardment, was already being tipped as a future First Naval Lord. Jackie Fisher possessed all Beresford's crusading zeal. But his excesses of language and behaviour, while colourful, were kept under sterner control than were Charlie B's. Fisher, too, was a close friend of the Prince of Wales's.

Fisher had no private means and lived on his pay of £660 a year, in contrast with Beresford's thousands. Fisher became brilliant at manipulating the Press in his campaigns to reform the Navy and increase the Navy estimates. The threats of war, especially those against Russia in 1885 and France in 1893, helped the cause of Navy reform.

These were years of imperial expansion and competition among the European powers. France and the newly united Germany had watched Britain increase her possessions all over the world. Since the Battle of Trafalgar in 1805, Britannia had indeed ruled the waves; and it was the Royal Navy that ensured her control of the world's trade routes and protected her as the world's richest nation. Jealousy led to a determination to emulate Britain. The "grab for Africa" was one result, with both France and Germany annexing vast areas and calling them their own.

France possessed the second most powerful Navy, and she and Russia—with her constant threats to India—seemed the most likely enemies in war. Germany, the greatest military power, was not yet openly hostile to Britain and had no Navy to speak of. But in 1888, the Prince of Wales's brother-in-law, Wilhelm, had succeeded to the Imperial throne of Germany. The Kaiser was no friend of the Prince and was jealous of Britain's might and empire. During the Sudan War and the Khartoum crisis in 1885, Wilhelm had written privately, "May the Mahdi chuck all the English into the Nile."

Buller would sometimes reflect on the odd chances that had brought about his two deepest and longest-lasting friendships and the contrast in the rank and background of his friends. His friendship with Prince George had been forged in the hard school of the *Britannia*, where they had stood up together against the ship's bullies; his friendship with Rod Maclewin had stemmed from their desperate fight for the railway station at Alexandria.

After one chance meeting with Prince George and his father at the entrance to the Marlborough Club, Buller saw Georgie (his nickname "Titch" had been dropped since he had achieved a reasonable stature) intermittently and never for long. The Prince had attended Buller's wedding in Westminster Abbey and had met Clemmie for the first time, congratulating Buller on her beauty and spirited nature. Then Buller had spent one weekend at Sandringham with Prince George, talking "Navy" incessantly between mammoth shoots over the estate, and they had met twice in London before the Prince, as a Lieutenant Commander, had been given his first ship.

Then, one more chance meeting: a few months later, in Montreal in June 1890. It was at a reception, and the heat was appalling.

Buller: "Georgie, how capital to see you! How is your ship? What sort of passage did you have out? Have you knocked your crew into shape? How are your father and mother? Isn't this a terrible 'do'? You look as hot as I feel."

Prince George: "Really, Archy, you don't give a fellow a chance! I will take those questions in order, and then ask you some."

They slapped each other on the back again and took their warm and rather sweet champagne to a quiet corner. After a while, Prince George said, "Father reports with pleasure that you are becoming a great one at baccarat. I hope you are winning, Archy. It is a terribly dangerous game. People lose their fortunes."

"I am glad your Papa is pleased. Clemmie hates the Marlborough Club—we have dreadful rows over it. So does my Papa—unlike yours. He has resigned now. But I like it. I like the excitement. I won three thousand pounds there one evening—the evening before I left."

The next morning, Prince George rejoined his ship, and Buller did not see him again until he heard of the Prince's brother's death; and, later, at the end of the Prince's naval career. By this time, Buller was in the Mediterranean.

Like the *Inflexible* before her, H.M.S. *Victoria* was one of the wonder ships of her day, an awesome and reassuring spectacle for the people of a maritime nation dependent upon its Navy for its security. As she lay at anchor in Valetta harbour in October 1892, fresh from maneuvers with the Mediterranean Fleet, she looked like some gigantic flat-iron miraculously floating on the still, blue water. Her nickname, however, was "the slipper"; and with her sister ship *Sans Pareil*, "the pair of slippers."

The age of sail-and-steam compromise was finally over. This 10,000-ton black-and-white monster, surely the ugliest warship ever constructed, did not carry a stitch of sail. Far belowdecks, her 14,500-h.p. triple-expansion engines could push her through the water at over 17 knots, the twin side-by-side funnels belching black smoke that trailed for miles astern, the water foaming over her low bows and forecastle deck.

Forward of the *Victoria*'s bridgework was the battleship's *raison d'être*, a pair of guns even larger than the *Inflexible*'s, of 16.25-inch caliber. In most previous ironclads, the barrels of the big guns were tucked into casemates or turrets or were little seen behind barbettes. There was none of that modesty about the *Victoria*. The Navy had at last come round again to breechloaders, and these guns projected prominently like twin probosci from some deadly insect.

It was clear that the *Victoria* was designed, with typical British self-confidence, for firing at a fleeing enemy. But in the unlikely contingency of having to fire astern, there was a ten-inch gun situated aft, and numerous smaller guns—six-inch and 6-pounder quick-firers—were ranged along the upper and the spar decks.

Rod had first seen her running down the slip at her launch in May 1887. She was the first ironclad battleship built in the Armstrong shipyard, and her guns, too, had been cast in the Elswick Works, the biggest guns ever to come from Armstrong. And because they were breechloaders, Rod felt a proprietorial pride in them. Hadn't his father given his life in the cause of the breech-loading gun? And now this much delayed acceptance of the more efficient gun structure, pioneered with the help of his father, seemed to go some way towards compensating for that terrible accident when Rod had still been an infant.

Rod, whose life for so long had been bound up in the sea and ships and guns, comforted himself with the belief that the Navy's return to breechloaders was his father's belated bequest to Britain. If there had been a major war at sea during the past quarter century, the Royal Navy would have been—perhaps fatally—at a disadvantage. Now, with ships like the *Victoria* with her Armstrong guns, Britain could win another Trafalgar against the French.

And now here she was, filling her intended function, Flagship of the Mediterranean Fleet, helping to ensure the free flow of trade from Gibraltar to Suez, ready to show the flag in any troubled area bordering this sea which Britain called her own—*mare nostrum*—in spite of a quaint French belief to the contrary. The whole might of the Fleet was anchored in columns in the harbour: the *Sans Pareil*, the *Edinburgh*, the *Nile*, the *Inflexible*, whose performance at Alexandria Rod remembered so vividly, the *Collingwood*, the *Phaeton*, and the *Dreadnought*, and there beyond the *Dreadnought*, the Flagship of the second-in-command, H.M.S. *Camperdown*.

She was one of the formidable "Admiral" class, only recently completed in answer to new French construction— twin white funnels in tandem, her four 13.5-inch breechloaders placed fore and aft in open barbettes, her bow sharp as a razor for ultraclose action ramming of the enemy.

Rod had witnessed this scene often—great black-and-white men-o'-war of 12,000 tons down to the little auxiliaries and torpedo boats, the bristling guns contrasting with gleaming brasswork and polished teak, the signal flags fluttering their messages, the white ensigns at the stern of every vessel, the union flag floating in the wind from the jack staff at the bows. But it never failed to impress him and fill him with pride.

The old fears he had experienced ten years earlier as he lay recovering from his wound had long since faded. Chief Petty Officer Roderick Maclewin, instantly recognizable by his short stature and broken nose, wearing the distinctive gilt buttons of his rank, with crossed guns and with stars and crown on his sleeve, was now a mature and steady twenty-eight years of age; a trusted and experienced member of the *Undaunted*'s company, who also knew as much about guns and gunnery as did the chief Gunnery Officer himself.

The *Undaunted* came slowly to her buoy, exchanging signals of courtesy with the Flagship. "Slow astern both!" the Captain ordered, the order at once recorded on the ship's telegraph, bells ringng far belowdecks in the engine room.

Lord Charles Beresford was standing on the starboard wing of his ship's bridge, surveying the scene with a glum expression. He turned to Rod. "What do you make of it, Midge?"

"Marvellous sight, isn't it, sir."

Beresford snorted. "All sham and glitter. Fine men, rotten ships. I keep tellin' 'em at home, we wouldn't stand a chance against the Frenchies at Toulon. They've better ships, better guns, better ammunition and more of it. It was before you joined us, Midge, but when we began this commission I checked the stores here—no spare guns for us, and only a single replacement outfit of ammunition. Two short engagements and we could have opened the sea cocks for all the use we'd have been, eh?"

"But the *Victoria*, sir," Rod protested loyally. "The French have got nothing as good as her, surely?"

"*Victoria, Dreadnought, Inflexible, Camperdown*—all the same, Midge," and he pointed in turn at the vessels that were the pride of the Mediterranean Fleet. "All armour in the middle, like a damned cummerbund. Nothin' at each end. One heavy shell, and they'd be like pricked balloons." He liked that analogy and repeated it more loudly to his Navigating Lieutenant. "Pricked balloons, eh, Pilot?"

"Yes, sir," said the officer obediently, "pricked balloons," and returned his attention to the capstan, its hawser, and the buoy.

"Wrote about it to *The Naval and Military Gazette* last week," continued Beresford. " 'Damn fool lot of ships we've got here,' I wrote. 'One shell or a ram in the right place and —glug, glug! The Good Lord knew better when he built us. A good big rib cage for the heart and lungs, eyes set well back in the skull, even the crotch's got the pelvis for protection against a beam shot.' "

"You wrote that, sir?" Rod asked in amazement.

Beresford turned and looked down at him, his plump face suddenly assuming a mischievous expression. "Somethin' like it. But *you'll* be all right. *We'll* all be all right. We can beat the Frenchies any time—you with your guns and your luck, eh, Lucky Midge?" Deep belly laugh.

They had picked up a buoy scarcely more than a cable from the Flagship, and—formalities completed—Beresford now put his glass to his eye and aimed it at the *Victoria's* fore superstructure. "Ah, there's the ol' boy, in his leather armchair on the chart-house roof. Always the same, ol' Georgie. And that chair—must've been made before Nelson was born." He was talking to himself now: "Damned if it wasn't." And he waved his hat in the direction of his Admiral and Commander-in-Chief.

Rod could identify Admiral Tryon with the naked eye, a tall, stout figure, now standing up and physically dominating his staff about him. Rod had never spoken to this august figure and had been close to him only once. There was no need for the rings on his sleeves or the glittering epaulettes to confirm that here was the master, the leader of men, the Commander-in-Chief of a great fleet. Everything about George Tryon spelled dominance and inborn self-assurance—at sixty years, more confident and commanding than ever. He had a full nose—almost a Buller nose—and had worn for decades a full beard, now grey like what still remained of his hair. A thick neck contrasted oddly with a rather feminine, cupid's bow mouth; broad shoulders; hard, muscular hands; short, spatulate fingers.

In the Petty Officers' mess everything there was to know about the Admiral had long since been discussed and dissected. If a course of success could be traced upon a chart, George Tryon had navigated it with a skill worthy of Captain Cook. "There never was such a nice place as Eton," he had once declared. He entered the Navy at sixteen, a top pass in his examinations, favouritism on the highest level, joined the Naval Brigade and thus saw a lot of hard fighting in the Crimean War, was selected by the Queen to serve in the Royal Yacht—sure passport to honours—and later was appointed Commander in the *Warrior*, first ever ironclad, premier fighting ship of the Navy of her time.

There was an old, grizzled Chief Petty Officer in the *Undaunted* who had served in the *Warrior* and told the tale of how she had been sent to escort Princess Alexandra from Denmark for her wedding to the Prince of Wales, and marvellously guided the Royal Yacht through the intricacies of the Thames estuary. "Princess is much pleased," came the welcome signal. The Tryon touch again.

Promotion to Captain over the heads of many of his contemporaries, the Companionship of Bath, and then appointment as A.D.C. to Queen Victoria. Applauded in all that he did, George Tryon was early destined for the highest honours and promotion, right up to Admiral of the Fleet and First Naval Lord.

Could there be a fault somewhere, concealed beneath this bounding self-confidence, this ironclad authority? In the hierarchical society of a distant fleet isolated from common life ashore, the Commander-in-Chief could assume a near-godlike stature; a god to be feared and respected at all times, and to such a degree that his word was unquestioned wisdom.

Nelson had dealt with this problem, which could become a danger in war, by creating his "Band of Brothers," his Captains and friends, who would meet in his cabin and talk strategy and tactics, the nature and the *matériel* of the enemy, and everything that related to the success and well-being of the Fleet: a forerunner of the twentieth century's Naval Staff.

In the *Victoria*, Tryon's Flag-Captain, his Flag-Lieutenant, his Staff-Commander, and the rest were all experienced and competent officers. But was there, lingering within the hearts of all of them, a fear of their formidable Admiral?

And—was there one other danger? Perhaps not, for alcohol flowed freely in the Royal Navy; heavy drinking was a historical tradition going back to the days when life was insupportable without the uplift of rum and wine, with "Dutch courage" issued to the lower deck before action. Yet, in a Navy of heavy drinkers, George Tryon was regarded as a heavy drinker: never to show it, of course, for that was beyond contemplation. But, all the same . . . It was something that was known in the Petty Officers' mess in the *Undaunted*, and in every mess in every ship of this great Fleet, where there were no secrets.

Beresford turned to Rod, angry and his expression transformed. "Where's my damn cox?" He did not like to be kept waiting.

Rod said smartly, "I'll send someone, sir. I'll—"

"You cox my gig." Brightening at the idea and mellowed by it as rapidly as the dark cloud had passed over his face seconds earlier: "Yes, that'll shock the old boy—coxed by a Chief Gunner. Put him off his dinner, shouldn't wonder."

The *Undaunted*'s well-disciplined crew had also learned to be adaptable to their Captain's unpredictable whims. When the leading seaman cox appeared, only half a minute late, he accepted the situation at once, backed away and saluted without a word. For his part, Beresford took not the slightest notice of him and tripped down to the waiting boat behind Rod.

There was a further break with tradition as Rod brought the gig alongside the battleship's platform. "Come on, Midge," Beresford called out cheerfully, just as if they were on a spree. "We'll go and meet the old man together."

So, instead of remaining with the boat, Rod ran up the companion ladder behind his Captain and was piped on board with him. Admiral Tryon had, quite properly, come out on deck to meet Beresford. After exchanging salutes, the Admiral glanced at Rod and said censoriously, "Really, Charlie, do you always use a Chief Gunner as cox?"

Although Beresford laughed cheerily at the question and appeared to enjoy the impression he had made, it was also clear that Tryon did not share his pleasure in the break with decorum.

Rod's reaction to the famous Admiral who had had such a brilliant career, was, "Oh, but he's an old man now!" He knew that the Admiral was sixty, but he looked much older, a man worn out before his time, face above his beard wrinkled, prominent broken veins on the big nose; the eyes, which must once have shone with good health, noting all about him shrewdly, now appeared slow to react. No diminution of authority. But . . . The Admiral stared doubtfully at Beresford for a moment before turning to his Flag-Lieutenant, Lord Gillford, a slight, dark, bearded officer who followed his master and his every word with tense concentration.

"Have you ever heard of a Captain employing his Chief Gunner as his cox, Gillford?" he demanded, determined not to let the subject drop.

"No, sir. I can't say that I have, sir."

Tryon swung his big head back towards Beresford slowly, like the bows of an ironclad in need of a tug. "You see, Charlie, my Flag-Lieutenant has never heard of a Chief Gunner acting as cox." There was silence between the two men for a moment; then, as if slowly awakening to the social requirements of the occasion, the Admiral brightened and put an arm across Beresford's shoulders. "Well, how are you, Charlie? How many ships have you saved this time? The Froggies'll be giving you a medal, shouldn't wonder." He was referring to Beresford's successful salvaging of the cruiser *Seignelay*, given up for lost by her Captain.

The two officers paced away together, their conversation

fading until they were out of earshot. Then Rod heard another voice, a familiar voice from the past.

"Well, cox, you really had the Admiral rattled then." There was a familiar laugh and Rod turned to find himself looking up at the figure of Lieutenant Buller. Tryon's staff had retired, leaving the old friends alone together on the battleship's upper deck.

"Sir, how very good to see you! I didn't know you were in the *Victoria*." Rod saw that Buller had put on weight and that his hair was receding. But the smile—friendly, conspiratorial, good-natured—was unchanged, making Rod feel the warmth he had just expressed in words.

"I'll tell you something else you don't know," said Buller. "You're transferring to the Flagship. Promotion, in a way."

"Under you?"

Buller nodded. "Well, under the Commander. How do you fancy being Chief Gunner in a battleship?"

The surprise was still showing on Rod's face, leading Buller to add with a laugh, "A-hundred-and-ten-ton guns—bigger than your nine point twos, eh?"

"But what about the *Undaunted*?"

"She's going home to pay off. And our gunner's gone down with Malta fever."

Tryon and Beresford returned from pacing the deck, and the Admiral prepared to descend to his cabin, Lord Gillford reappearing like a ghost ship from behind a ventilator to accompany him.

Buller saluted Beresford, who said to Rod, "Well, Midge, we're losing you. I'm taking the *Undaunted* home to stir up some mud about the state of this Fleet." He nodded towards the fore part of the ship where the 16.25-inch guns projected menacingly from their turret. "And you'll help look after these peashooters." He winked at Buller. "They shake the ship about when you let 'em off, eh?"

"We've only had firing practice once or twice, sir. Starts so many rivets and breaks so much glass that the Captain doesn't like it."

Beresford said grimly, "That's something else I'll take up when I get home. 'Battleships in the Mediterranean, when they *do* have ammunition, don't dare fire it off in case they shake to bits.' That'll be one for the First Lord to answer."

Whatever the faults of the Mediterranean Fleet's ships might be, at evolutions they were unsurpassed. Reincarnated, Admiral Tryon would have made a marvellous choreographer. Precision and complexity were the twin watchwords of his philosophy in maneuvers, and he practiced the Fleet constantly and tirelessly. He was not a man who was easily satisfied, but he derived the greatest pleasure from his command in observing his Captains moving their ships in elaborate evolutions and making geometric patterns with their wakes on the surface of the Mediterranean Sea.

Tryon had recently created a new and simplified form of signalling. It was called "The T.A. System" and was intended to make the response of his ships even speedier. "The design and object of the T.A. System," he once wrote, "is to provide for the time when no signals are reasonably to be relied upon." All he had to do was to hoist the T.A. signal, and from that moment the ships of the Fleet or a squadron merely observed the movements of the Flagship, or of the guides of the divisions, and conformed to their movements without further communication.

"A very little practice," continued Tryon's introduction, "will show that sufficient accuracy for safety and all practical purposes is easily secured."

No signals? "Outrageous!" "The man's mad!" muttered old Admirals. The Earl of Huntley sent Tryon a five-page telegram of invective when he heard of it. *The Times* called T.A. "Unsound in theory and perilous in practice."

All this only served to encourage Admiral Tryon to redouble the use of T.A. and further intensify his demands for absolute perfection.

Rod observed T. A. for the first time the following day. He had said good-bye to Beresford and to his shipmates on board the *Undaunted* and moved his gear into the battleship. The *Undaunted*'s commission had been an eventful one, like all of Beresford's commissions, full of crises, excitements, and honours, from Royal visits to Greece, to further policing activities in Egypt and the first experiments in high-speed mine-dropping from the ship.

Besides, Beresford was one of Admiral Tryon's oldest friends and deserved the splendid send-off his ship was given. Soon after 8:00 A.M., the entire Mediterranean Fleet raised steam and then raised anchors and proceeded out of Valetta harbour, and—under T.A.—formed up into single line ahead, making a line of men-o'-war miles long, with the *Undaunted* as rear guard.

Then, with masterly precision, which no other Navy in the world could have matched, and with no signal fluttering from the Flagship, each vessel turned 16 points to port in succession, reversing its course. As the first, and then the second and the third in turn passed Beresford's cruiser, the ship's company cheered.

When it was the *Victoria*'s turn, Rod was in the chart house. He put a telescope on the *Undaunted*'s bridge as the two vessels swept past each other, the smoke from their funnels joining and rising into the blue sky as one. There was Lord Charles Beresford on the bridge wing, his Navigating Lieutenant beside him. He saluted the Flagship smartly, then turned to his Lieutenant. Rod could imagine what he was saying, "Damn fools seem to like us, or somethin', Pilot."

Rod decided that he would miss his old Captain, as he always did: he would miss his passionate interest in everything and in everyone, his fanatical determination to make the Navy strong and efficient, his broad humour and eccentric ways, his self-confident skill, his indiscretions even, but above all, his kindness. Rod went out of the chart house to the rail, took off his cap, and cheered with the rest.

Buller was sharing a bottle of Madeira in the *Victoria*'s wardroom with Mark Holly and the ship's Padre, Alan Jones, a genial Welshman from Cardiff. The wardroom was one of the largest in the Navy, panelled in fumed oak upon which there were numerous paintings and photographs of naval harbours, naval vessels, and notable naval figures. Admiral Cuthbert Collingwood stared stonily from one wall, over a dozen chintz-covered armchairs, at his one-time Flagship, H.M.S. *Victory*, whose painting hung above the mahogany fireplace. Scattered about on the tables—some of Indian marble with legs shaped like an elephant's, others of dark teak with elaborately carved legs—were copies of *The Illustrated London News*, *The Army and Navy Gazette*, *Vanity Fair*, and month-old copies of *The Times*. The *Victoria* was still at anchor in Valetta harbour, and they might have been in the United Services Club in Pall Mall, except that the temperature was in the upper 90s, a level which the slow-moving ceiling fan did very little to ease. The Padre had just arrived from the sick bay where he had been giving spiritual comfort to a number of ratings and the ship's Commander, John Jellicoe, for Malta fever. "Well, gentlemen, when are we leaving for our summer maneuvers?" he asked the two Lieutenants. "The sooner we get away from this unhealthy island and get some air moving through the ship the better."

Holly unwound his long legs, stretched, and ordered another glass for Buller and himself. "The day after tomorrow, a little birdie tells me. But if you think Malta is unhealthy, wait until you try Beirut or Alexandria. At least Malta is an island and gets a bit of a breeze."

"Is that where we're heading?" The Padre was new to the Navy. Known to all as Jones the Priest, he was also the object of near-continuous teasing.

"Buller said, "Padre, in Alex last time I was there the temperature was a hundred and thirty. And the entire ship's company converted to Islam. Not a Christian left on board. That's what the heat did to them."

Eight bells sounded and officers on the forenoon watch entered the wardroom. The whole ship was discussing the imminent summer maneuvers, their likely itinerary, and above all, the competitive element between the two divisions. The second-in-command of the Mediterranean Fleet and Commander of the second division was Admiral Albert Hastings Markham, cousin of the explorer and geographer Sir Clements Markham. Markham was a talented officer and sailor who gave the impression that he did not very much enjoy being either. In a service notable for robust philistinism, Bertie Markham most enjoyed reading works of philosophy and of archeology. He would dearly have liked to join his cousin in his work, but—penurious all his life—he lived on his service pay. One of his few pleasures since he had been appointed second-in-command of this Fleet was his expeditions ashore to some of the great archeological sites of the Middle East, and he was known to be looking forward to the summer maneuvers for this reason.

But rumour from his Flagship, the *Camperdown*, suggested that the Admiral was not looking forward to the maneuvers for another reason, and that was his fear of George Tryon. Bertie Markham was physically bold, as he had proved in Arctic expeditions and in military campaigns in China. But he was also of a nervous disposition, and like some other bachelors, tetchy and overconcerned with the routine of his life. His staff found him difficult. Buller had heard from one of them that he had never been known to give praise to anyone.

Admiral Markham was easily intimidated by powerful personalities. Some years earlier, he had been outwitted by Tryon on maneuvers and had not enjoyed the experience. During the year in which he had served in his present command, the whole Fleet had observed that he found it difficult to stand up against the powerful and dominant personality of the Commander-in-Chief.

A fellow Gunnery Lieutenant, who sat down next to Buller and ordered a bottle of champagne from a waiter, said, "I don't know about you, Archy, but I think old Tryon's temper gets fouler every day." He then recited the details of an incident in which the language had been "perfectly horrid."

"It's his leg," said Buller.

"What's the matter with his leg?"

"The Doc was in his cups the other evening and told me he's got an ulcer on his leg. 'As big as your fist,' he said. But he was drunk and of course told me later I mustn't breathe a word to anyone or the old man would be hopping mad. So I said, 'Hopping with pain with that size ulcer.'"

The gong sounded for luncheon and they arose from their chairs, chatting on the way to the table—shining white cloth, fine-cut decanters and wine glasses, silver cutlery, and silver competition cups and a model of the *Victoria* down the center.

"You know old Pommie Davies in the *Camperdown*—he says Markham'll apply for a shore appointment if—"

"It's obvious what'll happen. Our old man'll make rings round the second div—"

"Onny Onslow says he's so nervous he shakes sometimes—"

"We're going to Beirut first."

"Tell that to the marines."

"A marines officer told me, actually, old boy."

Laughter, rumours, rumours of rumours. Only Grace put an end to it. Suddenly dignified in his professional role, the Padre, head lowered, said, "For what we are about to receive . . ."

Someone's guess had to be right, and it was Buller's. His prediction was that it would be May 27 when they left Malta, and so it was; and he won ten guineas. He gave the whole lot to the *Victoria*'s charity fund for the sick children of Newcastle. It was like Buller to gamble, to win, and then to give away his winnings. (Back at home, Clemmie still sometimes despaired of his gambling and his extravagance.)

The *Victoria* led out the Fleet from Valetta harbour in the afternoon, and everyone was relieved to be at sea again.

The *Camperdown* took up the rear guard, already watched critically by Tryon, who was in his customary position in his old leather armchair on the deck over the chart house. Earlier in the day, someone had overheard the Admiral say to his Flag-Captain, the Honourable Archibald Maurice Bourke, "The only way we'll get the second division up to the Mediterranean form is to go on and on at 'em. And that's what I'm going to do."

Soon, they would rendezvous with the other four battleships of the second division, which had been away in the Levant, and then the exercises and evolutions would begin in earnest.

On June 17 the combined Fleet was at Beirut, where at last they rested and were given shore leave for five days. Admiral Markham was the first ashore, and one of those most in need of a rest. Archeology would occupy him until it was time to leave, and it was said that he looked a new man after the relaxation of his hobby and first love.

The only special ceremony occurred on June 20, the fifty-sixth anniversary of the accession of Queen Victoria. The ship named after her, and all her consorts, too, dressed in honour, and at noon the citizens of Beirut were shocked into believing their last moment had come when the eleven battleships simultaneously fired a twenty-one–gun salute.

At 9:45 A.M. on June 22 anchors were weighed, and slowly and in stately procession the *Victoria*, the *Nile*, the *Dreadnought*, the *Collingwood*, the *Phaeton*, the *Edinburgh*, the *Camperdown*, and the rest proceeded out of the harbour into the open sea. They were due to make the short passage to Tripoli, Lebanon, and to anchor there to show the flag and the might of the Royal Navy that same evening.

Three-twenty P.M. Nearly the end of the afternoon watch. Buller had no duties to perform, no business on the chart house deck. But he reckoned that it would be cool up there, with an awning rigged above, and it would be interesting to observe at close hand his Admiral conducting the last evolutions before entering the harbour.

On the way up, Buller passed through the starboard seamen's mess deck where the men off watch were yarning or darning or lying half-asleep on the mess tables. Those who saw him in time got up and stood briefly to attention. He exchanged words with several ratings he knew by name, gunners mostly—a fat, jovial leading seaman straight out of *H.M.S. Pinafore*; a youngster from Leeds named Broughton whom Buller had seen grow from a frightened, half-starved boy to a fit, hard, brown young man in a few months.

"Ever been to Tripoli, sir?" called out another. "Are the girls tasty, sir?" A gust of laughter. Buller climbed up to the bridge, satisfied, as always, to be at ease with these men. There was a dead flat calm, the sea scarcely ruffled so that the *Victoria*'s stem was a diamond scoring a clean straight line across glass. Ahead, the white buildings of Tripoli could be clearly distinguished, though pulsing in the heat haze, the Tower of the Lions rising high above them.

The Fleet was already entering the wide bay north of the city, the purple rolling foothills rising and fading with the distance to the mountains of Lebanon—Mount Aruba, and to the south and higher still, Qurnet es Sauda; a land heavy in heat and history.

Buller was joined on the chart-house deck by Holly, who was as curious as he was about the Admiral's plans to anchor the Fleet. "Bertie Lanyon told me he's got a new trick up his sleeve," Holly said conspiratorially. "And look, here they come."

Tryon, Captain Bourke, Staff-Commander Hawkins-Smith, Officer-of-the-Watch Charlie Collins, Midshipman Lanyon, who was acting as Captain's *aide-de-camp*, and the Yeoman of Signals were all walking purposefully and in strict order of rank from the after bridge along the gangway above the spar deck to the fore bridge. Disregard the evidence of rank on sleeve, epaulette, and headgear; still no one could have doubts about who was in command. George Tryon, mighty in girth, height, and presence, vanguard officer in vanguard Flagship, paced towards his rightful station of command.

Though they were behind the party and half-obscured by funnels, stays, and masts, Buller could identify the other battleships of the first division: Gerard Noel's *Nile*, *Dreadnought*, *Inflexible*, *Collingwood*, and *Phaeton* in undeviating line-ahead and only two cables apart. And to port and very close—a mere six cables—the stately *Camperdown*, white upper works shimmering in the sun, Admiral Markham clearly identifiable with his staff on the fore bridge; astern the four battleships of his Second division: eleven battleships in all, the priceless cream of the Royal Navy about to demonstrate once again the precision and the unmatched skill of the great Fleet coming to anchor in a foreign port.

"We'd better leave," said Holly, making his way towards the iron ladder that provided a quick route to the deck below. The chart-house deck was no more than a small platform four or five yards square and this space was obstructed by stays and shrouds supporting the mainmast signalling yard above. The area was further confined by the wheel, compass binnacle, Tryon's armchair, and Tryon himself.

Buller hesitated, and before he could follow Holly down the ladder, Tryon burst onto the deck from the after ladder, red-faced and panting from the exertion; and suddenly the area was so crowded that Buller decided to remain quietly in the corner, watching the Yeoman bending on two signals in swift succession.

Buller saw the little coloured flags fluttering out on the yardarm above, and read:

> Second division alter course in succession 16 points to starboard preserving the order of the Fleet.

The second signal, addressed to the five battleships astern, was identical, except that the order was to turn to port.

So that was what Lanyon meant by the Admiral's having a new trick up his sleeve! With the coast looming ahead, the entire Mediterranean Fleet speeding towards it at 9 knots, the two divisions were to turn inwards, in succession, ship by ship, so that they would reverse course but keep the same order for anchoring. Very neat! A brilliant display, that would make.

Tryon was holding and leaning heavily on the rail at the after end of the deck, swaying slightly though there was no motion, at his side Captain Bourke, whose offer of the leather armchair was shrugged aside. Then both men gave their silent attention to the vessels of the *Victoria*'s own division. Among the rest of the officers there was quiet but anxious conversation, no more than a murmur until Lord Gillford suddenly called out loudly to Lanyon, "Take the distance to the *Camperdown*."

Buller glanced to port. He had not until this moment realized how uneasily close was Admiral Markham's Flagship. "We can't all turn *inwards*," he said to Charlie Collins. "Not at the same time."

Lanyon, holding the angle board, called out to the Flag-Lieutenant, "Six cables, sir," emphasizing the number as if to draw special attention to it. But the broad back of the Admiral did not turn, and he remained in silence, or in inaudible conversation with his Captain, their heads close together.

"Six cables!" Buller exclaimed quietly to Charlie Collins. "Why that's madness—it's suicide!"

The Quartermaster gave the wheel a light touch, glanced at the bearing, glanced at Buller and Collins, the anxiety clearly showing in his steady blue eyes. He knew. They all knew. The twin signals must now have been read with mixed disbelief and dread by the whole Fleet, the message passed with the speed of an electric telegraph from deck to deck, clear down to the engine rooms. Six cables, 1,200 yards. And as the most ignorant new boy-recruit knew, the turning circle of all these great ships was not less than four cables. Multiply four by two . . .

"Of course it's suicide," said Collins. The Staff-Commander

and all the other officers were standing as if paralyzed by the heat and by the imminence of their inevitable fate. Only the Quartermaster appeared alive, beefy hands on the wheel's spokes, adjusting to port, to starboard, a shade port, steadying the 12,000 tons of steel on its course to destruction, either on the rocky coastline rapidly approaching, or, if they turned, on the collision course with the *Camperdown*.

For a few seconds it was so quiet that Buller could hear the distant beat of the engines and the swish of the sea along the side of the hull. Nine knots, more than 10 miles an hour, steady trotting speed. Why didn't anyone say something?

Then Tryon suddenly turned, pulling himself up to his full height. Buller recorded this picture of him for all time in the pictorial library of his memory: eyes staring angrily, face scarlet, hat slightly askew. "What are we waiting for?" he demanded of the company generally in a thick voice.

A pause. Then Lord Gillford: "I believe the *Camperdown*, sir. I'll just go aft and see if all the ships in our division have hauled up."

The two signals would have been repeated "at the dip" by each ship, then hauled close-up to confirm that they were understood.

Tryon stared at the officers about him—was it in challenge? or defiance? or . . . Momentarily his gaze rested on Buller's eyes only ten feet distant, and there was no trace of recognition or acknowledgment. More a wild blankness.

Admiral Tryon: "Yeoman, semaphore the *Camperdown*, 'What are you waiting for?' And instruct her to show her pendants." (The last, in effect, a public rebuke.)

This did the trick. The moment the clack of the semaphores ceased high up the masthead, Buller saw the *Camperdown*'s repeat hoist hauled close-up. The delay of about three minutes had brought the fleet far past the lines of bearing of their anchorage, and the coast looked now critically close.

Lord Gillford: "Yes, sir. The *Camperdown* is the only ship we are waiting for, sir." Tryon gave no sign of hearing this confirmation of news that was already out of date. Instead, the Admiral ordered the Quartermaster, "Go on to starboard," indicating an immediate turn to port.

Buller wanted to cry out, "No! That is fatal, sir!" The paralysis on the chart-house deck had suddenly been broken. As the great ship began to turn, jack staff moving from right to left across the configuration of the Syrian coastline, and the *Victoria* began to heel—causing Tryon to stagger—the officers began to talk among themselves, the Captain to his Admiral.

Captain Bourke: "We had better do something, sir." He pointed at the great black-and-white bulk of the *Camperdown*, already turning inwards towards them, the funnel smoke a black, ever-growing cloud. "We shall be too close to that ship."

No response from Admiral Tryon, only a tilt of the head towards Admiral Markham's Flagship. For a mad moment Buller asked himself, "Is he testing him? Testing his initiative? But, by God, it's already too late!"

Captain Bourke, urgently, desperately: "Take the distance, Mr. Lanyon." Perhaps five seconds, then, "Hurry, hurry!"

Midshipman Lanyon: "Three and a quarter cables, sir."

Captain Bourke: "We had better do something, sir. We shall be very close to the *Camperdown*." But still no response. "We are getting too close, sir. We must do something, sir."

For the first time there came the sound of shouting from below. Instead of strolling about, the men were standing stock still or running. And the cries already contained a note of alarm.

The *Camperdown* was for one moment bows dead on, the sun shining on her decorated stem above the lethal ram bow, and the brass tampions of her big guns, a massive object of destructive power bearing down upon them.

"May I go astern with the port screw, sir?" asked Captain Bourke, this time repeating the question more rapidly when there was no reply.

Admiral Tryon contemplated the *Camperdown* again on

her collision course. There could be no avoidance now, only a reduction of impact. "Yes," he said in a dead voice. "Yes, go astern."

In rapid succession, Captain Bourke gave the orders, "Full speed astern port screw!" and "Full speed astern both screws!" Then the sound of the telegraph being put over and the bell ringing out.

For the first time, Lord Gillford noticed Buller standing in the far corner of the chart-house deck. "Hold on here, will you?" he said. "You may be needed."

Buller nodded and turned to look at the approaching bows of the *Camperdown*. He could see down the full length of the port side of Markham's Flagship, from the jack staff, past the fore barbette with the exposed pair of 13.5-inch guns, the bridge crowded with officers—standing as if supervising a Royal Review rather than helplessly observing an imminent catastrophe; past the open six-inch gun ports to the white ensign at the stern. Her silhouette was changing at every passing second as both ships closed the distance on full helm. But the laws of geometry made avoidance impossible, by a matter of two cables or more, 400 yards, a bit less than a quarter of a mile.

"She'll strike us just beneath the bridge," Buller found himself calculating. "Or perhaps forward." But well outside the armoured belt—Lord Charles Beresford's cummerbund.

Bertie Heath on the bridge below was shouting to the bo'sun's mate, "Pipe 'Close the watertight doors and out the collision mat.'"

At every moment new sounds—alarm sounds of the *Camperdown*'s foghorn, of the *Victoria*'s bugler sounding the "Gs"; the deep, rough sound of men's voices and the patter of bare feet on teak decks that evoked scenes of mass games or of gymnastics rather than of crisis.

Buller called out to a group of ratings running aimlessly towards the bows, "Look sharp to the collision mats, you men." White faces looking up, fear and indecision upon them. Pause. Then, the habit of years of discipline still gripping them: "Aye aye, sir." A quick salute. Running fast for the port side of the forecastle where the mats were stowed and where others were already at work.

"Go astern! Go astern!" It was Admiral Tryon's voice. The Commander-in-Chief was shouting through cupped hands—not even with a megaphone—at his second-in-command, petulantly, like a prefect at a recalcitrant junior. But the voice would be inaudible on the *Camperdown* above the sound of the foghorn, which still blared mournfully as if crying, "Look out, I'm coming!"

The *Victoria's* helm had been put over at exactly 3:31 P.M. and forty-five seconds by the ship's chronometer. At 3:34 the ram of the *Camperdown*, like a butcher's cleaver, stove into the starboard side of the *Victoria* sixty-five feet from her stem, and just forward of the gun turret, with a power of almost precisely 17,500 foot-tons.

Buller watched it slice into his ship's hull with clinical fascination, and a certain satisfaction, too, because the blow had come exactly where he had predicted it would. From his knowledge of the ship's geography, he also now calculated that the base of the ram would penetrate in turn the carpenters' stores in the hold, the number one reserve coal bunker (situated there to diminish the damage from a shell hit, but not an 11,000-ton battleship travelling at 6 knots), and the Petty Officers' mess.

"The ram," Buller had read in a manual not so long ago, "is the prime weapon of destruction at sea." He had laughed at this outdated statement. But, under these peacetime circumstances, it was proving correct.

The impact was more of a nudge than a crash. No tearing, rending sound. A bump, as if the ship had come alongside a quay a touch too fast. The sound better matched the occasion—an explosion, but not a very loud one. The visual effect, too, was of a modest-caliber shell hit, black dust, chunks of metal flying, the heavy teak deck crushed at the center of the impact and folding back untidily on each side. The two battleships were locked in a deadly embrace; and—it crossed

Buller's mind—if they had been in combat, Royal Marines would now be advancing across the forecastle deck preparing to board, bayonets fixed, perhaps with drawn cutlasses even, just as in Nelson's time.

A semaphore signal was being made from the *Camperdown*, a delayed explanation of delay to the Admiral, as irrelevant now as the cry of a dead man: "Because I did not quite understand your signal."

Tryon had managed to acquire a megaphone and put it to his lips. "Go astern, go astern," he shouted again. "Go astern with both engines." Then, "Why didn't you . . . ?" The voice was lost at a dozen feet, the distance Buller stood from him; at 150 feet, the distance to Admiral Markham, standing surveying the scene with an inscrutable expression upon his face, not a word would have been heard: an inaudible, unanswerable question.

Buller said to Lord Gillford, "That'll be like uncorking a bottle."

"And that'll be no worse than what's happening now," replied the Flag-Lieutenant. He was referring to the slow, implacable closing together of the two battleships' sterns, causing the ram to tear the breach open wider.

Then Admiral Tryon spoke, still clutching the megaphone but no longer using it. He was addressing his Staff-Commander, and Buller could hardly believe his ears. "D'you think she'll continue to float?"

Hawkins-Smith, once the sound, steady Commander, replied, "I think she ought to keep afloat as the damage is so far forward. Shall we steer for the land and try to beach her, sir?"

They continued to discuss the matter—Buller and Gillford exchanging incredulous glances—as if planning a commonplace evolution on maneuvers, while the *Camperdown* slowly dragged herself clear, and the sea poured into the bowels of the Flagship in a torrent, and the *Camperdown*, the nearby *Nile*, and other ships began lowering boats as fast as they could to pick up survivors of the inevitable catastrophe.

Lord Gillford said to Tryon, reporting good news, "The *Dreadnought*'s lowering boats, sir."

The Admiral turned angrily on his Flag-Lieutenant, as if he were personally responsible for this affront, this issuing of orders without his authority. "Make a signal to annul sending boats," he shouted.

Of course they were not going to sink, here in front of the Fleet; the Fleet which mercifully had changed course again in time, and so failed to complete the turn inwards that must certainly have sunk the first five battleships of the division in turn; all in front of thousands of the citizens of Tripoli and of the coastal villages along the Lebanon shore.

The attempt to place the collision mat over the twelve-foot-wide gash in the *Victoria*'s side was like hoisting a main-sail in a hurricane, and one by one the men were dropping it and wading clear of the water rising above the forecastle deck.

Every scuttle, every vent, every port in the *Victoria* had been open in the heat of the afternoon, and the tonnage rate of water pouring into the ship was increasing. Yet, in the fantasy world of the chart-house deck, the orders came from the Admiral as if they had suffered no more than a passing mishap. Seven knots was ordered, 38 revolutions was the instruction to the engine room, where already men were drowning by the score. "Go astern with the port engine, ahead with the starboard, and point her clear of the *Nile*. And annul sending boats," he repeated, as if the suggestion of sinking was an outrage.

But reality was men struggling for their lives through the rising waters, it was Captain Bourke running aft and then below-decks to check that the watertight doors were being closed, it was Buller and Gillford ordering boats to be lowered, it was the Quartermaster, straining every muscle, crying out helplessly to Hawkins-Smith, "I cannot move the helm, sir. The pressure's off."

"Ring down to the engine room and tell them to keep the hydraulic pressure on," ordered the Staff-Commander. But as anyone must know—anyone but the Admiral and his Staff-Commander with his faith in Tryon undimmed—the pressure was off because the engines were already underwater, the fires doused.

It was five minutes since the collision, the list was 20 degrees, the gun turret, the gun barrels, were all but submerged. The *Victoria* gave a lurch, almost as if she had been struck a second blow. But a second blow was not needed. Some giant and no doubt vital part of the battleship's anatomy had shifted below, and Buller and Lord Gillford, almost thrown, clutched at the rail.

It also appeared to awaken Admiral Tryon to the reality of the situation. Buller heard him say, "I think she's going."

"Yes, sir, I think she is," confirmed the Commander, parrot-wise.

Lord Gillford, his mouth close to Buller's ear, "Yes, I think she is," in a mockery of his senior's voice.

"And I think it's time we left," said Buller, intending to help supervise the lowering of the boats.

Tryon was calling and Buller turned, attempting unsuccessfully to stand to attention. But it was Midshipman Lanyon he was addressing. "Don't stay there, youngster, go to a boat."

Buller glanced at his Admiral. He was standing awkwardly on the sloping deck, one arm clutching the rail, the other the megaphone, a grave, stately, great figure, all dignity intact in spite of the angle, all dress correct if cocked hat still a touch rakish, staring forward at no one and nothing in particular, as if posing for the portrait that would hang for all to admire in the hall of the family seat.

But the last words gave the lie to this impression of imperishable authority, of unquestioned accomplishment, of unbroken success. "It is entirely my doing," he said suddenly in a broken voice, "entirely my fault . . ."

Buller took the quick route down to the bridge, which was still deserted, then to the spar deck, where parties working under the direction of Midshipmen and Petty Officers were attempting to launch boats. No panic, no disorder; but increasing confusion as the water rose faster and faster, causing men to leave their posts and scramble for space. Buller saw a pair of Maltese bumboatmen canteen workers shouting and pushing, and then throwing themselves, terror-struck, into the sea. And at the same time, he recognized that there was no sense in fighting a losing battle with the boats, not at this angle.

Jimmy Collins was shouting, "Jump! jump!" and Buller joined him, chivying the men back from the davits. "Get clear and jump. Every man for himself but don't panic. Get clear of the ship."

The men had formed groups of varying size, finding comfort in numbers, and there were plenty of signs of mutual help. One of the surgeons was half carrying a rating suffering from Malta fever, and the Welsh chaplain had his arms about the shoulders of two boys, no more than fourteen, who were clearly alarmed. There was a big group at the stern, too, drawn there no doubt because it appeared as the place that would be last flooded by the sea, although already several had jumped from the great height above the rising stern, turning over and over in the air.

On the port side of the quarterdeck, the Captain had got a large group of men to form ranks of four. As Buller watched, they turned "Right about turn" as if on the parade ground at Portsmouth barracks, and marched forward, climbing over the rails, and were all gone from sight within seconds.

A voice from behind caused Buller to turn. It was Holly, a wry smile on his face, up to his knees in water and holding a davit stave for support. "Well, we've made a mess of things this time."

"Are we dreaming, Mark? I can't really believe it."

There was nothing dreamlike about the cries rising from the ventilator beside them, from men who were not fortunate enough to be able to form fours on the quarterdeck, but were trapped below by bulkheads and watertight doors screwed shut by their shipmates, and of stokers in the hell of the engine rooms.

"A bad do, old man."

A leading seaman splashed past, clutching his trousers round his waist, fresh from his off-watch sleep, and threw himself into the sea, striking out strongly.

Holly said, "He'll be all right." He bent down to untie his shoe laces. "There's nothing more to do here." Now he ripped off his jacket and slipped the braces from his shoulders. They were bright scarlet, his pride and joy although they had been the subject of much ribbing. "Come on, we'd better obey our own orders." The sea was already lapping at his waist and breaking over his shoulders, and he just bent down and swam away from the side of the ship with his strong breast stroke.

The *Victoria* was listing 50 degrees to starboard and was tilted at about 18 degrees forward. At any moment she must capsize. Buller looked up and saw smoke still pouring from the twin funnels high above as if she were still bravely leading the fleet at 9 knots. The sinister rumble of mighty movement from below blended with the fading sounds of anguish still rising from the ventilators, and there was much shouting both from those in the water and the few left on board.

High above, on the chart-house deck, Buller could make out two figures. They were the Admiral, as still as if transformed into the *Victoria*'s figurehead, and his Flag-Lieutenant.

"Richard, for God's sake, Richard, jump for it," Buller shouted. Lord Gillford looked down, and when he spotted Buller half-submerged on the deck below, waved in acknowledgment.

"The fool," Buller said aloud, "the damn fool. He's not the Captain or the Admiral—he doesn't have to . . ."

Buller's inability to swim was known by very few people, and certainly not by Holly or Lord Gillford. He scarcely bothered to acknowledge it to himself, so long had he taken it for granted. It was, after all, a family tradition. When he had given the matter thought, he had always assumed that he would chance on a spar or something to keep him afloat until he was picked up. At the last moment, he used his knife to sever a length of rope lying coiled on the deck and tied it round his waist. He was, after all, no worse off than hundreds of the *Victoria*'s ratings who were unable to swim— actually thought it a bit effete to be able to swim. And, anyway, the sea was warm and calm, and there would be plenty of debris to support him. There were already several chairs in sight, wooden folding ones, and he could always lash himself to one.

He decided he would just let the water come. He certainly felt no trace of fear, only a sadness at the loss of all those lives—the men belowdecks—and the loss of this great ship. And, inevitably, her Admiral . . .

In the Petty Officers' mess at 3:30 P.M. the ten armchairs were occupied by sleeping figures, weary from the heat and the rigours of the long summer maneuvers. All but two of them would be on watch in half an hour, but by then the Fleet should be safely at anchor, and many of the ship's company could expect shore leave for the evening. Not that Tripoli had much to offer . . .

The mess had a mock Tudor simulated fireplace with imitation coal. In cold weather, a concealed electric fire could be switched on. They were all proud of this fireplace, which was consideerd very up-to-date. Rod was one of the two who were awake. No warning of the alarm that was spreading on deck had reached the mess, and the first intimation of the collision was the crash and the shudder—much less than the concussion from firing the main armament, someone recalled later—and the simultaneous piercing of the ship's side.

The *Camperdown*'s ram split the bulkhead between the mess and the coal bunker, hurling great quantities of coal into the mess, tipping over chairs and unsecured tables, and half-filling the fireplace that had never known real coal. Rod was thrown out of his chair and—bruised and dazed and covered in black dust—found himself lying some distance away. By the time he sat up, the dust had sufficiently cleared to reveal the upper part of the ram and the torn great stem no more than twenty feet away.

Because naval messes are retreats from the public hurly-burly of shipboard life, their privacy is sacred, and Rod's first instinctive reaction was one of outrage at this intrusion. He was brought to his senses by the muffled groaning on all sides and the new sound of rushing water. Catastrophe had struck the *Victoria* in the shape before him of part of a huge ram that was grossly out of scale with the friendly domesticity of tables, chairs, and pictures.

A number of Petty Officers had been badly knocked about and needed help. One of them, First Class Petty Officer Wheeler, was incapable of movement. A large strip of jagged-edged iron had fallen across his leg. With three others, all as black with coal dust as he was, Rod managed to clear the debris. Someone else had brought a stretcher from the emergency store, and they raced him, half-conscious, to the sick bay.

By the time Wheeler was in the hands of the sick orderlies, the angle of the decks told Rod that the ship could not last for long. When he reached the upper deck, the sounds were not those of emergency action to save the ship, but of even more desperate action to save lives. His mind went back to that day fifteen years earlier on board the *Eurydice*. A flat calm now, blazing sun instead of biting northeast wind and snow, a new great Flagship—"unsinkable" they had said—instead of an old converted frigate. But the same scent of mass fear in the nostrils: *sauve qui peut*, every man for himself. And a Lieutenant just beyond that group struggling to launch a boat was shouting, "Jump! jump!"

One of the men attempting to launch a boom boat without the aid of the hydraulic machinery suddenly turned and sat down on the deck, head between his knees. Then he looked up and stared at Rod, and a weak smile spread across his face. "Well, you look a proper gollywog, Maclewin."

It was the ship's Commander, John Jellicoe, pale from weeks in his cabin, dressed only in shirt and trousers.

"Let me give you a hand, sir."

"I'll be all right. I'm a good swimmer." He turned to one of the gunnery Lieutenants and said, "Hullo, Arthur, we had better go down the side of the ship as she turns over."

A lot of the crew were doing this. It was the gentle way of going in. Rod saw the Commander holding on to the jackstay as the battleship capsized and began to go down bow first. As soon as Rod was in the water, he struck out strongly in order to get clear of the ship. There was already a lot of debris about, life-giving to the nonswimmers, obstructive to those who wanted only to get clear.

After a hundred yards, Rod turned and, treading water, looked back. It was the most dreadful sight he had seen in his life, awful in its scale, piteous in its agony, calamitous in its inevitability. The *Victoria* had all but gone, only the after end of her keel and her stern quarters were still above water, the twin four-bladed propellers seen through the smoke and steam clouds were still rotating. There were figures on the steeply sloping hull plates, the men most fearful of the water that was rising, white and frothing, like a tide about a rock.

The sea between this last vestige of the sinking Flagship and Rod was thick with debris and the heads of those still swimming and alive as well as little half-submerged humps, all that could be seen of those who had succumbed.

Most of the men nearest to Rod were exhausted. Some had found an object to support them; others still swam wearily and called for help. Rod put an arm under the shoulder of one young rating whose face was vaguely familiar and helped him to a piece of debris, part of a spar and rigging from the target he had helped to riddle with blank six-inch shells before they had gone to Beirut.

"The boats'll soon be here," he told him. "Hold on."

Some had put their faith in debris that was insufficiently buoyant and, with lungs full of water, had lost consciousness.

Rod, still swimming with strength and total confidence, approached several of these. Two men had lashed themselves to an oar from the whaler that had broken loose, but their heads were submerged, and when Rod turned them over, they slipped away in turn, their faces white, their eyes wide open in disbelief at their own end.

Another seemed more hopeful, lashed to a half-submerged chair that might have come from the Petty Officers' mess. Again, while treading water, Rod raised the head from behind and held it clear of the water. The first encouraging sign was the water escaping from his mouth. The man was spitting and retching, the sudden violence to his body causing him to utter a string of curses.

The line was securing him too tightly to the chair, which was losing its buoyancy anyway, and Rod, half-blinded with stinging salt water, managed to untie the knot and get the man's shoulders under his arms to drag him clear in the classic stance of life-saving.

"Just relax," he called. "Relax, and you'll be all right." He was a big fellow, quite limp in his arms, but Rod could hold him for a while, until the boats came. It would not be long. There was a lot of shouting close by, and he thought he had caught a glimpse of a ship's launch before he had taken on this burden.

The man lay close above him, in intimate embrace, his long hair against his face and over his eyes. It was better to keep moving; the weight seemed to ease when he kicked out. He was swallowing a lot of water himself now, and each time he spat out it interrupted the deep rhythm of his breathing, which led to more water getting into his lungs. At one moment of near-surrender Rod found himself saying, "I'm going —we're both going." Then he remembered those words of the swimming instructor in the *Implacable*—"Panic is the worst enemy if you get into a tight corner . . ."

But Rod was close to the end when he heard voices very close. "A couple more here, Jack—easy now." Strong hands under his shoulders now, other hands taking the suffocating weight from his chest. A wonderful feeling of liberation, of relief.

Then he was on the launch's gunwale. "You're all right, Jack. We've got you—and the fellow you saved." Rod raised his head, opened his eyes.

Someone else was saying, "There she goes—oh God!" Rod dimly saw, as if through a thin screen, a massive cloud of smoke and debris rising like an erupting volcano from the mouth of a crater, the crater itself a circular wall of water spreading out, sweeping all before it. Then, a few seconds later, top hamper, bits of boats and whole boats, lockers and spars, anything buoyant and loose from below—from furniture to corpses—shot up as if every scuttle and vent, every opening in the battleship was the muzzle of a gun; shot up into the sky, killing and maiming many more who had survived the earlier convulsions.

When the smoke and spray began to clear, there was the *Camperdown* beyond, not more than two cables from the scene of the catastrophe which she had caused, herself hard down by the bows, her forecastle awash.

The voices in the rescue launch, dimly audible to Rod, were in clashing chorus. "Easy, easy to port there—right, I got 'im." "Look at the old *Camperdownlilly*—she's going, too." "Nah, she'll be all right." "This bloke's dead, Jock."

Then, clearly, an officer's voice. "Charlie, look. We'll get a medal for this—look at this one. Recognize him? Yes, look, he's nodding."

"And the bloke who saved him'll get a medal, too. His father'll see to that. Is he all right?"

Rod turned from gazing at the last scenes of the disaster and focused his eyes on the contrasting close-up scene of rescue and survival.

The bottom of the launch was littered with prone figures, the faces of the dead covered with blankets or pieces of clothing, others alive and receiving comfort from the crew. One of them, almost at Rod's feet, his head held up, was looking at him quizzically, a faint smile on his full lips. Yes, it was true. The *Victoria* had had a complement of 550 officers, Warrant Officers, Royal Marines, and ratings. Of these, say a half were still in the ship when she went down; and of those in the water, say half drowned, or were killed by debris or torn up in the screws. Still, it remained long odds on the one man Rod had been able to rescue being his old friend Archy Buller.

A croaking voice said, "That makes it one all, Midge."

Chapter XIII

"How many more?" asked Rod.

"A hundred—perhaps a hundred and fifty."

"And it'll be dark in half an hour."

The minister's wife, Mrs. Courage (and well named), dropped the bread knife and said in a despairing voice, "Would you take over, Roddy? My hand's got the cramp again."

They were all dead tired. A thousand children must have passed through the old Armstrong's frame-shop—great machines gaunt, still, silent—hands holding up bowls, like the scene in *Oliver Twist*. Rod and Rosie poured out a ladle of soup each, and Mrs. Courage cut half slices from the big loaves and dropped them into the bowls.

The everlasting queue was a river of pinched, pale faces beneath caps or plain bonnets ("You're to look *smart* for the kind ladies and gentlemen what're feeding you"), grubby hands clutching the bowls, some shaking from the cold so badly that Rod had to take the bowl from them before pouring.

All day it had been like this, ever since the minister had opened the great iron double doors at ten o'clock in the morning. Two policemen had been there at first, but the children were well behaved and had filed in, barefoot every one, chattering away cheerfully enough considering their condition. The frame-shop, disused for nearly eighteen months for lack of orders, before the slump had rung to the sound of metal upon metal and the clank of hydraulic machinery. Now it echoed all day long to the chirrup of children's voices.

Soup kitchens like this, in village halls or in any large empty buildings that had a roof, had spread all over the country where men worked in factories and yards, or down mines. The coal strikes had been on for nearly eleven weeks now, begun by a reduction in wages of 17.75 percent, and becoming more bitter and violent with the passing of every day. Mine owners' houses were wrecked, their lives threatened; the Dragoon Guards were called out in Nottinghamshire, the Inniskilling Dragoons in South Wales. Soldiers and police were at full stretch all over the country, and starvation—real starvation with working men's families dying—stalked the land. Revolution, it seemed, could not be far away.

At Armstrong's Elswick yards there had not been a ship on the stocks for months, and no orders were in sight. When Rod had come home in September with his medal for bravery, he had found Tyneside in a worse state than he had ever known it, and there was desperation in the face of many of the people he knew. His mother, recovering from the shock of the news of the *Victoria*'s sinking and the sharp relief that her son had been spared again, was one of the few who were not affected directly by the slump. Rod's allowance came through to her regularly, and he was earning £210 a year now, and Kate and William and their children were all right in their cottage at Cragside. But Doris Maclewin, now fifty-three, suffered as much in her heart as many of her neighbours from the hunger and cold and lived almost as frugally as they did, spending all her time and most of her money on local charities, on visits to the sick with food, and in helping the minister with calls on the most distressed.

As always, it was the children who worried her most. When Rod had arrived in Groom Road, his mother had been working for at least fourteen hours a day on charitable work of one kind or another and with the help of the Courages had just been getting the big soup kitchen going—though she refused to call it that. "Hot Food for Children" was the simple sign painted in white on the big iron doors. Doris Maclewin was tired and looked older than she was. Rod had at once ordered her to rest for a few hours a day, and then hurled himself into the work.

On that Saturday evening of October 1893, the soup and bread gave out as darkness fell, and there were still some twenty children waiting patiently.

Doris Maclewin was asking them gently to come back the next day, taking their names and promising they would be first to be served, when Kate and William arrived. Between them they carried a bag packed with leftovers from the Armstrong dining table—a great ham with scarcely a slice cut from it, a saddle of mutton, a cake that had never been cut, a pile of smoked salmon sandwiches—all the evidence of culinary riches the people of Elswick would never know.

"Come back, children," Doris Maclewin called out into the darkness from the doors. "You won't be going home hungry tonight."

Rod attacked the joints with the bread knife and cut up small portions of the cake, fearful that the richness of the food might be too much for these empty stomachs. William produced a lantern, and the seven of them portioned out this windfall among the children. Each child, as he or she came within the pool of yellow light from the lantern, looked up with eyes staring in wonderment at this sight of luxury that might have been the gold of Aladdin's cave.

That night, as Rod and Rosie lay in each other's arms, too tired to make love, Rod said, "I sometimes wonder whether this country is worth fighting for if there was a war."

"Why do you say that? England's a wonderful country." Rosie was genuinely shocked. "Nobody says things like that in the Navy. They would fight."

"Yes, I think they would fight," said Rod after consideration. "They would fight, and probably fight well, as British sailors always have. And I hope I would, too. But when you see how we live here, on Tyneside. And then how they live up at places like Cragside—fat and heavy with booze. The miners' strike could go on forever and they wouldn't notice."

"There'll always be poor and rich, Roddy."

"Not so poor, and so rich." He wondered whether to tell her. He did not want her to think he was growing bitter. And heaven forbid that she should think he did not want to go back to the Navy, as he hadn't, once long ago, for a different reason. In the end, he told her; he always did, in the end. She was his wife, he loved her, and he kept no secrets from her, just as he had kept no secrets from his mother in the past.

"I lost a lot of friends when the *Victoria* went down."

"Yes, I'm sorry," said Rosie, who had been half-asleep.

"And it need never have happened."

"Accidents do happen, and that was a terrible one. But you did all that you could—and more, Roddy." Wide awake now, she stroked his hair and kissed him. "And I'm very proud of you."

"It need never have happened. But there are a lot of Flag Officers in the Navy who have too much admiration, have too many toadying officers around them, and have too much to eat and drink—unlike our children today."

Rosie was genuinely shocked. "You mustn't say things like that, Roddy. You'll be court-martialled if you're heard."

"Oh, I don't," he said, and his laugh had an edge of bitterness. "But there are plenty who do. And there are plenty who said everyone was too frightened to tell Admiral Tryon that his order was suicidal, including Admiral Markham.

And there are others who say Admiral Tryon didn't know what he was doing."

"But he was a wonderful Admiral—everyone says so. He only thought of others at the end. That's what the newspapers said."

"And some of those others who were near to him say he had eaten too much luncheon. And drunk too much port—as usual. Three hundred and fifty-eight drowned, Rosie."

The mournful sound of a hooter from the river was a cry of lament for those trapped inside the battleship and for those who had succumbed before the boats could reach them. Of course, the court-martial at Malta had declared that no blame could be attached to Admiral Tryon—or to anyone else for that matter. "A proper old bloody whitewash," was the general opinion on the lower deck.

Other night sounds came through the window of the house next door to that of Doris Maclewin that Rod and Rosie rented. The cries of children, some of them no doubt from the pain of hunger; the sound of voices raised in anger down the alley; and in increasing volume, the sound of shouting and singing from the nearest pub round the corner, where some of the men out of work still had money to squander and to help them forget the misery of their lives.

Rosie was breathing regularly, her breath against his face. Now Rod wished he had not spoken. He had sounded bitter, he knew it. He had already said his prayers, as he always did before sleep; but he added another now, thanking God for his own good fortune and for the satisfied appetites of Tom and the two girls—Tom's younger sisters—in the next room.

Clemmie and Buller both liked May. She had seemed rather cool and distant at first when they had arrived to stay at Osborne, Queen Victoria's residence in the Isle of Wight. "Very shy," had been Clemmie's comment. But May had soon relaxed, helped by the teasing and easy ways of her host, Prince George, now Duke of York. She spoke quite frankly of her disappointment and sorrow at Eddie's death after she and Prince Albert Victor had become engaged. "But then—" she said, looking at her husband, "see what a nice brother he had! So nice he asked me to marry him instead. And only last May."

"'May I ask May in May?' I said to Papa," said Georgie lightly, and they all groaned. "And she said 'Yes,' bless her."

"I wish I had been home for the wedding," Buller said.

"It was such a lovely day," said the Duchess. "And everyone was so kind and sweet. Especially the crowds. I have never seen so many people in all my life, all cheering and waving and throwing kisses."

Clemmie said, "We *are* rather good at that sort of thing. Of course Papa pretends to hate the Monarchy and all that, but even *he* came up to Town, though he didn't tell anyone, and booked a private room at his club. We had to peek through a crack in the curtains in case we were recognized."

They all laughed at this nonsense. "Dinner is served, Your Grace." The butler's white head almost touched the floor.

"We *are* a small party tonight," said May in her attractive, soft voice. "Just eighteen. Dear Clemmie, I hope you won't be bored."

Dinner lasted for an hour and three quarters, course following course, smoked salmon from Abergeldie, pheasant from Sandringham ("A record bag last Saturday, Archy"), a great side of Scottish beef from the Balmoral estate, eggs, butter, and cream for the cakes and puddings from the home farm here at Osborne—Royal riches from Royal rivers and dairies and farms. Footmen flitted silently, replacing plates of scarcely touched food with fresh plates for new courses, all presided over with calm unobtrusiveness by the butler.

The Duke, still sorely missing the Navy, asked Buller again about the *Victoria*'s sinking. "If you had got the collision mat over earlier," he asked, "would that have saved the ship?"

The guests were suddenly silent, eager to hear from an

officer who had been there, who knew the truth, unlike those whose gossip had distorted the affair over the past months.

"No, nothing could save her," said Buller, "nothing but armour plate at the bows and stern instead of concentrated amidships." All eyes were on him, a sea of faces round the table, the glitter of the chandeliers matched by the sparkle of diamond tiaras, necklaces, shirt studs, and rings. "You can't imagine how quick it was, Georgie. It seemed like seconds from the time the *Camperdown* struck us to the time we were listing so steeply that we had to capsize. The Petty Officer who saved me, a marvellous little Geordie I've known off and on for years, was in the *Eurydice*—remember, back in '78? He said it was just the same then. All's well one moment—disaster the next."

The guest on Buller's right, not to be outdone by Buller, said proudly, "I was at Lady Tryon's reception on the evening of the disaster. And I saw the Admiral, quite distinctly. So did lots of others."

Puzzled, Buller turned to her. She was a small, attractive American, to whom Buller had only briefly spoken. She was Mrs. Weightman, the wife of an immensely wealthy landowner in Norfolk adjoining the Sandringham estate. "Which Admiral, ma'am?" he asked.

"Sir George Tryon, of course. Loads of people saw him, in full dress uniform, walking down the stairs to greet us. He even spoke my name."

"It's true, Archy," confirmed their hostess. "Several people have told me. And they kept remarking to Lady Tryon, 'How nice to see your husband here. I thought he was in the Mediterranean.' She became quite upset. And then a few hours later she heard he was drowned, and so gallantly."

The Duchess arose from her seat, her chair deftly lifted away from behind her. "Don't believe a word of it, any of you. Ghosts indeed! We'll leave the gentlemen, shall we?"

Mrs. Weightman, Buller noticed, glanced across the table to see that Clemmie was exchanging a last word with her neighbour, then lightly brushed her hand against his, just momentarily, as she arose. "How very nice to talk to you," she remarked in her attractive American accent. "I do so hope that we meet again." And there was no mistaking her meaning.

For a further hour the port went round, and then, led by the Duke of York, six of them, including Buller, retired for a hundred up on the billiards table. The Duke took the game lightly, clearly preferring to exchange what he called "salty tales" with the other naval guests. By far the best player was a young German Count and naval Lieutenant, whose wife was a close friend of the Duchess's and who had early made clear that he was a great influence in naval affairs in his country.

Count "Sonny" Reitzberg-Sönderlong knocked up a confident break of twenty-four to win the first game and shook his bullet head in mock modesty. "I was just lucky," he said. "Unlike your poor Admiral Tryon."

"What do you think was the cause of the accident, Sonny?" the Duke asked.

The Count retrieved his cigar and puffed at it thoughtfully. Buller feared the worst. "You know, Georgie, you must not mind when I say this. I say the cause was incompetency. Your Navy has gone slack with size and—how you say?—self-indulgence and self-satisfaction. No battles, and too big. Like your dear Papa, Georgie," and he laughed at his own tasteless joke, while Buller glanced nervously at the Duke.

"Your Navy is very big and very pleased with itself. You know how much I admire it," continued the Count sanctimoniously. "And in the numbers—how you say?—the statistics?—it is bigger than all the world together. But in its efficiency?" The German shrugged hs shoulders, grimacing at the Duke and at the other players in turn.

Buller was delighted to hear the Duke ask, "And your great Fleet? How efficient is that, Sonny?"

The Count was not in the least put out. "Ah, our Fleet.

Now it is very small. Just a few warships. Very, very efficient. But just you wait, Georgie. Like you, we have an Empire now, and great trade that must be protected. I was saying to the Emperor only recently, 'We need a great Navy, sir.' And he answered, 'We shall have a great Navy. A Navy as great as Queen Victoria's Navy. I shall see to it.' "

Buller went on half pay for most of the winter of 1893–4, hoping for a ship in the spring. Like most people in his social class, he found that boredom was the great enemy. At home in London, he enjoyed playing with his two children, Lucy, now four and a half, and Harry, two years younger. But they were too young to divert him for long; and then he would go to the Marlborough Club for a bottle or two of champagne and a game of whist, leading later to backgammon for most of the afternoon.

Clemmie was expecting their third child and was now able to go out very little. Their marriage was a happy-go-lucky light-hearted business, like those of so many wealthy young people, and there was a great deal of mutual tolerance, although Clemmie always worried about his gambling and sometimes worried about the fast company he kept among "the Marlborough Set." "Darling, you *are* so very late and so very drunk," she might say and then laugh and invite him to kiss her.

They moved down to Weir Park for Christmas, Clemmie with her two favourite maids, Buller with his valet, and the nurserymaid with her two "unders." The twins had been married recently, on the same day to sisters. There were no children yet, but even Weir Park felt fully occupied. It was also cold, and fires were lit in the bedrooms by 7:00 A.M. and kept going all through the day, old George Buller calculating that they were burning more coal than a battleship.

Junus had died of old age but Clarke had found a biddable puppy spaniel to replace him, and Lucy played with him for hours on end. It was a boisterous, happy Christmas, with a lot of games and present-giving—a new hunter for Buller from his parents, a diamond brooch for Clemmie from Buller. The tenants all came and sang carols on Christmas Eve and were given presents by Sir George and Lady Buller, and the whole family was invited downstairs to the servants' hall for hot toddy on Christmas morning before they trooped off through the snow to church.

The riots in mining and industrial areas had died down with the end of the coal strikes; and the vicar had made reference to what he called "a return to Godliness and obedience in time for the Holy day of the birth of Our Lord." Buller and his brothers and their mother hunted between Christmas and New Year. Then Guy and Henry and their wives left on a round of visits, and early in the new year Buller left, too, for a couple of visits in the Midlands.

Clemmie was still in bed, all lace and unpinned hair about her shoulders, when Buller came to say good-bye. Lucy and Harry were crawling about the floor with the new Junus, much to the disapproval of the nurserymaid on duty.

"Behave yourself, Archy, and give my love to the Wigmores," said Clemmie, holding out her arms.

"You'll promise to telegraph me if there are any signs."

"I wish there was a chance of that," Clemmie said ruefully. "Not due till the first week in February. You can bear the next child, Archy. I'm fed up no end with this whole business."

The train from Cirencester took him to Paddington, and Buller dropped in for luncheon at his club before taking a hansom to King's Cross, where a First Class carriage had been reserved for the Wigmore House party. A crowd of a dozen or more barefooted urchins clustered round the hansom as soon as it came to a halt. "Carry your bags, sir?" "Let *me* carry 'em, sir." Buller brushed them aside cheerfully, tossing a handful of coins, which cleared the way for a professional porter to deal with his luggage. He had always loved railway stations, more than ever since the fight in Alexandria. He loved the noise and movement and the expectation of excitement, even if it was to lead only to a weekend party at Wigmore House.

"Archy, darling, how lovely you could come!"

"Hullo, Archy old man. Left your better half at home, eh?"

The carriage was already half full, and Buller recognized most of the faces, all well established in Society.

"Yes, poor Clemmie—not really suitable for her to rush about in trains."

A minute before the train was due to leave, a very grand carriage drew up beside them, and servants jumped out to help their master and mistress, and get down the luggage. It was Mr. and Mrs. Weightman, he florid and bewhiskered and middle-aged and very large, she looking very young and lovely in a walking dress with plain skirt, three-quarter jacket and balloon-topped sleeves. A quick glance down the open carriage, and she made straight for the empty seat opposite Buller, who got up to greet her.

"Ah, my friend from Osborne. My gallant sailor from the poor *Victoria*." She smiled at him through her veil.

They talked all the way to the little Leicestershire station, which had been built by their host's father to serve Wigmore House. On the way, Buller became increasingly enchanted by this American woman's charm and her teasing ways. She teased him for not having been to any London theaters since he had gone on half pay. "Not even dear Oscar's *A Woman of No Importance*? Really, Lieutenant Buller. It is the wittiest play ever written."

Then she had produced a copy of *The Studio* magazine. "Now don't tell me you have never *heard* of Aubrey Beardsley!"

Buller shook his head. "Does he do portraits?"

"Portraits!" A light trill of laughter. She showed him some examples of Beardsley's pen-and-ink work, which secretly Buller found rather improper, and he hoped that no one else was looking.

Their keen-eyed and experienced hostess maneuvered them together that evening at late supper, a meal of cold meats and pastries, champagne or China tea, which was served at 11:30 for those who felt that they had not dined sufficiently well.

Mrs. Weightman, smelling heavily of the most expensive and delicious scent, apologized for being so boring about the arts. "I do go on so—my husband tells me. And it is not everything in life. It is much more important to be brave and dutiful, like you have always been, I am sure. I have heard of your wonderful courage in Alexandria during that awful war. And I am sure you saved many of your shipmates in the *Victoria*."

"As a matter of fact—no," said Buller. "I can't swim, and I was saved by one of my shipmates, a Geordie called Maclewin."

Mrs. Weightman laughed so much that her plate slipped from her knees and she had to dab at her eyes with a handkerchief; a footman whisked away the broken china and its contents. "Oh, that is too lovely! A sailor who cannot swim! Who is this Maclewin? Is he a Lieutenant, too? Is he here? You must introduce me to this gallant swimmer."

Buller, bewitched and heady with champagne, laughed with her. "No, I'm afraid not. This is not his sort of a party."

The inevitable occurred in the small hours of the morning. There were a dozen or more guests in the wrong beds at Wigmore House on that first night by 4:30 A.M. (and there would be still more on the second night). Buller, practiced now at interpreting any glance of invitation when saying "Good night," flitted along the half-lit corridor towards the room in which he knew Mrs. Weightman slept apart from her husband. He stood still for a moment, hand on the door handle, and heard the sound of a distant door being gently closed. He thought he heard, too, the muffled sound of a woman's laugh; and he certainly saw a figure moving swiftly and silently at the far end of the corridor on one more errand of love.

"Ah, my dear Lieutenant! My dear nonswimming Lieutenant."

"I hope I have not woken you up."

"Indeed you have, and I am very, very glad. Why do you have on all those pyjamas and thick dressing gowns? How very English of you."

There was still a faint flame from the fire, and the room was indeed warm, even when one stood naked in the near-darkness of this sumptuous bedroom.

It was warmer still in the bed, and this attractive little American woman's body was all that Buller had judged it would be: very soft and supple, the little hands very understanding in their hold and movements.

Mrs. Weightman was becoming quite breathless when she said, "I have no doubt that all sailors are really better in bed than in the sea . . ."

And, a good deal later: "Yes, I was right. Poor swimmer, good lover. Ah, my lovely boy."

The night "arrangements" at country house weekends were rarely discussed among the men. They were, on the other hand, much discussed, in a circuitous style and in lowered, excited voices, among the women. And there was plenty of time for doing so in the long day that lay ahead, even if few of the women guests came down before 11:30 A.M.

At Wigmore House, the party took on a new tone with the arrival, in his usual splendid and swashbuckling style, of the Prince of Wales, and the independent but not coincidental arrival of his mistress, Lady Warwick, more beautiful (even the most reluctant woman had to admit) than ever.

The Prince had not seen Buller for some time, but with the Prince's unerring eye for recognition and with his remarkable memory for faces, he came straight up at the first opportunity (in fact, in the drawing room after luncheon) and said, "Archy, my boy. My congratulations! I was so relieved to see your name among the survivors. What a blessing for the Navy! But poor old Georgie Tryon! A great man. My Georgie says he would have been First Naval Lord—a great tactician."

The Prince of Wales looked more than five years older. He wheezed at almost every breath, and his step and his movements seemed to have lost their pace and responsiveness. "Yes, sir, a great loss," said Buller. "I was very lucky to be saved."

Lady Warwick came up, solicitous for the comfort of her paramour. She looked at Buller, her dark eyes appraising him with unselfconscious favour. "Introduce me to this handsome, tall man, Bertie."

But for Buller, it was Mrs. Weightman again that night; and they lay for a long time together. Afterwards, as he crept back to his own room, Buller wondered how she could have brought herself to marry the red-faced landowner who seemed to have nothing to recommend him and was rarely even seen during the day. Status, he supposed. Only status, for she had plenty of money.

Later still, in the train to Mark Holly's place, he decided he very much wanted to get to sea again. After a while ashore, it was always the same. He felt slack and livery from too much food and drink, his appetites satiated. His sense of right and wrong was as primitive and little developed as that of most of his contemporaries in his class. But he could not feel happy when he knew that his physical fitness was being undermined. Hunting three times a week and lawn tennis were not enough to offset the effects of these long meals and drinking on these long weekends. He was getting fat. He had noted this ugly fact in the bath that morning—fat and over-indulged.

"Holly," he said. "We must get us a ship. I'm fed up and bored with lounging about. What we need is a proper old-fashioned sea war—against the Dons or Frenchies, with frigate actions and prize money . . ."

252

Chapter XIV

Buller got his appointment late in January 1894. And, to his delight, it was his first command. H.M.S. *Cobra* was one of the Navy's new torpedo boat catchers, armed with a single four-inch gun and six 3-pounder quick-firers. She was one of a class built in answer to the enormous French construction of torpedo boats, which now numbered over 200. Her displacement was a mere 550 tons, her complement only forty-eight Petty Officers and men. But, as his brother Henry remarked, "Archy might be C.-in-C. Channel Fleet he's so off his chump over that tin can."

Rod received an appointment early in the new year, too; a shore appointment to H.M.S. *Excellent*, where for two years he instructed new ratings in the art of gunnery. Rosie later brought the family down to stay in lodgings in Gosport. It was a happy time for the Maclewins.

The Newcastle that Rosie left behind was a happier place, too, after the miseries and strikes and lock-outs and unemployment and desperate hunger and cold and austerities of

1893. That year had been a time of political crisis as well as of industrial distress for the country. The Russian advance into the Pamirs was regarded as yet one more threat to India. France was giving much anxiety over her occupation of Siam and (once again) over Egypt. The Russian Fleet's visit to Toulon added greatly to British concern, and this led to a reexamination of the strength and efficiency of the Navy, both of which had earlier been in question with the accidental loss of the two battleships, one of them permanently.

The "Navy Scare" of 1893 resulted in an avalanche of orders for new ships. There had been nothing like it since the Napoleonic Wars. By the end of the year, steel mills, sawmills, ordnance shops, engine shops, fitting shops, pattern shops, frame-shops, and anglesmith's shops were reverberating to the clatter of presses, rivetters, lathes, cranes, and engines. The cage wheels at coal mineheads in Wales, the Midlands, the Northeast, and Scotland were everywhere turning again, and the skies were filled with smoke from countless chimneys. Vickers' profits rose from £55,000 in 1893 to a quarter of a million twenty-four months later; Armstrong's from 10 percent to 20 percent.

Between December 1893 and June 1894, no fewer than seven battleships, the largest ever designed, were laid down. They had names like *Majestic*, *Magnificent*, *Mars*, and *Victorious*, and (to Buller's special satisfaction) *Prince George*. A program presented by the First Lord of the Admiralty on December 8, 1893, also called for thirty cruisers, up to giants of 14,000 tons, 112 destroyers and torpedo boats, and numerous auxiliary and smaller craft.

Two senior naval officers, who had figured so largely in the careers of Buller and of Rod Maclewin and had been their Captains, were highly influential in bringing about this unprecedented "scare" program of construction in the teeth of the opposition of Gladstone's Liberal Government.

When the *Undaunted* was paid off at the time of the *Victoria-Camperdown* collision, Captain Lord Charles Beresford was given a shore appointment, from which he harassed the Government with tempestuous speeches and articles revealing British naval weakness.

Jackie Fisher worked as intensely and as effectively from within the naval establishment, persuading senior politicians that it was their absolute duty to strengthen the Navy, and also persuading the Board that they should threaten to resign *en masse* if the program was not passed.

The effect of all this was the final resignation of "the grand old man" Gladstone. The Admirals got their ships, the nation was strengthened and reassured; the forceful and fiery Fisher was knighted and appointed Director of Naval Construction to see the program through.

Beresford was cock-a-hoop; and up at Elswick the friends and neighbours of his "Lucky Midge" were at work again, their stomachs no longer aching for food. The frame-shop where for months Doris Maclewin and the Courages helped keep the Geordie children alive now echoed to the crash of steel and machinery instead of spoons rattling against tin bowls. The following five years continued to be prosperous for the Armstrong Elswick Works and for the nation that was suddenly anxious about its readiness for war. But when war came, it was not against the French or the Russians or even the new challengers to British sea power, the Germans. It was not the "proper old-fashioned sea war" Buller had referred to laughingly to Holly, and certainly there were to be no frigate actions or prize money. It was not even a sea war . . .

On September 19, 1899, the modern protected cruiser H.M.S. *Proud* was commissioned at Devonport, Captain J. D. Drury, Commander A. Buller; and, thanks to Buller's influence in higher quarters, Chief Gunner, Warrant Officer R. Maclewin.

"Looks like a bloody 'ulk, sir," a young A.B. said to Buller. "A bloody 'ulk wivout masts and upperworks, sir."

Buller smiled and nodded. They were looking at the mighty rock citadel towering above mist-shrouded Cape Town. Most of those without duties below had come up on deck, dressed in their Number 9 white working jumper and duck trousers, to witness this memorable landfall, a sight that had comforted mariners since Bartholomew Diaz doubled the Cape in 1488.

The *Proud*'s Chief Gunner climbed the ladder to the upper bridge where Buller was standing with the cruiser's Navigating Lieutenant, the Yeoman of Signals, two young snotties, the Quartermaster at the wheel, and the "bloody 'ulk" A.B.

"Is it your first time, Midge?" Buller greeted Rod.

"Once before, sir. When I was just a lad."

Buller laughed and glanced down at him, noting the hint of lines about his dark eyes and the broken blood vessels on the nose that he had suffered in a fight long ago in Malta. "Ah, the rheumaticky old veteran, just waiting for his pension! They'd still refuse you as underage if you tried to join the Navy today, Midge."

"I'm thirty-seven next year, sir."

Buller smiled and said, "Bunkum, Midge. Don't believe it." He turned to the Yeoman. "Make a signal to the harbour master, 'The Navy's here, your troubles are over.' Better use the lamp—they won't see anything else in this muck."

On the way out they had heard from the Canary Islands that there was trouble in South Africa, and three days earlier a passing P & O liner had signaled the *Isis*, "Boers have invaded English colonies." On his own initiative, the *Proud*'s Captain had ordered speed up from an economical 10 knots to 14, judging that the crisis justified the increase in coal consumption.

Now as the sun rose higher, the haze was dissolved, revealing Table Mountain in clear silhouette, with the invariable puff of cloud just above it, like a man who wears a hat indoors. Suddenly revealed, too, were the streets of the town —open-top horse trams, wagons drawn by oxen down at the docks, bicyclists everywhere, people on the pavements, wooden verandah houses, warehouses, big two-floor stores, the cathedral with columned spire. Then, later, the massive cliffs leading to Cape Point slipped by, and the *Proud* doubled the Cape.

Captain Drury joined the party on the upper bridge to take over from Buller and supervise the anchoring at Simonstown. The cruiser *Terrible* and two other men-o'-war were already anchored in the beautiful wide bay, and through his glass, Buller could make out a torpedo gunboat in the dry dock among the wharves and cranes and warehouses.

Rod asked the Captain, "I'll see to the signal guns, shall I, sir?" A twelve-gun salute was due to the Governor-General of the Cape Colony.

"Do that, Mr. Maclewin." Then Captain Drury added, "Hold it, Guns, they're signalling us."

The big signalling lamp above the superintendent's office was flashing Morse. Buller read, "Greetings Proud do not anchor required Durban urgently Natal threatened good luck."

"Acknowledge that," Captain Drury ordered the Yeoman, "and thank them."

As the *Proud* put her helm over 12 degrees and steadied on an easterly course, black smoke pouring from her three tall funnels, Buller reflected: so, it looks as though we're to get our war. A war that surely must soon be over, for what could a few invading Boer farmers from the Transvaal and Orange Free State do against the might of the British Army? Still, it was a war. And perhaps, like that echoing boyhood dream, once fulfilled at Alexandria seventeen years ago, Buller would again hear a gun fired in anger.

This likelihood increased when they arrived at Durban fifty-five hours later. If there was to be no war at sea, the Navy—so it appeared—was taking its weapons ashore instead. The 14,000-ton sheathed cruiser *Powerful*, Captain the Honourable Hedworth Lambton, was already anchored in Durban roads, and as the *Proud* anchored close alongside her big consort, they could see her winching a 4.7-inch gun, complete with a wheeled iron mounting, over the side into a lighter.

Captain Drury, watching the operation through his telescope, said, "Someone's been pretty sharp. I wonder who put that lot together."

"I've no doubt they'll be asking us to do the same thing," Buller remarked. "We'll soon know."

A steam launch was putting out from the *Powerful*, its little brass funnel puffing smoke, and the boat rose and fell through the Indian Ocean rollers towards them.

"Stand by to pipe the sides," ordered the officer-of-the-watch. And a minute later, "Stand by to hoist him in."

It was Lambton himself, a dapper man in white undress uniform, his Lieutenant standing at his side in the well of the launch. Buller knew him and his family well, but it did not appear that this was going to be an occasion for gossip. As the launch drew near, Buller glanced again at the shore, where the rollers broke massively along the beach. To the north, there were two- and three-storied hotels with decorated ironwork and long verandahs and striped awnings. Opposite the *Proud* and beyond the harbour bar that prohibited any sizable ships from reaching the quays were the cranes and warehouses of the busy port; beyond, the rising purple rolling hills of Natal. Natal—a rich jewel in the Imperial Crown, fought over by Boers and English and native Zulus, first occupied by the British sixty-five years earlier, and now threatened again by the Boers.

Lambton's news was even more serious than they had expected. Upcountry at Ladysmith, the British Army had been beaten back by the Boers, the town invested, the railway line cut. Natal was preparing for the worst; the Governor, Sir Walter Hely-Hutchinson, was concerned for Durban itself.

At the meeting in Captain Drury's cabin, Lambton told of the urgency to get as many guns as possible ashore rapidly to defend the city and to support the inadequate artillery of the Army. "Percy Scott made up these mountings at the Cape. Just a simple wood trail, an axle-tree, and a pair of ordinary Cape-wagon wheels," Lambton explained. He turned to Buller. "You and your Chief Gunner had better go ashore and see how it's done. There're four point sevens and twelve-pounders on the quay. The whole gun is sat on the ship's carriage and bolted down. Quite simple. And it works. Scott will be here himself with the *Terrible* in a few days."

As yet another British man-o'-war steamed into the roads in the afternoon, Buller and Rod went ashore with half a dozen gunnery ratings to study the mountings at first hand. One of the 4.7s was mounted on a railway truck. There were three more 4.7s, with names like Lady Randolph Churchill and Princess Louis, after the wife of Captain Prince Louis of Battenberg, and other names of notable society women —always women—painted on the mountaings. For two hours, Buller and Rod busied themselves with ordering the necessary timber and wheels. Behind the double and treble wharves, there was a big ornamental drinking fountain and a clock to celebrate Natal's discovery by Vasco da Gama 400 years earlier.

Everywhere they went there were khaki-uniformed troops from the regiments recently landed from the troopships still lying in the roads, waiting for a train to take them up to the front. They appeared cheerful enough. Some had put up crude signs saying "Avenge Majuba" (referring to the humiliating British defeat in an earlier Boer rising), and "Krush Kruger"; and one group was singing favourite music hall songs loudly and out of tune.

Phaetons and surreys were everywhere, and the trams were packed, as if the city were *en fête*. Durban might be threatened, but everyone seemed cheerful and business was brisk among the Indian shopkeepers and the rickshaw drivers with their fancy costumes and horned headdresses.

The *Proud*'s gunnery party had no time for the city's

pleasures, however. Buller was conscious of the sense of energy and purpose that now filled his men. When they had sailed from Devonport three weeks earlier, this was to have been a peacetime cruise to Trincomalee in Ceylon to take over from another cruiser due to pay off. Now half the ship's gunners were to form part of the Naval Brigade to fight the Boers.

The sun was low in the sky, though the heat was unabated, when the cox took the boat back towards the harbour bar. A steam launch was coming in, cutting a way through the numerous fishing boats. It slowed down as it neared them, and the cox called out through a megaphone, "Are you from the *Proud*, sir?"

Buller called back, "That's right. Commander Buller. What can we do for you?"

Both coxes eased their boats so that they rose and fell on the waves fifty feet apart. There was a tall, stout, very smart Commander standing in the launch's well. Buller was puzzled for a moment about his identity. The stance and figure were faintly familiar, but he was confused by the officer's heavy girth and the full beard with flecks of grey in it. The voice, when it carried across the water, was indisputably that of Alan Marchmount.

"Will you oblige me by coming over to the *Bengal* when I return to my ship, Commander Buller?" he shouted. "I've been asked to form a division from our ships. There's a lot to talk about and not much time."

Over the twenty years since they had passed out from the *Britannia*, Buller had rarely seen his old adversary—once in the foyer of the Army and Navy Club, briefly in Malta, at Henley Regatta about five years earlier, but never professionally. Buller had heard that Marchmount, inheritor of his father's millions and a noted dandy, had been in the Mediterranean in 1882 but had been too late for the bombardment and had left again before the land fighting hotted up. And now? Now, the same rank as Buller but a year senior to him, and

Buller was to be his second-in-command. Well, it was a long time since he had exchanged blows with him. They had both grown up since then and matured in the finest club in the world—better than the Marlborough or the "Senior." To go to the front with Alan Marchmount, Commander R.N., complete with his stock of freshly laundered shirts and immaculate white uniform no doubt, added another fresh dimension to a future that had suddenly become mighty interesting.

"Do you know Commander Marchmount, sir?" asked Rod when the two boats had resumed their course and speed.

"Not for many years, Guns—not really since I was a cadet and you were in the *Eurydice*. But he's a very experienced Gunnery Officer. Served under Captain Percy Scott at one time, I believe." Assuming the professional stance again, Buller added, "I think we'll take a couple of Nordenfelts and a Maxim with us. If you remember Alexandria, machine guns can come in handy."

On December 1 after a number of frustrating delays, Commander Marchmount's Second Naval Division was ready to leave for the front. Captain Lambton's division had left earlier, had fought outside Ladysmith, and—it had been reported—had given sterling support to General White's forces with its long 12-pounders and 4.7s. Now it was trapped within the town, and it would be the Second Naval Division's task to assist the Army in relieving Ladysmith and in rescuing their fellow sailors.

Now at last they were ready to entrain. Four 4.7s—two from each cruiser—and six long 12-pounders had been brought ashore. The Captain Scott mounting had been completed for each gun: two stout lengths of timber formed into a cross with the ship's mounting bolted through to a plate underneath. Then they were winched up and secured in the flatcars, each of which took on the appearance of a battleship on wheels, the whole train looking like a battle fleet in line-ahead formation.

At midday on this burning hot morning, the train of flatcars and eight wagons of ammunition and equipment drew slowly out of the harbour station and headed towards the city. The officers and Warrant Officers shared one carriage, and two more open carriages accommodated the gunnery ratings drawn from the *Proud* and the *Bengal*. Sandbags suspended from ropes slung across the closed carriages and steel plates built up the sides of the open carriages partly protected the division from snipers and fire from ambushes. Even in Durban itself there were many Boer sympathizers, and on the long winding route upcountry they had to be prepared for surprise attacks at any time. Buller had ordered the Maxim and two Nordenfelts to be mounted in the open carriages to provide counterfire.

In the foremost seats in the officers' carriage Rod drew his head in from the window and remarked to Buller, "It's nearly twenty years since we went into action in our first armoured train—d'you remember, sir?"

"Never forget it," said Buller, laughing. "That was some fight— and that fellow nearly did for you, eh?"

Marchmount was clearly put out by this talk of a past battle, although he did no more than glance at them superciliously. Then he gave his beard its habitual gentle stroke and turned to a young Lieutenant who had been listening and said pointedly, "Whatever these gallant gentlemen accomplished nearly twenty years ago, Thomson, we've got to think about the present—and these Boers." He laughed, but to Buller the sound had a sharp edge. "And unlike the Gippos, they know how to fight, so it seems."

Buller had no more taken to Alan Marchmount now than he had all those years ago in the *Britannia*. Although Marchmount had a year's seniority over him, Marchmount appeared always to need to score off him.

After Merrivale, the gradients became more severe and they were climbing, sometimes circuitously, high into the hills through raw cuttings in red rock. Buller sent Rod to check that the machine guns were manned and the men alert. Dusk was fast approaching, the favourite time for an ambush. Only two weeks earlier an armoured train similar to their own had been subjected to a surprise attack not far from here, and among those captured was the man Buller had seen as a boy at Lord Huntley's ball, Winston Churchill, now a newspaper correspondent who had fought at Omdurman and was making a name for himself as a politician, like his father. ("The Boer continued to look along his sights. I thought there was absolutely no chance of escape, if he fired he would surely hit me, so I held up my hands and surrendered.")

The night passed with nothing worse than the flashing of falling sparks from the engine's smokestack shooting past the windows, and a halt for water. Buller nodded off to sleep once or twice but not for long. His mind was tight with expectancy, with images of battle, with reflections on past scenes from the Egyptian war. If his generation, like his father's, was not going to be offered action at sea, then at least he was being offered again the chance to distinguish himself on land instead; just as his great-great-uncle, Horace Buller, Lieutenant R.N., had done at the Siege of Calvi alongside Nelson when The Hero had lost an eye.

It was said, after the fighting, that this Buller had been asked by a French courtesan if he had been afraid, and had replied, "Madame, forgive me, I know not of what you speak but am eager to learn all things from one so beautiful. Pray tell me." More than a century later, Archy Buller might have replied similarly, though perhaps less gracefully.

But beautiful French courtesans seemed as remote and unattainable at Frere as a jug of iced lemonade. The train steamed into the station of this little township of wooden and iron-roofed bungalows at nine o'clock on the morning of December 2. The sun was already high in a sky that was a bright-blue crucible of reflected heat. They got out of the train to stretch and to cook breakfast on the mobile field kitchen they had brought with them. Besides the heat and the dust that lay heavy in the still air, Frere seemed to emanate a sense of fatalism and gloom. Wounded on stretchers were being loaded silently into a train that had the Red Cross painted on the side of every carriage. They were being watched in equal silence by a squatting group of infantrymen in khaki uniforms and puttees, grey pith helmets pushed to the back of their heads, dead cigarettes between their lips. They looked a dejected crew, bereft of discipline and spirit alike, and when Buller approached them, none attempted to get up.

"Stand to attention in the presence of an officer," he barked at them.

The men got wearily to their feet and took the cigarettes from their mouths, eyeing him with hostility.

"Where is your officer?"

"We don't 'ave one," said one of the privates sullenly. "Sir."

"What do you mean?"

Another soldier nodded his head towards the train. "Lieutenant Hodges's in there, sir. An' our platoon Sergeant, 'e got a Mauser bullet in 'is 'ead two days ago."

Suddenly there was a *whooshing* sound, as if the air were being torn apart above them, and a concussive crack as a shell burst a hundred yards away, stirring up the dust and shaking leaves from a nearby eucalyptus tree.

"That'll be old Long Rob—usually starts about now," remarked another infantryman. None of the men stirred. It was as if they had been stunned by noise and battle and had given up caring for their lives. A line of 4-pounder guns, each drawn by four horses, thudded along the road to the north, and when the dust behind them settled, Buller saw for the first time the terrain on which they would soon be fighting—harsh, remorseless veldt, strewn with russet rock, spotted with Natal bottlebush and sword-leaved buddleia scrub, protea and eucalyptus trees, and tambookie grass where rare water, the same russet colour, flowed sluggishly. Hillocks like warts thrust up from a landscape that was beyond disfigurement. Remorseless yet hopeless. Why would anyone want it, why would anyone fight for this land which might have been the surface of some sun-tortured planet?

Buller put his telescope to his eye in the hope of finding something to break the monotony and picked out distantly a line of undulating hills, or kopjes, beating in the heat haze like the chest of some prone panting beast; Mount Alice in the extreme northwest to Nhlangwini in the northeast, the barrier —the natural line of fortresses—separating British forces from Ladysmith beyond.

A Colonel in the Inniskillings rode up on a sweating horse, his staff reining in behind him. They all looked dusty and disconsolate, but were evidently attempting to put on a show for the Navy.

"Good-day Commander," he greeted Buller. He sported a tight, waxed moustache and looked questioningly at Buller with red, protruding eyes. "Good trip up, eh? The artillery wallahs need the help of your big jobs. Damn Boers have got six-inchers—Creusots and Krupps. Outrange everything we've got." He cast an eye along the line of flatcars, the tarpaulined barrels, the manned Maxim and Nordenfelts. "Can you get this lot up to Chieveley? Oxen can take over from there. Plenty of conductors and Kaffirs—if they haven't done a bunk."

Marchmount came up, clearly put out that the Colonel was addressing Buller. "Well, what is it, Colonel? What is it? I'm in command here. Marchmount's the name—H.M.S. *Bengal*. Chieveley is it? That looks damn close to the front line." He had a map in one hand, a finger on Frere. "I hope the General knows what range we have—fourteen thousand yards is nothing for our four point sevens. Not like those little whipper-snappers that've just gone past."

In the short interval before the Colonel replied, Buller heard the distant rumble of heavy guns, with musket fire like a crackling soprano chorus accompanying it. This was no small affair, no Kaffir war, no Ashanti campaign, no Zulu uprising; this was real war on a scale the British Army had not known for decades, and against a tough adversary. These Boer farmers were well organized and had modern equipment. And here was Commander Marchmount R.N. telling this Colonel how to run his war.

"Arrangements have been made for you at Chieveley, Commander." The Colonel gave his moustache a dashing little twist and reined in his mount. (Buller was enough of a horseman to know that the mare was being stirred into restlessness.) "A camp's been laid out. Bit primitive." He gave a high-pitched laugh. "Not quite the comforts of your wardroom, eh? But it's what we're used to up here at the front." He pronounced it "frarnt."

The train was steadily shelled by Boer artillery all the way across the veldt to Chieveley, the spouts of russet earth rising into the sky as if punched out from below by a sharp fist—*whoomph* to the right, *whoomph* to the left, another much closer. Marchmount had ordered all windows open, but someone had left one closed and it was at once smashed into a thousand pieces, badly cutting a couple of ratings. Twice they felt the blast of concussion, and stones and shell fragments smacked against the carriage. Someone shouted "Shrapnel!" above the sound of the locomotive straining forward at top speed, and at once the roof of the carriage was beaten as if in a hailstorm, several big chunks of the shell piercing the wood.

Chieveley offered trees and concealment. Marchmount, peering through the window, said with relief in his voice, "That's good. Now, the sooner we get the guns off the better." His beard was thick with dust and he was looking pale and weary with anxiety. "Commander Buller, will you be so good as to discover the location of our camp. I'd like to get the men fed and washed as soon as we have the guns winched off."

"Of course," said Buller quietly. Yes, he, too, would like to get the men fed and washed, but not so that they sounded like horses.

It was still six miles to the forward Boer positions on the slopes of the kopjes, three times maximum rifle range. But there was a frontline feel to this township, from which the civil population had been evacuated. There were hundreds of men of Lancashire regiments, of the Dublin Fusiliers, and of the 1st Dragoons encamped around the town; and R.H.A. and officers' horses were tethered in long lines to hitching fences and eating the fodder scattered about their feet.

The smell in the still air was the very essence of heat and war; horse sweat, man sweat, horse urine and manure, gun oil, and steaming stew and tea; and, above all, the burning rock scent of the veldt. The camp and the town were being desultorily shelled, but everyone had learned to distinguish the dangerous ones by the note of the warning whine and went about their tasks as if nothing were happening.

Chieveley was alive with rumours of the big offensive that must come soon, the attacks that would drive the Boer General Botha and his burghers from the hills and break their grip on Ladysmith. The arrival of this new Naval Division with its guns struck a note of excited anticipation. "When are you getting them into position?" "What's your maximum range?" "It'll be capital to get our own back on Long Rob!"

The winching off of the 12-pounders and 4.7s aroused great interest, and there was no shortage of willing help. Ox wagons dragged the stacks of common, lyddite, and shrapnel shells to the scattered dumps about the town, and the guns themselves were dispersed on their limbers ready for moving when the order came.

The G.O.C. would give the general order but the artillery, including the guns of the Naval Brigade, were to be under the command of Colonel Charles Long, R.A. Meanwhile, Marchmount was determined to keep his officers and men busy and smart. "Got to give a good impression," he would say to Buller several times a day. And "Maclewin" (it was always Maclewin, never "Guns"), "Maclewin, I run my ship with a taut hand, and don't you forget it. The *Proud*'s standards may not be the *Bengal*'s but we're going to run this ship according to *Bengal*'s standards."

The men would be paraded several times in the heat of the day, with rifles, ammunition, and full pack drill, and Marchmount would be out there—observed by amazed Army officers —inspecting their puttees and webbing, checking their personal cleanliness as well as the barrels of their Lee-Metfords and Colt revolvers.

"I'll be glad when we get out of here—Boer guns'll be nothing compared with this," Rod confessed to Buller one evening as they took a stroll round the Naval Division encampment to the west of the town.

"Are the lads getting restless?"

"The *Bengal's* men are used to it," Rod replied. "But our boys are about ripe for mutiny. Say they'll be too dead beat to move when the order does come to advance."

Marchmount had continued to command the division in isolation and was never to be seen with any other officer but his Lieutenant, a frail-looking self-contained young man, Wallace Windsor. Marchmount confined his conversation with Buller to formalities; and Buller, with little to do for the time being, looked up acquaintances in the Dragoons and made a study of the terrain, riding with officers over the veldt and tracing out the Boer positions among the kopjes through binoculars. Sometimes he was the target of rifle fire at extreme range, and he was impressed by its accuracy.

On December 14, twelve days after they arrived at Chieveley, Buller became aware of a quickening of activity. A five-inch howitzer battery arrived. In the afternoon, he observed a splendid figure riding into the town, along with his staff. He had heard a great deal about Colonel Long already, his total recklessness, whether at pig-sticking in India (fifty boars in one day, it was said) or at the Battle of Omdurman, where he had handled the guns almost up to the rifle barrels of the dervishes and been highly commended by Kitchener. His appearance, Buller noted, matched his reputation as a fearless fire-eater—gleaming eyes, gaunt expression, waxed moustaches that might have been used as short range stabbing weapons if the need arose, a long straight back as he rode by on a great grey stallion.

That evening, Marchmount and Buller were summoned to the Colonel's presence in the R.A. Headquarters encampment. It was a chilly encounter from the moment the Colonel cast his eyes, with a good deal of doubt and suspicion, over Marchmount and gave Buller only a perfunctory glance. Sailors mixed up in Army affairs? he appeared to be thinking with every appearance of distaste. Wrong fellers in the wrong place. Ought to be at sea.

But there was also no denying the unappetizing fact that the R.A. was in dire need of heavy artillery and that only the Navy could fill the gap.

"Well, gentlemen, we open the offensive tomorrow before dawn," began the Colonel. "Perhaps you would be good enough to glance at this. . . ."

A pointer moved across the large-scale map of the terrain leading to Colenso on the River Tugela, the ridge of kopjes on the far side, the winding railway line—now broken in several places—leading north to Ladysmith. The Boer positions were marked with black shading but were mostly speculative, like the configuration of the kopjes themselves, which had never been properly surveyed.

"I'll be bringing up my fourteenth and sixty-sixth batteries to here, gentlemen. I would be so glad if you follow as close behind as you can with your twelve-pounders—you won't keep up with your oxen but keep 'em hard at it." The pointer was still. "Your four point sevens will be opening fire from here at six A.M. precisely." His pointer moved forward significantly across the map. "Your twelve-pounders from here, right beside my field batteries."

Buller heard Marchmount's sudden intake of breath and the edge of dismay in his voice as he exclaimed, "But that's only about a thousand yards from the river. That's suicide."

"I'm sorry you should think that, Commander. I happen to believe in close action and rapid fire, despite the Navy's notions. What is it? Five thousand yards opening range?"

"I wouldn't like you to think we're not prepared to support you . . ."

Marchmount was cut short. Long's voice was icy. "It is

not what you think that concerns me, sir," he said so that everyone in the big tent could hear. "It is what I ask you to do. And that is to close support me with your twelve-pounders. The only way to smash these beggars is to rush in at 'em. I'm not new to this game, Commander. Had a bit of experience in Afghanistan in '79 and '80, and last year in the Sudan."

There was a moment of total silence, and then far away a Boer heavy gun—a six-inch Creusot, Buller judged—fired a single shot. It might have been a punctuation mark—a full stop—in their conversation. A staff officer shuffled some papers, as if to indicate that the meeting was over, that there was nothing left to be said.

"Don't misunderstand me, Colonel Long," Marchmount said as they left. "We'll be there right behind you." His laugh was stiff with unease. "Trust the Navy."

It took a span of thirty-two oxen to draw each 4.7 gun—128 in all, with the conductors in command and the Kaffir drivers with their long whips. Sixteen oxen were needed for each of the 12-pounders, and many more for the Cape wagons carrying the ammunition. There was still no light in the sky when the division began to move, accompanied by the chorus of sounds from the Kaffirs, the complaining grunts of the oxen, the creaking of the leather harness, and the rumble of the wheels on the hard-packed road.

The air was already dusty from the beat of the infantry's marching feet, advancing in three columns across the veldt, the Lancashire regiments, 2nd Dublin Fusiliers, 1st Dragoons, Lord Dundonald's 2nd Life Guards and 13th Hussars, and the rest. There was no attempt at silence, no attempt at concealment. Close order over the open ground to the river where they hoped they would find drifts to make a crossing. And then up the kopjes, bayonets fixed, to drive the enemy from their burrows . . .

Buller and Rod were on horseback in the vanguard with

the 12-pounders; the men marched behind the limbers, ready to help if the oxen got into trouble. "Just stick as close to Colonel Long as you can," had been Marchmount's instructions. "I'll look after the heavies." So that was to be it. "We'll be there right behind you." But for the present "we"—Commander Marchmount R.N.—was looking after the 4.7s, which were to halt at 5,000 yards range from the Boer positions and open the assault at dawn.

The heat of the day crept in ahead of the sun, as if to give warning of what was to come. Buller felt his shirt damp against his back long before sunrise and, at the same time, those other discomforts of the veldt: the first tickle of thirst, the first breath of dust.

"It's going to be hot, sir."

Buller turned in his saddle and smiled at Rod. Rod's horse was much too big for him, and he had an uneasy seat anyway: a small, vulnerable figure—too small, too vulnerable, too young . . . "I'm thirty-seven, sir." Uttered with pride. Buller remembered the little Geordie at Alexandria, revelling in his knowledge of the locomotive; as bold and as authoritative as he had been in the sea off Tripoli, saving his life. Tough little "Guns," with his wife and three children—as he had confided to Buller once—up in Newcastle. Mrs. Maclewin wouldn't like to see him now, riding to within a thousand yards or less of the Boer lines. Or would she? Would she be more proud than fearful for his safety? Midge Maclewin didn't seem to care; even looked as if he were enjoying himself.

"Yes, Guns. Hot. Hot from the Boers, hot from the sun."

"We'll give them a taste of the Navy, sir."

The men seemed cheerful enough, too. Some had wrapped their scarves round their mouths to keep out the dust, while others, 300 miles from the sea, were singing sea shanties and "Jolly young Jacks are we . . ."

Hooray for the Queen's Naveee! Yes, Buller decided, he was going to enjoy this.

Dawn came suddenly, as if impatient for the proceedings

to begin. One moment it was all grey, the kopjes ahead a faintly darker grey. Then the sun heaved itself over the eastern horizon like an early spectator, and at once Buller felt the sweat running into his eyes and down inside his breeches. There would be half an hour, and no longer, when distant targets would be undistorted by heat shimmer, and the heavies, sights still accurate, would take advantage of this fact.

The 4.7s, far to their rear, opened fire together rapidly. Buller could imagine Marchmount standing behind the battery, hands over his ears, a tall, erect if portly figure, barking out the order to his Lieutenant; between salvos, putting the telescope to his eye to check the fall of shot. An odd, unloved man, blessed with wealth and privilege, up now close to danger where so many naval officers would give ten years' seniority to be. But joyless—yes, that was it, joyless. And perhaps something worse . . . ?

Buller thrust the image aside. This was war, this was his battery, and there was a job to be done. He glanced at Midge beside him, nodded, thrust in his spurs and cantered forward, urging on the teams.

The 4.7 shells sang high overhead. You could see them if you looked carefully. Buller felt the concussion through his horse, saw the sudden thrusts of smoke on the kopjes ahead. That would shake up the burghers.

It was wonderful how the little Kaffirs kept their spans of oxen on the move and the wheels out of the rougher patches of rock and scrub, dominating the great harnessed beasts yet showing an understanding for their difficulties, like sheepdogs with their flock. Some of the Kaffirs were content with little more than a loin cloth; others were more elaborately dressed for the occasion, many with cast-off European clothes. Shouting and laughing, uncomprehending of the dangers and enjoying the unusual nature of this work, they required little guidance from their bosses, the conductors.

Buller reckoned they were 2,000 yards from the river bank, 200 or 300 yards farther still from the Boer dugouts, when the Mauser musket fire first cracked out; a few ranging shots at first, then more rapidly. There was no question of halting here, however. Colonel Long had ordered: "Your twelve-pounders are to range parallel with my field batteries. When you see us halt on your left—that's the time to unlimber. Not before."

And there, beneath the dust cloud of their own making, were Long's two batteries, the 14th and the 66th, moving forward at a steady pace, faster than the Navy could make with their oxen teams. Ahead of them, dimly seen mounted figures, were the battery ground scouts, and between them and the guns, Colonel Long and his staff; all the artillery for the attack, except Marchmount's 4.7s, now far ahead of the infantry: Devons, East Surreys, and Scots and Irish Fusiliers, who were supposed to support them, but could never catch up at this rate.

Buller turned to Rod. The repeated, irregular sound *phut, phut, phut*, the series of little gouts of red earth spitting out of the soil, the occasional whine of a ricochet from a rock, were the evidence of the intensity of Boer fire already. "Looks as if we'll be getting the brunt for a while," he said with an encouraging smile. He noticed that a number of the Kaffirs who wore coats had put their collars up, as if—poor devils—facing a natural veldt hailstorm instead of this hail of Boer lead.

"There goes one, sir." Rod pointed to the nearest span, where an ox had keeled over and lay on its back, legs feebly kicking, bringing the team to a confused standstill. The Kaffirs, under the direction of the conductor, were cutting the traces and attempting to get some order to the span. One of them was shot while doing this work, spinning round and falling to the earth, at once still.

To the northwest Buller could see, not a mile away, the railway bridge over the Tugela and the railway station and the scattered wooden houses of Colenso. The sound of the musket fire drifted from the kopjes like hard rain on iron roofs, a continuous riffle, only rising and falling slightly in its intensity.

"They're halting, sir," Rod called to him. "Shall I give the order to unlimber?"

Buller saw across the undulating veldt, not 400 yards distant, the well-drilled gunners bringing round their guns and taking the horses and limbers back towards a protective donga, a wide pit in the veldt, to the rear. It was as if they were on the parade ground at Aldershot for inspection by the old Duke of Cambridge. The sharp crack of their first salvo sounded out before Buller replied, "Yes, unlimber, smart as you can."

Suddenly, it had become too much for the Kaffirs. This was not their battle, not their war. They had been hired to bring these strange, fierce weapons across the veldt, not to be killed by unseen missiles from unseen places. The panic of several, stemming from more injuries and deaths, spread rapidly, was transmitted to their charges, which fought to get free of their traces, and turned the well-ordered teams into a shambles of heaving animals and running black figures, into which the enemy poured an intense fire, every hit adding to the confusion.

"Cut them loose!" "Cut the traces!" The orders shouted by Buller and by Rod and by the other officers were not necessary. The ratings were tackling the pandemonium as if they were the crew of a dismasted sailing ship in a hurricane, knives slashing at the leather, beating the backs of the oxen to encourage them to break free, seizing the limbers and manually turning their big guns to face the enemy.

Buller caught a glimpse of oxen and black figures spreading out across the veldt like a stain, some towards the river and the Boer lines, others west towards Colonel Long's batteries, and the rest fleeing to the rear and the advancing infantry. "Steady the wagons there!" He drew in his horse and supervised the positioning of the ammunition supplies. "Petty Officer Rivers, organize a chain to the guns and keep the men at it."

Rod was up at the guns, where the crews required no encouragement to get into action swiftly in order to avenge their losses and to reduce the enemy fire. "Shrapnel every third round," he called out, racing along the line to repeat the order. Shrapnel to keep their heads down, common to blow them out, and lyddite to burn them up. That was the theory.

Ah, but that was good! Sharp thinking, good discipline, those could work wonders. For a few minutes, it had looked as if the chaos could never be cleared. Now they might have been in action on the gun deck of H.M.S. *Proud* living up to her name, steady salvos, breechblock open, smoke rising, fresh shell in, ram home the charge, breechblock closed, captain of the gun holding the taut lanyard with one hand and firing by jerking down the other hand on the lanyard, the click of the striker, the punching recoil that could kill, and the forward movement almost as punishing, the stirring of red soil into a cloud by the muzzle blast, the acrid yellow haze floating up from the muzzle . . .

The rhythm of the guns. They might not be at sea, but this was what all these years of practice and training, the teamwork and target practice, the remorseless polishing of their skill—this was what all that had been leading to. To this: rapid open fire against the enemy. Gunshot range. Point-blank, a distance Nelson would have approved.

Through the smoke and dust and heat haze, Buller could observe their hits, the sudden grey puff—yellow-grey for lyddite—on the slopes of the kopjes, the yellow-spark heart of the shrapnel bursts above. Colonel Long's fire on the western slopes of the kopje could be distinguished by its reduced impact and smaller bursts.

They were cutting down the musket fire, no doubt of that. But still the Mauser bullets rained down on them, the Boers' only target until the infantry came within range. And their artillery was answering, too. Buller saw a cloud belch up from the veldt a hundred yards to the east, and another in front. Two of his men had fallen by the nearest 12-pounder, the gun captain ordering ammunition runners to take their place. Others were down, too. They were taking heavy losses. But, by God, they were keeping up the rate of fire, keeping the burghers' heads down.

Buller cantered along to the extreme eastern guns, shouting encouragement to the men, laughing when a man tripped with a charge. "You'll have us all blown up, Jack!" Then, "Well done—keep it up!"

He met Rod on the way back. "Well, Guns?"

"It's not coming up, sir. And we're nearly out."

The shell supplies should have been replenished by the reinforcement teams. There must have been trouble to the rear. More panic perhaps. Couldn't blame 'em, not those Kaffirs. But . . .

"How much left?"

"Another three minutes' firing."

"Keep the rate to a round every minute and a half."

"Aye aye, sir."

The musket fire increased again with their own reduction of fire, and the division was taking savage casualties. Buller caught a glimpse of an A.B.—a good man, married, from Devonport, three children, name of Jackson—writhing on the ground with a stomach wound. One of his mates was trying to quieten him, his water bottle to his lips.

It was getting rougher, no doubt of that. A Mauser bullet whipped through Buller's shirt, just nicking the flesh, like the passing sting of a nettle. Ready ammunition down to three shells, all common, and nothing coming up. Number four gun was reduced to a team of three. The men looked up questioningly as he passed, waiting for orders, but ready to carry on if required . . .

The battery's fire was down to intermittent firing. Suddenly Buller saw that, to the west, Colonel Long's guns had been abandoned. They stood out in the open, in neat parade-ground lines, unprotected by shields like their own 12-pound-ers, not one firing, not one manned. Out of ammunition, like they were. Insupportable casualties. That old fire-eater abandoning the guns! Before the Navy? But what was to be gained by waiting until every man was dead or wounded? And with no ammunition . . .

"Mr. Maclewin, please order the cease-fire. Every man to the donga."

It was like lowering the flag in a sea battle. A painful order he had never expected he would have to make.

Buller reined in his horse and turned to repeat his order to the crews behind him. Sweating, dusty, panting figures, sennit hats thrown back on their heads, set expressions on their faces, baptism-of-fire faces, aching now with frustration and the need to avenge the deaths and injuries of their shipmates. He had seen these faces at Alexandria at the height of the battle. Hard-fighting faces.

"Cease fire—retreat to the rear." Buller's voice sounded raw and harsh. And then his horse was hit, and he was thrown hard to the rocky ground. Stunned momentarily. A hand on his shoulder. "Are you all right, sir?"

"I'm all right. Get moving, Skinner."

There was no need to give the order, "Help the injured!" No need at all. There were sometimes four men to every man down, the Mauser bullets *phut*, *phut*, *phut*, all round them— killing a man there before he could be lifted.

"God, I'm proud of these men today." Buller felt like saying it out loud: "I'm proud of you. D'you hear me—I'm *proud* of you." He helped a leading seaman to his feet. "Where did they get you, Arkwright? Right, take it easy, arm round my shoulder. Soon have you out of here."

And so they came back, "out of here," out of that hell of bullets and shrapnel and shell splinters on the open veldt, in the cannon's mouth, suicidally far ahead of the infantry that never came. And now all the guns lost? Maybe half the men gone, too. Or more. It would take time to make the count.

And the Naval Division lay beneath the burning 7:00 A.M. sun, some in agony, some in pain, some only bruised or nicked like Buller, all with their hearts broken at the knowledge of defeat, lying panting their lungs out, throats dry and dusty. Guns abandoned.

The donga was a saucer of heat scooped out of the veldt, scattered with rocks too hot to touch and Natal bottlebrush shrubs that offered a few square yards of shade. Small lizards and copper-red mole snakes—all that this place was fit for—moved over the rocks disregarding the sprawled figures and the surviving horses that stood about, shining with sweat, heads lowered.

At the extreme west end of this donga there was a renewal of activity among the survivors of Colonel Long's batteries. There was much shouting, and through the rising dust, Buller caught sight of limber teams being collected.

Rod returned from that direction on horseback. He had lost his cap and the sweat was pouring down his face. "The General's arrived and asked for volunteers to recover the army's field guns," he told Buller. "Colonel Long's among those wounded—seriously, I was told."

"Why doesn't the General get the infantry up? Damn the guns. What we need is support and ammunition. How can a few guns fight the whole Boer Army?" Buller looked about him, at his exhausted men, the worst wounded lying in the precious shade, tended by their shipmates until the R.A.M.C. arrived to carry them back. Buller saw the rocky lip of this donga, all that protected them from the frightful Boer fire; the final preparations for the suicide ride ordered by a General who must have gone mad in the heat; the veldt to the rear, stretching out endlessly, and not an infantryman, not a supply wagon, in sight. What a shambles! What a God-awful shambles!

"Guns, will you find a fit man who can ride well and send him back to Commander Marchmount. Tell him we've been driven from the 12-pounders, are out of ammunition, and need food and water."

"Aye, aye, sir."

Buller seized one of the stray horses and climbed into the saddle. He rode towards Colonel Long's survivors, where there were even more wounded gunners than his battery had suffered, and then took his horse up to the lip of the donga. He was in time to witness an act of desperate courage that was to earn seven V.C.s, including a posthumous V.C. for Field Marshal Roberts's only son, who was among the first to volunteer.

The teams of horses and riders had just reached the abandoned field guns and were attempting to limber up in a hail of Mauser bullets that spattered round them like drops of storm rain on dry sand so intensely that they set up a waist-high dust cloud. Buller saw one man fly out of the saddle of his horse as if struck by a dozen bullets—as he could well have been. He picked himself up and seized the limber pole of a gun and grabbed a drag with his other hand; and then was hit and lay still.

Half a dozen horses had already fallen, throwing their riders. One team had a gun limbered up and moving before the two leading riders were shot. Faintly from this scene of gallantry and carnage, there came the screams of wounded horses and the shouts of straining men.

Buller broke into a trot, and then a gallop, in the direction of the guns, as automatically as if the sound were the view hallo. Who could tell? One extra pair of hands could mean the recovery of a gun. And here, miraculously, came one limber, and then another, horses' heads stretched forward, eyes wide with terror, their riders lying low over their necks and beating the horses' flanks with their crops.

Buller cheered as they went past, one on either side, but he did not hear his own voice in the thunder of hooves, the clatter of limbers, and the shouting. Beyond was a confusion of figures, of horses, of gun barrels, of carriages, of limber poles, and of check ropes. Men and horses lay on all sides, dead or soon to die. Bullets filled the air as if a hundred Gatlings were concentrating on this tiny sector of the open veldt; and shrapnel bursts cracked like thunder directly overhead.

Buller reined in his horse and dismounted, seizing a limber pole. "Get out, you bloody fool!" A Lieutenant glanced at him wildly. "It's no good. No bloody use."

The man at his side fell as he spoke, his body tumbling onto a horse whose intestines lay spread over a rock. "Just get out!" repeated the Lieutenant. He had a ginger moustache and freckles. He had lost his hat and there was a streak of blood across his forehead. "Where's your horse? Ah, there. Get up . . . Room for me behind . . ."

One of the nearby guns was on its side, the muzzle of another had been smashed by a direct hit. Two guns saved before the Boers saw what was happening—or could not believe their eyes. Now there was nothing much left to recover. Buller remembered thinking, "This is a bloody place to be. What am I doing here?" But, through it all, fear remained as unidentified and remote as the ammunition wagons.

He saw no one else alive near the guns. Were they the last out? Who was to know, or care? He let the horse have its head, and they were back in the donga in two minutes. The Lieutenant slipped off the back of the horse and said between gasps, "What the hell's the Navy doin' here?" Then he caught a glimpse of Buller's rank insignia. "Frightfully sorry, sir. Thanks for bringin' me along. Rough do, what?"

There were other officers of the 66th Battery standing where they had halted. "The General's lost his Staff-Surgeon while you were away. Shot right beside him," recounted one. "He just sits there on his horse, with everything singing round him, staring towards the Boer guns. Never does anything, never says anything."

A Captain said to Buller, "That was a decent thing to do, sir." The Captain laughed and gave the Lieutenant with the ginger moustache a nudge in the ribs. "Not that old Jock's worth savin'. Just so happens he owes me a couple of guineas . . ."

Chapter XV

At eleven o'clock, Commander Marchmount rode up to the donga, where the survivors of the Naval Battery had been lying for four hours in the heat, without food or water beyond what was left in their bottles. Buller saw him coming with Lieutenant Windsor at his side, two figures shimmering and unnaturally tall in the heat distortion. When they were nearer, Buller, who was some distance from any of his men, asked out loud, "How on earth does he do it? For God's sake, he's not even *dusty!*"

"Commander Buller, what do you propose to do about your guns?"

"I have no immediate plans."

"You mean the Navy is to present them to the enemy?"

Buller could hardly believe his ears. The man was not joking, there was no irony in the question, which had been asked rather more sharply than was customary to an officer of equal rank.

"I mean we've no ammunition and too few men left to man them. I take it that the attack has failed. Your guns have ceased fire. There's no sign of the infantry. The Boers are still entrenched in the kopjes. And my men are awaiting orders. They are also done in."

Buller looked up at Marchmount on his horse as he recited this message coldly. Marchmount was gazing about the donga as if inspecting the quarterdeck for tarnished brightwork and finding the scene disagreeable.

"The orders are that we must save the guns."

Now Buller rediscovered that old enemy, his temper, an enemy that had lain low for so many years. It was rising uncontrollably, just as if he were a boy again. "What do you mean, 'save the guns'? You put your head out there in the open, Marchmount. You'll see the frying corpses of our men. You'll see them, if the Mausers don't get you first. And where're the oxen and the Kaffirs? Do you expect my men to drag the guns back—what's left of them?" He stared up at the impassive figure in his recently pressed white morning dress uniform, as if Marchmount was ready to have his Admiral piped on board. "You're mad. The sun's done in your brain."

Marchmount turned his head slowly towards his Lieutenant and spoke in a calm voice: "Kindly note those words, Mr. Windsor. I have no doubt that they will be used in evidence at the court-martial after this is over."

"And I know who'll be the accused, Marchmount—dereliction of duty, cowardice in the face of the enemy, and a few other charges." Buller's words were pouring out uncontrollably. Marchmount snapped back, as if not listening, "I understand the Army saved some of its guns. What the Army can do—"

"They saved two guns and lost more than half their men. Go and look for yourself—and count the corpses."

"With respect, sir. With your permission, sir . . ." A third voice broke in, a voice with a strong Geordie accent, hoarse now with dryness. Buller turned and saw Rod at attention, capless, sweat-streaked, and filthy. Marchmount nodded permission, and Rod continued. "I don't think we can recover the guns, sir. But we might deny them to the enemy."

"How's that, Chief Gunner?"

"We could wait until dark and incapacitate the guns. Take out the strikers from the breechblocks, sir. The Boers are unlikely to have spares—not of naval long-twelve-pounders."

"What do you think, Mr. Windsor?"

"Well, sir—it's a compromise."

A shrapnel shell burst overhead, the steel fragments rattling against the rocks and causing the two horses to rear. A second later a heavy common shell burst just beyond the lip of the donga, throwing up a cloud of dust and rock fragments.

While still settling his horse, and speaking more rapidly than before, Marchmount said to Buller, "Commander Buller, will you be so good as to have your Chief Gunner and a small party proceed to your abandoned"—and he laid special emphasis on the word—"your abandoned guns and recover the strikers. I would like them by luncheon time, please."

With the intervention of Rod, Buller had succeeded in controlling himself. "I will gladly do that tonight and report when the operation has been completed. Meanwhile, may I please request—"

"Now, not after dark. That may be too late. The General has cancelled the attack and the Boers may overrun this ground later today."

Buller listened aghast to this calm pronouncement, but determined not to repeat the weak stroke of losing his temper. "They won't last two minutes out there, Marchmount. There are more than a thousand Boer Mausers within range."

Marchmount ignored him and addressed Rod as if Buller had not spoken. "Chief Gunner, will you form a party without delay and send back a message when completed." Then, without another glance at the surviving officers and ratings lying about the donga, or at Buller, he pulled round his horse and trotted away, Lieutenant Windsor trailing him like a dog at heel.

"You're under my orders now, Guns," Buller said grimly, "and you are forming no party of my men. Those Boers wouldn't leave their safe positions, cross the river, and advance over open ground in a million years. Not against a single battalion, let alone half the British Army."

"I'm not afraid, sir. The job's to be done, but I'll do it alone." He smiled up at Buller: "I'm nippy with the striker —you know that, sir."

"Don't talk rubbish, Midge. The job needn't be done, but it will be done. And it'll be done by me and no one else. Then I shall have the greatest pleasure in serving the strikers, not for luncheon but for dinner to Commander Marchmount, along with his best quality mutton chops."

Rod laughed. "We could make it for luncheon, sir, if we hurry."

"You're not coming, Guns."

"Not 'Guns,' sir. 'Lucky Midge.' Remember what Lord Charles calls me. You won't get along without me."

As they were lying out there, the sun burnt down on them as if the sky were a blast furnace poised above the veldt, cruel, implacable, fierce, agonizing. Once, Buller glanced up at it in the old belief that you should know your enemy, and all that he saw was a searing white glow that filled the heavens and possessed no definition.

The only way to retain your senses was to talk. They had run from the donga before Marchmount and Windsor were out of sight, unarmed for speed and without even water bottles, deciding that it would be done quickly or not at all. Buller had told only one of his two surviving Lieutenants, leaving him in command.

They were halfway to the guns before some sharp-eyed burgher spotted the two figures 800 yards distant and fired the first shot. More shots followed within seconds, rising to a soaring, rattling climax—hundreds of Mauser bullets in the air at once—before they dropped behind the limbers.

Momentarily, as he lay there panting, Buller's mind again went back twenty-five years, to those boyhood dreams of hearing a shot fired in anger. Well, today at least, and not for the first time, those dreams were being fulfilled—"Yes, in full measure, full measure!" he told himself with a touch of self-mockery.

Later, they moved a few feet to gain the benefit of the shelter of one of the gun's wheels. Only partial shelter, from the sun as well as from the musket fire. It saved their lives, but there was no question of moving farther, of working on the guns' breechblocks and removing the strikers, let alone of returning to the donga. That would have resulted not just in being hit but of being riddled and torn apart within half a second.

There, secure in trenches and emplacements, behind rocks, were those hundreds of Boers, dirty, bearded, in their filthy old slouch hats, and no doubt as hot as they were. But each one a crack shot with his Mauser or Lee-Metford and with nothing else to shoot at but two mad Englishmen lying trapped out there within comfortable range. Even now, two hours later, they continued to shoot. But, evidently uncertain of their enemies' fate and anxious to avoid wasting ammunition, the Boers' volleys were only intermittent.

Yes, talk. Talk could save your mind, even if it further dried your parched throat.

Awhile back—it seemed like days ago—Buller had said, "Tell me about your family, Midge. Three children, you once told me, is that right?"

Then, later, Buller said, "Yes, I've three—Lucy, Harry, and another boy of four, Richard." And later still: "Tell me about your home—in Newcastle, Midge."

Rod moved an inch to the right, to keep his neck in the shadow of the gun carriage's wheel. "Just a little place. Two rooms up, two down. But we like it there. It's friendly. Though it can be hard, on the Tyne. A lot of hunger."

"Like us now."

Rod said, "Worse and for longer." And Buller felt ashamed of his flippancy. He could not remember ever having been hungry, except puppy hungry as a boy and in the *Britannia*, and always soon satisfied. And, of course, among his friends, four rooms for a family of five was beyond consideration as a house.

They talked then, and more easily, of their Navy life, of the chance that had got Rod past the height minimum, of life in the *Implacable*, of voyages about the world, of friends and enemies; and when Rod pressed him, Buller told of life in the Cotswolds, of hunting and hunt balls, of house parties, of the eccentricities of naval officers and those of noble birth, including his own father-in-law.

They laughed and fell silent for a few minutes. The heat beat down, surely worse than ever, but as if by some unspoken promise, neither uttered a word of complaint. Shortly after three o'clock and for no apparent reason, a heavy gun from far behind the nearest kopje opened fire and landed three shells very close, covering them with dirt and fragments of a eucalyptus tree that had stood fifty yards away.

Then Rod began to talk again, his voice very hoarse now, and strained. "How often have you been frightened, before this, sir? When you were in the water that time? At Alexandria?"

Buller was surprised by the question and bought time by saying with a laugh that was more a croak, "Out here—like this—with our Maker so close—we can drop the 'sir.' "

"Yes, sir. I mean—"

"Just call me Buller. Only a few people call me Archy and it's a terrible name."

But Rod just stopped saying 'sir,' and even that seemed unnatural.

"Since you ask me, I have to say I don't know. I remember long ago taking a big gate on my father's hunter—I wasn't more than ten. And one of my elder brothers told me I ought to have been scared, and I didn't understand what he meant. And I was supposed to feel scared standing on the old *Britannia*'s truck one evening when I was a cadet. But I just felt rather good up there."

When Buller moved, even an inch or two, it was like shifting from red-hot steel plate onto white-hot steel plate, and the stones seemed to drill through his puttees like pokers from a fire into his skin. He noticed that Midge, Guns, Warrant Officer Roderick Maclewin, far from his wife Rosie and his three little children and his smoke-blackened four-roomed house on the banks of the Tyne—Midge was looking awful: two days' beard dusty red over gaunt white cheeks; eyes unnaturally large and wandering—wandering like those of an Arab he had once picked up in the desert on the point of death. He was suffering much worse than Buller was. "Not the same reserves as me."

Poor little Midge. "Lucky Midge" sounded mocking in its inaccuracy now. Nice name Rosie. Can't have her a widow.

Then Rod seemed to revive. But his question was even more unexpected than the last one. "Have you always loved you wife?"

"Oh yes." Buller thought it as well to reply at once. For the sake of truth, he conditioned this. "Of course I've had lots of affairs, like everyone else. So has she. But, yes. Oh yes, we love one another. I mean, we're married."

"That's very interesting. I mean life is very interesting." Rod's voice was low and Buller lost several words as some Boer marksman, with nothing else to do, loosed off a couple of rounds at them.

"We're about the same age, you and me," Rod continued huskily and almost inaudibly. "Both in the Navy all our lives, both gunners, both been in tight corners like this—and together. Both married. Both love our wives and children. And now stuck behind this damn gun in this damn heat with this damn thirst. As we're probably both going to die, it doesn't much matter what we say."

"And both friends. I hope," added Buller. He had never heard Rod swear before. Clean-tongued young man, unlike most sailors. Clean-living, too. No slipping in and out of other women's beds. No delicious flirtations at dances. Or, for that matter, no putting a hundred guineas on a throw at baccarat, and laughing at the loss, and lighting up the third big Havana of the evening, and ordering another jeroboam of Mumms Extra Dry from Charles at the Marlborough at three in the morning. No inherited title in the family, along with acres of best Cotswold farming land and a house in Belgravia, no . . .

"Oh my God, how much the same we are!" exclaimed Buller to himself, with the afternoon sun torturing his head, his shoulders and back, the back of his legs, even the bottom of his feet through his boots. "How much the same we are, this steady Warrant Officer from Northumberland, and me. And, my God, how different!"

Buller felt impelled to express this thought to Rod, and turned his head. His old friend was lying still, on his right side, slightly curled up, only the top of his head in the shade, one hand lying in the dust, the other against the gun carriage wheel, eyes half-open and seeming to see nothing.

His lips, dry and cracked as ancient parchment, moved to prove that he was alive and that he could talk. But all he said was to repeat, now with a note of delirium, "Life is very interesting."

"He is burning to death, this friend of mine," Buller told himself. "This little Chief Gunner who is my friend and who saved my life and has a wife called Rosie—he is burning to death. And I am his senior officer, and I brought him here."

Very slowly, Buller sat up and stripped off his shirt. Then, even more slowly he secured one sleeve to a length of torn leather harness and the other through a spoke in the wheel. "A jury rig, but it'll have to do." Then he drew on the leather and secured that, creating shade for Rod from the waist up.

Any number of corpses, as he had pointed out to Marchmount. No shortage. And no shortage of water bottles attached to them. It had crossed his mind earlier, but the calculation of survival odds seemed as high as drawing four aces in a row. Now the odds did not seem to matter. Rod would not last until dusk, would not last for another hour without water and shade.

Buller moved so slowly, like a lethargic veldt mole snake, that he raised no dust, not a grain of dust, head up only high enough now and again to check his direction. Like a frying mutton chop. That's what he was, a sizzling, frying mutton chop. It took him fifteen minutes to reach the nearest corpse. It happened to be a rating named Wilf Robinson, a particularly happy-go-lucky leading seaman from Goole on the Humber, whom Buller had always liked, although it was difficult to recognize the blackened face and the sightless eyes as his. It was typically frugal of the man that he had not touched his water bottle.

Buller unstrapped it, and that took another five minutes. Then he began scraping his way back to the 12-pounder, over the same rocks. He even saw some of his own blood, already hardened and congealed like a healing wound; and he followed the red trail with his eyes. "Very convenient," he told himself. "This way I don't even have to raise my head."

It took longer to get back, not because he was being even more careful to avoid raising dust or be observed moving, but because his strength was beginning to drain away. "Like a damn ship's boilers when the bunkers are empty," he said softly to himself, thinking of old Lord Huntley. He could even hear his father-in-law's voice, the words slurred: "What happens when the bunkers are empty, eh?"

But there was never any doubt that he would complete the journey. "Can't waste all this good Buller blood. And all this good Wilf Robinson water. And all this time . . . My God, Buller, you're going delirious, too. Pull yourself together." He laughed soundlessly. "No, don't do that. It'll cause dust, and Mauser bullets."

Rod's eyes were closed. He was very light to hold up, against his chest. And to hell with being seen now. We've got to get this water down.

When Buller attempted to unscrew the felt-covered cap, he noticed to his astonishment that his hand was shaking. Shaking! He held it up for a moment, the wicked sun casting the shadows of his fingers against Rod's face, and the shadows were shaking, too. "I am," he said aloud, half unbelievingly, half knowing it to be true, "I am shaking with fear! Not just from weariness and strain, but from *fear!*"

At the same time, he felt a chill coursing through his body, as if the temperature had turned Arctic from tropic. It was a new sensation, a new experience, like the ache in his crotch and the prickling sensation beneath his tortured skin.

A few shots were fired from the kopje as the sun went down and a few more after it had set, the muzzle flashes like distant sparks, as if the Boers wished to remind the English once again, "This is the sunset of the British Empire. We are here now as we were this morning and as we shall be tomorrow morning."

Later, when it was dark, Buller quickly unscrewed the 12-pounders' strikers, working from one gun to the next. Press the knob of the spring catch, revolve the striker one sixth of a turn to the left. Then withdraw firmly.

He tied them together round his neck with a length of severed trace, the steel still hot from the day's sun. When he picked Rod up, he seemed to weigh little more than these hardened steel spikes. Buller hoisted him onto his own burnt back and held his arms over his shoulders.

Rod groaned and seemed to utter a few words. Buller, thinking his mind was wandering, said nothing in reply. But in this new dark silence of the veldt, the words were spoken again, insistently and more clearly.

Buller said, "What is it, Midge?"

"I said, 'That makes it two to one, sir.'"

Buller's laugh was like the stirring of dry gravel. Then he began to feel his way across the veldt, taking it steadily, scraping against a harsh shrub here, avoiding a rock there, the strikers jabbing the torn flesh of his chest and knocking against one another like a clanking steel anthem of survival.

❧ ⚜ ❧

The Funeral

On the first day of the second month of the new century—Friday the first of February, 1901—Lieutenant Buller D.S.O., R.N. and Warrant Officer Maclewin C.G.M., R.N. were among the company of the smallest and prettiest of the Royal Yachts, *Alberta*, who watched the coffin of Queen Victoria being placed on a dais on the quarterdeck of the vessel.

Earlier on this clear, beautiful winter day, Buller had said to Rod, "It doesn't seem possible—it's not true." Yet ten days had already passed since the Queen had died, surrounded by her closest relations. This tiny, frail figure, this Queen-Empress, had ruled England and half the world for so long that she had seemed to many to be immortal. Since she had ascended the throne as a mere girl in 1837, thousands of her people had grown up, grown old, and died knowing no other sovereign.

"It doesn't seem possible . . ." But it had happened. Her eldest son, Bertie, the Prince of Wales, had been proclaimed King outside the Royal Exchange in London and in every town in the land. In St. Paul's Cathedral, the Archbishop of

Canterbury had preached a sermon in which he had said, "She was a great Queen because she was so good a Queen. She respected our freedom, she won our hearts . . ."

Rod, head lowered, cap in hand, watched out of the corner of his eye as an officer straightened the white-and-golden pall, embroidered with a cross and the Royal Arms, over the coffin and stepped back in line. Rod could also see, beyond, the coast of the Isle of Wight stretching east towards Foreland, near the waters where he had miraculously survived as a boy—when this Queen whose body lay before him was scarcely an elderly woman.

Slowly, with her reciprocating engines turning over at minimum revolutions, the *Alberta* eased away from the jetty, and the sequence of actions which governs the movement of any vessel at sea, even if she carries the coffin of a dead Queen, was now followed. Rod felt the slight tremor from the engine room, felt the stir of wind caused by her movement, heard the orders spoken softly, heard the gentle footfalls of the yachtsmen's rubber-soled shoes. The Queen was on her last voyage.

And now the *Alberta* was approaching the double line of warships drawn up at Spithead, manned overall, black and white paint and brasswork gleaming in the last of the sunlight: the battleships *Alexandra, Camperdown, Rodney, Benbow, Collingwood, Colossus, Sans Pareil, Nile,* and *Howe,* echoing great admirals and great victories of the past and reminding Rod of events in his own life—the *Camperdown* ramming the *Victoria,* the *Alexandra* at the Egyptian bombardment.

The following day was bitterly cold, and the dark sky was more in keeping with the solemnity of the occasion. The Queen's coffin had been brought to London, had passed through the silent, packed streets, and had embarked again in the Royal Train to Windsor. Again, as Royal Yachtsmen, Buller and Rod were in the select escorting party in the procession to the chapel, headed by the Life Guards, massed bands, the Heralds, and notables of lofty eminence including the Ulster King of Arms, the Earl Marshal of England and the Lord Chamberlain, the coffin being followed by Kings, Emperors, Princes, Grand-Dukes, and Peers of the Realm.

As they waited outside the station for the arrival of the train, the raw cold began to penetrate the thickest uniform, the tallest bearskin. The Royal Horse Artillery horses were pawing the cobbles and shaking their heads restlessly by the time the locomotive entered the station with a hiss of steam like a great sigh of relief that the important journey was over.

Now there could be no more stamping of feet or swinging of arms against the cold, and the escort drew to attention as the coffin emerged, followed by the dignitaries in their uniforms and decorations and orders.

Buller, who had inherited his mother's special understanding of horses, recognized the first hint of trouble as one of the lead horses shied when the carriage moved slightly before the coffin was lowered onto it. A moment later the horse shied again, raising its forelegs, pawing the air, whinnying in fear compounded by the cold it had endured for an hour and a half. Its restlessness was transmitted to the others, and suddenly all the horses began to strain at their harness and to lunge against the restraining traces.

Behind, the gun carriage began to rock on its wheels. In a moment the coffin itself might be thrown off—the ultimate indignity and a scandal that would blot the records of the R.H.A. for all time. The officer in command snapped out an order and ran towards the lead horses, drawing his sword. In a moment the troopers in charge had cut all the traces and were struggling to hold and to calm their horses.

The disorder lasted for no longer than a minute. During that time the horses were led away, and as the stunned crowd and discomfited royalty looked on helplessly, Buller observed Prince Louis of Battenberg in the full dress uniform of Captain R.N. hasten to the King's side and consult with him. A Guards officer, after a deep bow, also attempted to talk to King Edward. There was much waving of arms before Prince

Louis swung round and barked out an order, "Ground arms and stand by to drag the gun carriage!"

Buller leapt into action, saw Rod seize an end of one of the severed traces and turn towards him, "There won't be enough, sir," he called out.

It would take a long time to locate rope or more leather traces for the men, and the Army was already protesting, as the officer had complained to the King at being deprived of the honour. But the King appeared to have decided that the Army had failed once and that it was up to the Navy now. Rope? Cord? Traces? Suddenly Buller had an inspiration and ran the short distance to the stationary train. He had always longed to pull the emergency communication cord. Now he severed it in the guard's van, and again in the forward end of the opulently furnished Royal Carriage, and pulled the stout cord through.

In a few moments it was doing service as a tow rope for the gun carriage, and the human team of sailors in boots and white puttees and sennit hats was hauling the late Queen's body on its long journey to St. George's Chapel. Only those present at the railway station knew that there had been a crisis as they observed the Royal Navy steadily and in perfect order draw the gun carriage up the steep, cobbled road to the castle.

The farewell luncheon for Kaiser Wilhelm II, Emperor of Germany, was entering its last phase, the appetite of even the greediest guest satisfied, though food, from cream cakes to mountains of fresh fruit and nuts, remained on the tables.

The new King's nephew had come to the bedside of his dying grandmother two weeks earlier. In the past he had given Queen Victoria much anxiety with his boasting and bombast and even threats against England and her Empire. But on this solemn occasion he had behaved impeccably, wearing dark civilian clothes instead of the brilliant uniforms in which he usually strutted about during his visits.

Buller had heard from Prince Louis of Battenberg that he

had been modest and kind throughout his stay, and had declared himself satisfied with his reception. Now he was returning home, and the King had ordered this last feast, which Buller had attended as First Officer of the *Alberta*.

Buller had found himself seated next to Count "Sonny" Reitzberg-Sönderlong, now a Korvetten-Kapitän in the Imperial German Navy, and an A.D.C. to the Kaiser. Like his master, the German appeared to have been mellowd by the nature of this visit and by the welcome the German party had received. Through the eight long courses of this luncheon, through the champagne and the hock, the rich claret, the port, and the brandy, they had talked of their adventures, their travels, and their families. Nothing hostile or provocative had been mentioned, and it seemed as if the two officers would part on the most amiable of terms.

A sudden hush in the dining room was followed by the Kaiser's and the King's rising to their feet. Both men were smoking big cigars. They made an oddly contrasting pair, these two, who ruled the most powerful and richest nations in the world, the Kaiser the taller and leaner with his clean-shaven chin and characteristic upturned moustache, King Edward suitably avuncular in his appearance, heavy grey beard and moustache, clever, hooded, self-indulgent eyes now on his guest.

Clearly, no speeches were expected, or the King would have remained seated, but, as if reluctant to let this opportunity pass, the Kaiser raised his hands and announced in English with a heavy German accent, "Gentlemen, we ought to form an Anglo-German alliance." His dark eyes flashed over the standing guests at the long tables. "You would watch over the seas while we would safeguard the land. With such an alliance, not a mouse would stir in Europe."

The King appeared momentarily nonplussed by these words but recovered himself as the good host, briefly put an arm across his nephew's shoulder, and led him away. There was no applause—that would never have done—but a murmur of approval rose from the guests.

The atmosphere seemed so warm and mellow that the remark of Count "Sonny," delivered to Buller in a voice that was part teasing, part threatening, sounded in extraordinary contrast. "I think we will watch over the seas, too—you will see, my friend."

Then the officer clicked his heels in Prussian style, bowed from the waist, and said, "Good-bye, my friend—we shall meet again, I have no doubt . . ."

More Fiction Bestsellers From Ace Books!